THE BEST OF GERALD KERSH

The Best of Gerald Kersh

Selected and with a Preface by Simon Raven

FABER & FABER

This edition first published in 2013
by Faber and Faber Ltd
Bloomsbury House, 74–77 Great Russell Street
London WC1B 3DA

A CIP record for this book is available from the British Library

ISBN 978-0-571-30448-6

CONTENTS

PREFACE

Gerald Kersh tells stories. Good and bad, long and short, neat, dramatic, bizarre, perverse, scientific, supernatural, historical, they have been flowing out almost without pause for the last twenty years. They range from full-length novels, such as the recent *Fowler's End* or the celebrated novel-documentary *They Die with their Boots Clean*, to little jokes of some fifteen hundred words. In between, there are short 'novels' of perhaps 30,000 words, long short stories of 10,000 or 12,000, and a great many short stories of what one might call classical length (4,000 to 8,000). All of them, from the novels proper to the little jokes, have three things in common: they are vigorous, they are inventive (sometimes to a point near lunacy), and they can be read with the greatest of ease.

First of all, then, Kersh's vigour. This is particularly in evidence when he is describing circumstances of squalor '*Busto is a Ghost . . .*' His phrasing, when he comes, for example, to describe a sleasy lodging house and its verminous inhabitants, has a near-Falstaffian richness which he never quite achieves at any other time. Which is not to say that he ever becomes flaccid. He may be careless, he may overplay his hand, he may be downright embarrassing; but he is never floppy. And indeed he could not afford to be: for Kersh's people, whether squalid or not, are always on the go; cheating, drinking, cruising, fornicating, making money or spending their immortal souls, they live in a world where it is always necessary, for good or ill, to act; and if they – or their creator – lost their vigour for one moment, then they would surely die.

As for Kersh's invention, this ranges from the ingenious devising of trick endings (*The Sympathetic Souse*) to the skilful presentation of phenomena. Occasional and brief excursions into Science Fiction (*Men Without Bones*) confront one with tiny yet cosmic horrors, at first sight of no importance in the scheme of things, but disquieting for days in their concentrated malevolence. With ghosts, again, he has a canny knack of persuasian (*Carnival on the Downs*). But it is with material and familiar freaks (human or otherwise) that he is at his best (*The Crewel Needle, The Queen of Pig Island*); for these are ready to hand and need not be created afresh, so that all the force of Kersh's invention is set free simply in order to *manipulate* them, to organise them to the most cruel advantage and to bring them to the most unlooked-for end.

And if, thirdly, you doubt me when I say Kersh is easy to read, then I shall merely invite you to examine this selection of his work. It is made up of what I myself consider to be the best of all his short stories published between 1939 and 1960. I have included one 'little novel' of some 22,000 words (*Clock Without Hands*) and three stories of just over 10,000 words. But if Kersh is a good stayer, he is nevertheless better over the shorter distances: most of the stories in this book are between 4,000 and 8,000 words, and it is in these, I think, that he is to be found at his most vigorous, Rabelaisian, readable, inventive and bizarre.

SIMON RAVEN

Neither Man Nor Dog

ONE day I asked Adze if he had ever known what it feels like to have a friend. 'I have had a friend; one friend, once,' he replied.

'Whom you loved?'

'Loved?' He paused. 'Well, yes: whom I loved.'

'A woman?'

Adze sneered. 'A woman!'

'A man, then.'

'Man? *Tfoo!* Men are dust and ashes.'

'Not a child, I suppose?'

'Children! *Ptoo!*' He spat. 'People are weeds, and children are the seeds of weeds.'

'I should have guessed,' I said. 'Horse or a dog.'

'Horses and dogs are as bad as men. They *like* men! They *admire* men! Fools! *Ketcha!*' He seemed about to burst with pent-up scorn.

He was silent for a while; for as long as it takes to smoke a cigarette he said nothing. There was always an oppressive and threatening quality about the silences of Adze. They made you think of wildernesses of broken stones; there was death and desolation in them. Then he laughed, and his laughter was short and harsh, like something splitting in a bitter frost. 'Friend!' he said. . . .

Friends are for cowards. You have friends because you are afraid to be alone. You value your friends because they are a kind of mirror in which you see reflected the

1

best-looking aspects of yourself. Friends! And as for women, bah! What is there in a woman that a man should lose his head over her? A woman is impossible to live with. She is always talking. You support her, and she expects you to be devoted to her body and soul. She smells. She gets fat. She whimpers like a pup, that she is all yours . . . and the moment your back is turned her lover comes out from under the bed. Listen to me. I am a very old man. I have known a lot of men and women, but never any to whom I could offer love or friendship. No, I am alone, me! Yes, I have known everybody, high and low, in all parts of the world . . . in fine houses and in gutters, on mountains and plains, in forests and on the sea, but I have always been alone, alone with myself.

Always, except just once. This was more than fifty years ago. I left Russia from Vladivostok, working on a stinking ship that sailed for the South Seas down past the Sea of Japan and the Riu-Kiu Islands. The name of the ship was *The Varvara*. The captain was a pig, and the crew were also pigs. The purpose of the voyage was to trade among the Islands. We had tobacco, beads, hatchets that would not cut, and some barrels of alcohol. This rubbish we intended to exchange for such things as pearls – because our white women loved to hang their necks with these little white sicknesses out of the bellies of oysters, and the South Seas are full of pearls and other nonsense.

Well, it was an unlucky voyage. Before we were out of the Sea of Japan we hit a storm, and the ship was rotten and the cargo was badly stowed, so that we were in a bad way when the winds died down. Everybody said that it was madness to go on, but the Captain swore that he would put a bullet into the guts of the first man who might dare raise a voice. I did not care. I had a feeling that, whoever died, I should live. So we repaired *The Varvara* as best we could and went on. And so we came to grief. Do not ask me where we were, because I do not know. Another wind came, howling like a devil out of hell, and it seemed to smash us like a bomb. The end of the matter was, that the crew, pigs and fools that they were, gave up hope. They cracked one of the bottles of vodka, and drank it out of their cupped hands, as the ship foundered. They died singing of sweet kisses, blue-eyed maidens, and love in the meadows, while the sharks were crowding round them like Society ladies around a millionaire. That was the end of them. Good. But the Captain, as I foresaw, had taken care of himself. He and the first mate got into the one remaining boat. Needless to say, I got in with them. They had half a mind to toss me out, only there has always been something in my face which makes men think twice before playing such games with me. The sea was heaving, but growing still now. Our little boat went up in the air like a cork and then down again between cliffs of green water. Yes, the sea is very powerful. The last I saw of our ship was a kind of scum of bits of wood. Good. Then I was alone with the other two men in the boat, and they were fast asleep exhausted. So I slept too. That was just before dawn. I awoke with the sun on my face. It was like the open door of a blast furnace when they let out the molten iron. The Captain awoke too, and said: 'Open that locker behind you and pass me the water.'

I did so; that is to say, I passed him one of two water-kegs in the locker, and also took out a little barrel of biscuits. He and the mate drank like fishes, and then handed me the keg. I also drank. Then we ate some biscuits. The sun rose higher. We lay and gasped. There was only half a gallon of water left in the keg, and the devil knew where we were. I said nothing. The day passed, and then the night, and then another day. The keg was drier than bones in a desert.

'The other keg,' the Captain said.

I looked at him, and said: 'There is no other keg.'

At that, they looked at each other like criminals in a cellar when they hear the police kicking down the door, and a sort of despair came down upon the mate, and he put his face between his hands and wept – only he was too dry to have any tears left. The night was a hundred years long, and the next day came like a flame-thrower, and the mate went mad, and jumped overboard, and the sharks were very pleased to see him. And the Captain raved and gasped and, for the first time in his life, cried for water. Then he too went. He thought, all of a sudden, that this blue sea was some stream or other where the women of his village used to go and do their washing, and leaned over the side of the boat. Sharks have a habit of leaping up and snatching. They leapt up. They snapped. His name, if I remember rightly, was Avert-chenko. But who cares?

So I was alone in the boat. I used the keg of water that I had hidden, sip by sip, and ate the biscuits. I do not mind being alone. I do not enjoy company. But then being imprisoned in that little boat, rising and falling and rising and falling, with nothing left but a sky like a house on fire, and a sea that covered the whole world . . . why, then, suddenly it seemed to me that I wanted company. I never felt like that before, and perhaps it was the sun that made me feel so. I kept looking out of my burnt-up eyes, and seeing nothing but this damned emptiness everywhere, this rotten emptiness for fire and salt . . . and it seemed to me that a hole had been bored in my chest, and some of this silence and emptiness had leaked into me.

I lay like this for days, drinking my water drip by drip. And then I was down to the last pint of water and the last biscuit, and also the last thread that held me to the world. In one day I knew that I also would start singing and babbling about snow and grass and trees. But I broke this last biscuit, determined to keep alive as long as I could, for it is a man's duty to save himself. I broke this biscuit, I say, and a cockroach crawled out. I watched it. It ran across my hand, dropped to the bottom of the boat and tried to find a place to hide. I followed it with my eyes, put out a finger and headed it off. It crawled up my finger, ran up into my palm, and stayed there, doing something or other with its feet. I put up my other hand to shelter it from the sun, and there it stayed. I made crumbs of a little biscuit and – devil take it – I actually moistened these crumbs with a finger dipped in water. I wanted that cockroach to stay with me. I wanted it to stay alive. Yes, of all created things, that thing is the only one which I wanted to live with me! It made me feel that the whole world was not dead, and that, somehow, there was land beyond the sea, the salty and murderous sea.

So the madness that was coming on me went away, and the night came with cooler air; and still the cockroach rested on my hand, which I did not dare to move for fear of frightening it away; and that night passed quickly until it cracked – my last night – cracked like my last biscuit and let in the dawn. And for the one time in my life, just for an instant, I felt that I also was small and resting as it were in the palm of some hand powerful enough to crush me.

I looked over the water; it was calm as glass, and saw a sail. It belonged to a Norwegian clipper-ship, but I was too weak to signal. My head went round and the darkness fell down, and I knew nothing more until I tasted water, and found myself lying on a deck looking up into the face as round and red as the sun, the face of a man with a yellow beard. There were men all around me, all offering me clothes, blankets, food, drink, sympathy. But I looked at the palm of my hand. The cockroach was gone. I had been lost and alone on an empty sea in an empty boat for forty days and forty nights. But when I saw that my cockroach was gone, then, for the first time in my life, I felt lonely.

The Devil that Troubled
the Chessboard

A SHOCKING book might be written about Pio Busto's apartment-house. It stands on a corner not far from Oxford Street. It stands. No doubt Busto, who knows all the laws pertaining to real-estate, has managed to find some loophole in the Law of Gravity; I can think of no other reason to account for the fact that his house has not yet fallen down. Pio Busto knows how to make a living by letting furnished rooms. He puts a sheet of wallboard across a small bedroom and calls it two apartments. His house is furnished with odds and ends raked from the junk-heaps in the Cattle Market. No space is wasted. He sleeps in a subterranean wash-house, and would convert even this into a bed-sitting-room if the coal-cellar were not crammed with spare furniture and bed-linen. He is something of a character, this Busto; he looks like Lorenzo the Magnificent, and sleeps with a savage old dog named Ouif; in case of burglars he keeps a service revolver under his pillow, and a cavalry sabre hung on a bootlace over his head. He keeps evil spirits at bay with a rusty horseshoe, the lower half of a broken crucifix, and a lithograph of the Mona Lisa whom he believes to be the Virgin Mary.

His rooms are dangerous. You sigh; they shake. You sneeze, and down comes a little piece of ceiling. What is more, the walls are full of holes, bored by tenants of an inquisitive turn of mind. The curiosity of these people is often highly irritating – your view is sometimes obscured by the eye of your neighbour, who is trying to peep back at you. But Busto's tenants rarely stay long. They are mostly rolling stones, and by the time they come down to Busto's house, which is very far from the bottom of things, they have acquired momentum. They come, and they go.

As for me, I lived for more than three months in one of the cheapest of those spy-hole-riddled bedrooms. I completed my education there. Through three or four tiny holes, which must have been bored by some neglected genius of espionage, I watched people when they thought they were alone. I saw things which walls and the darkness were made to conceal; I heard things which no man was ever supposed to hear. It was degrading, but impossible to resist. I stooped. I stooped to the keyhole of hell, and I learned the secrets of the damned.

Among the damned was Shakmatko.

.   .   .   .   .

Picture for yourself this terrifying man.

I saw him for the first time in the saloon bar of the 'Duchess of Duoro'– long-drawn-out, sombre, pallid, and mysterious; dressed all in black. He had the unearthly, only partly human appearance of a figure in a Japanese print. I glanced at him, and said to myself, with a sensation of shock: 'Good God, this man is all forehead!' Imagine one of those old-fashioned square felt hats without a brim: his skull was shaped exactly like that. It towered straight upwards, white and glabrous. His forehead conveyed an impression of enormous weight – it seemed to have pressed his face out of shape. You can reproduce something of his aspect if you model a human face in white plasticine, and then foreshorten it by squashing it down on the table. In plasticine that is all very well; but alive, in a public-house, it does not look so good.

And if all this were not enough, his eyes were hidden behind dark-blue spectacles.

As I looked he rose from his chair, stretching himself out in three jerks, like a telescope, and came towards me and said, in a hushed voice, with a peculiar foreign intonation:

'Can you please give me a match?'

'With pleasure.'

He recoiled from the light of the match-flame, shading his concealed eyes with a gloved hand. I thought of the Devil in Bon-Bon. The tightly clamped mouth parted a little, to let out a puff of smoke and a few more words.

'I find the light hurts my eyes. Will you drink?'

'Oh, thank you.'

He indicated a chair. When we were seated, he asked:

'Pardon me. You live in this vicinity?'

'Almost next door.'

'Ah. In apartments?'

'That would be a polite name for them.'

'You will excuse my asking?'

'Of course. Are you looking for a room?'

'Yes, I am. But it must be cheap.'

'I live on the corner. They have one or two rooms vacant there. They're cheap enough, but——'

'Are there tables?'

'Oh! Yes, I think so.'

'Then I will go there. One thing: I can pay in advance, but I have no references.'

'I don't suppose Busto will mind that.'

'You see, I never stay long at one place.'

'You like variety, I suppose?'

'I detest variety, but I have to move.'

'Ah, landladies are often very difficult to get on with.'

'It is not that. A large number of people live in this house of yours?'

'A good few. Why?'

'I do not like to be alone.' At this, he looked over his shoulder. 'Perhaps you would be kind enough to tell me the address?'

'I'm going that way. Come along with me, if you like.'

'You are far too kind.' He reached down and picked up a great black suitcase which had been standing between his feet. It seemed to drag him down as if it were full of lead. I said:

'Can I give you a hand?'

'No, no, no, thank you so very much.'

We walked back to the house.

.   .   .   .   .

'First afloor fronta vacant, thirteen bob. Very nice aroom. Top floor back aten bob, electric light include. Spotless. No bug,' lied Busto.

'Ten shillings. Is there a table in that room?'

'Corluvaduck! Bess table ina da world. You come up. I soon show you, mister.'

'As long as there is a table.'

We went upstairs. Straining at his suitcase the stranger climbed slowly. It took us a long time to reach the top of the house, where there was a vacant bedroom next to mine. 'Ecco!' said Busto, proudly indicating the misbegotten divan, the rickety old round table and the cracked skylight, half blind with soot. 'Hokay?'

'It will do. Ten shillings a week; here is a fortnight's rent in advance. If I leave within a week, the residue is in lieu of notice. I have no references.'

'Hokay. What name, in case of letters?'

'There will be no letters. My name is Shakmatko.'

'Good.'

Shakmatko leaned against the door. He had an air of a man dying of fatigue. His trembling hand fumbled for a cigarette. Again he recoiled from the light of the match, and glanced over his shoulder.

Pity took possession of me. I put an arm about his shoulders, and led him to the divan. He sat down, gasping. Then I went back to pick up his suitcase. I stooped, clutched the handle; tensed myself in anticipation of a fifty-six-pound lift; heaved, and nearly fell backwards down the stairs.

The suitcase weighed next to nothing. It was empty except for something that gave out a dry rattling noise. I did not like that.

.   .   .   .   .

Shakmatko sat perfectly still. I watched him through the holes in the wallboard partition. Time passed. The autumn afternoon began to fade. Absorbed by the opacity of the skylight, the light of day gradually disappeared. The room filled with shadow. All that was left of the light seemed to be focused upon the naked top of Shakmatko's skull, as he sat with his head hanging down. His face was invisible. He looked like the featureless larva of some elephantine insect. At last when night had fallen, he began to move. His right hand became gradually visible; it emerged from his sleeve like something squeezed out of a tube. He did not switch the light on, but, standing a little night-light in a saucer, he lit it cautiously. In this vague and sickly circle of orange-coloured light he took off his spectacles, and began to look about him. He turned his back to me. Snick-snick! He opened the suitcase. My heart beat faster. He returned to the table, carrying an oblong box and a large board. I held my breath.

He drew a chair up to the table, upon which he carefully placed the board. For a second he hugged the box to his breast, while he looked over his shoulder; then he slid the lid off the box, and, with a sudden clatter, shot out on to the board a set of small ivory chessmen. He arranged these, with indescribable haste, sat for a while with his chin on his clenched hands, then began to move the pieces.

I wish I could convey to you the unearthly atmosphere of that room where, half buried in the shadows, with the back of his head illuminated by a ray of moonlight, and his enormous forehead shining yellow in the feeble radiance of the night-light, Shakmatko sat and played chess with himself.

After a while he began to slide forward in his chair, shake his head, and shrug his shoulders. Sometimes in the middle of a move the hand would waver and his head would nod; then he would force himself to sit upright, rub his eyes violently, look wildly round the room, or listen intently with a hand at his ear.

It occurred to me that he was tired – desperately tired – and afraid of going to sleep.

Before getting into bed I locked my door.

.   .   .   .   .

It seemed to me that I had not been asleep for more than a minute or so when I was awakened by a loud noise. There was a heavy crash – this, actually, awoke me – followed by the noise of a shower of small hard objects scattered over a floor. Then Shakmatko's voice, raised in a cry of anguish and terror:

'You again! Have you found me so soon? Go away! Go away!'

His door opened. I opened my door, looked out, and saw him, standing at the top of the stairs, brandishing a small silver crucifix at the black shadows which filled the staircase.

'What is it?' I asked.

He swung round instantly, holding out the crucifix. When he saw me, he caught his breath in relief.

'Ah, you. Did I disturb you? Forgive me. I – I——May I come into your room?'

'Do,' I said.

'Please close the door quickly,' he whispered as he came in.

'Sit down and pull yourself together. Tell me, what's troubling you?'

'I must leave here in the morning,' said Shakmatko, trembling in every limb; 'it has found me again. So soon! It must have followed on my very heels. Then what is the use? I can no longer escape it, even for a day. What can I do? Where can I go? My God, my God, I am surrounded!'

'What has found you? What are you trying to run away from?' I asked.

He replied: 'An evil spirit.'

I shivered. There are occasions when the entire fabric of dialectical materialism seems to go phut before the forces of nightmarish possibilities.

'What sort of evil spirit?' I asked.

'I think they call them Poltergeists.'

'Things that throw – that are supposed to throw furniture about?'

'Yes.'

'And does it throw your furniture about?'

'Not all my furniture. Only certain things.'

'Such as——'

'Chess-pieces and things connected with the game of chess. Nothing else. I am a chess-player. It hates chess. It follows me from place to place. It waits until I am asleep, and then it tries to destroy my chess-pieces. It has already torn up all my books and papers. There is nothing left but the board and pieces: they are too strong for it, and so it grows increasingly violent.'

'Good heavens!'

'Perhaps you think that I am mad?'

'No, no. If you had told me that you had merely been seeing things I might have thought so. But if one's chess-board flies off the table, that is another matter.'

'Thank you. I know I am not mad. My name may be unfamiliar to you. Are you interested in chess?'

'Not very. I hardly know the moves.'

'Ah. If you were you would have heard of me. I beat Paolino, in the tournament at Pressburg. My game on that occasion has gone down in history. I should certainly have been world champion but for that Thing.'

'Has it been troubling you for long?'

'My dear sir, it has given me no peace for twenty years.

Conceive; twenty years! It visited me, first of all, when I was in Paris training with Ljubljana. I had been working very hard. I think I had been working nearly all night. I took a hasty lunch, and then lay down and went to sleep. When I woke up I had a feeling that something was wrong: a malaise. I went quickly into my study. What did I see? Chaos!

'All my books on chess had been taken out of the bookcase and dashed to the floor so violently that the bindings were broken. A photograph of myself in a group of chessplayers had been hurled across the room, torn out of the frame, and crumpled into a ball. My chess-pieces were scattered over the carpet. The board had disappeared: I found it later, stuffed up the chimney.

'I rushed downstairs and complained to the concierge. He swore that nobody had come up. I thought no more of it; but two days later it happened again.'

'And didn't you ever see it?'

'Never. It is a coward. It waits until nobody is looking.'

'So what did you do?'

'I ran away. I packed my things, and left that place. I took another flat, in another quarter of Paris. I thought that the house, perhaps, was haunted. I did not believe in such things; but how is it possible to be sure? From the Rue Blanche, I moved to the Boulevard du Temple. There I found that I had shaken it off. I sighed with relief, and settled down once again to my game.

'And then, when I was once again absorbed, happy, working day and night, it came again.

'My poor books! Torn to pieces! My beautiful notes – savagely torn to shreds! My beloved ivory pieces – scattered and trampled. Ah, but they were too strong for it. It could destroy books and papers; it could destroy thought; it could destroy the calm detachment and peace of mind necessary to my chess – but my ivory pieces and my inlaid ebony board; those, it has never been able to destroy!'

'But what happened then?'

'I ran away again. I found that by moving quickly and suddenly, I could avoid it. I took to living in streets which were difficult to find; complicated turnings, re-mote back-alleys. And so I often managed to lose it for a while. But in the end, it always found me out. Always, when I thought I had shaken it off for ever; when I settled down to calm work and concentration; there would come a time when I would awake, in horror, and find my papers fluttering in tiny fragments; my pieces in chaos.

'For years and years I have had no permanent home. I have been driven from place to place like a leaf on the wind. It has driven me all over the world. It has become attached to me. It has learned my scent. The time has come when it does not have to look long for my track. Two days, three days, then it is with me. My God, what am I to do?'

'Couldn't you, perhaps consult the Psychical Research people?'

'I have done so. They are interested. They watch. Needless to say, when they watch, it will not come. I, my-self, have sat up for nights and nights, waiting for it. It hides itself. And then – the moment comes when I *must* sleep – and in that moment——

'Coward! Devil! Why won't it show its face? How can I ask anybody for help? How can I dare? Nobody would believe. They would lock me up in an asylum. No no, there is no help for me.

'No help. Look, I ran away from it last night. I came here today. Yet it found me, this evening. There is no escape. It has caught up with me. It is on my heels. Even at this moment, it is sitting behind me. I am tired of running away. I must stay awake, but I long for sleep. Yet I dare not go to sleep. If I do, it will creep in. And I am tired out.

'Oh, my God, what can I do? It is with me now. This very night. If you don't believe me, come and see.'

Shakmatko led me out, to the door of his room. There, clinging to my arm, he pointed.

The chessboard lay in the fireplace. The pieces were scattered about the room, together with hundreds of pieces of paper, torn as fine as confetti.

'What *can* I do,' asked Shakmatko.

I picked up the chessmen, and, replacing the board on the table, arranged them in their correct positions. Then, turning to Shakmatko, I said:

'Listen. You're tired. You've got to get some sleep. You come and sleep in my bed. I'll watch.'

'You are a man of high courage,' said Shakmatko. 'God will bless you. And *you*, damned spirit of anarchy——'
He shook his fist at the empty room.

I took him back, and covered him with my blanket. Poor old man, he must have been nearly dead for want of rest! He gave a deep sigh, and was asleep as soon as his head touched the pillow.

I tiptoed to his room and sat down. I did not really believe in ghosts; but for all that, I kept my eye on the chessboard, and turned up the collar of my coat so as to protect my ears in the event of flying bishops.

An hour must have passed.

Then I heard a sound.

It was unmistakably a footstep. I clenched my fists and fixed my eyes on the door. My heart was drumming like rain on a tin roof. A floorboard creaked. The handle of the door turned and the door opened.

I had already steeled myself to the expectation of something white, something shadowy, or some awful invisibility. What I actually saw proved to be far more horrible.

It was Shakmatko. His eyes were wide open, but rolled up so that only the bloodshot white parts were visible. His face was set in a calm expression. His hands were held out in front of him: he was walking in his sleep.

I leapt up. I meant to cry out: 'Shakmatko!' but my tongue refused to function. I saw him walk steadily over to the table sweep the pieces off the board with a terrific gesture, and fling the board itself against the opposite wall.

The crash awoke him. He gave a start which shook him from head to foot. His eyes snapped back to their normal positions, and blinked, in utter terror, while his voice broke out:

'Damn you! Have you found me out again? Have you hunted me down again so soon? Accursed——'

'Shakmatko,' I cried, 'you've been walking in your sleep.'

He looked at me. His large, whitish eyes dilated. He brandished a skinny fist.

'You!' he said to me, 'you! Are you going to say that, too?'

'But you were,' I said. 'I saw you.'

'They all say that,' said Shakmatko, in a tone of abject hopelessness. 'They all say that. Oh, God, what am I to do? What *am* I to do?'

18

I returned to my room. For the rest of the night there was complete quiet, but it was nearly dawn before I managed to fall asleep.

.   .   .   .   .

I awoke at seven. I was drawn, as by a magnet, to Shakmatko's room. I dressed, went to his door, and tapped very gently. There was no answer. It occurred to me that he had run away. I opened the door and looked in. Shakmatko was lying in bed. His head and one arm hung down.

He looked too peaceful to be alive.

I observed, among the chessmen on the floor, a little square bottle labelled *Luminal*.

In that last sleep Shakmatko did not walk.

'Busto is a Ghost, Too Mean to Give us a Fright!'

THERE was no such man as Shakmatko, but there really was Busto's lodging-house. It was just as I described it: a rickety, rotting melancholy old house not far from New Oxford Street. The day came when Busto was kicked out: his lease had expired five years before, anyway. He fought like a trapped lynx to retain possession of the place, but the Borough Surveyor and the Sanitary Inspector had it in iron pincers. It was condemned and executed, torn to pieces, taken away in carts. And a good riddance, I say! Yet in retrospect one half regrets such demolitions. 'Where is the house in which I lived?' one asks; and, walking past, looks up at the housebreakers, and sighs . . . 'Ahhhhh. . . .'

Pah!

Time is more than a healer. It is a painter and decorator; a gilder and a glorifier. It converts the gritty particles of half-forgotten miseries into what sentimental old gentlemen call Pearls of Memory. Memory! Memory; Fooey on Memory! What a smooth liar it is, this Memory! I have heard a shrapnel-tattered veteran recalling, with something suspiciously like sentimental regret, the mud of Passchendaele. I could feel twinges of pleasurable emotion about Busto's, if I let myself go. Yet I endured several miseries there. The place was chock-full of my pet aversions. Bed-bugs, of which I have always had a nameless horror, came out at night and walked over me. For some reason unknown to science they never bit me. But other insects did. I used to lie in bed, too hungry and tired to sleep, and look out of the window over the black roofs, and listen to the faint, sad noises of the sleeping house; and marvel at the fearsome strength of vermin. Sandow, Hackenschmidt, gorillas, whales; they are nothing. For truly awful physical force watch insects. Compare the heart-bursting sprints of Olympic runners with the effortless speed of the spider; the bloody and ferocious gluttony of the wolf with that of the louse; the leap of the panther with the jump of the flea!

Busto's ghoulish presence filled the house. One worried about the rent. Sometimes I wrote verse at night, in true poetic style, by the light of a halfpenny candle – oh, most execrable verse, full of inspissated, treacly, heavy blue-black gloom. . . .

In whose dim caves God and the ghosts of hope
Hold panic orgy and forget the earth

– that kind of thing. What green caves? I forget. I think they were to be found in a 'sea to sink in'. What sea? Sink what? I don't remember. I also wrote a novel called *The Blonde and Oscar*. It was so sordid that it made publishers' readers scratch themselves. Compared with it, *L'Assommoir* was like something by Mrs Humphry Ward, and *Jude the Obscure* a kind of *Winnie the Pooh*. Prostitutes? Millions of 'em. Degenerates? On every page. I left no stone unthrown; explored every drain-pipe; took three deep breaths, attached a stone to my feet, exhaled, and sank to the bottom of the cesspit with a hideous gurgle. I tell you, publishers dropped it with muffled cries, and afterwards scrubbed their hands, like men who reach for pebbles on a beach and accidentally pick up something disgusting.

I was always having fights with other lodgers. My nerves were on edge. I was, in any case, a bit of an idiot, foolish with an uninspired foolishness – hell is full of such. I was unbelievably bumptious, arrogant, loud-mouthed, moody, quarrelsome, bull-headed, touchy, gloomy, and proud in a silly kind of way. At the prospect of a rough-house I boiled over with murderous joy. Only one man on earth inspired me with fear, and that was Busto.

.   .   .   .   .

Pio Busto used to cross himself before a lithograph of the Mona Lisa. He thought it represented the Virgin Mary. But in any case it was generally believed that Busto had no soul to save.

How small, how bent, and how virulent was Pio Busto, with his bulldog jaws, and his spine curved like a horse-shoe! How diabolical were the little eyes, hard and black as basalt, that squinted out of his pale, crunched-up face! Ragged, dirty, and lopsided, he had the appearance of a handful of spoiled human material, crumpled and thrown aside, accidentally dropped out of the cosmic dust-bin. It was said of him: 'Busto is not human. Busto is not alive. Busto is a ghost, too mean to give us a fright.'

He really seemed to have no thought beyond wringing out the rents of his abominable little furnished rooms. As soon as the money was due, up popped Busto like the Devil in a legend: '*My* landlorda gim*me* time to pay?

Hah? Hooh!' If you asked him for a match he would say: 'Buy a box.' There was a quality of doom about his avarice. Professional bilkers took one look at Busto and ran for their lives. Unemployed waiters – always habitual grumblers and irrepressible mutterers-under-the-breath – remained silent in his presence. He uttered few words, but his thin lips, corrugated like the edges of scallop-shells, sawed off a whole repertoire of formidable noises. His *Hooh!* expressed all the scorn in the world: his *Hah?* was alive with malice.

About once a month he used to get drunk on Red Lisbon – a deadly and incalculable wine concocted of the squeezed-out scrapings of rotted port-casks and laced with methylated spirits – a terrible drink of doubtful origin, which smites the higher centres as with a sandbag. It is otherwise known as Lunatic's Broth, or Red Lizzie. Busto would consume bottles of it, and even offer small saucers-full to his dog, Ouif. This, also, was a taciturn animal; shaggy, half-deaf, suspicious, and altogether badly formed. It was as if some amateur Creator had tried to piece together a bull-terrier with odds and ends of Airedale, Saluki, Dachshund, and jackal. Ouif shared his master's bed. Dogs have no æsthetics, so it is easy for them to be noble. Besides, it is physically necessary for a dog to attach himself to somebody, if only a man like Busto, just as a man must love some living thing, even a dog like Ouif.

Without Ouif, how could Busto have lived in the atmosphere of hate with which he surrounded himself? He trailed a tradition of pitilessness. Extortion was his métier. As he went his rounds, his feet seemed to squeeze out of the squeaking stairs all the squealing notes in the gamut of human misery. Hopelessness had soaked into

23

the pores of his ancient house; multitudes of passing tenants had left behind them the ghosts of their anguish and despair. Busto's was the step before the bottom. People came, lingered, clinging desperately as to a rock overhanging an abyss; then weakened and dropped out of sight. The time always came when Busto said: 'Clear out before twellovaclock!' Almost every rent-day, some unhappy defaulter was thrown out.

My rent-day was Saturday. One Saturday evening I was hurrying in with the necessary nine-and-six, when I met Mr Butts in the passage. He was an addresser of envelopes, a man with a booming voice, no shirt, and a monocle, most of whose earthly possessions were contained in a four-pound biscuit-tin. He was carrying this tin under his arm.

'Going?' I asked.

'Yes, my dear sir, I am,' said Mr Butts.

'Did Busto——'

'Of course. But he is sorry, now. You know, my dear sir, I never go out of my way to do anybody any harm, but people who wrong me always suffer for it afterwards. Busto throws me out into the street. Very good. An hour ago, his dog was run over. You see?'

'No! His dog?'

'Run over, my dear sir, by a taxi. Could you lend me fourpence?'

'Twopence?'

'A thousand thanks, my dear sir. . . . Good-bye, good-bye!'

The door slammed heavily. The rickety umbrella-stand vibrated to a standstill. Silence, darkness, and the evil odours of dampness and decay settled upon the passage. I went downstairs to the disused wash-house in which Busto lived and slept. I knocked. He tore the door open and cried: 'Yes? Yes?' But when he saw me his face fell, and he said: 'Oh, you. Hooh! I toughta you was da vet.'

'The vet?' I said. 'Why, is Ouif ill?'

'Yes.'

'May I see him? I know a little bit about dogs.'

'Yeh? Come in.'

Ouif lay on Busto's bed, surrounded with pillows and covered with a blanket.

'Run over, eh?' I said.

'Ah-ah. How you know?'

Without replying, I lifted the blanket. Ouif was crushed, bent sideways. Practically unconscious, he breathed with a strenuous, groaning noise, his mouth wide open.

'Whacan I do?' asked Busto. 'I touch 'im, it 'urts. You tella me. What I oughta do?'

I passed my hand gently down the dog's body. Ouif was smashed, finished. I replied: 'I don't think there's anything much you can do.'

'A hotawatta-bottle?'

'A hot-water bottle's no use. Wait till the vet comes.'

'Hooh. But what *I* do? Dis is *my* dog. Brandy?'

'Don't be silly. Brandy'll make him cough, and it hurts him even to breathe.'

'Hell!' exclaimed Busto, savagely.

I touched Ouif's stomach. He yelped sharply. I covered him again.

'How did it happen?'

Busto flung up his big, earth-coloured fists in a help-less gesture. 'Me, I go buya one-two bottla wine ova da road. Ouif run afta me. Dam taxi comes arounda da corner. Brr-rrr-oum! *Fffff!* Run aright ova da dog, without a stop!' shouted Busto, opening and closing his hands with awful ferocity. Hell, Ker-*ist*! If I getta holda diss fella. Gordamighty I tear 'im up a-to *bits*! Lissen; I tear outa diss fella's 'eart an' tear *dat* up a-to bits too! Yes!' shrieked Busto, striking at the wall with his knuckles and scattering flakes of distemper. 'Lissen, you tink 'e die, Ouif?'

'I'm afraid he might. All his stomach's crushed. And his ribs. All the bones——'

'*Basta, basta,* eh? Enough.' Busto slouched over to the table, seized a bottle of wine and filled two teacups. 'Drink!' he commanded, handing one to me; and emptied his cup at a gulp. I swallowed a mouthful of the wine. It seemed to vaporise in my stomach like water on a red-hot stove – *psssst!* – and the fumes rushed up to my head. Busto drank another cup, banging down the bottle.

'You like this dog, eh?' I said.

'I send my fraynd for the vet. Why don't dey come, dis vet?'

There was a knock at the front door. Busto rushed upstairs, and then came down followed by a wizened man who looked like a racing tipster, and a tall old man with a black bag.

'Dissa my dog.'

'What happened?' asked the vet.

'Run over,' said the little man, 'I told yer, didn't I?'

'Well, let's have a look.' The vet stooped, pulled back the blanket, and began to touch Ouif here and there with light, skilful hands; looked at his eyes, said 'Hm!' and then shook his head.

'So?' said Busto.

'Nothing much to be done, I'm afraid. Quite hopeless.'

' 'E die, hah?'

'I'm afraid so. The best thing to do will be to put him out of his misery quickly.'

'Misery?'

'I say, the kindest thing will be to put him to sleep.'

'Kill 'im, 'e means,' said the wizened man.

'Lissen,' said Busto. 'You mak this dog oright, I give you lotta money. Uh?'

'But I tell you, nothing can possibly be done. His pelvis is all smashed to——'

'Yes, yes, but lissen. You maka dis dog oright, I give you ten quid.'

'Even if you offered me ten thousand pounds, Mister . . . er . . . I couldn't save your dog. I know how you feel, and I'm sorry. But I tell you, the kindest thing you can possibly do is put him quietly to sleep. He'll only go on suffering, to no purpose.'

'Dammit, fifty quid!' cried Busto.

'I'm not considering money. If it were possible to help your dog, I would; but I can't.'

'Dammit, a hundreda quid!' yelled Busto. 'You tink I aina got no money? Hah! Look!' He dragged open his waistcoat.

'Nothing can be done. I'm sorry,' said the vet.

Busto rebuttoned his waistcoat. 'So what you wanna do? Killum?'

'It's the only merciful thing *to* do.'

'How mucha dat cost?'

'Mmmmm, five shillings.'

'But make 'im oright, dat aina possible?'

'Quite impossible.'

'Not for no money?'

27

'Not for all the money in the world.'

'Hooh! Well, what you want?'

'For my visit? Oh, well, I'll say half a crown.'

'Go way,' said Busto, poking half a crown at him.

'The dog will only suffer if you let him live on like this. I really——'

'I give-a you money for cure. For killum? No.'

'I'll do it for nothing, then. I can't see the dog suffering——'

'You go way. Dissa *my* dog, hah? *I* killum! You go way, hah?' He approached the vet with such menace that the poor man backed out of the room. Busto poured another cup of Red Lisbon, and drained it at once. 'You!' he shouted to me, 'Drink! . . . You, Mick! Drink!'

The wizened man helped himself to wine. Busto fumbled under one of the pillows on the bed, very gently in order not to disturb the dog, and dragged out a huge old French revolver.

'Hey!' I said. 'What are you going to do?'

'Killum,' said Busto. He patted the dog's head; then, with a set face, stooped and put the muzzle of the revolver to Ouif's ear. With clenched teeth and contracted stomach-muscles, I waited for the explosion. But Busto lowered his weapon; thought for a moment, rose and swung round, all in the same movement, confronting the lithograph of Mona Lisa.

'Twenna-five quid ada Convent!' he shouted.

Mona Lisa still smiled inscrutably.

'Fifty!' cried Busto. He returned to the table, poured three more drinks, and emptied another cup. Nobody spoke. Fifteen minutes passed. Ouif, brought back to consciousness by pain, began to whine.

'No good,' said Busto. He clenched his teeth and again aimed at the dog's head. 'Gooda dog, hah? Lil Ouif, hmm?'

He pressed the trigger. There was a sharp click, nothing more. The revolver had misfired. The dog whined louder.

'I knoo a bloke,' said Mick, 'a bloke what made money during the War aht o' profiteerin' on grub. Done everybody aht of everyfink, 'e did. So 'e 'as to live; this 'ere dawg 'as to die.'

The walls of the room seemed to be undulating in a pale mist; the wine burned my throat. Busto opened a third bottle, drank, and returned to the bed.

'You look aht you don't spoil that there piller,' said Mick, 'if you get what I mean.'

I shut my eyes tight. Out of a rickety, vinous darkness, there came again the brief click of the hammer on the second cartridge.

'Now, agen,' said Mick.

Click. . . . Click. . . .

'For God's sake call that vet back, and let him——'

'You minda you biz-ness, hah?'

'It's 'is dawg. 'E's got a right to kill 'is own dawg, ain't 'e? Provided 'e ain't cruel. Nah, go easy, Busto, go easy——'

I hunched myself together, with closed eyes.

Click, went the revolver.

'Last cartridge always goes orf,' said Mick. 'Try once agen. 'Old yer gun low-*er*. . . . Nah, *squeeeeeeze* yer trigger——'

I pushed my fingers into my ears and tensed every muscle. The wine had put a raw edge on my sensibilities. I shut my eyes again and waited. I heard nothing but the pulsing of blood in my head. My fingers in my ears felt cold. I thought of the revolver-muzzle, and shuddered. Time stopped. The room spun like a top about me and the Red Lisbon wine, the Lunatic's Broth, drummed in my head like a boxer with a punching-ball – *Ta-ta-ta, ta-ta-ta, ta-ta-ta.*

I opened my eyes. Busto was still kneeling by the bed. The revolver, still unfired, remained poised in his hand; but Ouif had ceased to whimper. He lay motionless, the petrified ruins of a dog.

'Anyway 'e die,' said Busto.

'Of 'is own accord,' said Mick. 'Bleedn war-profiteers is still alive. So 'e 'as to die, if yer see what I mean.'

'Some people complain,' I said, 'because men die and dogs go on living.'

Busto made an unpleasant noise, with his tongue between his lips: *'Pthut!* Men is rubbish. Dogs is good.'

He drank the last of the wine. Then, pensively raising the revolver, he cocked it and let the hammer fall. The last cartridge exploded with the crash of a cannon; the big bullet smacked into the ceiling, bringing down an avalanche of plaster; the revolver, loosely held, was plucked out of Busto's hand by the recoil and fell with a tremendous clatter and jingle of broken crockery among the teacups. For a moment we all sat still, stunned with shock. The clean piercing smell of burnt gunpowder cut through the close atmosphere of the underground bedroom. Busto jumped to his feet, kicked over the table, jerked his elbows sideways in an indescribably violent gesture and, raising his fists to the ceiling, yelled:

'Ah, you! Death! Greedy pig! Wasn't you a-belly full yet?'

Then he grew calm. He pointed to the body of Ouif and said to Mick: 'Chucka disaway.'

'Where?'

'Dussbin.'

'Wot, ain't yer goin' to *bury* 'im?'

'Whagood dat do?' Busto turned to me, and made a familiar gesture. Raising his eyebrows and sticking out his chin, he pointed with the index finger of his left hand to the palm of his right, and uttered one sound:

'Hah?'

I remembered; paid him my rent, nine shillings and sixpence, and went up the creaking stairs to bed.

.   .   .   .   .

I should say, I suppose, that there was a great deal of good in Pio Busto – that a man who could love his dog must have something fine and generous somewhere in his soul. It may be so, but I doubt it. I said I feared him. That was because he was my landlord, and I had no money and knew that if I failed to pay my rent on Saturday I should be in the street on Sunday as surely as dawn follows night. How I detested him for his avarice, his greed, his little meannesses with soap, paint, and matches! Yet I admit that I felt a queer qualm of pity for him – that grimy, grasping, hateful little man – when he gave away cups of Lizzie Wine that night in the wash-house when the little dog Ouif lay dying in his bed. I don't know . . . there are men whom one hates until a certain moment when one sees, through a chink in their armour, the writhing of something nailed down and in torment.

I have met many men who inspired me with much more loathing than Busto, several of whom passed as

Jolly Good Fellows. It is terrible to think that, after the worst man you know, there must always be somebody still worse.

Then who is the Last Man?

The same applies to places. The insects at Busto's drove me mad. But, say I had been at Fort Flea? You will not have heard the story of Fort Flea, for it was hushed up. I got it from a man who learned the facts through an account written by a Mr de Pereyra, who knew the Commanding Officer. It went into the official reports under the heading of *Fuerte di Pulce*, I think.

During the Spanish campaign in North Africa, in the latter years of the Great War, a company of Spanish soldiers occupied a fort. There was the merest handful of Spaniards, surrounded by at least two thousand Kabyles. Yet the tribesmen retreated and let them take the fort. Later, a Kabyle, carrying a flag of truce, approached the soldiers and, screaming with laughter, cried: 'Scratch! Scratch! Scratch!' They didn't know what he meant, but they found out before the day was over.

The Doctor, who had been attending two men who had been wounded, came to the Captain and, in a trembling voice, asked him to come to the improvised hospital. 'Look,' he said. The wounded men were black with fleas – millions of fleas, attracted by the smell of fresh blood. They were coming in dense clouds, even rising out of the earth – countless trillions of fleas, which had their origins in a vast sewage-ditch which, for centuries, had received the filth of the town. They were mad with hunger; attacked everybody, swarming inches deep; drew pints of blood from every man; killed the wounded, devitalised the rest, made eating impossible by pouring into the food as soon as it was uncovered, prevented sleep, made life intolerable. And nothing could be done. The Spaniards had the strictest orders to hold their position. A desperate dispatch was rushed to the General – General Sanjurjo, I believe – who sent a scathing reply. What kind of men were these, he wondered, who could let themselves be driven back by the commonest of vermin? So at last, when reinforcements arrived, there were only twelve men left, all wrecks. The Kabyles hadn't attacked: they had stood by, enjoying the fun. The rest of the men had been eaten alive; nibbled to death.

And I complained of the polite little insects in the bedrooms at Busto's.

Thicker than Water

PART ONE

'You always were such a confounded milksop,' said my uncle. 'I shall never forget that time when you came down from Cambridge, pure as a lily. I gave you a ten-pound note, and told you: "Here's a tenner, Rodney – go to the West End, find some lively company; have a good time, make a man of yourself!" And out you went, buttoned up like a blessed parson. And you were back by midnight, all flushed. . . . What? You're blushing again, are you? Better watch out, Rodney. You make me think of the little train that used to run between Wittingley and Ambersham – when the driver blew the whistle, the engine lost steam, and stopped. Don't blush; you can't spare the blood for it. Oh, you curd, you!'

I said: 'Oh, Uncle – please!'

But he had no mercy. He was in one of his savage, comic humours. He went right on, in apostrophe, talking to the crystal chandelier: '. . . He comes back by midnight, does this Rodney, all of a glow. I say to myself: "Well, now, at last this bookworm has made a bit of a fool of himself. About time! Let's have a little vicarious pleasure . . ." And I ask him to tell me how he has spent his evening – not, mark you, that he can have sowed many wild oats between tea-time and the Devil's Dancing Hour. "Been dissipating, Rodney, my boy?" I

34

ask him. And: "Oh yes, Uncle Arnold!" says this little nobody. And, as I am a living sinner, he puts down nine pounds-three-and-six, with – Lord help us! – a look of guilt, saying: "Here is the change!" '

He laughed his great, coarse laugh, and the crystals of that detestable chandelier vibrated with it, seeming to titter in sympathy. Knowing that it would be useless now to beg for mercy, I remained silent.

He continued: 'Change, I ask you, *change*! – the chandelier sang: *Change!* Nine pounds-three-and-six out of a ten-pound note. And had he dissipated? "Oh yes, Uncle Arnold." . . . On sixteen shillings and sixpence, this fellow had had his first big night in town, by all that's marvellous! . . . "The cost-of-living must have dropped," I say, "because when I was twenty-two, forty-odd years ago, and if *my* uncle had given me a tenner to blue in town, *I'd* have come home with an empty pocket and an unpaid bill from Gervasi in the Strand – yes, and had to borrow half a sovereign from the butler to pay the cabbie. . . . What in the world," I ask this tame mouse, "what in the *world* can a gentleman do, to have an evening in town on sixteen-and-six?" And he tells me, does this Rodney: "I met my friend, Willikens, of Jesus College, and we went to a picture palace. We saw Rita Anita in *Passion's Plaything*, and after the show we went to a café in Soho and had ham and scrambled eggs." '

I cried: 'Oh, Uncle——'

' – Oh, nephew!' he snarled, glaring at me again. 'I decided, from that moment on, that you were a beastly little prig. I promised my dear sister – your unhappy mother – that I'd look after you. Poor girl! Your father, whom she went and married – bolts and bars wouldn't hold her – against all our advice, was a blackguard and a scoundrel and a rogue and a vagabond. But at least he had the decency to go to the devil like a man, if not a gentleman. Whereas you – you whey-faced marigold——'

' – Uncle, I cannot help the colour of my hair!' I said.

'You can't help anything, you!' said he. 'I wonder that you have the nerve to interrupt me. Why, you spaniel, for less than half of what I've said to you, I would have struck my own father in the face! My elder brother practically did so to my father for much less, and was kicked out of doors, and went and made his fortune in Africa . . . and I wish I'd gone with him. . . . Oh, you spiritless thing – I'd have thought better of you if you had knocked me down, just now, instead of whimpering: "Uncle, Uncle, Uncle!"'

And I could only say: 'But, *Uncle!*'

' – And yet,' my uncle said, 'there must be some kind of a spark of spirit in you, somewhere, or you wouldn't have had the nerve to fall in love with this Mavis of yours. All the same, you should have got that kind of nonsense out of your system, the time I gave you that ten-pound note. "He who commits no follies at twenty will commit them at forty." Whoever said that was quite right. So here you are, infatuated, at your age——'

' – Uncle, I'm only thirty-nine!' I said – and, to save my life, I could not have stopped my voice breaking – 'and it isn't infatuation. It's true love!'

'That would make it a thousand times worse, if it were true. Only it isn't. It can't be. True love, indeed – you, of all people!'

'And why not me, as well as anyone else?' I asked.

'Why not you?' he replied. 'Because . . . you are *you*. True love's for men. And what are you? A marigold, a carrot – aha, there he goes, blushing again like a tomato! – a weed, a vegetable; anything you like except a man. Love, young Rodney, takes blood and fire. All the fire in you has gone into your ridiculous hair; and all the blood in your body you need to blush with. . . . Infatuation, I say – don't dare to interrupt – infatuation with a common dancing girl, who gets paid a couple of pounds a week for showing her fat legs to every Tom, Dick, or Harry who has sixpence to pay for a ticket!'

Even if I had not been choked with misery and rage, I dare say I should have held my tongue. My uncle was in one of his moods, and if I had told him that Mavis had slender and beautiful legs, he would have corrected himself into further offensiveness by saying: *I beg your pardon, skinny legs.* If I had argued that, say, Pavlova was also, by his definition, a 'dancing girl', and that Mavis was a serious Artiste in Ballet, he would have said, with an unpleasant leer: *Oh yes, we know all about that! So was Signora Scampi, when my father set up an establishment for her in Brook Street, in* 1883. . . . Brutal ignoramus as he was, he had a talent for turning any word to his own purpose. So I was silent, while he went on:

'Now, if you'd been anything like a Man, I'd have been the last to object to your marrying a dancer. I nearly did myself, once – wish I had – she had legs, at least, to recommend her, which is more than my barren scrub of a Lady had . . . and, as for morals, if any: better. At least, La Palestina was frank, which is more than could be said for our own skinny-shanked, goose-fleshed womenfolk . . . curse and confound them, from their droopy eyelids to their long cold feet! . . .

'However, let's not waste words. Marry your dancer,

and not only will I strike you out of my will, but I cut off your allowance. Now then! Decide.'

'But, Uncle!' I said. 'I *love* Mavis, and she loves me.'

He said, with a sneer: 'You are infatuated with your Mavis, and she is in love with the eight hundred pounds a year I allow you. I ask you, you radish, what else could any full-blooded woman find in you to love?'

I might have said that Mavis was not the type of ballet dancer of my uncle's turbulent youth; that she was by no means what he, and his type, would have described as 'full-blooded', being dark and slender, petal-pale and serious. But then he would only have snarled a laugh and cursed himself, saying that it was just as he had thought all along – the girl was anæmic, unfit to breed from, and he would see himself damned before he countenanced such a blend of milk and water.

'Rodney, my boy,' he said, 'I want your word, here and now. Give up any idea you might have of marrying this girl. If not, I send a note to Coote tomorrow, and that will cost you eight hundred a year while I'm alive, and my money when I'm dead. You know me, Rodney. I'm a bull-terrier when I lay hold, and my mind's made up. . . . Well?'

I said: 'I'll do as you say, Uncle Arnold. I'll give her up.'

Then he struck the table a blow with his purple fist, and shouted: 'I knew you would! Oh, you milksop! If you had defied me, I'd have raised your allowance to twelve hundred, and given you my blessing; and kissed your bride for you. As it is, you stick of rhubarb, your allowance is henceforward reduced to six hundred pounds a year. And let this be a lesson to you. . . . True love, eh? And you'd sell it for eight hundred a year!'

'Oh, but, Uncle——' I began.

' – Oh, but, Uncle! Why, do you want to know something? If I had been you, I would have confronted my old uncle with a *fait accompli*. I'd have said: 'Uncle, I have married such-and-such a girl. Take her, or leave her! And then – I'll tell you something – I'd have been for you one hundred per cent. Oh, you . . . !'

And, of course, it must be at this wrong moment that I find the courage to say: 'Uncle, Mavis and I were married three months ago.'

He started to puff out his cheeks, but, remembering that his doctor had warned him to control his temper, sucked them in again. When he subsided, I had never seen a more terrifying mixture of malignancy and mirth than his face expressed. He said: 'Oh, you did, did you? And you have the gall to tell me so, now?'

I protested: 'But, Uncle! You just said——'

' – I just said, you worm, that if you had had the spirit to tell me so in the first place, I'd have thought better of you. But no, not you! You've got to sniff and fumble your wormish way, you have; until I let fall a word, and then you're as bold as brass, you copper-headed Thing! . . . Oh, so! You married the girl, did you? Well, if I could half-guess that she loved you for yourself (as she might have loved me for myself) instead of for the money I provide you with, blast my eyes but I would have allowed you twenty-four hundred a year! But as it is, just because you're such a sniveller, I cut you down to . . . did I say six hundred a year? Beg pardon: four hundred. Your allowance is cut in two, young Rodney. And for every time, hereafter, you whine *Oh, Uncle,* I cut you another fifty. Now then!'

He knew my old servile habit; he tore the protest out

of me, as surely as if he had me on the rack. 'Oh, Uncle!' I cried.

'Three hundred and fifty pounds a year,' he said, with satisfaction.

'You don't do me justice,' I said. 'You have always made a mockery of me, just because I have red hair and never liked to hunt or shoot!'

Talking to the chandelier, again, my uncle murmured, making a burlesque of my accent: 'He didn't think it was fair for the Hunt to ride after one poor little fox . . . and when I winged a partridge and knocked its head against my boot, he burst into tears. . . . Poor boy!'

'I damned you, for a brute!' I shouted, and was appalled by the reverberation of my voice in that big old house. 'A brute, a brute! Keep your dirty money! Damn you, keep it!'

His old servant, coming in with a great silver tray at that moment, stood aghast. But my uncle laughed, and said: 'A show of spirit, Rodney, what? Back you go to four hundred a year. . . . Bring in the oysters, Lambert!'

Lambert put down the tray. There were three oval silver platters, each platter indented at the periphery with twelve deep hollows. In each hollow lay a fat Colchester oyster in the deep-shell. In his ceremonious way, Lambert uncorked a bottle of Chablis, and poured a little into my Uncle Arnold's glass. He, sniffing and mouthing the wine, grunted: 'Sound! . . . Lambert, wine to Mr Rodney.' Then, to me, with a sardonic twist of the mouth: 'You won't take an oyster, by any chance, will you, Rodney?'

I said: 'Not for any consideration, thank you, Uncle

Arnold. You know oysters disagree with me. They make me ill. No, thanks, really!'

He was at me again like a bull-terrier. 'Oysters disagree with him!' he said, to the chandelier. 'Disagree! As if any self-respecting oyster would condescend to agree or disagree with this grain of grit! An oyster would turn him into a seed pearl for a little girl's bracelet. . . . Oh, bah! Last of the season – isn't it, Lambert?'

Lambert said: 'The last oysters of the season, Sir Arnold. This is the thirtieth of April. We'll not have oysters again until there is an R in the month – September first, Sir Arnold, as you know.'

When Lambert had left the room, my uncle grumbled: 'May – June – July – August . . . four months, before the oyster season opens in the autumn. And what am I to live on until then? . . . Chicken, I suppose . . .' Then he glowered at me, and said: 'Oysters disagree with you, Rodney, do they? They make you ill, what?'

'Yes, Uncle,' I said. 'I am what they call "allergic" to shell-fish. They make me . . . they give me convulsions.'

'Then I'll tell you what,' my uncle said. 'Here's three dozen oysters, the last of the season. I'm going to eat two dozen. You eat the third dozen, and I'll give you back your eight hundred a year. What say?'

The very smell of the oysters nauseated me. I could only say: 'I can't, I won't!'

Eating greedily, my Uncle Arnold said: 'I'll tell you what, young Rodney: for every oyster you eat, I'll raise your allowance fifty pounds a year. . . . Come on, now!' And he held out, on a three-pronged fork, a fat Colchester.

'Go to the devil!' I cried, starting back, and striking the fork out of his hand.

He grinned, taking up another fork, and said: 'Spirit! Bravo! Your allowance is now four hundred and fifty.'

'Oh, Uncle!'

'Four hundred,' said he, swallowing another oyster. 'Oh, dear me, how we go to the dogs, poor us! . . . What wouldn't I give, now, for a Saddlebag! You don't know what that is, do you, Rodney?——' my uncle slavered most unpleasantly, in reminiscence. 'You take a great, thick, tender steak, and slit it down the middle on two sides so that it opens like a pocket. Stuff it with eight or ten succulent Whitstable oysters, with their juice, and sew up the open edges. Grill, preferably over charcoal. . . . Oh, the very idea of it turns *your* stomach, doesn't it? We used to wash it down with porter, and chase it with port, you milksop. . . . And all the damned quacks allow me, now, is fish and white meat. Not even salt. My blood pressure is high, they say, and my arteries hard. . . . I never noticed that my arteries were hard.'

Here the old man held out a gnarled left fist, bulging with blue veins. He touched one of these veins with the forefinger of the other hand, and said, quite pathetically: 'Springy as a pneumatic tyre. What's hard about that? . . . Doctor says red meat and wine will make me drop in my tracks. . . . Salt, too, they deny me. And what is life without salt? . . . *No excitement*, they say. So what is left? Other people's excitement, vicarious pleasure . . . and you, Rodney, deny me even that. . . . Ninety-eight per cent water, you vegetable! At least I can live to watch you wriggle. . . . An oyster would make him ill. Go to bed, Rodney, go to bed – I'm sick to the heart at the sight of you! Go away!'

He looked so lonely as he sat there, feeling the big blue veins in his clasped hands, that I said: 'Oh, my dear Uncle, forgive me if I have offended you——'

' – What was that you said?'

'Oh, Uncle——'

' – I thought you would come around to that again. Three hundred and fifty a year it is now. Go to bed.'

Such was Sir Arnold Arnold, my uncle: a brutal old man, who had lived only for pleasure; a savage hedonist, whose appetites had outlived the means of gratifying them. Lusty, in spirit, as an uninhibited *bon vivant* of thirty, here he sat, at eighty, with half a million in the bank, and nothing to look forward to but the oyster season next September. For the fear of death was upon him. The doctors had warned him that, although he might be good for another ten years of life, if he took care of himself, a little over-indulgence in food, or wine, or emotional excitement could kill him as quickly and as surely as a bullet in the heart. Much as I hated him that evening, I was sorry for him. Going to bed, I reflected: *Why, I don't believe that even his oysters give him any great pleasure, now that he can't spice them with pepper sauce. . . .*

I thought of his many kindnesses to me – he may have been a ruffian, but his heart was in the right place – and, although he had just ruined me, I forgave him. In a way, I loved him – even admired him; and if I ever hated him, it must have been because I envied him. Examining my inner heart now, I come to the conclusion that he was the man I should have inclined to be if Nature and Circumstances had given me half a chance.

I swear, I never really meant to kill my uncle.

.   .   .   .   .

43

. . . I could not sleep. I lay awake, reproaching my-self, attacking myself from every angle. . . . There was no doubt about it, my uncle was right in his estimate of my character. I *was* a milksop, a weakling, a vegetable, ninety-eight per cent water. I *did* cut a ridiculous figure. I *had* made a fool of myself that very evening, with my evasions, and my confessions which were not con-fessions. . . .

. . . But was my marriage to Mavis something to con-fess, like a crime?

. . . I felt my face growing hot in the dark; and, re-membering my uncle's constant allusions to my incur-able habit of blushing, burned hotter. No one had the right, I told myself, to make game of a man because he blushes at a word. There is cruelty in that – schoolboy insensibility. You might as reasonably make mock of a man because he has one leg shorter than the other. . . . And as for making a joke of my red hair – why, if you condoned that kind of humour, you condoned, in effect, the persecution of negroes because they are black. . . .

I remembered a boy who was at school with me, at Eatonstowe. His name was Ward, and he was an albino. None of the other boys bore him any grudge – yet how pitilessly they persecuted him! One day somebody sent him a message saying that his cousin had come to see him; and there was a pink-eyed white mouse in a card-board box. . . . Yet he was silent. He made a pet of this mouse, kept it in his pocket. It used to run up his sleeve and sit on his shoulder. He used to take the mouse to bed with him. . . . One morning, poor Ward woke us all up before the bell, I remembered: he had turned over in his sleep, and smothered the mouse; and that was the first time I had ever heard that lonely boy cry . . . and oh, the desolate hopelessness of it, the woe, the helpless grief! It struck us silent, and afterwards we offered Ward toffee and fruit; but he would never speak to us any more, and soon his guardian took him away from school. . . . *Us,* I remembered; because I – God forgive me – had been among the worst of Ward's persecutors. Why? Because, before he had come to school, it had been I who was the butt of the form, on account of my fantastically red hair. It had been a relief to have some-one else to persecute. . . .

Then I remembered Fatty Onslow, who had been the worst bully of the lot – a monstrously fat boy who, having been mercilessly teased for three terms, suddenly developed a giant's strength, which he tyrannously used like a giant. I had thought I should never forgive the things he did to me. . . . Yet, when I ran into him fifteen years later, in Pall Mall, he was as quiet and gentle a fellow as you ever met . . . and died, as I wished I might die, heroically, in the North Sea. 'Stand by to ram!' he roared, bleeding to death – and, with his destroyer, rammed and sank a German cruiser.

Such, again, was my Uncle Arnold, I thought. Only there was, perhaps, too much of the fourth-form bully left in him – that was all. I blamed myself for letting him treat me so. There was, I reasoned, never a man on earth who would not respect another, however puny, who was devoid of fear . . . and I was rotten with fear, eaten up with it!

In this respect, only Mavis understood me, because she was sensitive, too. It was she who made it clear to me that I was not really a coward; only sensitive. She loved the colour of my hair, she said, because it reminded her of something out of Dubinushki's setting for the *Valse des*

Fleurs. . . . My heart ached then as I thought of Mavis.

She had had a hard life, poor girl. Almost literally, she had danced herself out of nowhere——

– *Hey, wait a minute!* I said to myself, trying to reason with myself – *what do you mean, out of nowhere? She is still nowhere. But she relies upon you to help her dance her way somewhere.*

Mavis depended upon me so absolutely. She had such faith in me, and relied so utterly upon my given word – and I had sworn to see her through her career. . . . It is generally an excellent thing to have a woman pin all her faith and hope on you . . . but it may be sometimes a very bad thing. It takes a broad back to bear the weight of a woman's trust. A woman's unstinted faith may put a strong man's head among the stars; on the other hand, it may put a weak man's head into the gas oven. And I am a weak man.

Yes, I contemplated suicide that night in my uncle's house; and I wish I had had the courage to commit it. . . .

I had come, paying my duty-visit, with the intention of borrowing a little money – a matter of some few hundred pounds. Before I knew Mavis, I had regarded myself as quite a rich man: my uncle allowed me eight hundred pounds a year, and over and above that I had my salary, four hundred pounds a year from the High Commissioner's office where I worked. Twenty-four pounds a week was affluence, to me. I had my little flat in Knightsbridge; my books and my gramophone records: my little self-indulgences. I could even lend a little to my friends. But after I fell in love with Mavis, somehow I could never make ends meet.

I met her at a meeting of the Little Ballet Group, in Russell Square. She performed the dance Riabouchinska used to do, with the little metal fawn . . . only Mavis was smaller than Riabouchinska: an animated ivory figurine, most beautiful! Mavis lived, she told me, only for The Ballet. But her health was not very good; one of her lungs was questionable – she had had a hard time of it in her early youth. Her father drank, her mother kept a little general store in a side street off the Gray's Inn Road. . . . She had been sent out to work in a factory at the age of fourteen. But she wanted to dance – dancing was her life, she said, again and again.

She did that Fawn Dance in a borrowed costume, stained with someone else's grease-paint. When I went to congratulate her, after the dance, and saw her weeping so forlornly in the little dressing-room, it was as if a hand came out of the foggy night and squeezed my heart into my throat.

Mavis had such humility. . . . Now, here is a joke: it was I, of all created creatures, who coaxed and persuaded her into artistic arrogance! Seeds of my own destruction? Yes, perhaps I sowed them. It was I who said to Mavis: 'You must not wait and hope; you must insist, demand!' *I*, mark you! . . .

She insisted. She demanded. I believe there is nothing quite so persuasive as the eloquence of a weakling who, genuinely despising himself for what he is, preaches in favour of that which he would be if he could.

I made Mavis hard. Soon my twelve hundred pounds a year was nothing. And, in talking my doctrine of *Strength – Strength – Strength*, I found that I had talked myself into contempt and out of existence as the man who had comforted the thin little girl when she was crying in the dressing-room.

I do not know whether Mavis had overestimated my

fortune. I am sure I made my financial position pretty clear: eight hundred a year from my uncle, four hundred a year from my office. She thought herself lucky, at that time, if she drew a hundred and fifty a year, and had enough, at the end of the week, to satisfy her landlady in Bernard Street.

But when Mavis and I came to be together, the money went like water. There had to be supper parties, cocktail parties, and luncheon parties; because she had to 'meet people'. And could she meet people in a shabby dress? Of course not. And could I do her discredit by appearing less elegantly turned out than an adagio dancer? No. I went to Savile Row for my suits, to St James's for my shoes, and to Bond Street for my shirts. Again, could we live in three little rooms in Knightsbridge? Knightsbridge, yes; three rooms, no. We needed a big lounge for 'people', and impressive furniture.

I got into debt. I mortgaged myself. And, at last, when the dressmakers, and the other tradesmen, were pressing for settlement of their accounts, I had gone to my uncle to borrow five hundred pounds, and found myself with my allowance cut in two.

Mavis would have something to say about this!

I had not lied when I told my uncle that I could not live without her. She was all I had ever loved. Weary of turning over in my mind what I should say to her when I returned home, I began to consider ways and means of killing myself.

And then – at half-past three in the morning – someone knocked at my door. Lambert came into my bedroom, and said: 'Oh, Master Rodney – Master Rodney – will you come down? Sir Arnold – I mean your uncle – is taken very bad!'

I put on dressing-gown and slippers, and followed him. As I went downstairs, I was aware of a sense of doom.

I wished my uncle dead, yes. I wished him dead, God forgive me, for his worth in money, considering the terms of his will. But I beg you to believe me – do, please, believe me – when I tell you that I loved the old gentleman very dearly, and had no intention of murdering him, as I did, that night.

PART TWO

You may imagine that, as I went downstairs – steadily, slowly, contemplatively – my thoughts were with my uncle. As a matter of fact, they were not. The date was 30 April, but the weather struck cold in the old house. I thought, first, that it might have been a good thing to put on my overcoat, over my dressing-gown; then it occurred to me how right Mavis was when she insisted that a woman had to have a fur coat. This being the case, therefore, I had bought her a fur coat.

Now there are fur coats and fur coats. Mavis had told me how a certain class of woman could not distinguish between musquash and mink, or between mink and sable. Such women were earmarked for oblivion. But Mavis had 'modelled' for furs, and knew what was what. She had a great deal of this kind of knowledge. Mavis knew, and wanted to be one with, the kind of woman that recognises – let us say – blue fox, blond mink, and Siberian sable. She could explain the difference between

49

the pelts of certain rodents – for example, mole and chinchilla. The difference, generally, ran into many hundreds of pounds. Mavis made a social difference of it.
. . . Chinchilla and sables, perhaps, might come
later. Meanwhile, she could wear nothing cheaper than
mink. And wearing mink, how could she ride in a bus?
Women wearing mink do not ride in buses – it is anti-
social to do so – the proletariat stares. And what is a
mink coat without a corsage of orchids, preferably
purple? . . . But what girl, who respects herself, wears
a suit by a lesser craftsman than Vallombroso under a
mink coat? Respecting herself in a Vallombroso suit,
how could she feel comfortable with something inferior
to Ambergh underwear next to her skin, a Bobini hair-
cut, and shoes by Dupuy? . . . The hat was another
item. Nobody who was anybody wore a hat that was not
made by Berzelius. And one became a Somebody by
mixing with Somebodies. This was Mavis's philosophy,
and I could not disagree with it.

'I always found,' she had told me, 'that when I had
supper for eighteen pence at the Café Mauve, I never
had more than eighteen pence to pay for my supper.
But when I started to have supper for three-and-sixpence
at the Café Impérial, I managed to find three-and-six-
pence . . .'

This operates, in a way; the only drawback is that
somebody must pay. . . .

It was of this that I was thinking when I went downstairs. My uncle was lying on his back, with his knees
drawn up. His face was blue with pain, but still he
fought. He said, gloatingly: '*You* would have been dead
three-quarters of an hour ago, I bet! It looks as if you
might come into your inheritance yet, you worm.'

'What is the matter, Uncle?' I asked.

He said: 'I don't know. My belly is hard as a pump-kin, and hurts like hell. . . . First I go hot, and then I go cold, and when I move my head . . . I seem to fade away, wash away on a kind of foggy wave. It pains, Rodney, it pains!'

Then Lambert came in with a hot-water bottle. (I write down these details to convince you that almost to the last I wished my poor uncle nothing but well.)

'This sounds like appendicitis,' I said. 'Take that bottle away, and make a pack of crushed ice in a towel.'

Even in his agony, my Uncle Arnold sneered: 'Male nurse!' You see, my eyes were weak, so that in the war I was only in the Medical Corps. He had been a rough-riding cavalryman, and had been shot in the thigh at Rorke's Drift – carried the Mannlicher bullet that dis-abled him on his watch chain.

'Call Dr Gilpin,' I said to Lambert.

He hesitated, and said: 'I wanted to, sir, but Sir Arnold said not to.'

Remember – all I had to do was temporise, humour my uncle in his obstinacy for three or four hours, and he would surely have been dead that day. But I said: 'Uncle, you have an appendicitis, very likely burst; and that "fading away" in waves is a hæmorrhage. Lambert, call Dr Gilpin this instant!'

'No damned quacks!' my uncle groaned. 'It's nothing but a belly-ache. I can't imagine why Lambert called you down, you Woman! . . . Lambert, don't call Dr Gilpin, call Mr Coote – if I die where I lie, I cut this milksop off with a shilling.'

That was the nature of the man; do you know, I honoured him for it! But I rose to the occasion, and said: 'You may cut me off, or you may cut me on, as you please; I am getting the doctor.' And so I did.

The old gentleman was delirious when Dr Gilpin arrived. The diagnosis was as I had foreseen – a burst appendix, with a serious internal hæmorrhage.

I went with my uncle and the doctor to the Cottage Hospital. The surgeon there said: 'We'll pull the old boy through, I dare say. But I'll want somebody to stand by for a transfusion of whole blood. . . . How about you?'

I said: 'My blood group is universal O.'

'How d'you know?'

'I found that out during the war,' I said. 'I was in the R.A.M.C.'

'You'll do,' said the surgeon.

At this point I murdered my uncle, Sir Arnold Arnold, for the sake of my love for Mavis. For, you see, an allergy may be transmitted in a transfusion of blood. I spoke the truth when I said that my blood group was Type O, which is universally transfusible. But some devil got hold of my tongue, so that when I intended to say, *I am violently allergic to oysters, and Sir Arnold lives on them; therefore, if he receives my blood in transfusion now – his heart being weak, and his blood pressure high – he will almost certainly die in a fit of asthmatic coughing, or of convulsive colitis, when he celebrates the opening of the next oyster season with three dozen Colchesters next September . . .* I was silent.

Premeditation here! When I let them siphon the blood from my arm into the bottle for transfusion, I knew that I was poisoning my uncle as surely as if I had been putting arsenic in his tea.

But I never spoke.

He was conscious by noon, and then he said: 'Rodney, my boy, I'm an old man, and a little testy at times. Don't mind every word I say. Blood is thicker than water, old fellow; and you must have good blood in you. You behaved like a man and a gentleman, by God! . . . Bring your Mavis to see me. I dare say she's a nice gel, really. Meantime, send Coote to me. I'm going to give you a thousand pounds for a wedding present.'

'Oh, no, Uncle!' I said, almost crying.

'Don't interrupt. I haven't the strength to argue. Get Coote. I'll leave the Cottage Hospital five thousand, I will. . . . Go away now. No, wait a second. Rod——'

'Uncle?'

'Your allowance, henceforward, is a thousand a year. You're a good boy. Now go home.'

Mavis was waiting for me when I got home. She said: 'Good Lord, Rod! You look like death warmed up. Your eyes are all red. Have you been crying, or something? And where were you all last night?'

'My uncle was very ill, so I got no sleep,' I said.

I was sick to hear her remark: 'If only the old fellow would pop off! We'd have fun then, wouldn't we?'

'Very likely,' I said heavily.

She asked me: 'But did the old bully come across? . . . He must have given you a hundred or two, at least, surely?'

Unfolding the cheque, I said: 'He gave me a thousand pounds, and has raised my allowance to a thousand a year. Does that please you?'

It did. 'Let's celebrate!' she cried. But I said that I was tired, and wanted to rest. I said nothing about the

53

blood transfusion – the thought of what I had done sickened me.

A little later, after she expressed a hope that my uncle might 'pop off' soon, we had our first quarrel. After that we had our first delightful reconciliation, and I agreed to take her for a holiday to the Pyrenees. In this, as you will see, there was the sure hand of God.

.   .   .   .   .

Ah, but that was a holiday! We spent a delightful week in Paris, and then went south. It is a wonderful thing, to leave the station under a fine rain, and wake up under a blinding sun. Mavis had never been abroad before. As you must know, the greatest pleasure that things give their possessor is the delight he finds in sharing them with someone he loves. . . . There was a forest, a road almost without perspective; a certain view of blue water, white foam, and yellow sand; above all, the little peak the peasants call 'La Dent Gâtée'; and this I loved beyond everything.

You may keep your Matterhorn, your Mont Blanc, and your Dent du Midi. Give me my Dent Gâtée. To look at, it is not much. If it were much, no doubt I should never have gone beyond the base of it. My beloved Dent Gâtée is a very minor mountain, from the point of view of a climber – there is nothing difficult about it – the herdsmen follow their goats over the peak, and down over the Spanish border, without thinking twice. To a true mountaineer, the Dent Gâtée is what soldiers call 'a piece of cake'. I loved it, though. It has hidden depths. Never mind the precipices that go rushing a thousand feet down, buttressed like the walls of the great cathedrals; never mind the icy torrents that spring out of the living rock and go, in blown spray, down into the terraced valley! I like the Dent Gâtée for its silence, and for its mysterious caves.

The old cavemen lived here, scores of thousands of years ago. The great M. Casteret, I believe, began to explore the caves of the Dent Gâtée; one of his predecessors, in 1906, in a hole named Le Chasme Sans Fond, discovered an antediluvian carving of a buffalo, and the carefully arranged teeth of three cave bears. . . . There was an animal for you, if you like! From nose to tail-root, the cave bear measured ten feet, and he stood five feet at the shoulder. His haunches were considerably higher than his shoulders; so that when he reared up to attack, his forepaws must have hovered twenty feet high, armed with hooked claws ten inches long. His canine teeth were bigger than bananas. But around this creature, which was much bigger than a bull, you must wrap a pelt about three times as long and dense as that of a grizzly bear. This nightmare our ancestors fought with chipped flints lashed to the tips of wooden poles! . . . All this made me feel that Man is not called Man for nothing.

I tried to convey this to Mavis, but she felt the cold. She wanted to be over the mountain, and into Spain; where, she said, she proposed to hear a flamenco, learn a gipsy dance, and see a bull-fight. So we hurried up and up that tricky road until, a mile before we were to touch the mountain village called Lô, we crashed.

It was not my fault. It happened like this: Mavis was hungry and thirsty, and I was preoccupied. . . . In my head something kept singing: *You murdered your Uncle Arnold – Murdered your Uncle Arnold – He will die in September – You have murdered your Uncle Arnold. . . .*

Changing into second gear, coming into low, I encountered a cow, and swerved. My right-hand turn, thoughtlessly twisted on, took me up a steep bank. The car turned over. It stopped rolling at the edge of the road, the rear wheels spinning over the cliff.

Mavis's arm had gone through the windshield. I was always a coward – I had ducked – I was merely stunned.

Coming to, I ran for help. It happened that an old man was going to Lô, mounted on a mule. I made a tourniquet of my tie, thrust five hundred francs into the man's hand, mounted Mavis on the mule, and followed her to Lô, where there was a doctor.

I trembled for her, when I saw him: he was a French doctor of the old school, who used his ear for a stethoscope, and did not believe in new-fangled drugs. A rugged old fellow, jack of all medical trades and master of none – but no fool. He said: 'Madame has lost too much blood and, what with that and the shock, I order a transfusion. But you are in no condition, m'sieur, to have half a litre of blood taken out of your arteries at the moment——'

'– No, no!' I cried. 'I gave blood for a transfusion only a month ago. I am not fit, doctor; not healthy.'

'– If you will allow me to proceed?'

'I beg your pardon, doctor.'

'*Il n'y a pas de quoi*, m'sieur. . . . As I was saying, since you are not in a condition to give blood to your wife, I have called in a woman of the village. A healthy animal, I assure you. She was wet-nurse to the Princesse de Bohemond's child, which I had the honour prematurely to deliver, after the Prince's motor-car crashed on this self-same road. The baby thrived – at eight months, mark you! We can't do better than take a little blood from young Solomona. They do not come much healthier than she – she is bursting with milk and blood.'

Then he introduced the woman Solomona, to whom I gave a thousand francs. She bared a powerful brown arm and giggled as the needle went home in the artery at the crook of the elbow.

A little colour came into Mavis's cheeks as Solomona's blood ran into her veins. It worked like magic. Her eyes opened, the lids fluttering, and she smiled.

I remember saying: 'Now I can die,' and after that I must have collapsed. When I was conscious again, a day and a half later, the doctor told me that I had concussion; for which, he said, the only remedy was ice-packs and rest.

But how could I rest until I had seen Mavis? I went into the room where she lay – and she looked even more beautiful than ever – and, taking her by the hand, begged pardon for my unskilful driving.

'It was all the cow's fault,' said Mavis. 'She wasn't looking where she was going . . .' Mavis was still a little light-headed. She rambled on, drowsily: '. . . Poor old cow. Didn't know where she was going. . . . But do any of us? Couldn't see what harm she was doing. . . . Can any of us? Kind of lost and frightened – her eyes looked lonely. . . . But aren't we all? . . . I hope I won't be too much scarred.'

I said: 'The doctor said that there'll be nothing that a bit of cosmetic won't cover. You'll be all right, my sweet.'

'. . . Lucky it wasn't my leg,' she said. 'I couldn't afford that. . . . Even so, Abaloni always kept nattering about my not knowing what to do with my arms and hands. Perhaps this will make me worse. Oh, Rod – don't let it!'

'Dearest Mavis, nothing is ever going to make you unhappy.'

'That would be nice, Rod . . . I *have* made sacrifices for my Art, you know?'

I nodded, not knowing exactly what she meant. To tell you the truth (it might have been on account of my bang on the head) I was a little irritated with her now. I could not help thinking: *Uncle Arnold, in her position, by this time would have been sitting up and shouting: 'A scratch, damme, a bloody scratch! Get some wine – red wine – that makes blood! And steak, bleeding, underdone! Bustle about, you dago dogs!'* . . . I couldn't banish from my mind the image of the old gentleman as he lay in the Cottage Hospital: every inch a proper man, but smiling with a kind of tenderness, and eager to give, to pay, all rancour forgotten.

I said: 'You have made sacrifices, Mavis, no doubt. For your Art. So have I made sacrifices, for your Art!'

She laughed, in a lightly-fluttering, high-pitched way, and said: 'Oh no! What, you? Sacrifices? Oh no! I sacrificed my body for my Art!'

A great cold came over me then. 'You sacrificed your body to whom?'

'To you, of course,' she said.

Quite calmly, I believe, I said: 'Very likely. But for your Art, and my love of you, Mavis, I have sacrificed my immortal soul.'

'Don't let's be intense,' said she, wearily, 'because I don't think I could bear it.'

A strange, unpleasant light made a sickly sunrise in

my disordered head. 'Why, I believe you were really in love with Abaloni!' I cried.

'Please, Rod, let's not go into that, now!'

And then I knew that it was the choreographer Abaloni whom Mavis had always truly loved. There surged up in me a great white hate – boiling bubble-to-bubble with my love for her. In circumstances such as this, a man feels at the tip of his tongue some stupendous speech . . . and comes out with something trite and silly.

I could only say: 'Abaloni's fat!'

'You're no oil painting,' said she.

Before I could find words to say in reply, Mavis sat up. For the moment, I thought that she was crying, because tears were running down her cheeks, and I said: 'Dear Mavis, forgive my inadequacies, and pardon me if I hurt you. I love you most dearly. If it will be better for you to be with Abaloni, then go. I thought you loved me. I was a fool to think so. Take half of what I have, and go to Abaloni——'

But she was not crying. She could not catch her breath.

I called for the doctor. He said: 'It happens, occasionally. There are people, especially women, who are affected like this in the mountains by changes in atmospheric pressure. Come away, and let her rest.'

I came away with the nurse, who put me to bed with cold towels on my head. Next morning, when I went to see Mavis, she said: 'I must have been sort of woozy yesterday. Rod, did I say all sorts of silly things? . . . I can sit up today. Let's go home soon. . . . But tell me – did I talk all kinds of silliness?'

'Not a word,' I said.

'I must have had a temperature,' she said. 'I don't know *what's* the matter with me, but I seem to have caught a virus, or something——' Mavis began to struggle for breath, and the sound that she made – how can I describe it? – was as if she had been caught at that fine point between breathing-in and breathing-out. She agonised, at last, in a convulsive combination of coughing and sneezing.

'The doctor says this has something to do with atmospheric pressure,' I told her. 'As soon as he gives permission, I'll take you home. I'm sorry our little holiday turned out so wretchedly.'

Mavis said: 'Please, Rod, let it be soon! I can't breathe here. . . . Do you very much mind not kissing me, Rod? This might be catching. Yes, that's it – it might be catching. Do you mind awfully leaving me alone a bit? Pretty please?'

I had to say: 'Look, Mavis – did you mean what you said last night about loving Abaloni?'

She became angry at this, and cried: 'Oh, for heaven's sake, *do* try to be *civilised* just for *once* in your life! Please leave me alone, Rod. Sort of go away, kind of, for the moment; and tomorrow, perhaps.'

So I left her, and went to see the doctor. He handed me a cablegram. It was from my uncle's solicitor, Mr Coote. My uncle, Sir Arnold Arnold, had died suddenly in Paris: would I, his heir and executor, return to London at my earliest convenience?

When I read this, I put my head between my hands and sat for a while rocking to and fro in deep grief. Then this grief was overlaid with black fear. *Was it I who killed him?* I wondered. But I reassured myself – this could not be: oysters would not be in season until the first of September. So I went back to Mavis's bed-side.

'Oh, please, Rod——' she began.

' – I must go back to England immediately,' I said. 'My uncle's dead.'

Her face was radiant as she cried: 'Oh, how – terrible! Oh, I'm so – sorry!'

I could almost have killed her then. But I stooped to kiss her. I hope I shall not long remember – I am sure that I shall never forget – the quick little gesture of re-vulsion with which she turned away as soon as my lips touched her cheek. 'Better hurry, Rod, darling,' she said: and began to weep.

'You're crying!' I said.

'So are you,' said she.

'I loved the old man very much, I think,' I said, 'and you even more, Mavis. Until soon. Good-bye.'

I arranged for transportation to the nearest airport. Before I left I sent for the woman who had given of her blood to my wife and, in genuine gratitude, put some money into her hand, and thanked her most warmly.

She burst into tears and rushed out of the room.

When I went to see Mr Coote in his office in Staple Inn, my worst fears were confirmed. Discreetly congratu-lating me upon my inheritance, which, even after death duties had been paid, would still leave me rich – Coote told me the story of my uncle's death:

'. . . As you no doubt know, the late Sir Arnold was of – *de mortuis nil nisi bonum* – an impatient, an im-petuous disposition. Oh dear! In a nutshell: the oyster season being over, he resented having to live on "slops" – he said he'd be damned if he would, and said in Paris they served oysters all the year round. "And what the devil's the matter with a fat Portuguese oyster, damn it all?" Sir Arnold said.'

'Go on, Mr Coote!'

'To proceed . . . Sir Arnold went to Paris. He went straight from the train to Fratelli's Restaurant, ordered three dozen of the finest Portuguese oysters and half a bottle of wine. He ate the oysters, drank the wine, and collapsed in a convulsion; a sort of asthmatic convulsion, but of the most violent kind. And this, I regret to say, was too much for his poor heart. . . . Now, please, oh, please, you really must pull yourself together! . . . Dunhill! A glass of water, quick!——'

For, at this, I fainted.

.   .   .   .   .

The Victorian novelists used to call it a 'brain fever'. Now, I believe, we refer to my condition then as a 'nervous breakdown'. I was put to bed and given opiates and sedatives – bromide of this, bromide of that. But always, when the world slipped away, and I slid out of it into the cool dark, I was snatched out of my black, drugged peace by fantastic nightmares.

In these, invariably, my Uncle Arnold appeared, curiously blue in the face and unpleasantly bloated, wheezing: 'Give me credit for it, Rod, my boy – never dreamed you had it in you to kill your old uncle! . . . But you ought to have done it with a poker, or even the paper-knife, face-to-face like a man . . . I could have forgiven you for that, Rod. But yours was a woman's trick, a poisoner's trick. . . . I'll lime you for that, my fine-feathered friend – I'll give you a taste of your own medicine – I'll give you a dose of your own poison, you woman, you!'

Then my uncle coughed himself into dissolution, and I awoke with a loud cry.

I might have lain there for a week or more; only on the third morning there came a telegram from Mavis, saying that she was arriving at Victoria Station by the boat train from Paris the following day. I got out of bed at once, and made myself presentable, and was pacing the platform a good hour before the train came in. She was more beautiful than ever. 'Oh, Mavis, Mavis!' I cried, kissing her.

To my horror and astonishment, her eyes filled with tears, and her chest heaved in a fit of coughing that sounded like thin steel chains being shaken in a cardboard box. 'For God's sake go away!' she said, as soon as she could talk. 'You make me ill!'

I am too tired to write more. What Mavis said is true. Literally, I make her ill. I understand, now, the sudden violent emotion of the woman who gave Mavis her blood in that transfusion – Solomona, her name was, I think. I have inquired since, and tests have been made. Solomona is violently allergic to my kind of red hair.

Therefore Mavis, who is all I have to live for, finds that my presence is poisonous to her. So she has left me, and I am dreadfully alone.

It is impossible for her to live with me. But it is impossible for me to live without her.

I see no occasion further to prolong my existence.

With this, I end the narrative of my confession: God is just.

The Crewel Needle

CERTAIN others I know, in my position, sir, have gone out of their minds – took to parading the streets with banners, and what not, shouting *UNFAIR*! Well, thank God, I was always steady-minded. I could always see the other side of things. So, although I really was unjustly dismissed the Force, I could still keep my balance. I could see the reason for the injustice behind my dismissal, and could get around to blaming myself for not keeping my silly mouth shut.

Actually, you know, I wasn't really sacked. I was told that if I wanted to keep what there was of my pension, I had better resign on grounds of ill-health. So I did, and serve me right. I should never have made my statement without first having my evidence corroborated. However, no bitterness – that ends badly, mark my words. Justifiable or unjustifiable, bitterness leads to prejudice, which, carried far enough, is the same thing as madness. . . . I started life in the Army, d'you see, where you learn to digest a bit of injustice here and there; because, if you do not, it gets you down and you go doolally.

Many is the good man I've known who has ruined himself by expecting too much justice. Now I ask you, what sane man in this world really expects to get what he properly deserves? Right or wrong?

· If I had been thirty years wiser thirty years ago, I might have been retired now on an Inspector's pension.

Only, in the matter of an Open Verdict, I didn't have the sense to say nothing. I was young and foolish, d'you see, and therefore over-eager. There was a girl I was very keen on, and I was anxious to better myself – she was used to something a cut above what I could offer her. D'you see?

I was supposed to be an intelligent officer, as far as that goes in the Police Force. But that isn't quite good enough. In those days all the so-called intelligence in the world wouldn't get a policeman very far – seniority aside – unless he had a kind of spectacular way of showing it.

I'm not embittered, mind you. Nothing against the Force. Only I ought to have known when to stop talking.

.   .   .   .   .

At first, like everybody else, I thought nothing of it. The police were called in after the doctor, merely as a matter of routine, d'you see. I was on the beat then, in Hammersmith. Towards about eight o'clock one Sunday morning, neighbours on either side of a little house on Spindleberry Road were disturbed by the hysterical crying of a child at No. 9.

At first there was some talk of the N.S.P.C.C., but there was no question of that, because the people at No. 9 were, simply, a little orphan girl, aged eight, and her aunt, Miss Pantile, who thought the world of her niece and, far from ill-treating the child, had a tendency to spoil her; because the little girl, whose name was Titania, was delicate, having had rheumatic fever.

As is not uncommon, the houses in Spindleberry Road are numbered, odd coming up and even going down. The neighbours in question, therefore, were Nos. 7 and 11. Spindleberry Road, like so many of them put up around Brook Green before the turn of the century, is simply a parallel of brick barracks, sort of sectionalised and numbered. Under each number, a porch. In front of each porch, iron railings and an iron gate. At the back of each and every house, a bit of garden. I mention this, d'you see, because these houses, from a policeman's point of view, present only an elementary problem: they are accessible from front or back only.

Beg pardon – I've never quite lost the habit of making everything I say a kind of Report. . . . Well, hearing child crying, neighbours knock at door. No answer. No. 7 shouts through letter-box: 'Open the door and let us in, Titania!' Child keeps on crying. Various neighbours try windows, but every window is locked from the inside. At last No. 11, a retired captain of the Mercantile Marine, in the presence of witnesses, bursts in the back door.

Meanwhile, one of the lady neighbours has come to get a policeman, and has found me at the corner of Rowan Road. I appear on the scene.

Not to bother you, sir, with the formalities: being within my rights, as I see them in this case, I go in, having whistled for another policeman who happens to be my Sergeant. The house is in no way disturbed, but all the time, upstairs, this child is screaming as if she is being murdered, over and over again: 'Auntie Lily's dead! Auntie Lily's dead!'

The bedroom is locked on the inside. Sergeant and I force the lock, and there comes out at us a terrified little golden-headed girl, frightened out of her wits. The woman from No. 11 soothes her as best she can, but the Sergeant and I concentrate our attention upon Miss Lily Pantile, who is lying on a bed with her eyes and mouth

66

wide open, stone dead.

The local doctor was called, of course, and he said that, as far as he could tell, this poor old maiden lady had died of something like a cerebral hæmorrhage at about three o'clock in the morning. On a superficial examination, this was as far as he cared to commit himself. He suggested that this was a matter for the coroner.

And that, as far as everybody was concerned, was that, d'you see. Only it was not. At the Inquest, it appeared that poor Miss Pantile had met her death through a most unusual injury. A gold-eyed crewel needle had been driven through her skull, and into her brain, about three inches above the left ear!

Now here, if you like, was a mystery with a capital *M*.

Miss Pantile lived alone with her eight-year-old niece. She had enough money of her own to support them both, but sometimes made a little extra by crewel work – you know, embroidering with silks on a canvas background. She was especially good at crewelling roses for cushion covers. The needle she favoured – she had packets and packets of them – was the Cumberland Crewel Gold Eye, one of which had found its way, nobody knew how, through her skull and into her brain. But how could it possibly have found its way there? – that was the question.

There was no lack of conjecture, you may be sure. Doctors cited dozens of instances of women – tailoresses and dressmakers, particularly – who had suddenly fallen dead through having needles embedded in various vital organs. Involuntary muscular contractions, it was demonstrated, could easily send an accidentally-stuck-in needle, or portion of a needle, working its way between the muscles for extraordinary distances, until it reached, for example, the heart. . . .

The coroner was inclined to accept this as a solution, and declare a verdict of Death by Misadventure. Only the doctor wouldn't have that. Such cases, he said, had come to his attention, especially in the East End of London; and, in every case, the needle extracted had been in a certain way corroded, or calcified, as the case might be. In the case of Miss Lily Pantile, the crewel needle – upon the evidence of a noted pathologist – had been driven into the skull *from the outside*, with super-human force. Part of the gold eye of the needle had been found protruding from the deceased's scalp. . . . What did the coroner make of that? – the doctor asked.

The coroner was not anxious to make anything of it but routine inquiry.

In the opinion of the doctor, could an able-bodied man have driven a needle through a human skull with his fingers?

Definitely, no.

Might this needle, then, have been driven into Miss Pantile's skull with some instrument, such as a hammer?

Possibly; but only by someone of 'preternatural skill' in the use of fine steel instruments of exceptional delicacy. . . .

The doctor reminded the coroner that even experienced needlewomen frequently broke far heavier needles than this gold-headed crewel needle, working with cloth of close texture. The human skull, the doctor said – calling the coroner, with his forensic experience, to witness – was a most remarkably difficult thing to penetrate, even with a specially designed instrument like a trephine.

The coroner said that one had, however, *to admit the possibility* of a crewel needle being driven through a middle-aged woman's skull with a hammer, in the hands of a highly-skilled man.

. . . So it went on, d'you see. The doctor lost his temper and invited anyone to produce an engraver, say, or cabinet-maker, to drive a crewel needle through a human skull with a hammer 'with such consummate dexterity' – they were his words, sir – as to leave the needle unbroken, and the surrounding skin unmarked, as was the case with Miss Pantile.

There, d'you see, the coroner had him. He said, in substance: 'You have proved that this needle could not have found its way into the late Miss Pantile's brain from inside. You have also proved that this needle could not have found its way into Miss Pantile's brain from out-side.'

Reprimanding somebody for laughing, then, he declared an Open Verdict.

So the case was closed. A verdict is a verdict, but coroners are only coroners, even though they may be backed by the Home Office pathologist. And somehow or other, for me, this verdict was not good enough. If I had been that coroner, I thought to myself, I would have made it: Wilful Murder by a Person, or Persons, Unknown.

All fine and large. But what person, or what persons, known or unknown, with specialised skill enough to get into a sealed house, and into a locked room, hammer a fine needle into a lady's skull, and get out again, locking all the doors behind him, or them, from the inside – all without waking an eight-year-old girl sleeping by the side of the victim?

Furthermore, there was the question of Motive. Robbery? Nothing in the house had been touched. The old lady had nothing worth stealing. Revenge? Most un-likely: she had no friends and no enemies – lived secluded with her little niece, doing no harm to any-one. . . . You see, there was a certain amount of sense in the coroner's verdict. . . . Still . . .

'Only let me solve this mystery, and I'm made,' I said to myself.

I solved it, and I broke myself.

.   .   .   .   .

. . . Now, as you must know, when you are in doubt you had better first examine yourself.

People get into a sloppy habit of mind. I once read a detective story called *The Invisible Man*, in which every-body swore he had seen nobody; yet there were footprints in the snow. 'Nobody', of course, was the postman, in this story; 'invisible' simply because nobody ever bothers to consider a postman as a person.

I was quite sure that in the mystery of Miss Pantile there *must* have been something somebody overlooked. I don't mean Sherlock Holmes stuff, like cigarette-ash, and what not. Not a clue, in the generally accepted sense of the term, but *something*.

And I was convinced that somehow, out of the corner of my mind's eye, I had seen in Miss Pantile's bedroom, a certain something-or-other that was familiar to me, yet very much out of place. Nothing bad in itself – an object in itself perfectly innocent; but, in the circumstances, definitely queer. Now what was it?

I racked my brains – Lord, but I racked my silly brains! – trying to visualise in detail the scene of that bedroom. I was pretty observant as a youngster – I tell you, I might have got to be Detective-Inspector if I'd had the sense to keep my mouth shut at the right time – and the scene came back into my mind quite clearly.

There was the room, about sixteen feet by fourteen. Main articles of furniture, a pair of little bedsteads with frames of stained oak; crewel-worked quilts. Everything neat as a pin. A little dressing-table, blue crockery with a pattern of pink roses. Wallpaper, white with a pattern of red roses. A little fire-screen, black, crewel-worked again with yellow roses and green leaves. Over the fireplace, on the mantelshelf, several ornaments – one kewpie doll with a ribbon round its waist, one china cat with a ribbon round its neck, half a pair of cheap gift-vases with a paper rose stuck in it, and a pink velvet pincushion. At the end of the mantelshelf nearest the little girl's side of the room, several books——

' – Ah-ah! Hold hard, there!' my memory said to me. 'You're getting hot!' . . . You remember the old game of Hot-and-Cold, I dare say, in which you have to go out of the room, and then come back and find some hidden object? When you're close to it, you're hot; when you're not, you're cold. When my memory said 'hot', I stopped at the mental image of those books, and all of a sudden the solution to the Spindleberry Road mystery struck me like a blow between the eyes.

And here, in my excitement, I made my big mistake. I wanted, d'you see, to get the credit, and the promotion that would certainly come with it.

Being due for a week-end's leave, I put on my civilian suit and went down to Luton, where the orphan girl Titania was staying in the care of some distant cousin, and by making myself pleasant and being tactful I got to talking with the kid alone, in a tea shop.

She got through six meringues before we were done talking. . . .

.   .   .   .   .

She was a pale-faced little girl, sort of pathetic in the reach-me-down black full mourning they'd dressed her in. One of those surprised-looking little girls with round eyes; mouth always part-open. Bewildered, never quite sure whether to come or to go, to laugh or to cry. Devil of a nuisance to an officer on duty; he always thinks they've lost their way, or want to be taken across a street. It's difficult for a busy man to get any sense out of them, because they start crying at a sharp word.

Her only true distinguishing mark or characteristic was her hair, which was abundant and very pretty. Picture one of those great big yellow chrysanthemums combed back and tied with a bit of black ribbon.

I asked her, was she happy in her new home? She said: 'Oh yes. Auntie Edith says, as soon as it's decent, I can go to the pictures twice a week.'

'Why,' I asked, 'didn't your Auntie Lily let you go to the pictures, then?'

Titania said: 'Oh no. Auntie Lily wouldn't go because picture houses are dangerous. They get burnt down.'

'Ah, she was a nervous lady, your Auntie Lily, wasn't she,' I said, 'keeping the house all locked up like that at night.'

'She was afraid of boys,' Titania said, in an old-fashioned way. 'These boys! What with throwing stones and letting off fireworks, they can burn you alive in your bed. A girl isn't safe with these boys around.'

'That's what your poor Auntie said, isn't it, Titania?

72

Now you're not afraid of boys, are you?'

'Oh no,' she said, 'Brian was a boy. He was my brother.'

'What, did Brian die, my little dear?' I asked.

'Oh yes,' she said. 'He died of the 'flu, when Mummy did. I had the 'flu, too. But *I* didn't die; only I was delicate afterwards. I had the rheumatic fever, too.'

'Your brother Brian must have been a fine big boy,' I said. 'Now about how old would he have been when he passed away? Twelve?'

'Thirteen and a quarter,' said Titania. 'He was teaching me how to spit.'

'And so he passed away, and I'm very sorry to hear it,' I said. '. . . And your Auntie Lily wouldn't let you go to the pictures, would she? Well, you must always obey your elders, as you are told in the Catechism. Who did you like best on the pictures?'

Her face sort of lit up, then, d'you see? She told me: 'Best of all I liked Pearl White in a serial, *Peg o' the Ring*. Oh, it was good! And John Bunny and Flora Finch——' She giggled at the memory. 'But we had only got to Part Three of *The Clutching Hand*, when Mummy and Brian died, and I went to live with Auntie Lily. . . . Apart from the danger of fire, picture palaces are unhealthy because they are full of microbes. Microbes carry germs. . . . Auntie Lily used to wear an Influenza Mask on her face when she went out – you know, you can't be too careful these days,' said this serious little girl.

'And kept all her windows locked up, too, I dare say,' I said. 'Well, your elders and betters know best, no doubt. . . . But I mean to say, what did you do with yourself? Play with dolls?'

73

'Sometimes. Or, sometimes, I did sewing, or read books.'

'Ah, you're a great one for reading, Titania,' I said, 'like your poor mother used to be. Why, Titania is a name out of a fairy story, isn't it? A clever girl like you could read anything she could get her hands on, if she were locked up with nobody to talk to. I bet you read your poor brother's old books, too. I remember noticing on the mantelpiece a bound volume of the *Boy's Own Paper*. And also . . . now let me see . . . a book with a black and yellow cover entitled *One Thousand Things a Clever Boy Can Do* – is that it?'

She said: 'Not *Things*! *Tricks*.'

'And right you are! *One Thousand Tricks a Clever Boy Can Do*. And I'll bet you mastered them all, didn't you?'

She said: 'Not all of them. I didn't have the right things to do most of them with——'

'There's one trick in that book, which I have read myself,' I said, 'which you did master, though, and which you did have the right apparatus for, Titania, my dear. Tell you what it is. You get a medium needle and stick it down the centre of a soft cork. Then you get a penny and place this penny between two little blocks of wood. Put your cork with the needle in it on top of the penny, and strike the cork a sharp blow with a hammer. The cork will hold the needle straight, so that it goes right through that penny. That's the way you killed your poor Auntie Lily, isn't it, Titania?'

Finishing the last of her meringue, she nodded. Having swallowed, she said, 'Yes,' and, to my horror, she giggled.

'Why, then,' I said, 'you must come back to London

74

with me, d'you see, and tell my Inspector all about it.'

'Yes,' she said, nodding. 'Only you mustn't say any-thing to Auntie Edith.'

I told her: 'Nobody will do anything dreadful to you; only you must confess and get it off your poor little mind.'

Titania's second cousin Edith, by courtesy called 'Auntie', came with the child and me to London . . . and there, in the police station, she flatly denied every word of everything, and cried to be sent home.

Put yourself in my position, stigmatised as a madman and a brute! I lost my temper, one word led to another, and I 'tendered my resignation'. . . .

I shall never forget the sly expression on the girl Titania's face when she went back with her Auntie Edith to Luton.

I have no idea what has happened to her since. She will be about thirty-eight or thirty-nine by now, and I should not be at all surprised if she had turned out to be quite a handful.

The Queen of Pig Island

THE story of the Baroness von Wagner, that came to its sordid and bloody end after she, with certain others, had tried to make an earthly paradise on a desert island, was so fantastic that if it had not first been published as news, even the editors of the sensational crime-magazines would have thought twice before publishing it.

Yet the von Wagner Case is commonplace, considered in relation to the Case of the Skeletons on Porcosito, or 'Pig Island', as it is commonly called.

The bones in themselves are component parts of a nightmare. Their history, as it was found, written on mutilated paper in Lalouette's waterproof grouch-bag, is such that no one has yet dared to print it, although it happens to be true.

In case you are unacquainted with the old slang of the road: a *Grouch-Bag* is a little pouch that used to hang about the necks of circus performers. It held their savings, and was tied with a gathered string, like the old-fashioned Dorothy-Bag. This was necessary, because circus-encampments used to be hotbeds of petty larceny. So, on the high trapeze, the double-back-somersault man wore his grouch-bag. The lion-tamer in the cage of the big cats might forget his whip or lose his nerve – he would never forget or lose his grouch-bag, out of which could be filched the little moist roll of paper-money that was all he had to show for his constantly imperilled life.

Lalouette carried her grouch-bag long after the gulls had picked her clean. It contained 6,700 dollars and a wad of paper with a scribbled story, which I propose to make public here.

It is at once the most terrible and the most pathetic story I have ever had to tell.

.   .   .   .   .

At first the captain of the ship who landed on Porcosito, who subscribed to a Popular Science magazine, thought he had discovered the Missing Link – the creature that was neither man nor ape. The first skeleton he found had a sub-human appearance. The thorax was capacious enough to contain a small barrel; the arms were remarkably long, and the legs little and crooked. The bones of the hands, the feet, and the jaw were prodigiously strong and thick. But then, not far away – it is only a little island – in a clump of bushes, he found another skeleton, of a man who, when he was alive, could not have been more than two feet tall.

There were other bones: bones of pigs, birds, and fishes; and also the scattered bones of another man who must have been no taller than the other little man. These bones were smashed to pieces and strewn over an area of several square yards. Wildly excited, happy as a schoolboy reading a mystery story, the captain (his name was Oxford) went deeper, into the more sheltered part of Porcosito, where a high hump or rock rises in the form of a hog's back and shelters a little hollow place from the wind that blows off the sea. There he found the ruins of a crude hut.

The roof, which must have been made of grass, or light canes, had disappeared. The birds had come in and pecked clean the white bones of a woman. Most of her hair was still there, caught in a crack into which the wind had blown it or the draught had pulled it. It was long and fair hair. The leather grouch-bag, which had hung about her neck, was lying on the floor in the region of the lower vertebræ, which were scattered like thrown dice. This human skeleton had no arms and no legs. Captain Oxford had the four sets of bones packed into separate boxes, and wrote in his log a minute account of his exploration of the tiny island of Porcosito. He believed that he had discovered something unexplainable.

He was disappointed.

The underwriters of Lloyd's in London, had, with their usual punctiliousness, paid the many thousands of pounds for which the steamship *Anna Maria* had been insured, after she went down near Pig Island, as sailors called the place. The *Anna Maria* had gone down with all hands in a hurricane. The captain, officers, passengers, cargo and crew had been written off as lost. Faragut's Circus was on board, travelling to Mexico.

Captain Oxford had not found the remains of an unclassified species of overgrown, undergrown, and limbless monsters. He had found the bones of *Gargantua the Horror, Tick and Tack, the Tiny Twins* and *Lalouette*.

She had been born without arms and legs, and she was the Queen of Pig Island. It was Lalouette who wrote the story I am telling now.

    .   .   .   .   .

Tick and Tack were tiny, but they were not twins.

A casual observer sees only the littleness of midgets, so that they all look alike. Tick was born in England, and his real name was Greaves. Tack, who was born in Dijon, Brittany, was the son of a poor innkeeper named Kerouaille. They were about twenty-five inches tall, but well-formed, and remarkably agile, so that they made an attractive dancing-team. They were newcomers to the Circus, and I never saw them.

But I have seen Gargantua and Lalouette; and so have hundreds of my readers. Gargantua the Horror has haunted many women's dreams. He was, indeed, half as strong and twice as ugly as a gorilla. A gorilla is not ugly according to the gorilla standard of beauty; Gargantua was ugly by any reckoning. He did not look like a man, and he did not quite resemble an ape. He was afflicted by that curious disease of the pituitary gland which the endocrinologists term *Acromegaly*. There is a well-known wrestler who has it. Something goes wrong with one of the glands of internal secretion, so that the growth of the bones runs out of control. It can happen to anyone. It could happen to me, or to you; and it produces a really terrifying ugliness. Gargantua, as it happened, was by nature a man of terrible strength; George Walsh has told me that he might have been heavy-weight weight-lifting champion of the world. An astute promoter realised that there was money in his hideousness: so Percy Robinson rechristened himself *Gargantua the Horror*, grew a beard – which came out in tufts like paint-brushes all over his face – and became a wrestler. As a wrestler he was too sweet-natured and silly, so he drifted into a side-show. Naked to the waist, wearing only a bear-skin loin-cloth, he performed frightening feats of strength. In a fair in Italy I saw him lift on his back a platform upon which a fat man sat playing a grand piano. That same evening I saw Lalouette.

I would not have seen her if I had not been in the company of a beautiful and capricious woman who said, when I told her I had a prejudice against going to stare at freaks, that if I would not come with her she would go in alone. So I bought the tickets and we went into the booth.

Lalouette was an aristocrat among freaks. She drew great crowds. Having been born without arms and legs she had cultivated her lips and teeth, and the muscles of her neck, back, and stomach so that she could dress herself, wash herself, and, holding a brush or pencil in her lips, paint a pretty picture in water-colours or write a letter in clear round longhand. They called her Lalouette because she could sing like a bird. One had the impression that she could do anything but comb her hair. She could even move a little, by throwing her weight forward and sideways in a strange rolling motion. Lalouette painted a little picture while we watched, and sang a little song, and my lady friend and I, overcome with admiration and with pity, agreed that a woman of her accomplishments might have been one of the greatest women in Europe if the Lord in His wisdom had seen fit to make her whole. For she was a lady, superbly educated, and extremely beautiful – a blonde with great black eyes and magnificent hair of white-gold. But there she was, a freak on a turn-table; nothing but a body and a head, weighing fifty pounds.

I had some conversation with her: she spoke five languages with perfect fluency, and had read many books. Enquiring into her history I learned that she came of a noble, ancient, overbred Viennese family. Indeed, royal blood ran in her veins, and some fortune-teller had told her mother the Countess that the child to which she was about to give birth would be a Ruler, a Queen.

But when the child was born they saw a monstrosity. The Count fainted. The Countess loved Lalouette and cherished her, devoting her wretched life to the unfortunate child, who, soon after she could speak, demonstrated a proud and an unyielding spirit. Conscious of her infirmity, Lalouette wanted to do things for herself, despising assistance – despising herself.

Her father could not bring himself to look at her. When she was seventeen years old her mother died and her father sent her away with her nurse. 'All the money that you need, take,' he said, 'only do not let me see this abortion.' Then, when the First World War came, the Count lost all his money and shot himself. The kind old nurse lost much of her kindness after that, and when an agent named Geefler offered her money if she could persuade the girl to go with him, the nurse, pleading sickness and poverty, had no difficulty in persuading Lalouette that this would be a good thing to do.

So the young lady changed her name. Geefler sold her to Gargamelov, who passed her on to Faragut; and she drew money up and down the world, until Faragut's Circus went towards Mexico, and the *Anna Maria* was wrecked, and she found herself with *Tick and Tack* and *Gargantua the Horror* on Porcosito, the Island of Pigs.

Then the prophecy came to pass. She was the Queen of Pig Island. She had three subjects: two dancing dwarfs and the ugliest and strongest man in the world; and she had no arms and no legs; and she was beautiful.

.   .   .   .   .

Gargantua was a man whose tenderness was in inverse

proportion to his frightful ugliness. As soon as the *Anna Maria* began to sink he went instinctively to the weakest of his friends and offered them his muscles. To Tick and Tack he said: 'Hold on to my shoulders.' They were in sight of land. He took Lalouette in his left hand, told the others to hold tight, and jumped overboard, and swam with his legs and his right hand. The ship went down. The Horror swam steadily. He must have covered five miles in the face of a falling high wind. At last his feet touched ground and he staggered up to a sandy beach as the sun was rising. The two little men were clinging to him still. His left hand, stronger than the iron which it could bend, held Lalouette. The dwarfs dropped off like gorged leeches, and the giant threw himself down and went to sleep – but not before he had made a hollow place in the soft, fine sand, and put Lalouette comfortably to rest.

It was then, I believe, that Gargantua fell in love with Lalouette. I have seen it happen myself – in less outrageous circumstances, thank God! The strong makes itself the slave of the weak. And he saved her life. It is the tendency of Man to love that which he has risked his life to save.

Unhappy Gargantua! Poor Horror!

.   .   .   .   .

Armless and legless, Lalouette was the Brain. In spite of her disability, she was the Queen of Pig Island. She was without hope and devoid of fear; so she could command, since everything was clear in her mind. And she had read many books. Lalouette said: 'Tick and Tack; there must be water here. One of you go to the left. The other goes to the right. Look for the place where things grow greenest——'

'Who d'you think you are, giving orders?' said Tick.

She said: 'Oh, yes, and another thing: empty your pockets.'

Tick had, among other things, a leather-covered loose-leafed notebook. Tack had a remarkably large-bladed knife which he carried, no doubt, to give himself confidence; but he was a fierce little man at heart. They all had money. Gargantua had a fine gold cigarette-lighter, and a few hundred sodden dollars in a sea-soaked pocket – he alone wore no grouch-bag. Lalouette had strung about her neck with her grouch-bag, a gold pencil.

'We'll need all these things,' she said.

'Who in the hell d'you think you are, giving us orders?' said Tick.

'Be quiet,' said Gargantua.

Lalouette continued: 'That lighter is of no use as a lighter, because it's full of water. But it has flint and steel! It strikes a spark. Good. Gargantua, leave it to dry.'

'Yes'm.'

'You two, on your way right and left, had better pick up dry driftwood – the drier the better. We can strike a spark with that lighter and make a fire. Having lit a fire we can keep it burning. It must not ever be allowed to go out. Your knife, Tack, will be useful too . . . You, Gargantua, will go up the beach. There is a lot of wood here from ships. So there must be iron. Wood from ships has always iron. Iron is always useful. In any case bring wood that has been cut. We will build a little house. You shall build it, Gargantua – and you too, Tick, and you also, Tack. I shall tell you how you must build it.'

Tick began to protest: 'Who d'you think——'

83

'Leave the lighter so that it dries in the sun,' said Lalouette, 'and take care that your knife is dry and clean, Tack.'

'Always,' said Tack.

Gargantua said: 'Here's my lighter; you can have it if you like – it's solid gold. A lady gave me it in France. She said——'

'You can have my notebook if you like,' said Tick sullenly. 'It's solid leather, that cover. Pull that gadget down and those rings open and the pages come out.'

'Please, if you will allow me, I will keep my knife,' said Tack.

'You may keep your knife,' said Lalouette. 'But remember that we may all need it, your knife.'

'Naturally, Mademoiselle Lalouette.'

'Who does she think——' began Tick.

'*Shush!*' said Gargantua.

'No offence, Lalouette,' said Tick.

'Go now, please. Go!'

They went. Tick found a spring of fresh water. Tack reported the presence of wild pigs. Gargantua returned with an armful of wreckage; wood spiked with rusty nails; a massive thing like a broken mast in which was embedded an enormous iron pin.

'Light the fire,' said Lalouette. 'You, Gargantua, make a spear of that long piece of iron. Make it sharp with stones. Then tie it tight to a stick. So you can kill pigs. You and you, Tick and Tack, go up to the rocks. I have seen birds coming down. Where there are birds there are eggs. You are light, you are dancers. Find eggs. Better still, find birds. When they sit on their nests they are reluctant to go far away from their nests. Approach

84

calmly and quietly, lie still, and then take them quickly. Do you understand?'

'Beautifully,' said Tack.

Tick said nothing.

'Better get that fire going first of all,' said Gargantua.

Lalouette said: 'True. Boats must pass and they will see the smoke. Good, light the fire.'

'If I could find another bit of iron, or something heavy,' said Gargantua, 'I could do better than this spiky sort of thing, Miss. I dare say I could bang it out to a bit of a blade once I got the fire going good and hot.'

'How?' said Lalouette.

'I was 'prentice to a blacksmith, 'm,' said Gargantua. 'My dad was a smith, before the motor-cars came in.'

'What? You have skill then, in those great hands of yours?'

'Yes'm. Not much. A bit, but not much.'

'Then make your "bit of a blade", Gargantua.'

'Thank you, 'm.'

'Can you make me a comb?'

'Why, I dare say, yes. Yes, I should say I *could* make you a bit of a comb, 'm. But nothing fancy,' said Gargantua, shutting one eye and calculating. 'Something out of a little bit of wood, like.'

'Do so, then.'

'Yes, 'm. If Mr Tack doesn't mind me using his knife.'

'Could you also build a house, Gargantua?'

'No, 'm, not a house; but I dare say I might put you up a bit of a shed, like. Better be near the drinking water, though. And I shouldn't be surprised if there was all sorts of bits of string along the beach. Where there's sea there's fish. And don't you worry – I'll bring you home a nice pig, only let me get that fire going nice and bright. And as for fish,' said Gargantua, plucking a nail out of a plank and making a hook of it between a finger and a thumb, ' – sharpen that up and there you are.'

'Clever!' said Tick, with malice.

'But he always was clever,' said Tack, tonelessly, but with a bitter little smile. 'We already know.'

Gargantua blinked, while Lalouette said: 'Be quiet, please, both of you.'

Then Gargantua nodded and growled: 'That's right. You be quiet.'

Tick and Tack exchanged glances and said nothing until Lalouette cried: 'Come! To work!' – when Tick muttered: 'Who the hell do they think they are, giving orders?'

'Come on, now, you two!' shouted Gargantua.

I believe it was then that the two midgets Tick and Tack began to plot and conspire against Gargantua the Horror, and I am convinced that they too in their dwarfish way were in love with Lalouette.

They followed Lalouette's instructions, and struck sparks out of Gargantua's lighter to kindle powdery flakes of dry driftwood whittled with Tack's big-bladed knife. Tick blew the smoulder into flame and the men fed the fire until it blazed red-hot, so that Gargantua, having found a thick slab and a pear-shaped lump of hard rock for his anvil and hammer, beat his iron spike into a good spearhead which he lashed to a long, strong pole. Then they had a crude but effective pike, with which Gargantua killed wild pigs.

Porcosito is not called Pig Island without reason. It used to be overrun with swine, bred from a pedigree boar and some sows that Sir John Page sent to Mexico in 1893, in the *Ponce de Leon*, which was wrecked in a squall. Only the pigs swam ashore from that shipwreck. Porcosito seems to be an unlucky island.

Gargantua hunted ruthlessly. The pigs were apathetic. The boars charged – to meet the spear. The four freaks ate well. Tick and Tack fished and caught birds, gathered eggs and crabs. Lalouette directed everything and at night, by the fire, told them stories and sang to them; recited all the poetry she could remember, and dug out of her memory all she had ever read of philosophy. I believe that they were happy then; but it makes an odd picture – the truncated beauty, the stunted dancers, and the ugliest man on earth, grouped about a flickering fire while the songs of Schubert echo from the rocks and the sea says *hush . . . hush . . .* on the beach. I can see the sharp, keen faces of the midgets; and the craggy forehead of the giant wrinkled in anguish as he tries to understand the inner significance of great thoughts expressed in noble words. She told them stories, too, of the heroes of ancient Greece and Rome – of Regulus, who went back to Carthage to die; of the glorious dead at Thermopylæ, and of the wise and cunning Ulysses, the subtlest of the Greeks, who strove with gods and came home triumphant at last. She told them of the triumph of Ulysses over Circe, the sorceress who turned men into beasts; and how he escaped with his crew from the cave of the one-eyed giant Cyclops. He was colossal; the men were small. Ulysses drilled his sailors to move like one man, and, with a sharpened stick, blinded the giant and escaped.

She let them comb her hair. The French dwarf Tack was skilful at this, and amusing in conversational accompaniment to the crackling of the hair and the fire. Tick hated his partner for this. Yet the gigantic hands of

Gargantua were lighter on her head than the hands of Tick or Tack – almost certainly because the little men wanted to prove that they were strong, and the giant wanted to demonstrate that he was gentle.

It was Gargantua who combed Lalouette's beautiful bright hair, evening after evening, while Tick and Tack sat exchanging looks. No words: only looks.

Sometimes the little men went hunting with Gargantua. Alone, neither Tick nor Tack could handle the heavy spear. But it must be remembered that they were a dancing-team, trained to move together in perfect accord. So, while Tick directed the fore-part of the shaft, Tack worked close behind him, and they put their combined, perfectly synchronised strength and agility into a dangerous leap-and-plunge. Once they killed a fat boar. This must have made them confident of their power to kill.

This is not all guesswork. I have ground for my assumption, in what Lalouette wrote in Tick's loose-leaf notebook, holding the gold pencil in her teeth and guiding it with her lips, before she bit the paper into a ball and pushed it with her tongue into her grouch-bag.

It takes courage and determination to kill a wild boar with a spear. A boar is fearless, powerful, unbelievably ferocious, and armoured with hard hide and thick muscle. He is wickedly obstinate – a slashing fury, a ripping terror – two sickles on a battering-ram, animated by a will to kill, uninhibited by fear of death.

Having killed a boar, Tick and Tack, in their pride, resolved to kill Gargantua.

Lalouette says that she, unwittingly, gave them the idea, when she told them the story of Ulysses and Cyclops.

But the foolish giant called Gargantua the Horror, billed as the strongest and ugliest man on earth, must have been easy to kill. He worked all day. When Lalouette's hair was combed and her singing ceased, he went away modestly to sleep in the bushes. One night, after he had retired, Tick and Tack followed him. Gargantua always carried the spear. Lalouette listened drowsily for the comforting rumble of Gargantua's snoring a few yards away; she loved him, in a sisterly way.

. . . *Ha-khaaa . . . kha-ha . . . khaaaa-huk . . . khaaaa . . .*

As she listened, smiling, the snoring stopped with a gasp. Then Tick and Tack came back carrying the spear, and in the firelight Lalouette could see that the blade of the spear was no longer clean. The redness of it was not a reflected redness.

Thus she knew what the little men had done to Gargantua. She would have wept if she could; but there was no hand to wipe away her tears, and she was a proud woman. So she forced herself to pretend to be asleep.

Later she wrote: *I knew that this was the end. I was sorry. In this place I have felt strangely calm and free, happier than I have ever been since my dear mother used to hold me in her arms and tell me all the stories I told here; stories of gods and heroes and pygmies and giants, and of men with wings. . . .*

But that night, looking through the lashes of her half-closed eyes, she saw Tick untying the blade of the spear. He worked for an hour before he got it loose, and then he had a sort of dirk, more than a foot long, which he concealed in a trouser-leg. Tack, she thinks, had been watching him also; for as soon as Tick closed his eyes and began to breathe evenly, he took out the knife which he

89

had never allowed them to take away from him, and stabbed his partner through the heart.

He carried the body out of the range of her vision, and left it where he let it fall. Lalouette never knew where.

Next morning Tack said to her: 'At last we are alone. You are my Queen.'

'The fire?' she said, calmly.

'Ah yes. The fire. I will put wood on the fire, and then perhaps we may be alone after all this time.'

Tack went away and Lalouette waited. He did not return. The disposition of his bones, and the scars on them, indicated that he was killed by a boar. There was no more driftwood near-by. Tack went into the trees to pick up whatever he might find. As I visualise it, he stooped to gather sticks, and looked up into the furious and bloody eyes of a great angry boar gathering itself for a charge. This must be so: there is no other way of accounting for the scattering of his shattered bones. Hence, the last thing Tack saw must have been the bristly head of a pig, a pair of curled tusks, and two little red eyes. . . .

.   .   .   .   .

The last words in what may be described as Lalouette's Journal are as follows:

A wind is blowing. The fire is dying. God grant that my end may be soon.

This is the history of the Queen of Pig Island, and of the bones Captain Oxford found.

.

The Sympathetic Souse

THE Carpathians have always been the rocky-breasted wet nurse of sombre and terrible fantasy. Dracula came out of these parts in which, as the peasants whisper, crossing themselves: 'The dead ride hard.' Hungary, and Austria, have always been breeding grounds for vampires, werewolves, witches, warlocks, together with their bedevilments and bewitchings.

Psychoanalysis started in these parts. There are hundreds of professional psychologists (witch-doctors) from most other countries in the world who have studied under Freud, Jung, Adler, Groddeck, and the rest. Most of them go away with unblinking conviction: a species of owl stuffed with conjecture curdled into dogma. It is interesting, by the way, to observe that most of these fumblers in the dark are in a state of permanent nervous breakdown – an occupational disease you get when you try to take someone else's soul to pieces and clean it and reassemble it. No man in the world ever emptied his heart and mind in an analyst's office or anywhere else – only madmen try, who do not know what they are talking about; their candour is fantasy.

Anglo-Saxons ought to leave psychology to take care of itself. They break their hearts trying to make an exact science of what – considering the infinite permutations and combinations of the human mind – can never crystallise out of mere philosophy. In the end, it all boils down to repetitive case-histories, reports, and other rubbish – sex in statistical tedium, with the spicy bits veiled in the obscurity of a dead language.

So, in effect, said that shrewd little mental specialist whom I will call Dr Almuna, when I met him in a select scientific group at a cocktail party. He runs the Almuna Clinic – a polite, expensive kind of looney bin not far from Chicago – and specialises in dope fiends and alcoholics.

Almuna is good company. This cheerful man who has kept clean because he has learned how to wash his hands in any kind of water – this Almuna, a kindly cynic, believes everything and nothing. There is nothing didactic about Dr Almuna: he admits that the more he knows he knows, the less he knows he knows.

Once, in the course of a conversation he said to me, in reply to a certain question: 'I know the lobes of a brain, and have followed the convolutions of many brains, and the patterns of behaviour of many men and women. And still I cannot pretend to understand. I try, believe me! But every human brain is a separate labyrinth. He would be a lucky man who, in a lifetime, got to the heart of anybody's brain. No, no; quite simply, I do not try to explain. I treat, and endeavour to understand. The other way lies theory. Hence, fanaticism; and so delusion . . .'

On the occasion to which I have referred, when earnest professional men made a group and discussed cases, Dr Almuna was there, cocking his head like a parrot; one eye shut; avidly attentive. Some practitioner whose name I forget was talking of a case of 'sympathetic pains'. He had investigated and thoroughly authenticated the case of a girl who, at three o'clock in the morning of 7 January 1944 uttered a piercing shriek and cried: 'I'm shot!' She pointed to a spot under the collar-bone. There, mysteriously, had appeared a small blue dot, exquisitely painful to the touch. It transpired that exactly at that moment her brother, who was serving overseas, had been struck by a bullet in that very place.

Dr Almuna nodded, and said: 'Oh, indeed, yes. Such cases are not without precedent, Doctor. But I think I can tell of an even more extraordinary instance of physical sympathy between two brothers . . .'

Smiling over his cigar, he went on:

.   .   .   .   .

These two brothers, let us call them John and William, they came to me at my clinic in Vienna, in the spring of 1924, before Mr Hitler made it imperative that I leave for foreign parts – even Chicago!

John came with his brother William. It was a plain case, open and shut, of dipsomania. Aha, but not so plain! Because there was such a sympathy between these brothers, William and John, that the weakness of the one affected the other.

William drank at least two bottles of brandy every day. John was a teetotaller – the very odour of alcohol was revolting to him. William smoked fifteen strong cigars a day. John detested the smell of tobacco smoke – it made him sick.

Yet account for this, if you like, gentlemen – William, the drunkard, and the smoker, was a harmless kind of fellow, while his brother John, the total abstainer, the non-smoker, showed every symptom of chronic alco-holism, cirrhosis of the liver, and a certain fluttering of the heart that comes of nicotine poisoning!

93

I do not suppose that any doctor has had the good luck to have such a case on his hands. There was William, breathing brandy and puffing cigar smoke like a steam engine, in the pink of condition; blissfully semi-comatose; happy. And there was John, with a strawberry nose, a face like a strawberry soufflé, eyes like poached egs in pools of blood, fingers playing mysterious arpeggios all over the place – a clear case of alcoholic polyneurotic psychosis – but John had never touched a drop.

It was John who did most of the talking – the one with the strawberry nose. He said: 'Dr Almuna, for God's sake, stop him! He's killing me. He's killing himself, and he's killing me.'

William said: 'Pay no attention, Doc. John's the man of nerves. Me, I take things easy.'

At this John cried: 'Nerves! Damn you, William, you've torn mine to shreds!'

William said, quite placidly: 'Give me some brandy, Doctor.'

And then you would have been amazed to see the play of expression on the face of John, the plaintive one. He folded his hands and gripped them tight to stop the tremor; and I have never seen a more remarkable combination of desire and revulsion in a human countenance.

'Don't!' he said; and then: '. . . Well, Doctor, if you think it's okay . . .'

Alas, that I should say it – to an inquiring mind, however well-disposed, all men are guinea-pigs. Besides, it might be argued, who was John to say what the suave and comfortable William might, or might not, have? Experimentally, if you like, I gave William three ounces of brandy in a measured glass. It went down like a thimbleful, and he smiled at me – a smile that was pleasant to see.

And believe me or believe me not, his brother John began to retch and hiccup and blink at me with eyes out of focus, while William, having lit a strong cigar, folded his hands on his stomach and puffed smoke!

Sympathy, what? Wow, but with a vengeance!

At last, after a fit of deep coughing, and something like nausea, brother John said: 'You see, Doctor? Do you see? This is what I have to put up with. William won't let me work. Do you appreciate that? He won't let me work!'

Both John and William were evidently men of sub-stance. They had arrived in a custom-built Mercedes-Benz, were tailored by Stolz, and carried expensive jewellery. It is true that William was covered with cigar-ash, and that his platinum watch had stopped in the afternoon of the previous day; but it was impossible not to detect a certain air of financial independence.

John, the strawberry-faced, the tremulous one, he was neat as a pin, prim, dapper. I wish I knew the laundress who got up his linen. He wore a watch-chain of gold and platinum and, on the little finger of his left hand, a gold ring set with a large diamond. There was about two carats of diamond, also, stuck in his black satin tie. . . .

How shall I describe to you this weird mixture of dandyism and unkemptness in John? It was as if some-one had disturbed him in the middle of a careful toilet. His clothes were beautifully cut and carefully pressed. You might have seen your face in the mirrors of his shoes. But his hair needed trimming – it came up to the neck in little feathers – and his finger-nails were not very tidy. William was flagrantly, cheerfully – I may even say atavistically – dirty, so as to be an offence to the eye and to the nostrils. Still, he too wore well-cut clothes and jewellery: not diamonds; emeralds. Only rich men can afford to be so elegant or so slovenly.

So I asked: 'Work, Mr John? Come now, what do you mean by "work"?'

William, rosy and contented, was smiling and nodding in a half-sleep – the picture of health and well-being. And his brother John, who had not touched a drop, was in a state of that feverish animation which comes before the sodden sleep that leads to the black hangover.

He said: 'Oh, I don't *need* to work – I mean, not in point of economy. Mother left us enough, and much more than enough. Don't you worry about your fee, Doctor——'

'You leave Mother out of this,' said William. 'Little rat. Always picking on Mother, poor old girl. Give us another bit of brandy, Doctor: this is a bore.'

Before I could stop him, William got hold of the bottle and swallowed a quarter of a pint. He was very strong in the hands, and I had to exert myself to take the bottle away from him. After I had locked it up, it was – believe me! – it was poor John who said, in a halting voice: 'I think I am going to be sick.' What time William, blissfully chewing the nauseous stump of a dead cigar, was humming 'O Doña Clara', or some such trash.

And upon my soul, gentlemen, John joined in, in spite of himself, making what is politely called 'harmony':

O Doña Clara,
Ich hab' dich tanzen gesehn,

Und deine Schoenheit
Hat mich toll gemacht . . .

Then John stopped, and began to cry.

He said: 'That's all he knows, you see? You see what he is? A pig, a vulgar beast. My tastes are purely classical. I adore Bach, I love Mozart, I worship Beethoven. William won't let me play them. He breaks my records. I can't stop him. He's stronger in the hands than I am – exercised them more. Day and night he likes to bang hot jazz out of the piano; and he won't let me think, he won't let me work – Doctor, he's killing me! What am I to do?'

William lit another green cigar and said: 'Ah, cut it out, will you? . . . Why, Doc, the other day this one ordered in a record by a guy called Stravinsky, or something.' He chuckled. 'It said on the label, *Unbreakable*. But I bust it over his head; didn't I, Johnny? Me, I like something with a bit of life in it . . . rhythm. You know?'

John sobbed. 'My hobby is painting miniatures on ivory. William won't let me. He mixes up my paints——'

'Can't stand the smell of 'em,' said William.

' – Jogs my arm and, if I protest, he hits me. When I want to play music, he wants to go to sleep. Oh, but if *I* want to sleep and *he* wants to make a noise, try and stop him!'

'Let's have a little more brandy,' said William.

But I said to him, solemnly: 'The stuff is deadly poison to you, Mr William. I strongly urge that you spend about three months in my sanatorium.'

97

'I won't go,' he said. 'Nothing the matter with me. *I'm* okay.'

'Make him go, *make* him go!' his brother screamed. 'Oh, William, William, for God's sake – for *my* sake – go to the sanatorium!'

'I'm okay,' said William, cheerfully. 'You're the one that needs the sanatorium. I'm not going. I'd rather stay at home and enjoy myself. A short life and a merry one. Ha?'

And the extraordinary fact of the matter was, William was, as he said, okay – liver impalpable, kidneys sound, heart in excellent condition – he, who drank two quarts of brandy every day of his life! A tongue like a baby's, eyes like stars, steady as a rock. It was John who showed the stigmata of the alcoholic and the cigar-fiend – he who had never tasted liquor or tobacco.

How do you like that for sympathy?

John whispered brokenly: 'I might have tried to bear it all; only last week this sot proposed marriage to our housekeeper! Marriage! To our housekeeper! I can't bear it, I can't bear it!'

William said: 'Why not? Nice woman. Johnny hates her, Doc, but she understands me. Past her prime, maybe, but comfortable to be with. Shares my tastes. Likes cheerful music. Don't say no to a highball. Cooks the way I like it – plenty of pepper, rich stuff with a lot of spice. This Johnny-boy, here, all he can take is milk and boiled weakfish. Yes, so help me, I'm going to marry Clara. . . . Sure you can't let me have another little bit of brandy, Doc? An itsy-boo?'

I said: 'No. For the last time, are you sure that you won't come to my sanatorium?'

98

'Sure as you're sitting there,' said William, while John sobbed helplessly on the sofa.

So, to conclude: The brothers John and William went out to where their great limousine was waiting in the dusk, and drove away.

Shortly afterwards, John died in delirium of cirrhosis, nephritis, dropsy, and 'the whole works' – as you put it. His brother William died soon after, and they were buried together in the Sacred Heart cemetery.

Curious, what?

.   .   .   .   .

The good Dr Almuna rubbed his hands and chuckled.

A listening psychiatrist said: 'Most extraordinary,' and began an explanation that promised to be interminable.

But Dr Almuna cut him short. He said: 'The explanation, my dear Doctor, is an exceedingly simple one. Perhaps I failed to mention that John and William were Siamese twins, and had only one liver between them. And poor John had the thin end of it, which cirrhosed in advance of William's.'

He added: 'Intriguing, what? Perhaps the only case on record of a man drinking his teetotal brother to death.'

The White-washed Room

SHE was one of those hearty, healthy young women whom you may see every day in towns like Guildford. You see them and you hear them. They wear good tweed execrably cut and, more often than not, are accompanied by pink-faced men in yellow turtle-necked sweaters and big flannel trousers, who wear – as it were with an air of astonishment – brushed-up gingerish moustaches. The men with the moustaches stand condescendingly filling foul old briar pipes, or lighting cigarettes, while conversing at the tops of their voices – usually with one big, booted foot on the running-board of a small, fast, yet dilapidated little car.

She came of an excellent family. She could out-ride, out-smoke, out-drink and out-think any other well-bred girl in the little town. She could ride and take care of a horse, and knew exactly what to look for in a dog. As her father said, Athene was a good girl with no damn nonsense about her. She was his only child, and after his wife died she was mother, daughter and son to him.

She had only one secret. This was the only thing of which she had ever been ashamed, or afraid. It was a dream. Normally, Athene didn't dream; she went to bed and pulled down a big, thick black curtain which rolled up at daybreak, when she awoke, bright like a struck match, and went storming and roaring about her daily business – which was the strenuous business of organised pleasure. It would have humiliated her to admit that she had dreams that troubled her.

From time to time – especially after a hard day's hunting – she would drop into a deeper sleep than usual, and, although this sleep was terribly deep, she felt until the last, that she was somehow standing aside from herself and watching herself. The dream took this form:

She dreamt that she had been asleep. Something at the back of her mind told her that she had been travelling, and was a long way from her home. As, in the dream, she came out of a deep blackness, with something like the gasp of relief of a swimmer who comes up to the surface from somewhere below his depth, she knew that she was in a remote and strange place, and that she was in danger.

In her dream she lay still and waited. Athene was an intelligent girl, accustomed to the frenzied patience of the hunter and the fisherman: she knew how to keep still.

She knew that she was dreaming, but she wanted to know what was to come.

Her eyes were open. She could see the foot-rail of a black iron bed. Beyond it stood a blank white-washed wall. She could not move her eyes, yet something informed her that, on the north side of the room, directly opposite the window, there stood a lectern with a small vase containing four dying chrysanthemums.

As she reached this stage of the dream the horror of the grave and the fear of death took hold of her, and she wanted to scream. But she couldn't scream.

She was paralysed. Athene was well aware that outside the sun blazed, and that there she would be free and happy. Here there was no sun. This place was dead.

One white-hot bar of light had poked itself between the bars of the window and made a little puddle somewhere behind her. She couldn't see it but she knew it was there; she couldn't move her eyes.

But she could hear.

She could hear little quiet feet approaching. Their scuffling began as a whisper, turned into a flapping, and at last became footsteps which stopped outside the door.

She heard the door-knob turn.

Slippered feet slapped the clean floor. Then she saw two little old ladies dressed in washed-out pale blue, who walked to the foot of the bed.

As this point she awoke, always wet with cold, biting off the beginning of a scream, because it would have been improper for such a woman to express terror, let alone scream.

Athene married. She bore her husband three children, two girls and a boy. Only one of her children went wrong – the girl, who went to live in sin with a politician who afterwards made a fortune out of advertising and thereby vindicated himself. Athene had never said anything about her hideous dream. The time had passed. She was desperately lonely. Her children were strangers to her and she could find no means of loving her husband. She went away.

She did not know where she was going; she knew simply, that she wanted to go away, anywhere away from her world.

She took the train. It was filled with soldiers. Athene had taken a ticket to the end of the line and was prepared to get out anywhere at all. The train was hot and stuffy; they had been crossing a great white desert – white because it was of fine sand under a white-hot sun.

It seemed to her that she read BERGVILLE on the sign in the station and she got out and drank ice-cold beer until the groan of coaches and the screeching of the wheels told her that the train had left without her, so she sent a telegram ahead, dealing with her luggage, found a hotel and went to sleep.

Athene slept heavily, and, as it always happened in her heavy sleeps, she had her dream.

She dreamt that she was in a strange town. She knew that she had missed her train. Athene had not the slightest doubt concerning what was to come; she had dreamt this dream too often before. She knew that she was going to have her nightmare of the white-washed room and the iron bed.

Surely enough, the dream came. . . . There she lay, rigid on the iron bed in the white-washed room, unable to move. Athene knew – having dreamed this dream a hundred times before – that she was going to hear footsteps in the passage.

She heard them. They were the old familiar shuffling footsteps that she had associated with the quiet old women in blue.

Athene was aware that she was dreaming, and that in a second or two she would be properly awake, laughing at herself and preparing to go out with the Chesterfield Hunt. So, in spite of the nightmare, she stayed calm.

She heard the footsteps approaching, heard the door open and heard the door close, strained her fixed eyes until the two old ladies in blue came into her field of vision, and then expected to wake up with a terrified shriek, as usual.

But she didn't wake up.

The dream continued:

The two old ladies in blue did not stop. Looking at each other and sadly shaking their heads, they advanced. One of them, with a dry and tremulous forefinger, closed Athene's eyes, and she heard one of the old women say to the other:

'What a lovely corpse she makes. I wonder where she comes from.'

And Athene knew that, when she awoke this time, no one would ever hear her scream.

The Ape and the Mystery

WHILE the young Duke had been talking, the aged Leonardo had been drawing diagrams with a silver point on a yellow tablet. At last the Duke said: 'You have not been listening to me.'

'I beg your pardon, Magnificence. There was no need. Everything is clear. Your water down there near Abruzzi is turbid and full of bad things, evil humours. Cleanse it, and this flux will pass.'

'What,' said the Duke, 'I must wash my water?'

'You must wash your water,' said Leonardo.

The young Duke stared at him, but he continued still drawing on his tablet: 'You must wash your water. Tell your coopers to make a barrel, a vast barrel, as large as this hall, and as high. Now in this barrel you must lay first, clean sand to the height of a man. Then charcoal to the height of a man. Above this, to the height of a man, gravel. Then, to the top, small stones. Now down here, where the sand is, there must be a pipe. The bottom of this great cask will incline at a certain angle. The pipe will be about as large as a man's arm, but a plate of copper, or brass, suitably perforated, will cover the end embedded in the sand and will be further protected by a perforated case so that it may be withdrawn, if choked with sand, and replaced without considerable loss of pure water.'

'What pure water?' asked the young Duke.

'The pure water of Abruzzi, Magnificence. It will pour in foul at the top and come out clean at the bottom.

These fluxes are born of the turbidity of the water.'

'It is true that our water is far from clear.'

'The purer the water, the smaller the flux. Now your water poured in at the top will purify itself in its downward descent. The greater pebbles will catch the larger particles floating in it. The smaller pebbles will take, in their closer cohesion, the lesser particles. The gravel will retain what the little pebbles let pass. The charcoal will arrest still tinier pollutions, so that at last the water – having completely purged itself in the lowest layer of sand – will come out pure and sweet. Oxen, or men (whichever you have most of) may pump the water by day and by night into my filter. Even your black pond water, poured in here, would come out clear as crystal.'

'I *will* do that,' said the young Duke, with enthusiasm. 'The coopers shall go to work, the rogues. This moment!'

'Not so fast, Magnificence. Let us consider. Where is the cooper that could make such a cask? Where is the tree that could yield such a stave for such a cask? Big pebbles, little pebbles, gravel, charcoal, sand . . . Yes, reinforce it at the bottom and construct it in the form of a truncated cone. Still, it crushes itself and bursts itself asunder by its own weight. No, Magnificence. Stone is the word. This must be made of stone. And –' said Leonardo, smearing away a design on his tablet and replacing it with another – 'between every layer, a grill. To every grill, certain doors. Bronze doors. The grills, also, should be of bronze. As for the pipes – they had better be bronze. A valve to control the flow of the water, a brass valve. Below, a tank. Yes, I have it! We erect this upon . . . let me see . . . fourteen stone columns twenty feet high, so that, since water must always run down to level itself, it would be necessary for your servants only to turn a screw, to open a spring of pure water, gushing out of a bronze pipe in twenty places at once in your palace, as long as the tank were full. I have also an excellent idea for a screw, designed to shut off the water entirely or let it in as you will, wherever you will, either in a torrent or in a jet no thicker than a hair's breadth. In this case, of course, your Magnificence will need a more powerful pumping engine. . . .'

The young Duke asked: 'What do you want all those bronze doors for?'

Leonardo said: 'Magnificence, you have seen the pebbles in a stream.'

'Naturally.'

'You have seen them, and you have touched them no doubt?'

'Well?'

'They are slimy, are they not? They are covered with little green plants, you will have observed?'

'Well, well?'

'So will be the big pebbles, little pebbles, gravel, charcoal and above all the sand in your Magnificence's filter. Slime and green stuff will choke it, or make it a source of even more noxious water than ever before. Hence, the bronze doors. Every month the stones, charcoal, sand and so forth, are raked out and the empty places refilled with fresh stuff.'

The young Duke did not know what to say. He was uneasy. Turning an enormous seal on the forefinger of his right hand he muttered: 'This is all very well. I have the greatest respect for your knowledge, and all that. But . . . stone, bronze doors, bronze gratings . . . I mean to say, bronze pipes, and God-knows-what made out of brass. You know all about these things, of course. But seriously, I really think we'd better let it drop. . . .'

'If you liked the pipes could be simply lead. The gratings would have to be copper, of course, but in about thirty or forty years . . .'

'Thirty or forty years!'

'What is thirty or forty years?' asked Leonardo, with a smile, combing his great beard with his fingers. 'If you build, build for ever. Long after you are dead, Magnificence, by what will you be remembered? The fight you fought with Colonna? The bad portrait of you which you hired poor little Ercole to paint? Oho, no, no, no! Your descendants will say: "Ah, that was the Duke who washed the water here in Abruzzi and cured his people of their belly-aches." Therefore I say stone of the hardest and bronze of the toughest. I know, Magnificence; I know.'

'You know everything, Leonardo.'

'I know a little of everything, and not much of anything – with the possible exception of the art of painting. Of that I know something. Yes, I know a certain something about painting pictures. But what is that worth? Little, Magnificence – so little! Your wall, upon which I smear my blood and tears, will fall. The bit of wood that I give my life to cover with pigments will warp, Magnificence, crack and rot. I grind my colours and I refine and refine my oils, and hope and hope for a few years more of life, as Leonardo da Vinci, when I have gone where I belong. But mark my words! One cup of sweet water out of your river down at Abruzzi – one cup of water, pure water, in the belly of a grateful ploughman – will make you immortal, and you will be remembered long after my colours fade. Simply because of a cup of clean water, Magnificence! So I talk in terms of hewn stone and mighty bronze, thinking of that cup of good water.'

The Duke found his opportunity to change this subject. 'Ah, yes,' he said. 'Now that you mention it. Speaking of colours, and what not. You are the man who painted that picture of the Madonna Lisa, are you not? I mean the wife of Francesco di Bartolommeo di Zanobi del Giocondo – that one. Yes, of course you are.'

'Yes,' said Leonardo.

The Duke said: 'Remarkable man that you are! To-day you make drains. Tomorrow you cast cannon. The day before yesterday you make a sort of Icarus Machine, so that a man can fly like a bird. Ah . . . can you? Did it?'

'No, Magnificence, not yet.'

'It would not surprise me if you could transmute metals. They say that you are something of an alchemist. Can you turn base metals into gold, Leonardo?'

'I have never tried.'

'Try! try! Who knows? They tell me that the Valentinois has a learned doctor from the Lowlands who——'

'The tank,' said Leonardo, making a diagram, 'could be of copper, lined with——'

The Duke said: 'Yes, yes, yes, of course. Monna Lisa was a Neapolitan, or at least she was from the South. Yes, she was a Gherardini. Do you happen to know whether she was related to the Florentine family of that name?'

'No,' said Leonardo de Vinci, 'I know only that she married del Giocondo – he bought a picture of Saint Francis from Puligo. I have seen worse pictures. He is something of a connoisseur, Giocondo.'

'I saw your picture,' said the Duke. 'Between ourselves, it's not at all bad. La Gioconda is by no means a bad-looking woman. She's his third wife, you know.'

'I know. Her predecessors were Camilla di Mariotto Ruccelai, and Tommasa di Mariotto Villana. They both died within four years.'

'Ah, yes. There are some queer stories about that,' said the Duke.

'But to return to the tank, Magnificence.'

'To the Devil with the damned tank! Tell me, Leonardo – what was she always grinning about?'

'Madonna Lisa? She never grinned, Magnificence. She smiled, yes. Grinned, no.'

'You must have been alone with her for a long time.'

'Never for a moment,' said Leonardo. 'Never for one little moment. There were always waiting-women, secretaries, musicians, dress-makers, and frequently the lady's husband.'

'A jealous man, that,' said the Duke.

'Yes. He is going the way to hell, as I nearly did, trying to find the bottom of a bottomless pit.'

'She always struck me as deep,' said the Duke, 'ever so deep – deep as the sea. D'you know what? She isn't by any means what you could call a beautiful woman. But, the few times I met her, I couldn't take my eyes off her. I am not,' he said, curling the point of his red-blond beard between two fingers, 'I am not altogether undesirable as far as women are concerned, and in any case . . . well, I should have . . . however, there was something about that woman that froze me. In a way, she frightened me. She never said anything. You know, I suppose, that if I want to be amusing – if I go out of my way to be sprightly and entertaining – I could make St Bartholomew roar with laughter at the stake. Well, d'you know what? With the Madonna Lisa I had no success whatever. I believe you must have heard that I tell a tolerably good story. I told her three of the raciest and best I ever knew. There was never anything but that strange little pinched-up smile. You caught it perfectly, Leonardo. God knows how you did it, but you caught it. I stood and looked at the picture for nearly five minutes, and I said to myself: "Aha – he has caught it. There is the smile. There she is. There is La Gioconda to the life. What is she smiling at? She might be the Mother of God or she might be the Devil's Wife." And a sort of cold shiver went up and down my spine. Fortunately, at that time I was . . . anyway it was lucky for me that I had a certain other distraction just then. But one or two gentlemen I know completely lost their heads over her. Yet I am of the opinion – tell me what you think, Leonardo, because you have seen all the beautiful women in the world and know everything – in my opinion the Madonna Lisa is not beautiful.'

'No.'

'When you say "no", Leonardo, do you mean "no, she is not beautiful" or "no, I disagree with you, she is beautiful"?'

'She is not beautiful,' said Leonardo.

'It seemed to me that her hands were coarse and bony, but you painted them as if they had no bones in them. But she must have been an easy person to paint, because she moved less than anyone else I ever met in my life.'

'Yes, nothing but the blinking of her eyes told you that she was alive,' said Leonardo. 'But sometimes she moved her hands. Occasionally she took her right hand

from the back of her left hand, and loosely locked her
fingers together. But generally she let her hands fall into
her lap, where they lay relaxed, with the palms upwards.
You see such a disposition of the hands in good old
women who have done their work and are content to sit
and look at their grandchildren. I have seen hands like
hers on death-beds – the death-beds of women who have
lived contentedly and died in peace with all their sins
forgiven.'

'Yes, she must have been easy to draw,' said the Duke.
'She kept so still. Now if you were drawing me, Leonardo, that would be quite a different matter, because
I can't keep still. I pick something up, I put something
down, I walk here, I walk there, I take hold of a curtain
or a piece of tapestry. . . .'

'On the contrary, Magnificence, that would make you
all the easier to portray.'

The Duke, putting forward his right hand, said: 'And
what do you think of *my* hand?'

'It is a perfectly good hand,' said Leonardo, without
enthusiasm. 'It will do everything you want it to do.
I see by the third and fourth fingers that you are a horseman. The first and second fingers, and the thumb, tell
me that you are a swordsman, and the tendons of your
wrist tell the same story.'

The Duke said: 'Her hands really were a little too
large and hard. What made you draw them so round and
soft?'

Leonardo replied: 'I softened them to make a symbol
of terrible strength.'

'I saw no terrible strength,' said the Duke, 'only pretty
hands – pretty, soft, yielding hands.'

Leonardo repeated: 'Terrible strength. Soft and yielding. What is softer and more yielding than a quicksand or a quagmire? And what is stronger? What is more terrible? In the sea, what is stronger and more terrible than those soft, yielding things that lie still in the dark and lay their pliable fingers, or tentacles, upon the diver?'

'I don't quite follow you,' said the Duke, 'but, as I was saying, I could have fallen in love with that woman. I couldn't get to the bottom of her.'

'You had better thank God that you did not fall in love with her, Magnificence,' said Leonardo, 'and as for getting to the bottom of her, that is impossible.'

'Yes, as I said, the Madonna Lisa is deeper than the sea.'

'No. She has no depth to which you could dive and no height to which you could climb. She is nothing at all. Del Giocondo will have discovered that much by now. She is, as you might say, God's judgment upon him, that poor devourer of women. He loves her insanely – and she smiles. He bites his fingers, beats his head against the wall, and goads himself into madness in his hopeless endeavour to find something in her that is tangible – something upon which he may lay his hand and say: "At last I have found you." And all the time she smiles, and is silent. He may fall on his knees and weep on her feet. She will smile. He may lock her in her chamber and starve her: she will smile. He may humiliate her, beat her with sticks, strike her before the servants . . . she will continue to smile. This I say with authority, because I have seen it all. And he knows that if he cut her throat, she would smile that enigmatic smile even in death . . . and he is exhausted, defeated. He is exasperated and worn out (just as I might have been) by his effort to know her.'

'But you know her, Leonardo?'

'By the grace of God and an ape.'

'How, an ape?'

Leonardo was tired of it all. He made a gesture like a man who is shaking water off his finger-tips, and said: 'Oh . . . like del Giocondo, like you, like a dozen others, I lost sleep thinking of her. The smile, the smile, the smile. I have seen every face in the world, from the Throne to the gutter. I can read faces as your secretary can read a book. As a cut key fits the wards of a lock, so the shape of a face falls into position in a keyhole in my mind. Very good, this one baffled me,' said Leonardo, laughing grimly. 'I saw the agony of del Giocondo and the calm of the Madonna Lisa, and I wanted to *know*. I talked to her, watched her, employed ten thousand artifices to get her off her guard. And still she smiled. That smile came between me and my sleep. I hated her bitterly because she was too much with me. Then, to be brief, when the portrait was finished and my brushes put away, God sent the ape.'

'What ape?'

Leonardo said: 'Del Giocondo filled his house with musicians, tumblers, dancers, and all that, in order to amuse his wife. There was a choir of little boys that sang. There was a man who made me laugh – even me. Madonna sat with folded hands, quietly smiling. I finished the portrait. Then something happened. Del Giocondo had several large hounds. One of them, a buff-coloured dog almost as big as a donkey, used to lie at her feet. This gigantic hound had hanging jowls and an expression of indescribable melancholy. When I showed the Madonna Lisa the finished picture, she nodded and said, through a pin-hole in her compressed mouth: 'That is good.' At this, the great dog, whose ears had caught some warmth in her voice, came forward lashing about with his great tail which disturbed a little sleepy ape no bigger than your two hands.'

The Duke looked at his hands.

Leonardo continued: 'This absurd ape, enraged as little things are enraged, leapt upon the dog's back and pulled his ears, grimacing and chattering. The patient dog looked up with such absurd melancholy that it was impossible not to laugh. There was this gigantic dog, which might have killed a leopard,' said Leonardo, half laughing at the memory of it, 'and there was this preposterous ape chattering and chattering with ape-like anger while the dog feebly gesticulated with his tail, one friendly touch of which had been sufficient to knock his assailant head-over-heels. I laughed. Monna Lisa laughed – and then, by God, in the bursting of a bubble everything was clear. Then, Magnificence, I was a happy man, because I had uncovered a trivial truth, so that a thousand unconnected pieces fell together and made sense. La Gioconda threw back her head and opened her mouth and laughed, and then I knew why she had always smiled that strange quiet smile.'

'Why?' asked the Duke.

'She has very bad teeth, that vain and empty woman,' said Leonardo, laughing, 'but I have been thinking——'

'*Very* bad?' asked the Duke.

'Rotten. Her smile is the secretive smile of a woman with bad teeth. Touching the matter of the water supply; I believe——'

'I detest women with bad teeth,' said the Duke, yawning. 'And to the devil with your pipes and water-tanks.'

The King Who Collected Clocks

SECRETS such as Pommel told me burn holes in the pockets of the brain. If I could tell you the real name of the King and his country, your eyebrows would go up and your jaws would go down – and then, more likely than not, you would damn me for a sensational rogue and a dirty liar.

I met the Count de Pommel in the Casino at Monte Estoril, in Portugal. At first I thought that he was a confidence trickster operating under a mask of shy reserve. The Count de Pommel had lost all his ready money on the third block of numbers, and was feverishly convinced that his luck was about to change. Offering me his watch as security, he asked me to lend him a thousand escudos; about ten pounds. In England, as things were then, almost any watch that ticked was worth ten pounds. I gave him the money. Then he began to win. In three-quarters of an hour he won eleven thousand escudos, stopped playing, and returned my money in exchange for his watch, with a thousand expressions of gratitude and the offer of a glass of champagne. He gave me, at the same time, six square inches of visiting card: he was the Count de Pommel, of the Quinta Pommel at Cascais and the Villa Pommel, Lausanne, Switzerland. The watch, he said, was worth four hundred pounds.

'Who made it?' I asked.

'I did,' he said.

'There is something about you that made me think you were a clever man with your hands,' I said.

He held out his hands. Transparent, bloodless, reticulated with narrow black veins, they seemed to vibrate like the wings of an insect. 'Once upon a time, yes,' he said. 'Now, no. A nervous disorder. There is nothing worse than nerves in my profession.'

'Your profession?'

'Or trade, if you prefer the word. I am, or was, a watchmaker. I got my title of nobility from King Nicolas, Nicolas the Third,' he said, and added: 'I am not a nobleman by birth. Actually, I was a Swiss.'

'Oh, of course,' I said, remembering. 'Nicolas the Third collected clocks and watches.'

'His was the finest collection in the world.'

'And you – of course, of course! Pommel – now I get it – Pommel is a name I associate with the Nicolas Clock.'

The Count de Pommel smiled and said: 'It was a toy rather than a clock in the proper sense of the word. Birds sprang out singing and flapping their wings, Father Time held up a mechanical calendar in the shape of an hour-glass; and I devised a barometer also worked by clockwork, so that figures representing the Four Seasons appeared according to changes of atmospheric pressure. The Nicolas Clock was over-complicated. I am far more proud to have made the watch I pledged with you this evening.'

'It seemed to me to be made of gold.'

'Only the case. It is a very simple watch, but perfect; foolproof and waterproof – absolutely accurate. It seems silly, perhaps. I am a retired man, and time does not matter to me. Still, I like accuracy for the sake of accuracy – it is something to be achieved. I cannot work any more; my hands are unsteady, as you see. So I have a regard for that watch. It is the only thing left to me of all that I have made. The others are museum pieces, collectors' pieces – dead!'

'Did you also make the figures on the Nicolas Clock, Count de Pommel? They are works of art.'

'No, a Belgian artist made those: Honoré de Kock. We worked together.'

'Ah, yes, Honoré de Kock. He died, didn't he?'

'Yes, Poor Honoré. . . . He was a very good fellow. I liked him very much. It was a pity.'

'He died in an accident, I believe?' I said.

'He died on purpose,' said the Count de Pommel.

'You don't mean to say he killed himself?'

'No, far from it.'

'Are you telling me that de Kock was murdered?' I asked.

'I would rather not talk about him just now, if you will excuse me.'

'I beg your pardon, Count,' I said.

He was troubled. 'No,' he insisted, 'no, no, no! You have been very kind, very accommodating. I liked your face as soon as I saw you; and you were very good, too, charming! I should never have been so bold . . . only when I start playing, which is seldom, I am carried away. I take only a certain sum with me, and if I leave the table – then I lose the thread of the game. I can't imagine what possessed me to . . . to . . . to . . . Will you dine with us tomorrow, sir?'

'With pleasure,' I said, and so we finished the bottle and parted; and I walked back to my hotel, thinking of incongruities. I remembered a temperamental plumber,

a clumsy oaf with a soldering iron, who convinced everyone that he was a great craftsman because he was feroci-
ously arrogant; and I thought of Pommel, the greatest
living master of his craft, clock and watchmaker to
King Nicolas himself – and singularly like a trapped
mouse in his pitiful humbleness, in spite of his title of
nobility.

I wanted to know more about him. Among other
things, I wondered what sort of woman he had married.
Pommel must have been more than seventy years old. I
imagined a bloated, faded woman of fifty or so, soured
by cumulative marital discontent.

I was wrong. She was fifty years old, and fat, but still
attractive. Pommel called her Minna. Her hair was dull
red, her eyes were blue and clear, and she had the
warm, creamy, calm air of a woman who has achieved
happiness, so that nothing can hurt or touch her. She was
a Hungarian, and had been a needlewoman in King
Nicolas's palace – the kind of a girl that sings as she
works and likes to sit still. She was well beloved, secure,
healthy and contented – a woman who could grow
festive over a crust, or dance to her own singing. Before
an hour had passed I gathered that she had been poor
Honoré de Kock's mistress, not because she liked him
but because he was so unhappy; that she loved Pommel
because he was happy with her and because he was kind-
hearted; and that there was a big, dark secret about
which she had promised not to speak.

This, of course, was the inside story of the death of
Nicolas, the King who collected clocks. In the end I got
that story.

.   .   .   .   .

When I was twelve years old (said Pommel, after dinner) I was apprenticed to Tancred Dicker, and I learned a lot from him. You have, perhaps, seen pictures of him – Tancred Dicker, the one that looked like a sheepdog. Soon he let me work for him as a journeyman; I had the knack. By the time I was twenty I worked *with* Dicker. I went with him when King Nicolas asked him to come and stay and work on clocks, more than forty-five years ago, when I was twenty-two. When Dicker and I arrived we had first to meet a gentleman named Kobalt, a distant relation of King Nicolas's Queen, a very powerful man indeed. The King relied upon him: the poor King was getting old, and had rheumatoid arthritis. He no longer cared very much for affairs of state, you see. He liked best of all his pastime, his hobby, which was collecting clocks and watches. Oh, yes, yes, the King had had other hobbies in his day; but he had got old – more than seventy-three years old – and turned his mind to higher things, being more or less tired out.

Before we saw the King we saw Kobalt, as I was saying, and Kobalt talked to us about what we had come for. You will have heard of Kobalt, no doubt – or it may be that he was a little before your time. It was Kobalt who ran away with Marli Martin, the wife of the Minister; your father, more likely, heard of that affair. Kobalt is probably no longer in the land of the living; he must have been fifty years old when I first saw him more than forty years ago, and he was still good-looking. He was wicked, and a pig, but all the same he was a nobleman and a gentleman – a dangerous beast, and cunning; very brave – a wild boar, as you might say. He had light hair and moustaches, light-coloured eyes, no eyelashes. As soon as I saw him I disliked him: there was badness all over him. He said to us:

'I am very happy to meet you. His Majesty is very anxious to consult with you. He is . . . but listen!'

He raised a finger, pulling out his watch with his free hand; smiled and said: 'Exactly five o'clock.' Almost before he had finished speaking, the place became full of music. Birds sang, bells rang, silver and golden gongs sounded – dozens and dozens of striking clocks chimed the hour. A German timepiece sent twelve lame-looking Apostles staggering out to strike a gold-headed Satan with bronze hammers. From a cheap wooden affair leapt a scraggy-looking little cuckoo with five hiccups, while a contraption under a glass dome let out five American-sounding twangs.

'His Majesty the King has a collection of more than seven hundred clocks,' said Kobalt, as soon as he could make his voice heard. 'He has a sort of weakness for clocks – like Louis the Sixteenth. But never mention Louis the Sixteenth in His Majesty's presence; the name of that unhappy monarch strikes a not-too-pleasant note in the King's ears. We'll see more of each other, I hope, my dear Monsieur Dicker. I am sure that we have much in common. Much!'

Dicker bowed low, and so did I. But I was full of a new idea. If His Majesty liked clocks, he should have clocks – toys, novelties, nonsense – clocks with figures and contrivances. That was when I first conceived the Nicolas Clock. Tancred Dicker and I worked on it for four and a half years. Some of the technical innovations are his, but it was I who got the credit for the whole; and so I became Watchmaker to King Nicolas the Third.

De Kock designed, modelled, and cast the case and the

figures. He had talent – almost genius, the genius of the old Dutch Masters who could portray a man, an apple, a monkey, a grape, a bit of linen or a ray of sunshine, exactly as it appeared. He had a photographic hand; and it was this that made him unhappy – he wanted to make his own things, you see – it humiliated him merely to imitate the handiwork of the Lord God Almighty. He ate his heart out in his longing to create something with life of its own, but he never could. It is a sad thing when a man like de Kock becomes at last convinced that *au fond* he is a mediocrity; it breaks his heart.

Although he was very popular and successful and made a great deal of money, poor Honoré was very unhappy. He had already taken to drinking. Personally, I liked him very much indeed, and had a great admiration for him. He was a craftsman rather than an artist, he could work in any medium. Bronze, ivory, wood, marble, glass, gold, iron – anything and everything. Yet, because he could not reconcile himself to the fact that God did not see fit to give him the divine spark, he was always deep in melancholy. So it may, after all, have been true that poor Honoré de Kock committed suicide in the end. But I am by no means sure of this.

.   .   .   .   .

But where was I? Ay, yes, Dicker and I were talking to Kobalt, that smooth, terribly dangerous nobleman. It was a marvellous thing to hear all those clocks striking at once, and afterwards, when the last chime had died away (there was one vulgar little beast of a clock that was always a little late, and arrived breathless after all the others had done) – it was marvellous, afterwards, to listen to the ticking of all those clocks. The whole Palace was full of it. At night, first of all, you could not sleep; you lay awake, listening, waiting for the concert that almost deafened you every quarter of an hour. There was one silly figurine of a dancing girl. Every hour she performed a little can-can, showing her underclothes, and kicking a tambourine which she held in her right hand. Another contraption – an old French novelty clock – was decorated with a dozen fantastic musicians. When their hour came they all went raving mad, throwing their limbs in all directions, while an extraordinarily strident musical box, concealed in their platform, played a lively jig. And there was a German clock – somehow a typically German clock – upon which there stood, in a painted farmyard, a farmer, his wife, his son, his daughter and a pig. Without fail, twenty-four times a day, the farmer beat his wife, the wife smacked the son, the son kicked his sister, she pulled the pig's tail, and they all shrieked. A crazy clock! I could see that Dicker and I would have our hands pretty full, because these tricky toy clocks tend to be too sensitive, and sometimes have to be nursed like quarrelsome old invalids. What a business! His Majesty employed a staff of nine highly-skilled men who had nothing to do but wind up his clocks and see that they were set at the correct time. But he would not let them tamper with the works. That is what we had been employed for, at a salary that took even Dicker's breath away; and Dicker was accustomed to eccentric millionaires to whom money was of no importance.

I am sorry. I am boring you with all this talk of clocks, clocks, clocks. But clocks, you see, are my whole life: I know nothing else. Also, if I am to tell you the really remarkable part of this story, I cannot avoid reference to clocks. His Majesty Nicolas III, in his old age, thought of nothing but his collection. You might have thought that a man, even a king, so old and broken (or, I should say, especially a king) would not like to be reminded of the passing of time. But no, his love of clocks was stronger even than his fear of death.

We were hurried to his presence. You might have thought that we were doctors and he was dying. Oh, dear me, how very old His Majesty was! He was sitting stiffly in a great velvet chair, wrapped from neck to ankles in a wonderful dressing-gown; and even with this, in spite of the fact that the windows were sealed and a fire was blazing, he seemed to be blue with cold. He was dried up, so to speak. There was no moisture left in him. Even his poor old eyes looked dry and he kept blinking as if he was trying to moisten them. The King was suffering from a sort of paralysis which, it was said, was the price he had to pay for certain youthful indiscretions. Also he had arthritis and moved with great difficulty, dragging his feet. I shall never forget how shocked I was when I first saw him. I had had some silly childish idea that a king in real life looks like a king. And there was this little, corpse-like man, old as the hills and weary of the world, quivering to the finger-tips, shuddering and sighing and groaning, swaying his tired old head from side to side like a turtle. Only his beard was magnificent; it was like floss-silk, and covered most of his face and part of his chest.

But when he saw Dicker and me he came to life. He brushed aside the formalities and came straight to business. Oh, that awful voice! It was like a death-rattle, punctuated with groans. From time to time, forgetting his afflictions in his excitement, he started to make a gesture; but his arthritis stopped him with a painful jerk and he let out a moan of pain. He said that we were welcome, very welcome. We could have anything we liked, all we had to do was ask; even for money. We were to live in the Palace, where a workshop had been fitted up. His clocks had been neglected. His beautiful collection of seven hundred rare clocks was going to the devil. We were to go to work at once. First and foremost, there was a job to be done on a unique Swiss clock. It had stopped. It was all the fault of one Fritz Harlin, who had poked his clumsy fingers into the works, pretending to repair it. This was to be put right at once, and he would watch while we worked. It was his only pleasure, that poor old King – watching workmen tinkering with clocks. He has sat and watched me for eight hours on end in my workshop; even taking his meals out of a vessel like a teapot – he could digest nothing but milk – on the spot.

We were conducted to this workshop, which was a workshop out of a dream. Upon the bench stood a silent clock upon which stood a bronze Father Time about two feet high, and a dozen other figures about four inches high. There was a King encrusted with jewels and wearing a golden crown; an enamelled Cardinal in a red robe; a Knight in silver armour; a Merchant carved out of lapis lazuli; a Surgeon with a knife in one hand and a human heart made of a spinel ruby in the other; a Nun of silver and ivory; an Infanta of ivory and red gold; a painted Harlot hung with oddments of jewellery; a Peasant, all sinews, in old ivory and bronze; and an aged Beggar made of bone and studded with sores which were little rubies. The idea was, at the striking of the hour, Time mowed these figures down, one by one, finishing with the King, who came under the scythe on the last stroke of midnight. It was a beautiful piece of workmanship, and we approached it with reverence.

Soon the King came in between two attendants. One of these was an old doctor and the other was a sturdy young man with a nondescript face; they supported him under the arms and led him to another red velvet chair. When Dicker and I began to bow the King said: 'No, no, no need, no need. Get on with the work.' Then, trying to make an imperious gesture with his hand, he cried out in agony and groaned with terrible oaths and curses. Dicker and I went to work. This Fritz must have been a fool. I will not try your patience with technical details; but he had not seen one dazzlingly simple thing – one steel wire, less than half an inch long, bent at an angle of about sixty-five degrees, upon which the movement of the main figures, and therefore the movement of the whole mechanism, ultimately depended. Wear and tear and tiredness – for even steel gets tired – had reduced this angle by half a degree. I adjusted it in thirty seconds with a pair of pliers, wound and set the clock, and then – swish went the scythe, down went peasant, soldier, priest and king while the clock was still solemnly chiming (it had little golden bells like church bells). His Majesty uttered a cry of delight, a groan of anguish, half a dozen shocking words and a gracious compliment. We explained that it was nothing; that we would make a new angle-pin of the finest tempered steel, and Time would cut down Men for another hundred years.

And after that, I can assure you, Dicker and I were established, under King Nicolas III. We could do no wrong. I really believe that even if Dicker and I had committed murder it would somehow have been hushed up and we could have got away with it. Poor Dicker – this went to his head. Once, for example, when the Chamberlain at the Palace, a terribly proud man with a very hasty temper, told Dicker to remember his place, Dicker threatened to go home. The Chamberlain was dismissed with ignominy.

This man, whose name was Tancredy, then conceived a frightful hate for the King, and secretly gave his support to the Liberal-Democrat Party. I dare say you will have read something about the political situation in that country in King Nicolas's time, especially towards the end of his reign when there was a great deal of discontent. King Nicolas, like his fathers before him, was an absolute monarch. In effect he was the Law.

After his father, King Vindex II, had been assassinated by a woman who threw a seven-pound bomb into his carriage, Nicolas, influenced by a wise old Minister, had brought about certain reforms in the country. He had started a system of free education, free medical services, sanitation, the encouragement of the fine arts and of heavy industry, the development of an export trade – all this and much more was associated with Nicolas III. Nevertheless, the ordinary man of the people was subject to restrictions which horrified me. I am Swiss, you see.

There was no real freedom of speech or of the Press. The average man had to glance over his shoulder before he felt that it was safe to say what he wanted to say. There was frightful corruption in the highest places – especially when the King had grown too old and feeble and sick to care about anything but his seven hundred fantastic clocks. Consequently discontent was driven out of sight as an acorn is driven into the ground by your foot when you tread on it. This acorn, if I may put it that way, sent out all sorts of underground roots and pushed up unforeseen shoots. There were the Anarcho-Liberals, the Terrorists of the Brutus Party; the Democratic-Socialists, the Independent-Anarchists; the Republicans; the Labour-Royalists; and a dozen others. But the most subtle and formidable force working against the King was that of the Liberal-Democrat Party, led by an ex-lawyer named Martin. This was a Party to be reckoned with. Its methods were unquestionably constitutional and its policy was not to dethrone the King but to take away his power – which meant that the King would become a mere puppet; a King in name only. The Monarchists, who kept a great deal of personal power mainly because the King was a proper King, hated these Liberal-Democrats; and had indeed, my dear sir, very good reason to hate them. They were afraid of the Liberal-Democrats and of Martin, whose Party was growing stronger and stronger. He was suspected of encouraging, and even of financing and inspiring, all kinds of anti-Nicolas propaganda – mysterious little newspapers, scurrilous and filthy books and pamphlets and cartoons printed abroad; riots, acts of terror, and sometimes strikes. But nothing could be proved. Martin was too clever.

It was believed that only the personality of King Nicolas III kept the System in one piece. And poor King Nicolas was senile, paralytic, crippled with arthritis, and not far from death. After he died – and he was expected to die fairly soon – all the quiet, pale things underground would rush out and overwhelm the country.

As long as the old King lived, the Monarchists had

something to stand on. You see, nobody was allowed to forget that old King Nicolas had been a much better man than his ancestors; that he was a humane, kind-hearted Father of his People, and meant to make everyone happy as soon as he could afford to do so. Also, he was the King; as such, he inspired the People with an almost superstitious veneration.

But he had no issue. There had been only one son, a pitiful, sickly boy, who was dead of anæmia.

It took me many months to learn all this, and, having learned it, I began to feel that, after all, Dicker and I were not as well provided for as we had thought.

By then I was working on the Great Clock of Nicolas. The old King came every day to watch while we worked. It is a strange thing: although I like a clock to be a clock and not a silly mechanical toy, I developed a kind of weakness for these ingenious little bits of machinery. It was very pleasant working in the Palace: everything was to hand. His Majesty had a passion for exclusiveness: he insisted that the inner workings of the clock we were making should be seen by himself, Dicker, and (of course) me. Honoré de Kock worked with us later, because he, as the sculptor and caster of the figures, had to know what made them work. There was not a great deal for de Kock to do in the beginning. He was a bored, melancholy man, as I have said; and he could not keep his hands still; he was always playing with something.

One day, when it was necessary for him to stand by until we had worked out the details of the knee-joint of the central figure of the Great Clock of Nicolas, he began to knead and fidget with a large lump of putty on the bench. An hour passed. 'What's that?' asked His Majesty.

'Nothing, Your Majesty,' said de Kock.

'Show me,' said the King.

Then we saw that Honoré de Kock with his fidgety, photographic hands had squeezed, gouged, and patted out of that lump of putty an exact likeness of Dicker. The King was childishly delighted and said: 'Do one of me.'

Poor de Kock bowed and said: 'With pleasure, Your Majesty, but not in putty. Putty will not hold its shape. If it would please you I could make your likeness in, say, wax – simply, Sire, as a little game to divert you.'

Although it was early in the day, de Kock had already drunk a whole bottle of Apricot Brandy, and scarcely knew, or cared, what he was saying.

'Yes,' he went on, 'it might amuse Your Majesty. One of the first commissions I ever had was from a lady who had her likeness made in wax – full-length.'

'What for?' asked the King.

'Why, her husband was suspicious of her, you see, because she was very much younger than he. She used to leave her room stealthily in the dead of night to visit someone else. Her husband was in the habit of peeping in at odd hours to see if she was still there. I made her a perfect likeness, movable at the joints like a dressmaker's dummy, so that she could put herself into all kinds of attitudes; and deceived her husband perfectly for three years.'

'And what happened then?'

'Your Majesty, one night the husband crept in to spy upon his wife as usual, and was so overcome by the beauty of my waxwork that he ventured to creep up and kiss it. And then he rushed out yelling that his wife was dead – just as she came creeping back along the passage.'

'And then? Did he kill her?'

'No, he broke up the wax model.'

That was the only occasion on which I ever saw the King laugh. It hurt him, and the laugh turned into a groan, and the groan into a curse. But de Kock's story had put him into a very good humour. King Nicolas had been a very gay fellow in his time, fond of practical jokes – you know, making fools of people; pouring water over them, setting booby-traps so that when they opened the door a pailful of something nasty emptied itself over them . . . and so forth.

'Yes,' he said to de Kock, 'you shall make me in wax, life-size. But you mustn't tell anyone about it, do you hear? You go on and model me – every hair, every line, everything. Then we'll have fun. Yes, we'll play tricks. I shall be in two places at the same time. I'll frighten them out of their wits, the rogues. . . .'

Later, the King sent de Kock a beautiful gold cigar-case, studded with diamonds, but de Kock was gloomy and furious. 'Why did I tell him?' he cried. 'Why in God's name? After all these years – have I come down to making wax dolls for old men in their second childhood?'

But I said: 'Wax doll or bronze doll, what is the difference? If it pleases the old gentleman, let him have it. You know how generous he is when he is pleased. You'll have to hang about in the workshop for several months, perhaps. You will be bored. Instead of playing with a bit of putty, play with a bit of wax, and do yourself some good at the same time.'

De Kock was mollified; and set up a great lump of clay on a stand and went to work on the King's head. His technique was, if I remember rightly, as follows: first he modelled the head with microscopic accuracy in sculptor's clay. When this was dry, he made with infinite care a plaster mould, into which a special sort of wax was poured. So, the mould being taken away, section by section, like pieces of a jigsaw puzzle, out came the head, looking so horrible that it gave me a nightmare. It did not look a bit like the King at that stage, because de Kock had made him without the hair and the beard.

The putting in of the King's hair was the most tedious part of the business, because in a real life-like waxwork image every hair must be put in separately. I should not have cared for the job of putting in King Nicolas's beard a hair at a time; but when de Kock was at work he was a fanatic in his thoroughness. That is why he was what he was, poor fellow. Also, in spite of his first angry reluctance, he became engrossed in the King's head. He went to a shop where such things were sold, and bought an enormous quantity of beautiful silky white hair. (The starving peasant women of the Balkans, some of whom have beautiful heads of hair, sell their crowning glory for a few copper coins in order to buy something to eat.) The old King watched, blinking, fascinated. Then, looking at him, an idea occurred to me. I said to de Kock: 'Since the old gentleman has taken such an interest in this doll, as you call it, why not let us combine our two arts? If you can fix your model constructionally, I can undertake to do the rest.'

'What do you mean?' asked de Kock.

'Why,' I said, 'it would be no trouble at all for me to devise a clockwork mechanism to make him blink his eyes, sway his poor old head, tremble all over, and move those stiff, shaky hands of his. To me, that would be as easy as making a cuckoo-clock.'

De Kock was delighted with the idea. We arranged it between us secretly, so as to give His Majesty a pleasant little surprise. If he wanted his harmless fun, he could have it. No one knew what we were doing. Dicker was very ill with a disease of the heart – of which, by the way, he died shortly after. So de Kock and I spent all our spare time playing with his dummy and, as a matter of fact, we really began to take quite a fancy to it – as a job, I mean. It had taken hold of us.

The machinery that made the eyes and the head move and the hands tremble was nothing: a mere toymaker's job. I always liked difficult, intricate pieces of work. So it occurred to me that it might be really amusing to fix the jointed figure so that it could stand up and even take a few stiff rheumaticky paces backwards and forwards. That also was easy – hawkers in the street sell tin toys which can do that very thing; and even turn somersaults. No, it was not complicated enough for me.

Having made the dummy tremble and blink and sit and stand and walk, I now wanted to make it talk.

Well, you know that the phonograph had been invented then, although it was a very crude affair and did not sound real. But then again, neither did the King's voice sound real – in fact it sounded rather like a scratchy old phonograph record. Also, the King's voice was the easiest thing in the world for any man to imitate. You can imitate it yourself if you like. Let a lot of saliva run to the back of your throat and groan – there is the King's voice. I say once again, it was easy. The entire mechanism fitted into the back of the figure between the shoulder-blades and the hips, and was operated by several levers. If you pressed one, the figure stood up. If you pressed another, it walked twelve paces forward and turned on its heel. So if you wanted the figure to pace up and down all you had to do was repeat the pressure on that lever.

Another lever made it sit down. As the thighs and legs made an angle of ninety degrees, the phonograph automatically started. Choking imprecations, together with groans of pain came out of the mouth. All the time the dummy shook and quivered, while a perfectly simple, concertina-shaped bellows inside the head sucked in the air and blew it out, so that the moustache that concealed the mouth was constantly in motion, and you could hear a kind of wheezy breathing.

It was all quite life-like, especially when we dressed it in clothes which we borrowed from the King's wardrobe. As the King's Clockmaker, I was a person of great consequence in the Palace. Everybody knew what had happened to Tancredy; they all went out of their way to be polite to me. I could even have had intrigues with Duchesses if I had been so disposed. I had no difficulty in getting from the Master of the King's Wardrobe a complete outfit of the royal clothes, including fur slippers, a sable dressing-gown and a round velvet cap such as His Majesty invariably wore. When the dummy was dressed we sat it in a deep red velvet chair in the workshop, covered it with a sheet, and waited. At last the moment came. De Kock and I were excited, like children who have prepared a wonderful surprise for a beloved parent and are impatient to reveal it.

The King came in, with his doctor and his attendant holding him up, and was lowered, groaning and cursing, into his usual chair.

'What have you got there?' he asked.

I said: 'A little surprise for Your Majesty.' Then I

pressed two of the levers and whisked away the sheet all in one movement, and the dummy got up, walked twelve paces, which brought it face to face with His Majesty, and turned scornfully on its heel. I had measured my distance. Following it, I pressed another lever and it walked straight back to the chair and turned on its heel again. Another touch and it sat down, and the gramophone started and the great groaning voice bellowed dirty language right into the King's face.

I looked towards him laughing in anticipation of his delight, but what I saw horrified me. His face had become blue. His eyes seemed to be trying to push themselves out of their sockets. His mouth opened, and he uttered a terrible rattling scream. I still hear that scream in my dreams.

'Your Majesty,' I cried, 'forgive me!'

But he did not hear me. He fell back, and seemed to shrink like a sack of flour ripped open with a knife; and the old doctor, with a face as blue and terrified as the old King's, felt his heart and stammered: 'Oh, my God! Oh, my God! Oh, my God! He's dead – the King is dead!' And I remember that the sturdy attendant, bursting into tears, threw himself on his knees and cried: 'Oh, Your Majesty, Your Majesty! Don't go without me! Take me with you! Oh, Your Majesty!' He shouted this a heartbroken voice, something like the howl of a dog in the night. Then I heard footsteps; the door opened. I saw Kobalt with a dozen others behind him. Kobalt naturally looked first towards the King's chair, and when he saw what was there, the blood ran out of his face. Yet he was a quick-thinking man, even at a moment like this. He swung round and shouted: 'Back to your posts! God help the man I find in this corridor! Colonel of the Guard, a double guard on the outer gates – no one leaves the Palace!'

After that he slid into the workshop, shut the door, approached the royal chair and said: 'Doctor Zerbin – is His Majesty——?'

'His Majesty is dead,' said the doctor, with tears on his face. I felt that it was I who had killed the King and I said: 'Your Highness, it was all well meant. His Majesty asked us, de Kock and me, to make a figure, for a joke. The King wanted to——'

Kobalt turned, quick as a snake, with murder in his eyes. But then he saw the figure in the chair and his mouth hung open. He looked from it to the dead King. You know how death changes people. His Majesty, poor man, was all shrunk and shrivelled and blue, and looked somehow less than half as big as he had been five minutes before. The dummy, in every hair and every baggy pouch and wrinkle, was the image of the King as he had been when he was alive. Kobalt came slowly towards me. I never was a brave man, and loathe violence. I thought Kobalt was going to kill me, and all in a rush I said: 'Don't be hasty! De Kock and I are perfectly innocent, I swear it. His Majesty wanted a waxwork figure just to play a trick. A figure . . . like this. . . .'

And I pressed levers. I made the wax image of Nicolas III stand up. It walked twelve rheumaticky paces, looked at the corpse of the King, turned on its heel, strode back, sat down groaning and trembling, and puffed at Kobalt all the vile words you have ever heard, in a voice like the voice of His Majesty. Then it was still, except for a swaying of the head and a continuous tremor. In a quiet place, of course, anyone could have heard the noise of the powerful clockwork that made it move. But in the Palace of poor King Nicolas III, where there were more than seven hundred clocks, the noise of cogs, ratchets and pendulums was perpetually in everybody's ears; even the members of the kitchen staff when they were out imagined that they were still hearing the ticking of clocks.

Kobalt actually bowed to the image and started to say: 'Your Majesty,' but he stopped himself after the first syllable, and said: 'How very remarkable!'

'It is only a doll,' said de Kock, and there was a certain gratification mixed with the terror in his voice, 'a wax doll, a mere nothing.'

'It looks real enough,' I said, pressing the levers again; whereupon the figure got up, stood, walked twelve paces, turned, walked back, sat, groaned with agony and damned our eyes. Kobalt touched its wax forehead and shuddered. He went over to the King and felt his hand. Then his keen eyes veiled themselves. I could see that he was thinking hard and fast. It was not difficult to guess what was in his mind; the end of the King was the end of Kobalt. He, too, was as good as dead.

Soon he looked at me and said: 'You made this machinery, did you? I want to have a word with you. And you, Monsieur de Kock, you made this waxwork figure? For the moment it deceived me. You are a very talented man, Monsieur de Kock . . . and His Majesty collapsed on seeing your little work, gentlemen? Few artists live to boast of a thing like that.'

If he had simply said: 'Few artists can boast of a thing like that,' I might not be here to tell you this story. But when he said 'live to boast,' I knew that there was something wicked in his mind. I knew that I was in frightful danger. Poor de Kock was already beginning to swell up like a pigeon, rolling his eyes and pushing out his chest. Kobalt went to a speaking-tube and blew into it, and then he said: 'Major Krim? . . . Come down here at once with four or five men upon whom you can rely.' Turning to me he said: 'When I give you the word, make that thing work again.'

With an air of reverence – smiling now – he threw the sheet with which we had covered the dummy over the dead body of King Nicolas. Footsteps sounded. 'Now!' said Kobalt to me and I pressed levers. Major Krim, a man with a scarred face, came in with four others. As they entered, the dummy got out of the chair and walked abstractedly a few paces while Kobalt, keeping a wicked eye on me, said: 'His Majesty commands that the Dr Zerbin and the attendant Putzi be put under arrest instantly, and kept *incommunicado*.'

The thunderstruck doctor and the grief-stunned attendant were taken away. As the door closed the unhappy Putzi began to weep again, looking back over his shoulder at the thing covered by the sheet.

'Oh, you may well cry, you scabby dog!' shouted Kobalt, and then the image sat down groaning and quivering with the inevitable asthmatic curses, and the door closed.

Kobalt opened it again very quickly and glanced outside; shut it again and locked it, and said to me: 'What a very remarkable man you are, my dear M. Pommel, to make something like that. Why, it is almost – if I may say so without irreverence – almost like God breathing the breath of life into clay. How does it work?'

I have always been a timid and obliging man, but now – thank God – something prompted me to say: 'Your Highness, that is my secret and I refuse to tell you.'

Kobalt still smiled, but there was a stiffness in his smile and a brassy gleam in his eyes. He said: 'Well, well, far be it from me to pry into your professional secrets – eh, M. de Kock? . . . How wonderful, how marvellous – how infinitely more important than the death of kings, who are only human after all and come and go – how very much more important is the work that makes a man live for ever! To be a great artist – only that is worth while. Ah, M. de Kock, M. de Kock, how I envy you!'

Poor foolish de Kock said: 'Oh, a mere nothing.'

He had been drinking Plum Brandy. His vanity was tickled. I could not help thinking that if he had a tail he would wag it then.

'How *does* that work?' asked Kobalt, and the very intonation of his voice was a gross flattery. I could not stop looking at the body of the King under the sheet; but de Kock, full of pride, said: 'What do I know of such things? Your Highness, I am an artist – an artist – not a maker of clockwork toys. Your Highness, I neither know nor wish to know, nor have I the time to get to know, the workings of an alarm clock.'

In quite a different tone of voice, Kobalt then said: 'Oh, I see.' And so he gave another order, and Major Krim conducted de Kock to his suite, where, three weeks later, he was found with his brains blown out and the muzzle of a pistol in his mouth. The verdict was suicide: de Kock had emptied three bottles of a liqueur called Gurika that day.

But that is not the point. As soon as the Major had led de Kock out of the workshop, Kobalt began to talk to me.

Oh, that was a very remarkable and a very dangerous man! You were asking me about de Kock, earlier in the evening, and I said that I was not quite sure whether poor Honoré really committed suicide. Well, thinking again, I am convinced that he did not. The butt of the revolver was in his hand, the muzzle was in his mouth, and his brains were on the wall. There was one peculiar aspect of this suicide, as it was so called: the revolver was held in de Kock's right hand, and I happened to know that he was left-handed. It seems to me that he would have picked up his revolver with the same hand that he used to pick up the tools of his trade. A man dies, if he must, as he lives – by his best hand. And then again: Dr Zerbin and the attendant Putzi disappeared.

I beg your pardon, all this happened later. I was telling you that when I was alone in the workshop with Kobalt, he talked to me. He said that he would give me scores of thousands, together with the highest honours that man could receive, if I would communicate to him the secret of that unhappy dummy that de Kock and I had made to amuse the King who now crouched dead in his chair. I have always been timid but never a fool. I became calm, extremely calm, and I said:

'I think I see your point, Your Highness. Without His Majesty, you are nothing. Naturally you want to be what you are and to save what you have – you want to be, as it were, the Regent in everything but name. If the news of His Majesty's death reaches Tancredy, you are out. You may even have to run for your life, leaving many desirable things behind you. Yes,' I said, 'I believe that

I can see to the back of your scheme. Once you are acquainted with the working of this doll, you will work it. King Nicolas III, the poor old gentleman, was the Father of his country, with half a century of tradition behind him. As long as King Nicolas could show himself to the people, the monarchy was safe. And as long as the monarchy was safe, you were great. This dummy here looks so much like His unhappy Majesty that even you, at close quarters, were deceived for a moment. If the real King had not been sitting over there, you would never have known anything. I may go so far as to say that the figure de Kock made and I animated is even stronger than the King because it can stand up and walk of its own accord, which His Majesty could not; and say the same things in the same voice. It can even write His Majesty's signature.'

This, in point of fact, was perfectly true. The arthritic fingers of the King had no suppleness left in them, so that he wrote with his arm. Keep your arm stiff, grip a pen between the thumb and the first finger of your right hand, write the name *Nicolas* and you will see what I mean. Like this:

I had saved this for a last surprise – God forgive me. To demonstrate the truth of what I was saying (for I felt that I was fighting for my life) I got an inked pen, put it between the fingers of the dummy, and squeezed the thumb inwards. Immediately, upon a piece of paper which I presented, the pen scratched out the royal signature, and then the fingers opened and the pen was tossed aside.

'I will not tell you as much as I know,' I said, 'because I know that if I do, I shall be a dead man. It is useless for you to pry into the inside workings of this dummy because you will never be able to discover three very important things. Only I can tell you how the clockwork is wound. There are nine different springs, which must be tightened in their proper order. There are certain very perishable parts, and these must be constantly replaced. I warn you that you had better leave me alone.'

I said all this out of the mad bravado of a very nervous man, you understand. Having finished, and feeling myself on the verge of hysterics, I picked up a bottle that de Kock had left on my bench, and gulped down a couple of mouthfuls of it.

'I don't suppose you know that I could make you talk,' said Kobalt, in a voice that made me shudder.

In reply I told him the honest truth. I said: 'I am sure you could. But please don't. I can't stand pain. Oh, it is not only that,' I added, as I saw him beginning to smile, 'I can't stand pain – that's perfectly true – but when I said I shouldn't do it if I were you, I meant to say that the things I handle are actually more delicate than feathers. You could make me talk easily – you could make me talk by threatening me only with your fist. But don't you see? – the things I would tell you to do need a certain sort of hand, a certain kind of skill, and the training of many years. You'd never be able to do what you made me tell you to do. And I couldn't do it myself because you would have thrown me out of gear. Honestly, Your Highness, you'd better leave me alone.'

Kobalt looked at me steadily and coldly for a long

time and then said: 'My dear Monsieur Pommel, heaven forbid that I should argue with an expert. You're the greatest man of your time in your profession or, for that matter, any other. Let it be exactly as you say. Let us be friends. You are a cleverer man even than I thought.'

And so it happened, my friend, that the real King Nicolas III – God rest his soul – was secretly buried somewhere in the country, having been carried out of the Palace in a wine cask, while the dummy made by de Kock and animated by me became a Head of State. The news was given out that the old King, miraculously recovered, could walk again, with only one attendant. I was that attendant. I had to be with him, to wind him up, keep him in good repair and press the proper levers. Every day I took him down to the workshop and he sat while I went on with my work on the great Clock of Nicolas, which – as all the world must know – I completed. Another artist took up work on the moving figures where de Kock had left off. That is why experts have observed certain discrepancies.

It is fantastic, when you come to think of it: I was the real ruler of that country. I was the hand, the voice, the presence and the personality of His Majesty, King Nicolas III! Kobalt continued to be a man of power. When he, in conjunction with the Minister of the Interior, put forward the Monopol Bill that included clauses involving the oppression and persecution of Jews, I caused King Nicolas to run a wet pen across the document. He tossed away the pen with a groan and an oath, without signing. After that, the whole world marvelled at the renewed vigour of this aged man.

At about this time, my dear Minna came into the story. I hate to say it, but old King Nicolas – like the aged King David in the scriptures – used to keep himself warm at night through the proximity of young women. I provided a young woman. His Majesty had always loved women of a certain shape with red hair. He said that their very presence kept him alive. It was necessary for me to have someone whom I could take into my confidence, because my nerves were giving way. Remember, all this went on for several years. My dear Minna kept company at night with the wax image of Nicolas III. I taught her how to work the levers that made it move, and cut for her a copy of the big key – it had a handle like a corkscrew – that went into the little hole in the region of the left kidney and wound him up. From the beginning there was a deep sympathy between us . . . was there not, Minna, my little love?

It was Minna, in fact, who made a nobleman of me. She said: 'Why should you not call yourself by the same title as others do?' She was right. I was a foreigner, and not well born. People were talking. It was impossible for me to discuss things with the gentry as man-to-man. I procured a Patent of Nobility and, over the signature of His Majesty, became the Count de Pommel.

Meanwhile, I believe, I was instrumental in bringing about more reforms. We taxed the big landowners, we built big blocks of flats for workmen, we sent an expedition to observe weather conditions; we brought engineers from Scotland to improve the tramway system and installed electric light, and we did a great deal to establish the paper industry. We cultivated tobacco in the south and were beginning to draw revenue from exports. I had always wondered why the whole world had not heard of *Aka*, the smoked roe of a fish that lived only in one of our lakes. *Aka* is delicious. We made a monopoly of it, salted it, bottled it and sold it back to our own country and to the world.

If all had been well, I might have made an earthly paradise. But it was too good to last. All the intrigues of Kobalt, all the agitation of the Liberal-Democrats could not hurt us. The monarchy had never been stronger. No, it was the will of God. In the first place, the surface of de Kock's dummy began, naturally, to show signs of wear and tear. I could have adjusted that. I could have found another waxwork artist and kept him perpetually incarcerated. I could easily have done this. It was not a matter of the first importance. A thousand times more important than the appearance of His Majesty was, in the long run, the way he behaved. How he moved, and what he said, you understand, depended on me.

One morning I awoke out of an anxious dream and found that my hand was unsteady. Do not misunderstand me – mine was not a drunken tremor, because I never used to drink. It was anxiety, I think, that made me shake. It was extremely serious. Everything depended on my skill. I began to worry. And the more I worried, the more I trembled. I could easily, no doubt, have employed a highly skilled watchmaker, and trained him, telling him exactly what to do . . . keeping him in confinement, *incommunicado*. But I did not dare. Also my magnifying glass began to be misty, and the mist would not wipe off. To be brief, my eyes were going. A tremor and a foggy eye – that is death to a watchmaker.

Yet again, in spite of everything, in spite of all I had done, the Liberal-Democrats had got stronger under Tancredy. Trouble was brewing. Still, I should have stayed on to the end if Minna had not been there.

Thank God, she made me see reason. Dear Minna said: 'What is all this to you, Pommel, my dear? You are a Swiss. Most of your money is in the Bank of Lausanne. You can retire and do what you like. The Great Clock of Nicolas is finished. The old King died years ago. Be sensible and get out now!'

It seemed to me that Minna was right. I could no longer trust myself to work as I used to. I arranged for Minna and for me what the French call a *coupe-fil*, a 'wire-cutter'– a diplomatic passport. Having plenty of money – my wages only, and no plunder – put away in Switzerland, I drove with Minna over the border, and so, after many years, came home.

A little later, I learned that Kobalt had led His Majesty to address a delegation of Liberal-Democrats. Kobalt pressed the wrong levers. His Majesty sat down, cursed abominably, got up, walked twelve paces – straight into the fire – and stood, his hair and clothes blazing. As he stood, he melted. The fire took hold of the wax. The burning wax ran over the thick carpet. One wing of the palace was burned down. After that, upon the slogan *The King is Dead: Long Live the People*, the Liberal-Democrats scrambled up to power, and then were overthrown by the Communal-Workers' Party. The Communal-Workers were later accused of having shot King Nicolas III in a cellar. Tancredy went into exile. The last time I heard of Kobalt, he was supposed to be running a very prosperous night-club in one of the Latin-American countries . . . but I do not know anything about this, and I do not care to know. I cannot think of that man without a shudder.

But, on the whole, it is a strange story in its way – No? A little out of the ordinary – Yes?

Clock Without Hands

SEVERAL years ago, when newspapers had space to spare for all kinds of sensational trivialities, John Jacket of the *Sunday Special* went to talk with a certain Mr Wainewright about the stabbing of a man named Tooth whose wife had been arrested and charged with murder. It was a commonplace, dreary case. The only extraordinary thing about it was that Martha Tooth had not killed her husband ten years earlier. The police had no difficulty in finding her. She was sitting at home, crying and wringing her hands. It was a dull affair; she was not even young, or pretty.

But Jacket had a knack of finding strange and colourful aspects of drab, even squalid affairs. He always appproached his subjects from unconventional angles. Now he went out on the trail of Wainewright, the unassuming man who had found Tooth's body, and who owned the house in which Tooth had lived.

Even the Scotland Yard man who took down Wainewright's statement had not been able to describe the appearance of the little householder. He was 'just ordinary', the detective said, 'sort of like a City clerk'. He was like everybody: he was a nobody. At half-past seven every evening Wainewright went out to buy a paper and drink a glass of beer in the saloon bar of the 'Firedrake'–always the *Evening Extra*: never more than one glass of beer.

So one evening at half-past seven John Jacket went into the saloon bar of the 'Firedrake', and found Mr Wainewright sitting under an oval mirror that advertised Bach's Light Lager. Jacket had to look twice before he saw the man.

A man has a shape; a crowd has no shape and no colour. The massed faces of a hundred thousand men make one blank pallor; their clothes add up to a shadow; they have no words. This man might have been one hundred-thousandth part of the featureless whiteness, the dull greyness, and the toneless murmuring of a docile multitude. He was something less than non-descript – he was blurred, without identity, like a smudged fingerprint. His suit was of some dim shade between brown and grey. His shirt had grey-blue stripes, his tie was patterned with dots like confetti trodden into the dust, and his oddment of limp brownish moustache resembled a cigarette-butt, disintegrating shred by shred in a tea-saucer. He was holding a brand-new Anthony Eden hat on his knees, and looking at the clock.

'This must be the man,' said Jacket.

He went to the table under the oval mirror, smiled politely, and said: 'Mr Wainewright, I believe?'

The little man stood up. 'Yes. Ah, yes. My name *is* Wainewright.'

'My name is Jacket; of the *Sunday Special*. How do you do?'

They shook hands. Mr Wainewright said: 'You're the gentleman who writes every week!'

' "*Free For All*"– yes, that's my page. But what'll you drink, Mr Wainewright?'

'I hardly ever——'

'Come, come,' said Jacket. He went to the bar. Mr Wainewright blinked and said:

'I take the *Sunday Mail.* With all due respect, of course. But I often read your efforts. You have a big following, I think?'

'Enormous, Mr. Wainewright.'

'And so this is the famous . . . the famous . . .' He stared at Jacket with a watery mixture of wonder and trepidation in his weak eyes. 'With all due respect, Mr Jacket, I don't know what I can tell you that you don't know already.'

'Oh, to hell with the murder,' said Jacket, easily. 'It isn't about that I want to talk to you, Mr Wainewright.'

'Oh, *not* about the murder?'

'A twopenny-halfpenny murder, whichever way you take it. No, I want to talk about *you*, Mr Wainewright.'

'Me? But Scotland Yard——'

'—Look. You will excuse me, won't you? You may know the sort of things I write about, and in that case you'll understand how this Tooth murder affair fails to interest me very much. What does it amount to, after all? A woman stabs a man.' Jacket flapped a hand in a derogatory gesture. 'So? So a woman stabs a man. A hackneyed business: an ill-treated wife grabs a pair of scissors and – *pst*! Thousands have done it before; thousands will do it again, and a good job too. If she hadn't stabbed Tooth, somebody else would have, sooner or later. But . . . how shall I put it? . . . you, Mr Wainewright, you interest me, because you're the . . .''

Jacket paused, groping for a word, and Mr Wainewright said with a little marsh-light flicker of pride:

'The landlord of the house in which the crime was committed, sir?'

'The bystander, the onlooker, the witness. I like to get at the, the *impact* of things – the way people are affected by things. So let's talk about yourself.'

Alarmed and gratified, Mr Wainewright murmured: 'I haven't anything to tell about myself. There isn't anything of interest, I mean. Tooth——'

'Let's forget Tooth. It's an open-and-shut case, anyway.'

'Er, Mr Jacket. Will they hang her, do you think?'

'Martha Tooth? No, not in a thousand years.'

'But surely, she's a murderess, sir!'

'They can't prove premeditation.'

'Well, Mr Jacket, I don't know about that . . .'

'Tell me, Mr Wainewright; do you think they *ought* to hang Martha Tooth?'

'Well, sir, she did murder her hubby, after all . . .'

'But how d'you *feel* about it? What would you say, if you were a juryman?'

'The wages of sin is . . . ah . . . the penalty for murder is the, ahem, the rope, Mr Jacket!'

'And tell me, as man to man – do you believe that this woman deserves to swing for Tooth?'

'It's the law, sir, isn't it?'

'Is it? They don't hang people for crimes of passion these days.'

At the word 'passion', Mr Wainewright looked away. He drank a little whisky-and-soda, and said: 'Perhaps not, sir. She might get away with . . . with penal servitude for life, Mr Jacket, do you think?'

'Much less than that.'

'Not really?' Mr Wainewright's voice was wistful.

'She might even be acquitted.'

'Well, sir . . . that's for the judge and jury to decide. But to take human life . . .'

'Do you dislike the woman, Mr Wainewright?'

Jacket blinked at the little man from under half-raised eyebrows.

'Oh good Lord no, sir! Not at all, Mr Jacket: I don't even know her. I only saw her for an instant.'

'Good-looking?'

'Good-looking, Mr Jacket? No, no she wasn't. A . . . a . . . charwomanish type, almost. As *you* might say, she was bedraggled.'

'As *I* might say?'

'Well . . . without offence, Mr Jacket, you are a writer, aren't you?'

'Ah. Ah, yes. Not a handsome woman, eh?'

'She looked – if you'll excuse me – as if she . . . . as if she'd *had children*, sir. And then she was flurried, and crying. Handsome? No, sir, not handsome.'

'This Tooth of yours was a bit of a son of a dog, it seems to me. A pig, according to all accounts.'

'Not a nice man by any means, sir. I was going to give him notice. Not my kind of tenant – not the sort of tenant I like to have in my house, sir.'

'Irregular hours, I suppose: noisy, eh?'

'Yes, and he . . . he drank, too. And worse, sir.'

'Women?'

Mr Wainewright nodded, embarrassed. 'Yes. Women all the time.'

'That calls for a little drink,' said Jacket.

He brought fresh drinks. 'Oh no!' cried Mr Waine-wright. 'Not for me: I couldn't, thanks all the same.'

'Drink it up,' said Jacket, 'all up, like a good boy.'

The little man raised his glass.

'Your good health, Mr Jacket. Yes, he was not a nice class of man by any means. All the girls seemed to run after him, though: I never could make out why they did. He was what you might call charming, sir – lively, always joking. But well; he was a man of about my own age – forty-six, at least – and I never could understand what they could see in Tooth.'

He swallowed his whisky like medicine, holding his breath in order not to taste it.

Jacket said: 'Judging by his photo, I should say he was no oil-painting. A great big slob, I should have said – loud-mouthed, back-slapping, crooked.'

'He was a big, powerful man, of course,' said Mr Wainewright.

'Commercial traveller, I believe?' said Jacket.

'Yes, he was on the road, sir.'

'Make a lot of money?'

'Never saved a penny, Mr Jacket,' said Mr Wainewright, in a shocked voice. 'But he could sell things, sir. He wouldn't take no for an answer. Throw him out of the door, and back he comes at the window.'

'That's the way to please the ladies,' said Jacket. 'Appear ruthless; refuse to take no for an answer; make it quite clear that you know what you want and are going to get it. He did all that, eh?'

'Yes, sir, he did. . . . Oh, you really shouldn't've done that: I can't——'

More drinks had been set down.

'Cheers,' said Jacket. Wainewright sipped another drink. 'Are you a married man, Mr Wainewright?'

'Married? Me? No, not me, Mr Jacket.'

'Confirmed bachelor, hm?'

Mr Wainewright giggled; the whisky was bringing a pinkness to his cheeks. 'That's it, sir.'

'Like your freedom, eh?'

'Never given marriage a thought, sir.'

'I shouldn't be surprised if you were a bit of a devil on the sly, yourself, Mr Wainewright,' said Jacket, with a knowing wink.

'I . . . I don't have time to bother with such things.'

'Your boarding-house keeps you pretty busy.'

'My apartment house? Yes, it does, off and on.'

'Been in the business long?'

'Only about eight months, sir, since my auntie died. She left me the house, you see, and I thought it was about time I had a bit of a change. So I kept it on. I was in gents' footwear before that, sir, I was with Exton and Co., Limited, for more than twenty years.'

'Making shoes?'

Mr Wainewright was offended. He said: 'Pardon *me*, I was a salesman in one of their biggest branches, sir.'

'So sorry,' said Jacket. 'Did Tooth yell out?'

'Eh? Pardon? Yell out? N-no, no, I can't say he did. He coughed, kind of. But he was always coughing, you see. He was a heavy smoker. A cigarette-smoker. It's a bad habit, cigarettes: he smoked one on the end of another, day and night. Give me a pipe any day, Mr Jacket.'

'Have a cigar?'

'Oh . . . that's very kind indeed of you I'm sure. I'll smoke it later on if I may.'

'By all means, do, Mr Wainewright. Tell me, how d'you find business just now? Slow, I dare say, eh?'

'Steady, sir, steady. But I'm not altogether dependent on the house. I had some money saved of my own, and my auntie left me a nice lump sum, so . . .'

'So you're your own master. Lucky fellow!'

'Ah,' said Wainewright, 'I'd like a job like yours, Mr Jacket. You must meet so many interesting people.'

'I'll show you round a bit, some evening,' said Jacket.

'No, really?'

'Why not?' Jacket smiled, and patted the little man's arm. 'What's your address?'

'77, Bishop's Square, Belgravia.'

'Pimlico . . . the taxi-drivers' nightmare,' said Jacket. writing it on the back of an old envelope. 'Good. Well, and tell me – how does it feel to be powerful?'

'Who, me? I'm not powerful, sir.'

'Wainewright, you know you are.'

'Oh, nonsense, Mr Jacket!'

'Not nonsense. You're the chief witness; it all depends on you. Don't you realise that your word may send a woman to the gallows, or to jail? Just your word, your oath! Why, you've got the power over life and death. You're something like a sultan, or a dictator – something like a god, as far as Martha Tooth is concerned. You have terrible power, indeed!'

Mr Wainewright blinked; and then something strange happened. His eyes became bright and he smiled. But he shook his head. 'No, no,' he said, with a kind of sickly vivacity. 'No, you're joking.'

Jacket, looking at him, said: 'What an interesting man you are, Wainewright! What a fascinating man you really are!'

'Ah, you only say that. You're an author, and you can make ex-extraordinary things out of nothing.'

'Don't you believe it, Wainewright. You can't make anything out of nothing. There's more in men than meets the eye, though; and you are an extremely remarkable man. Why, I could make fifteen million people sit up and gape at you. What's your first name?'

'Eh? Er . . . George Micah.'

'I think I'll call you George. We ought to get together more.'

'Well, I'm honoured, I'm sure, Mr Jacket.'

'Call me Jack.'

'Oh . . . it's friendly of you, but I shouldn't dare to presume. But, Mr Jacket, you must let *me* offer *you* a little something.' Wainewright was leaning toward him, eagerly blinking. 'I should be offended. . . . Whisky?'

'Thanks,' said Jacket.

The little man reached the bar. It was his destiny to wait unattended; to be elbowed aside by newcomers; to cough politely at counters.

At last he came back with two glasses of whisky. As soon as he was seated again he said:

'Mr Jacket . . . you were joking about . . . You weren't serious about making fifteen million people . . .'

'Sit up and gape at you? Yes I was, George.'

'But Mr Jacket, I . . . I'm nobody of interest; nobody.'

'You are a man of destiny,' said Jacket. 'In the first place – not taking anything else into account – you are an Ordinary Man. What does that mean? All the genius of the world is hired to please you, and all the power of industry is harnessed in your service. Trains run to meet you; Cabinet Ministers crawl on their bellies to you; press barons woo you, George; archbishops go out of their way to make heaven and hell fit your waistcoat. Your word is Law. The King himself has got to be nice to you. Get it? You are the boss around here. All the prettiest women on earth have only one ambition,

George Wainewright – to attract and amuse you, tickle you, excite you, in general take your mind off the harsh business of ruling the world. George, you don't beg; you demand. You are the Public. Let anybody dare lift a finger without keeping an eye on your likes and dislikes: you'll smash him, George! Rockefeller and Woolworth beg and pray you to give them your pennies. And so what do you mean by saying you're nobody? Where do you get that kind of stuff, George? Nobody? You're *everybody!*'

Mr Wainewright blinked. Jacket drank his health, and said: 'So now tell me more about yourself.'

'Well . . .' said Mr Wainewright. 'I don't know what to say, I'm sure. You know everything already. You want my opinion, perhaps?' In Mr Wainewright's eyes there appeared a queer, marsh-light flicker of self-esteem.

'Perhaps,' said Jacket.

'In my humble opinion,' Mr Wainewright said, 'the woman deserves to die. Of course, I admit that Tooth was a bad man. He was a drunkard, and a bully, and went in for too many women. He ill-treated them, sir; and he was a married man too. I couldn't bear him.'

'Then why did you let him stay in your house?' asked Jacket.

'Well . . . I don't know. I had intended to give Tooth notice to quit more than once, but whenever I began to get around to it . . . somehow or other he managed to put me off. He'd tell me a funny story – never a nice story, but so funny that I couldn't help laughing. You know what I mean? He had a way with him, Mr Jacket. He must have. He sold Poise Weighing Machines. He told me, once, how he had sold a sixty-guinea weighing-machine to an old lady who had a sweet-shop in a little village – it was wicked, but I couldn't help laughing. And then again, his success with the women. . . . But all the same, you didn't ought to be allowed to get away with murder. I mean to say – he was her husband, wasn't he? And a human being, too. And I mean to say – the fact remains, doesn't it? She stabbed her husband to death with a pair of sharp scissors.'

'All right,' said Jacket. 'But can we prove that Martha Tooth *meant* to do it, eh? Can we prove premeditation?'

'I don't know anything about all that, I'm afraid,' said Mr Wainewright.

Jacket said: 'They don't hang you for murder without malice aforethought in a case of this sort. And incidentally, there isn't any actual proof that Martha Tooth really did stab her pig of a husband, is there?'

Mr Wainewright was shocked. 'She must have!' he said. 'Who else could have, if she didn't?'

'Anyone might have done it, my dear George. I might have done it. You might have done it. The charwoman might have done it. Did anyone *see* her do it?'

'Well, no, I suppose not,' said Mr Wainewright. 'But the evidence! The evidence, Mr Jacket!'

'Call me Jack, George old man.'

'Jack,' said Wainewright, shyly and with some reluctance.

'But go on, George,' said Jacket. 'What evidence?'

'*The* evidence, J-Jack. (Jack, sir, since you insist.)'

John Jacket felt a strange, perverse desire to provoke, to irritate this respectable little man. 'Evidence,' he said, 'evidence! I spit on the evidence. A woman comes into a house; a woman goes out of a house. The man she visited is found, stuck like a pig – which he was – with a pair of long, sharp, paper-cutting scissors in his throat near the collar-bone. So what? So what, George? He was in the habit of smuggling women into his room. Isn't that so?'

'Yes, that's true.'

'Say, for example, this man Tooth had a woman in his room before his wife – this wretched Martha Tooth – turned up unexpectedly. Say, for example, he hides this hypothetical woman in a cupboard. . . . Was there a big cupboard, closet, or wardrobe in Tooth's room?'

'There *is* a big wardrobe,' said Mr Wainewright, meditating.

'Say, then, that Tooth, hearing his wife's voice downstairs, hid his concubine in the wardrobe. The wife comes in. She talks to Tooth. She goes away. As the door closes, the enraged woman in the wardrobe comes out fighting, with a pair of scissors, and – *jab*! An overhand stroke with something like a stiletto, striking the soft part of your throat just where the big artery runs down. A child could do it. What?'

'Possible, I dare say,' said Mr Wainewright, tapping his foot in irritation, 'but I don't see the point. Mr Jacket – I'm sorry, I mean Jack. Jack, since you say I may call you Jack. If there *had* been any other lady in Tooth's room *I* should have known it.'

'How could you know?' asked Jacket.

Mr Wainewright meditated, marking off points with his fingers: he was somewhat drunk. He said, laboriously: 'In the first place, I have a respectable house. When my auntie died I converted it into little furnished flatlets. People can do as they like in my place, within reason, Mr Jacket. I mean to say Jack, Jack. By "within reason" I mean to say that people can have visitors . . .

within reason, visitors. As the person responsible for the house, I was always on the spot – or nearly always. A person can't be sure of anybody, and you don't want your house to get a bad reputation. So I . . . to be frank, I listened to how many footsteps were going up to this floor or that floor. And as it happened my little room was next door to Tooth's. And I can assure you that Mrs Tooth was the only visitor Tooth had that night. Mrs Madge, the lady who does the cleaning, let Mrs Tooth in. I passed her on the stairs – or rather, I stood aside to let her pass on the first-floor landing. I had seen Tooth only about two minutes before. He'd just got home from Bristol.'

'Did he say anything?' asked Jacket.

'He . . . he was the same as usual. Full of jokes. He was telling me about some girl he met in Bristol, some girl who worked in baker's shop. The, ah, the usual thing. Mrs Madge let Mrs Tooth in while he was talking to me. He said: "I wonder what the – the Aitch – *she* wants." And he said that she had better come on up. He'd been drinking. I went down because, to be quite frank, I'd never seen Tooth's wife, and wondered what kind of a woman she could be.'

'And what kind of a woman was she, George?'

'Not what I should have expected, Mr Jacket – I mean J-Jack. One of the plain, humble-looking kind. You wouldn't have thought she'd have appealed to Tooth at all: he went in for the barmaidish type, sir.'

'You never can tell, George, old boy. After that you went up to your room, if I remember right.'

'That's right. My room was next door to Tooth's. I mean, my sitting-room: I have a little suite,' said Mr Wainewright, with pride.

'Have a little drink,' said Jacket, pushing a freshly-filled glass over to him.

'I couldn't, really.'

'No arguments, George. By the by, remind me to let you have some theatre tickets. You and I'll go to the first night of *Greek Scandals* next week. Drink up. Well, go on, George.'

'Where was I? Oh yes. I had some accounts to do, you see, so I went to my sitting-room. And I could hear them talking.'

'What were they saying, George?'

'I couldn't quite get what they were saying, Mr Jacket.'

'But you tried?'

Mr Wainewright fidgeted and blushed. 'I did try,' he admitted. 'But I only gathered that they were having a quarrel. Once Tooth shouted. He said "Go to the devil." She started crying and he burst out laughing.'

'A nice man, your friend Tooth, George.'

'Yes, sir. I mean no, Mr Jacket – not at all nice.'

'And then?'

'About a quarter of an hour later, I should say, they stopped talking. They'd been raising their voices quite loud. I knocked on the wall, and they stopped. Then Tooth started coughing.'

'Was that unusual?'

'No, not at all unusual. He was a cigarette-smoker. In the morning, and at night, it was painful to listen to him, sir. And then his door opened and closed. I opened my door and looked out, and Mrs Tooth was going downstairs crying, and there was some blood on her hand. I asked her if she had hurt herself, and if she wanted some iodine or anything, and she said "No, no," and ran downstairs and out of the house.'

'She'd cut herself, it appears.'

'That's right, ah . . . J-Jack.'

'That's it, George. Call me Jack and I'll call you George,' said Jacket. 'What made you go into Tooth's room later on?'

Mr Wainewright said: 'He always borrowed my evening paper. I nearly always used to hand it over to him when I'd done with it.' He held up a copy of the *Evening Extra,* neatly folded. 'When I got back from here – I come here just for one quiet drink every evening, and read the paper here as a rule, you see – I went to his door and knocked.'

'And, of course, he didn't say "Come in,"' said Jacket.

'No. So I knocked again. No answer. I knocked again——'

'– And at last you went in without knocking, eh?'

'Exactly. And there he lay across the bed, Mr Jacket – a horrible sight to see, horrible!'

'Bled a good deal?'

'I never thought even Tooth could have bled so much!'

'That shook you, eh, George?'

'It made me feel faint, I assure you, sir. But I didn't touch anything. I phoned the police. They were there in ten minutes.'

'Detective Inspector Taylor, wasn't it?'

'Yes, that's right. A nice man.'

'He collects stamps for a pastime. Have you any hobbies, George?'

Mr Wainewright giggled. 'It sounds silly,' he said.

'When I haven't got anything else to do I cut pictures out of magazines.'

'And what do you do with them when you've cut them out, George?'

'I stick them in a scrap-book.'

'An innocent pastime enough.'

'In a way, sort of like collecting stamps – in a way,' said Mr Wainewright.

'Yet you never can tell how that sort of thing may end,' said Jacket. 'Look at Tooth. He got his by means of a pair of scissors – editorial scissors, paper-cutting scissors. Lord, how often have I wanted to stab the Sub with his own scissors!'

'That's right,' said Mr Wainewright. 'Long pointy scissors. They were part of a set – scissors and paper-knife in a leather case. I'd borrowed them myself a few days before. Very sharp scissors.'

'Little did you think,' said Jacket, 'that that pair of scissors would end up in your lodger's throat!'

'Little *did* I, J-Jack,' said Mr Wainewright. 'It makes a person think. May I ask . . . are you going to put something in the paper about me?'

'I think so,' said Jacket.

Mr Wainewright giggled. 'You wouldn't like a photograph of me?'

'We'll see about that, George. We'll see. What are you doing on Saturday?'

'Next Saturday morning I get my hair cut,' said Mr Wainewright.

'Matter of routine, eh?'

'Yes, sir. But——'

'No, no, never mind. You get your hair cut on Saturday, George, and I'll give you a tinkle some time. Right.

And now if I were you I'd go and get some sleep, George, old man. You don't look quite yourself,' said Jacket.

'I'm not a drinking man . . . I oughtn't to drink,' muttered Mr Wainewright, putting his hat on back-to-front and rising unsteadily. 'I don't feel very well . . .'

Poor little fellow, thought Jacket, having seen Mr Wainewright safely seated in a taxi. *This Tooth affair has thrown him right out of gear. Bloodshed in Wainewright's life! A revolution! It's almost as if he found himself wearing a bright red tie.*

Jacket, who was on the edge of the haze at the rim of the steady white light of sobriety, began to work out a story about Mr Wainewright. He thought that he might call it *The Red Thread of Murder.* Never mind the killer, never mind the victim – all that had been dealt with a hundred times before. What about the Ordinary Man, the Man In The Street, who has never seen blood except on his chin after a bad shave with a blunt blade, who opens a door and sees somebody like Tooth lying dead in a thick red puddle? Jacket laughed. In spite of everything Mr Wainewright had to get his hair cut on Saturday. There was, he decided, something ineffably pathetic about this desperate doggedness with which people like Wainewright clung to the finical tidiness of their fussy everyday lives.

He went to sleep thinking of Mr Wainewright. Mr Wainewright lay awake thinking of John Jacket, but went to sleep thinking: To-morrow is Friday: *I put a new blade in my safety-razor.*

.   .   .   .   .

So that Saturday, Mr Wainewright went to his barber. Friday was New Blade Day; Monday was Clean Shirt

Day; Sunday morning was Bath morning; and he had his hair cut every third Saturday. This was law and order; a system to be maintained. System; routine – in the life of Wainewright inevitable laws governed collar-studs, rubber heels, sheets of toilet-paper, the knotting of neckties, the lighting of pipes, the cutting of string and the sticking-on of stamps. He ate, drank, walked and combed his hair in immutable rhythm. He was established to run smoothly for ever. Every habit of Wainewright's was a Bastille; his every timed action was housed in a little Kremlin. Therefore, to-day, he had to get his hair cut. But Jowl's display made him stop for a few minutes.

Jowl, who owned the antique shop on the corner, had stripped some bankrupt's walls of a great, gleaming yataganerie of edged and pointed weapons. They hung on sale: double-handed swords, moon-faced battle-axes, mailed fists, stilettos, basket-hilted Italian daggers, Toledo rapiers, needle-pointed Khyber knives, adze-shaped obsidian club-axes, three-bladed knuckle-duster daggers, arquebuses, and a heap of oddments of sixteenth-century body-armour. Wainewright stood, smoking his pipe, looking hard. He stopped and examined some assassin's weapon of the fourteen hundreds – a knife with a spring. You stabbed your man, and – *Knutch!* – it flew open like a pair of scissors.

At the back of the window stood a complete suit of jousting-armour, with a massive helmet shaped like a frog's head. Wainewright looked up and, as it happened, he saw the reflection of his face exactly where his face would have been if he had been wearing the armour.

Then, in his breast, something uncoiled. He gazed, whistling. 'Ye Gods!' he said. 'Ye Gods!' But even as he looked he was inclined to laugh: his reflection was wearing a bowler hat.

Still, why not? thought Mr Wainewright. But then he remembered that he was an important person, that the glaring eyes of the world were focused on him. He walked across the court and pushed open the door of Flickenflocker's Select Saloon.

Calm! thought Wainewright. *Calm! Keep calm!* The door of the barber's shop was fitted with a compressed air brake: it hissed behind him and closed with a gentle tap.

As the door hissed, Wainewright stood still, tense. Then he also hissed: he had been holding his breath. When the door closed, he also made a tapping noise: he had been standing on his toes.

Flickenflocker said: 'Harpust one! Quarder-nour late! For fifteen years so I never knew you to miss a second! Eh? *Tsu, tsu, tsu!*'

'Am I late?' asked Wainewright.

'Fifteen minutes in fifteen years,' said Flicken-flocker. 'One minute every year. In a hundred-twenty years, so you could save enough time to go to the pictures.'

'The usual,' said Wainewright, sitting in a chair.

'Nice and clean back and sides,' said Flickenflocker.

Wainewright nodded. But as he did so he noticed that a peculiar quietness had come over the people in the shop. They were exchanging hurried words in lowered voices, and looking at him out of the corners of their eyes. Deep in the breast of Mr Wainewright something broke into a glow which spread through him until he felt all his veins were burning brilliantly red like neon-tubes. He knew exactly what was being said: *That is*

Wainewright, the witness for the prosecution in the Tooth murder case.

In a clear, slightly tremulous voice, he said:

'And I'll have a lavender shampoo.'

'Why not?' said Flickenflocker, as his long sharp scissors began to nibble and chatter at the fine, colourless hair of the little man in the chair. 'Why not?'

.   .   .   .   .

Flickenflocker worked with the concentration and exalted patience of a biologist cutting a section, and as he worked he whistled little tunes. His whistle was a whisper: he drew in the air through his teeth, for he had been taught never to breathe on customers. At all times he seemed to be working out some problem of fabulous complexity – breathlessly following a fine thread through infinite mazes of thought. Occasionally he uttered a word or a mere noise, as if he had found something but was throwing it away . . . *Tss!* . . . *Muhuh!* . . . *Tu-tu-tu!* . . . *Oh dear!* Wainewright liked this strange, calm barber who demonstrated no urge to make conversation; whose shiny yellow hands, soft and light as a pair of blown-up rubber gloves, had touched the faces of so many men whose pictures had filled posters while their names topped bills.

For Flickenflocker's was a theatrical establishment, or had been. A hundred photographs of forgotten and half-remembered actors hung on the walls. As small boys cut their names on desks and trees, actors and sportsmen pin their photographs to the walls of pubs and barber-shops. Thus they leave a little something by means of which somebody may remember them . . . until the flies, in their turn, deface the likenesses which Time

166

has almost wiped away; and the dustbins, which gape around the relics of little men like sharks in a bitter sea, close with a clang. Even in the grave nothing is completely lost as long as somebody can say: *Lottie had a twenty-four-inch thigh;* or *Fruitcake bubble-danced;* or *J. J. Sullivan could have eaten Kid Fathers before breakfast.* We hang about the necks of our to-morrows like hungry harlots about the necks of penniless sailors. So, for twenty-three years, singers, boxers, actors, six-day cyclists, tumblers, soubrettes, jugglers, dancers, wrestlers, clowns, ventriloquists and lion-tamers had given Flickenflocker their photographs – always with a half-shrug and a half-smile of affable indulgence. Flickenflocker hung up every one of them: he knew that the day always came when a man returned, if only to look at the wall and dig some illusion about himself out of the junk-heap of stale publicity.

They always came back to Flickenflocker, whose memory was reliable and unobtrusive as a Yale lock. One sidelong look at a profile opened a flap in his head and let out a name. After ten years he could glance at you, name you with matter-of-fact enthusiasm, and make appropriate casual chatter. As soon as the shop door closed and your heels hit the street he kicked the flap back and waited for the next customer . . . looked up, segregated; silent except for hisses, gulps, and monosyllables.

Yet Flickenflocker could talk. Now, while Pewter's flat French razor chirped in the lather like a sparrow in snow and, on his left, the great hollow-ground blade of Kyropoulos sang *Dzing-dzing!* over the blue chin of a big man in a pearl-grey suit, Flickenflocker talked to Mr Wainewright.

167

The barber made conversation with the least distinguished of all his customers.

.   .   .   .   .

'You're the man of the moment, Mister Wainewright.'

'Nonsense, Mister Flickenflocker.'

'I can read the papers, thank God, Mister Wainewright. I'm not *altogedder* blind yet, God forbid. Hm!'

'It's all got nothing to do with me.'

'No? Your worster enemies should be where that poor woman is now. In your hands is already a rope. A . . . a . . . a loop you can tie; you can tie a noose round her neck.'

'It's the Law, Mister Flickenflocker.'

'You're right there, Mister Wainewright. That's what the law is for. That's what we pay rates and taxes for. You want to kill somebody: right, go on. But afterwards don't say: "Huxcuse me, I forgot myself." Don't say: "Once don't count – give me just one more charnsh." A huxcuse me ain't enough – murder ain't the hee-cups. Murderers get hung: good job too. Poor woman!'

'But if she's guilty?'

'Mmmmyes, you're right. But a woman's got a lot to put up with. With a certain class of man a woman can put up with a lot, Mister Wainewright.'

'But murder!'

'Murder. . . . Mnyup. Still, in a temper. . . . I knew a baker, a gentleman. In . . . in . . . in the electric chair he'd of got up to give a lady his seat. So one day in a temper he put his friend in the oven. They found it out by trousers-buttons; by trousers-buttons they found it out. Afterwards, he was sorry. Still, I didn't say it was *right*; only I don't like hanging ladies. N-hah, mmmmyah! Well, you got nerve!'

'Why? Why have I got nerve?'

'Judge, juries: I'd be frightened out of my life.'

'But why?'

'They can make black white. White black they can make.'

'I've nothing to fear: I can only tell the plain truth.'

'And good luck to you! What class of people is a murderer? No class. A man in the prime of life, so she goes and kills. With scissors, eh? She kills her husband with scissors! It shows you. Scissors, pokers – if somebody wants to murder a person, hm! Daggers they can find in . . . in . . . in chocolate cakes, if they put their minds to it. Even a razor they can kill somebody with. Present company excepted. With a murderer, everything is a revolver. But what for? Why should she do it to her own husband?'

'For love, I think, Mister Flickenflocker.'

'Eeeeh! Love. People should settle down, with a home, and plenty children, with plenty work; happy they ought to be, people. If there's an argument, so sometimes one gives way, sometimes another gives way. For peace in the house, you got to give way. It looks bad to fight in front of the kids. So in the end you have grandchildren. What do they mean, *love*? To *kill* a person for love? In a book they read such rubbish, Mister Wainewright. For hate, for money, for hunger kill a person. For your wife and children kill a person. But love? Never heard of such a thing.'

'We'd better leave that to the judge and jury,' said Wainewright, coldly.

'We got no option,' said Flickenflocker. 'We got to leave it to the judgen-jury. Anyway, it didn't have nothing to do with you, thank goodness.'

169

'No?' said Wainewright.

'No,' said Flickenflocker, easily.

'It happened in my own house. I was in the next room. It does affect me a *little* bit,' said Wainewright, frowning.

'It's all for the best I dessay,' Flickenflocker picked up a pair of fine clippers. 'Lots o' people'll want to live there now.'

'More likely they'll want to stay away from my house, Mister Flickenflocker.'

'Don't you believe it! If there was a body (God forbid) in every cupboard, people'd pay double to stay there. For every one that don't like a murder, there's ten that'd rather have a murder than a . . . a . . . a hot-water-bottle. Don't you worry. I know people, so they'd give fifty pounds to have a murder in their place.'

'Dry shampoo, please,' said Wainewright.

Flickenflocker unscrewed the top of a bottle. 'Curiosity,' he said.

'Hm?'

'Curiosity. Were they open or shut?'

'Were what?'

'The scissors. The scissors the lady killed the gent with.'

'Shut.'

'It only shows you, eh? What can cut, can cut out lives from people. *Psss!* . . . *Hwheee!* Even a road – fall on it from a high roof, and where are you? . . . Scissors, eh? Temper, that's what it is: temper. A stab and a cut, and there you are: you've hanged yourself.'

Wainewright did not want to talk any more. He was looking into the mirror. Two men, awaiting their turn, were exchanging whispers and looking in his direction.

He knew what they were saying. *That's Wainewright,* they were saying; *that quite ordinary-looking man having the lavender shampoo is Wainewright, the Wainewright who has the house where Tooth was murdered by his wife.*

He smiled. But then old Pewter flipped the linen cover from the man in the chair on Wainewright's right – a big, swaggering man with a humorous, rosy face. One of the whispering men got up and said, in a voice that shook with awe: 'Excuse me, but aren't you Al Allum?'

The big man nodded gravely. '*That* is my name,' he said.

'May I shake hands with you? Would you mind?'

'Not at all.' The big man held out a heavy, manicured fist, caught the stranger's hand in a grip that made him jump, gave Pewter a shilling, and went out with a cordial and resonant 'Good-bye'.

The man who had shaken hands with him said to Pewter: 'I'll give you two shillings for that shilling Al Allum gave you just now.'

The old man handed him a shilling with a faint smile. The other man, putting it in his breast-pocket, explained: 'It's for my boy. He's crazy about Al Allum: you know what kids are.'

Somebody else said: 'The greatest comedian alive today, Al Allum. Ever see his fake conjuring sketch? Brilliant!'

'Brilliantine?' asked Flickenflocker.

'Cream,' said Wainewright.

'Mmmmmyah! . . . There.'

As Wainewright was paying his bill he said to the cashier: 'Is your clock right?'

The girl replied: 'It wouldn't be working in a barber-shop if it was.' Everybody laughed. A man said: *'Dead clever, that!'*

Mr Wainewright went out.

The city muttered under dry dust and blue smoke; the day was warm. Girls passed looking like bursting flowers in their new summer dresses. Wainewright looked at them. Here – passing him, jostling him and touching him with swinging hands in the crowded street – here walked thousands of desirable young women with nothing more than one-sixtieth of an inch of rayon, linen, or *crêpe de Chine* between their bare flesh and his eyesight. Why – ah, why – did his destiny send him out to walk alone? *What's wrong with me?* Wainewright asked himself. *Tramps, cripples, hunch-backs, criminals, horrible men deformed and dis-coloured and old – they all know the love of women. What's wrong with me? What have they got that I haven't got? I am a man of property . . . still a young man.* He stared piercingly at a pretty girl who was slowly walking towards him. Wainewright felt that his eyes were blazing like floodlights. But the girl, looking at him incuriously, saw only a small ordinary man with mild, expressionless eyes; if she thought of him at all, drawing conclusions from what she saw, she thought of him as a dim and boring little family man – a nobody – the same as everybody.

Mentally addressing the passing girl, *That's what you think*, said Wainewright. *If I told you who and what I am you'd change your ideas quickly enough, Blondie!* He stopped to look at hats in a shop window. A furry green velour caught his eye, and he decided to buy a hat like that – a two-guinea hat, a real Austrian hat and not a ten-shilling imitation such as Tooth used to wear. That, and a younger-looking suit, a tweed suit; a coloured shirt, even. . . . *Why have I waited so long?*

Wainewright was not a drinking man. Alcohol gave him a headache. But now he felt that everything was changing inside him: he was getting into step with life. Now he wanted a drink. He walked jauntily to the 'Duchess of Douro'. Tooth had taken him there once before, one Saturday afternoon several months ago. Wainewright remembered the occasion vividly: he had not yet come into his inheritance; he worked for his living then. His aunt was still alive. He was waiting: she could not live for ever. His little Personal Expenses Cash Book said that Wainewright had had seven hair-cuts since then. This made five months since his last drink of beer with Tooth.

Tooth was a tall dark man, strongly built, bright with the sickly radiance and the good-fellowship of the travelling salesman. He resembled one of those wax models that make cheap clothes attractive in the windows of mass-production tailors: he had the same unnatural freshness of complexion, the same blueness of chin, agelessness of expression, and shoddy precision of dress. Tooth wore Tyrolean hats and conspicuous tweeds. He liked to be seen smoking cigars. Yes, with his fivepenny cigars he was a man of personality with a manner at once detestable and irresistible – a way of seeming to give himself body and soul to the achievement of the most trivial objects. He could not accept the finality of anybody's 'No'. Argument, with Tooth soon became acrimonious, full of recrimination. Women described him as 'masterful'; Tooth would shout for twenty minutes over a bad penny, a bus ticket, or an accidental nudge of the elbow.

'Have a drink,' Tooth had said.

'I couldn't really, Tooth.'

'You can and will, cocko. There's a girl in the 'Douro' I want to introduce you to. A blonde. Genuine blonde: I found out. Eh? Ha-ha! Eh? Come on.'

On the way to the public-house Tooth talked:

'Having the car painted. Just as well: I always seem to get myself into bother when I'm out in the car. Be lost without it, though. Tell you about the other night? Listen: I'm on my way to Derby. Listen. Listening? Well . . . listen:

'On the way I meet two girls, sisters. Both ginger; one slim and the other plumpish. So I say: "Want a ride?" And so they say: "Yes". And well . . . after a few miles we pull up . . .' Tooth became briefly but luridly obscene. 'But listen: the joke of it was this; I ran 'em about fifteen miles farther on and we pulled up at a sort of tea-shop place and went in for a cup of tea. Listening? Well, I order tea and cakes and things, and I say: "Excuse me, my dears, I've got to see a man from the Balkans about a boarhound," I say. "Pour my tea out and I'll be right back," I tell 'em. So I nip out, start up the old jam-jar, and scram before you can say knife. Eh? Ha-ha! Eh? Eh?'

'But what happened to the girls, all that way from home?'

'That's their look-out. I told you I had to get to Derby, didn't I? What was I going to do with 'em in Derby? Have a heart! Ah-ah, now you're coming in here to meet the nicest barmaid in London. No nonsense. Shut up. Come on in now.'

He crashed through the grouped drinkers, pulling

Wainewright after him. A tall young woman with honey-coloured hair, whose face was strangely expressive of lust and boredom, dragged languidly at the handle of a beer-engine. But when she saw Tooth she smiled with unmistakable sudden joy. Only a woman in love smiles like that.

'Baby,' said Tooth, 'meet Mr Wainewright, one of the best.'

'Why, Sid! Why haven't you been to see me for such a long time?'

'Been busy. But I've been thinking of you. Ask George Wainewright. We met in the City. He wanted me to go with him to a posh week-end party in Kingston. (He's a very well-to-do man.) But I insisted on coming here. Did I or did I not, Wally?' said this pathological liar.

The compulsion of Tooth's glance was too strong. Wainewright nodded.

'See, Baby? Now, what'll we have?'

'I, ah, a small shandy.'

'Oh, no, George. Not if you drink with me, you don't. None of your shandies. Drink that stuff and you don't drink with me. You're going to have a Bass, a Draught Bass. That's a man's drink. Baby, two Draught Bass.'

'He always has his own way,' said the girl called Baby.

'Skin like cream,' whispered Tooth, with a snigger. When the girl returned with the beer he leaned across the bar and stroked her arm. 'This evening?'

'No, I can't.'

Tooth grasped her wrist. 'Yes.'

'Leave go. People are looking.'

'I don't care. I'll wait for you after eleven.'

'I shan't be there. Let go my arm, I tell you. The manager's coming over.'

'This evening?'

'Stop it, you'll get me the sack.'

'I don't care. This evening?'

'All right, but let go.'

'Promise?'

'Promise.'

Wainewright saw four red marks on the white skin of her arm as Tooth released her. She rubbed her wrist, and said in a voice which quivered with admiration: 'You're too strong.'

'Eh, George?' said Tooth, nudging Wainewright and grinning.

'You must have one more drink with me,' said Wainewright, emptying his glass with a wry face, 'and then I must be off. . . . Excuse me, miss. One more of these, please.'

'Eh? Eh? What's that? Oh no, damn it, no, I don't stand that. You make it two more, Baby. Do you hear what I say?' Fixing Wainewright with an injured stare, Tooth added: 'On principle, I don't stand for that kind of thing.'

'Very well.'

'So I should think! No! Fair's fair! Well, and where are you staying now?'

'In my aunt's place still.'

"Hear that, Baby? Looking after his old auntie, eh? His nice rich old auntie. Ha-ha! He knows which side his bread's buttered, George here. No offence, George. I'm going to look you up in a week or two. I want a nice room, reasonable.'

'We're full right up just now, Tooth.'

176

'Ah, you old kidder! Isn't he a kidder, Baby? You'll find me a room all right. I know.'

And surely enough, a fortnight later Tooth came, and by then Wainewright's aunt was dead, and there was a room vacant in the solid and respectable old house in Bishop's Square. So Tooth had come to live with Wainewright. Yes, indeed, he had blustered and browbeaten his way into the grave, as luck ordered the matter; for there Mrs Tooth had found him.

And therefore all Britain was waiting for a Notable Trial and, under rich black headlines, the name of George Wainewright was printed in all the papers, called by the prosecution as witness in the Victoria Scissors Murder.

Mr Wainewright smiled as he entered the 'Duchess of Douro': this pub had brought him luck. In this saloon bar he had found power.

.   .   .   .   .

The barmaid called Baby was still there. Wainewright stood at the bar and waited. 'What can I get you?' she asked.

With a gulp of trepidation Wainewright said. 'Whisky.'

'Small or large?'

'Ah . . . large, please.'

'Soda?'

'Yes, please.'

'Ice?'

'Please.'

He looked at her. She did not recognise him. He said: 'You don't remember me.'

'I've seen you somewhere,' she said.

'I was in here some time ago with a friend of yours.'

'Friend of *mine*?'

'Tooth.'

'Who?'

'Tooth. Sid Tooth.'

'Sid! I didn't know he was called Tooth. I thought his name was Edwards. He told me his—— Well, anyway . . .'

'If you didn't know his name was Tooth, you don't know about him, then,' said Wainewright, gulping his drink in his excitement.

'Know what?'

'Victoria Scissors Murder,' said Wainewright.

'What's that? Oh-oh! Tooth! Was that Sid? Really?'

'Yes, that was Sid. It happened in my house. I'm Mr Wainewright. I'm witness for the prosecution.'

She served another customer: Wainewright admired the play of supple muscles in her arm as she worked the beer engine.

'Want another one?' she asked, and Wainewright nodded.

'Will you have one?'

'Mustn't drink on duty,' she said. 'So *that* was Sid! Well.'

'I'm sorry to be the bearer of sad tidings,' said Wainewright.

'Sad tidings? Oh. I didn't know him very well. We were just sort of acquaintances. Scissors, wasn't it? Well, I dare say he deserved it.'

Wainewright stared at her. 'I was in the next room at the time,' he said.

'Did you see it?'

'Not exactly: I heard it.'

'Oh,' said the barmaid. 'Well . . .'

She seemed to bite off and swallow bitter words. 'WELL what?' said Wainewright, with a little giggle.

She looked at him, pausing with a glass in one hand and a duster in the other, and said:

'That makes one swine less in the world.'

'I thought you liked him,' Wainewright said.

'I don't like many men.'

'Oh,' said Wainewright. 'Um . . . ah . . . oh, Miss,'

'Yes?'

'Tooth. Did he . . . ah . . .'

'Did he what?'

'Oh, nothing.'

'Yes, he did,' said the barmaid.

'Did what?'

'Nothing,' She turned away. 'Excuse me.'

Wainewright wanted to talk to her. 'May I have another?' he asked. 'Do you mind?'

He emptied his third glass. 'You don't like me,' he said.

'I don't know you.'

'Do you want to know me?'

The barmaid called Baby said: 'Not particularly.'

'Don't go,' said Wainewright.

She sighed. There was something about Wainewright that made her uneasy: she did not like this strange, dead-looking empty-eyed man. 'Do you want something?'

He nodded.

'Another double Scotch?'

Wainewright nodded absently. Baby replenished his glass: he looked at it in astonishment, and put down a ten-shilling note.

179

'You've got some silver,' she said.

'I haven't got anything at all,' said Wainewright, 'I'm lonely.'

The barmaid said, in a tone of hostility mixed with pity: 'Find yourself somebody.'

'Nobody wants me. I'm lonely.'

'Well?'

'I've got eight thousand pounds and a house. A big house. Big, big . . .' He spread his arms in a large gesture. 'Twenty years I waited. God, I waited and waited!'

'What for?'

A buzzer sounded. A voice cried: 'Order your last drinks please, gentlemen! Order your last drinks!'

'She was eighty-seven when she died. She was an old woman when I was a boy.'

'Who was?'

'Auntie. I waited twenty years.'

'What *for*?'

'Eight thousand pounds. She left it to me. I've got eight thousand pounds and a house. Furnished from top to bottom. Old lease. It brings in seven pounds a week clear.'

He groped in a fog, found himself, and dragged himself up.

'Pardon me, Miss,' he said. 'I ought not to drink.' He felt ill.

'That's all right,' said the barmaid.

'Will you excuse me, Miss?' asked Wainewright.

The girl called Baby was turning away. Something like rage got into his throat and made him shout: 'You think I'm nobody! You wait!'

A doorman in a grey uniform, a colossus with a persuasive voice, picked him up as a whirlwind picks up a scrap of paper, and led him to the door, murmuring: 'Now come on, sir, come on. You've had it, sir, you've had enough sir. Let's all be friendly. Come on, now.'

'You think I'm nobody,' said Mr Wainewright, half crying.

'I wish there was a million more like you,' said the doorman, 'because you're sensible, that's what you are. You know when you've had enough. If there was more like you, why . . .'

The swing-door went *whup*, and Mr Wainewright was in the street.

He thought he heard people laughing behind him in the bar.

'You'll see, tomorrow!' he cried.

The doorman's voice said: 'That's right. Spoken like a man. Here you are, then, sir. Where to?'

A taxi was standing, wide-open and quivering.

'77, Bishop's Square, Belgravia,' said Mr Wainewright.

'Bishop's Square, Victoria,' said the taxi-driver.

'Belgravia,' said Mr Wainewright.

The doorman was waiting. He fumbled and found coins. 'Here,' he said. The doorman saluted and the taxi-door slammed. Everything jolted away. At Whitehall, Mr Wainewright realised that he had given the doorman four half-crowns instead of four pennies. He rapped at the window.

'Well?' said the driver.

'Oh, never mind,' said Mr Wainewright.

Let them all wait until tomorrow. They would know then to whom they had been talking.

But on that Sunday, for the first time in ten years, the editor of the *Sunday Special* cut out John Jacket's article. Twenty minutes before midnight, formidable news came through from Middle Europe. Jacket's page was needed for a statistical feature and a special map.

Mr Wainewright went over the columns, inch by inch, and found nothing. He telephoned the *Sunday Special*. A sad voice said: 'Mr Jacket won't be in until Tuesday – about eleven o'clock. Tell him what name, did you say? Daylight? Maybright? Wainewright. With an E, did you say, did you say? E. Wainewright? Oh, George. George E. Wainewright? Just George? George. Make your mind up. George Wainewright, I'll give Mr Jacket the message. 'Bye.'

On Tuesday, Mr Wainewright arrived at the offices of the *Sunday Special* before half-past ten in the morning. Jacket arrived at a quarter to twelve. He saw that the little man looked ill.

'How are you, George?' he asked.

'Mr Jacket,' said Mr. Wainewright, 'what's happened?'

'Happened? About what?'

'I hate to disturb you——'

'Not at all, George.'

'We met, you remember?'

'Certainly I remember. Hm?'

'The piece you were going to put in the paper about . . . about . . . my views on the Tooth case. Did you . . . ?'

'I wrote it, George. But my page was cut last Sunday. On account of Germany. Sorry, but there it is. Feel like a drink?'

'No, nothing to drink, thank you.'

'Coffee?'

'Perhaps a cup of coffee,' said Mr Wainewright.

They went to a café not far away. Jacket was aware of Mr Wainewright's wretchedness: it was twitching at the corners of the nondescript mouth and dragging down the lids of the colourless eyes. 'What's up?' he asked, as if he did not know.

'Nothing. I simply wondered . . . I wondered . . .'

'About that story? Take it easy, George. What is there that I can do? Bigger things have happened. As for this Tooth murder case – if you can call it a case. Martha Tooth is certain to get off lightly. Especially with Concord defending. I must get back to the office.'

In Fleet Street Mr Wainewright asked him: 'Is the trial likely to be reported?'

'Sure,' said Jacket.

'I suppose I'll be called, as witness?'

'Of course.'

'But I'm detaining you, J-Jack.'

'Not at all, George. Good-bye.'

'Good-bye, sir.'

Jacket hurried eastwards. Mr Wainewright walked deliberately in the direction of the Strand.

.   .   .   .   .

Sumner Concord was perhaps the greatest defender of criminals the world had ever known. He could combine the crafty ratiocination of a Birkett with the dialectical oratory of a Marshall Hall, and act like John Barrymore – whom he closely resembled. The louder he sobbed the closer he observed you. In cross-examination he was suave and murderous. Birkenhead himself was afraid of Sumner Concord. Yet Concord was an honest man. He would defend no one whom he believed to be guilty.

'Tell me about it,' he said, to Martha Tooth.

'What do you want me to tell you?' she asked.

'You must tell me exactly what happened that evening at Number 77, Bishop's Square. The truth, Mrs Tooth. I want to help you. How can I help you if you do not tell me the truth?'

She said: 'There isn't anything to tell.'

'Now you are charged——' began Sumner Concord.

'Oh, what do I care? What do I care?' cried Martha Tooth. 'Charge me, hang me – leave me alone!'

Sumner Concord had strong tea brought in before he continued. 'Tell me, Mrs Tooth. Why did you visit your husband that night?'

Martha Tooth said: 'I wasn't well. I couldn't work. There were the children. I wanted Sid to do something about the children. I *was* his wife. He *was* my husband, after all. . . . I only wanted him to give me some money, just a little, till I could work again.'

'Work again at what, Mrs Tooth?'

'I'd been doing housework.'

'And it had been some time since your husband had given you any money?'

'Three years.'

'You had been supporting yourself and your two children all that time?'

'Yes.'

'He had sent you nothing?'

'Not a penny. I left Sid over three years ago.'

'Why did you leave him, Mrs Tooth?'

'He used to beat me. I couldn't stand him beating me in front of the children. Then – it was when we had two rooms in Abelard Street near the British Museum – he brought a woman in.'

'Are there, Mrs Tooth, by any chance, any witnesses who could testify to that?'

'Mrs Ligo had the house. Then there was Miss Brundidge; she lived downstairs. I ran away with the children and went to my aunt's place. She still lives there: Mrs Lupton, 143, Novello Road, Turners Green. Her friend, Mrs Yule, she lives there too. They both know. We stayed with them once. Sid used to knock me about. The police had to be called in twice. He wanted to kill me when he'd been drinking.'

' . . . *In twice*,' wrote Sumner Concord. 'Novello Road. Novello Street Police Station, um? Take your time. Have some more tea. A cigarette. You don't smoke? Wise of you, wise. He was a violent and dangerous man, this husband of yours, then?'

'Yes.'

'He threatened, for instance, to kill you, no doubt?'

'No,' said Martha Tooth, 'he never threatened. He just hit.'

'And on this last occasion. You called to see him. Hm?'

'Yes, that's right.'

'You hadn't seen him for some time?'

'About three years.'

'How did you find out his address?'

'From his firm, Poise Weighing Machines.'

'You hadn't tried to find out his address before, eh?'

'All I cared about was that Sid shouldn't find out my address.'

'But you were at the end of your tether, hm?'

'I was supposed to be having an operation. I've still got to have an operation. And I thought Sid might let me have something . . .'

'There-there, now-now! Calm. Tears won't help, Mrs Tooth. We *must* be calm. You saw Sid. Yes?'

'Yes, sir. But . . . he'd been drinking, I think.'

'Tell me again exactly what happened.'

'I called. A lady let me in. I went up, and Sid was there. He said: "What, you?" I said: "Yes, me." Then he said – he said——'

'Take your time, Mrs Tooth.'

'He said: "What a sight you look." '

'And then?'

'I suppose I started crying.'

'And he?'

'He told me to shut up. And so I did. I think I did, sir. I tried to. I asked him to let me have some money. He said that I'd had as much money as I was ever going to get out of him – as if I'd ever had anything out of him!' cried Mrs Tooth, between deep, shuddering sobs.

'There, there, my dear Mrs Tooth. You must drink your tea and be calm. Everything depends on your being calm. Now.'

'I said I'd go to his firm. I told him I was ill. I told him I'd go to his firm in the City. Then he hit me, sir.'

'Where?'

'In the face – a slap. I started to cry again. He hit me again, and he laughed at me.'

'He hit you in the face again?'

'Yes, with his hand.'

'This is very painful to you, Mrs Tooth, but we must have everything clear. Your hand was wounded. How did you hurt your hand?'

'All of a sudden . . . I didn't want to keep on living. I was so miserable – I was so miserable – I was——'

Sumner Concord waited. In a little while Martha Tooth could speak again.

'You hurt your hand.'

'I wanted to kill myself. There was a knife, or something. I picked it up. I meant to stick it in myself. But Sid was quick as lightning.'

There was a ring of pride in her voice, at which Sumner Concord shuddered, although he had heard it before.

'What happened then?' he asked.

'He hit me again and knocked me over.'

'You fell?'

'Against the bed, sir. Then Sid hit me some more and told me to get out. He said: "I hate the sight of you, get out of my sight," he said.'

'Above all, be calm, Mrs Tooth. What happened after that?'

'I don't know.'

'After he hit you the last time – think.'

'I don't know, sir.'

'You got up?'

'I can't remember.'

'You can't remember. Do you remember going out of the room?'

'I sort of remember going out of the room.'

'You got back to your home?'

'Yes.'

'You remember that?'

'Yes, sir. I know, because I washed my face in cold water, and moved quietly so as not to wake the children up.'

'That, of course, was quite reasonable. That would account for the blood in the water in the wash-bowl.'

'I dare say.'

'Your throat was bruised, Mrs. Tooth. Did your husband try to strangle you?'

'He got hold of me to keep me quiet, I should think, sir.'

'Before you picked up this knife, or whatever it was? Or after?'

'I couldn't say. I don't know. I don't care.'

'I suggest that you picked up this sharp instrument, knife, scissors, or whatever it may have been, *after* your husband took you by the throat.'

'Very likely,' said Martha Tooth, drearily, 'I don't know. I don't care.'

'You must pull yourself together, Mrs Tooth. How can I help you if you will not help yourself? You picked up this knife, or pair of scissors, *after* your husband began to strangle you with his hands. Is that so?'

'I should think so.'

'He was an extremely powerful man, I think?'

'My Sid? Sid was as strong as a bull, sir.'

'Yes. Now can you give me a list of the places – rooms, flats, houses, hotels, any places – in which you and your husband lived together from the date of your marriage until the date of your separation?'

'Yes, I think I could, sir.'

'You lived together for several years, didn't you?'

'Nearly seven years, off and on.'

'He ill-treated you from the start?'

Martha Tooth laughed. 'He beat me the first time two days after we were married,' she said.

'However, you managed to keep this matter secret?'

'Oh, everybody knew.'

'Hush, hush, Mrs Tooth. Everything depends upon your self-control! He can't hurt you now.'

'I'm not crying because of that . . .' Martha Tooth bit her sleeve and pressed the fingers of her free hand into her eyes. Still, tears came out between her fingers.

'Why are you crying, then?'

'You're so good to me!'

'*You must be calm,*' said Sumner Concord, in a cold, hard voice.

She stopped crying. 'Everybody knew how he treated me,' she said.

'You must try and remember everyone who might make a statement concerning the manner in which your husband treated you, Mrs Tooth. You must try and remember. Is that quite clear?'

'Yes, sir, but I'm afraid. I'm afraid of being in the court. They'll make me swear black is white. I don't know what to do. I don't know what to say. I don't——'

Sumner Concord stopped her with a gentle, but imperious gesture, and said: 'Mrs Tooth, you mustn't persuade yourself that there is anything to be afraid of. You will be given a perfectly fair trial. The clerk of the court will say to you: "Martha Tooth, you are charged with the murder of Sidney Tooth on the 7th May of this year. Are you guilty or not guilty?" And you will say: "Not guilty." This I believe to be the truth. I believe that you are not guilty of the murder of your husband. I believe that, desperate with grief and pain and terror, you picked up the scissors intending to kill yourself, and not to kill your husband.'

Martha Tooth stared at him in blank astonishment and said: 'Me, pick up a pair of scissors to kill Sid? I shouldn't have dared to raise a hand to Sid.'

'Just so. He had you by the throat, Mrs Tooth. He was shaking you. Your head was spinning. You struck out wildly, blindly, Mrs Tooth, and it happened that the point of that sharp pair of scissors struck him in the soft part of his neck and penetrated the subclavian artery. You had not the slightest intention of hurting him in any way,' said Sumner Concord, holding her with his keen, calm, hypnotic eyes. 'What happened after that, Mrs Tooth?'

'I don't know what happened,' she cried. 'As he let go of my neck, I ran away from him, that's all I know.'

'Exactly. You ran away blindly, neither knowing or caring where you were going. Is that not so? And later they found you wringing your ice-cold hands and crying, while the children lay asleep in your poor furnished room. Is that not so?'

'My hands were ice-cold,' said Martha Tooth in a wondering undertone. 'How did you know my hands were ice-cold?'

Sumner Concord smiled sadly and with pity. 'Be calm, my dear lady, be calm.'

'But how did you know my hands were ice-cold?'

'They frequently are in such cases,' said Sumner Concord. 'And now you must eat your meals and rest and get your poor nerves in order again, Mrs Tooth. You are to banish this matter from your mind until it is necessary for us to talk about it again. You are to leave everything in my hands. I believe that you have been telling me the truth, and in that case I give you my word of honour that I believe that no great harm can come to you. Now you must rest.'

'I don't care what happens to me, sir, but the children – what about the children?' asked Martha Tooth, twisting her wet handkerchief in her skinny, little chapped hands.

'Put your mind at rest, they are being well looked after, I promise you.'

A shocking thought seemed suddenly to strike her and she gasped: 'They can send me to prison for years. And then what would happen to them?'

Rising, and laying large, gentle hands on her shoulders, Sumner Concord replied: 'Even if you had known that you were striking your husband, you would have been striking him without premeditation, and in self-defence, because in the hands of this crazy drunken brute you were in peril of your life, and if there is any justice in the world, you need not necessarily go to prison at all.'

Then he went away and obtained the statements of Mrs Ligo, Miss Brundidge, Mrs Lupton, Mrs Yule, and half a dozen others. He obtained certain evidence from the police at the Novello Street Police Station. A few days later, everybody began to take it for granted that Martha Tooth would get away scot-free.

.   .   .   .   .

Because it was Sumner Concord who was defending Martha Tooth, the Central Criminal Court was crowded. Mr Wainewright, glancing timidly from wig to horse-hair wig, felt his heart contract and his stomach shrink, and when his fascinated gaze fell upon the hard, white, turtle-face of Mr Justice Claverhouse, who sat in his great robes under the sword, he was seized by an insane impulse to run away and hide. Yet, at the same time, he was aware of a certain spiritual exaltation as witness for the prosecution in Rex v. Tooth.

Mr Sherwood's speech for the prosecution was longer than one might have expected. He had put a lot of work into it. If he could hang Martha Tooth, snatching her from the protective arms of Sumner Concord, he was a made man. His manner was cold and precise. His voice was – as one journalist described it – winter sunlight made articulate. As he spoke, members of the public who had hitherto believed that Martha Tooth could not possibly be convicted changed their minds. One or two sportsmen who had laid five to four on her acquittal began furtively to try to hedge their bets. Mr Sherwood's sentences struck home like so many jabs of an ice-pick. Here was an angry woman, may it please His Lordship and the members of the jury. Here was an embittered woman, a jealous woman. Here was a woman scorned. She had brooded over her real or imaginary wrongs until at last she had decided on a bloody revenge. Under the cover of the gathering darkness, she had gone stealthily out of her house, to the house of her husband. And there she had stabbed him to death with this pair of scissors, paper-cutting scissors with a shagreen handle. (The pair of scissors was unwrapped from some tissue paper in a little cardboard box, into which they had been packed with loving care.) She left the scissors in the wound, knowing that no fingerprints would be visible on the rough shagreen handle. Then she slunk out of the house. But her cunning had not been quite deep enough. She had forgotten to wipe her fingerprints from the door-knob on the inside of Mr Tooth's bed-sitting-room door. There were witnesses who could swear to having seen her come and seen her go. Medical evidence would prove that this murderous stab in the throat, which had gone down through the subclavian artery, had been inflicted at such-and-such a time. She was arrested almost literally red-handed, for she had not yet had time to empty certain blood-stained water from a basin in her room. While her husband's innocent children lay asleep in her bed, the murderess had crept back to wash away the evidence of her guilt, and so on and so forth. And now with the assistance of his learned friend, Mr Bottle, he would call the evidence before the court.

At this point, Mrs Madge was called. She remembered everything. She had let Mrs Tooth in on the evening of the murder. She knew at exactly what time she had let that party in. How did she know the time? She had every reason to know the time because it was time for Mrs Madge to go home and she had paid a certain amount of attention to the clock. She was not a clock-watcher but she did her duty, and was not paid to stay more than a certain number of hours. On this particular evening she had an appointment with a friend, Mrs Glass, with whom she had arranged to go to the pictures in time for a certain performance. Therefore she had particularly desired to get away in time to change her clothes and make herself decent. Therefore – give or take half a minute – she could fairly exactly say at what time the lady came to the door and asked for Mr Sidney Tooth and she could swear to the lady: she was in the habit of keeping her eyes open; it was her hobby, sizing people up. Mrs Tooth was wearing a very old loose black coat, the sort that the Jewish shops sell for a guinea, and one of those black hats you could get for three-and-six-pence at Marks and Spencer's. She was carrying an old black handbag, and her shoes must have been given to her by a lady, a bigger lady than Mrs Tooth who had worn them out and was about to throw them away. She could take her oath on it that Mrs Tooth was the person she had let in on that fatal evening.

Then came Mr Wainewright. He had bought a new

suit for the occasion – a smart, well-cut suit, with the first double-breasted coat he had ever worn. He had gone to the West End for a shirt that cost eighteen shillings. His tie must have cost as much again, and there was a pearl pin stuck into the middle of it. An equilateral triangle of white handkerchief protruded from his breast pocket. He looked respectable and intensely uncomfortable as he gave his evidence, which was as he had outlined it to John Jacket that evening in the 'Firedrake'.

Cross-examined, he gave the defence nothing to work on. It was apparent that Wainewright was telling the truth. Then came the turn of the defence.

To the astonishment of the public, Mr Sumner Concord did not attempt to break down the evidence for the prosecution. There was no doubt at all, he said, that the unfortunate Mrs Tooth had called on her husband at that time. But he happened to know that she had called in order to plead with him. Tooth had callously deserted her and his two children. He was earning a good salary and substantial sums in commission, which he devoted entirely to dissipation. Mrs Tooth, the deserted woman, had been compelled to support the children and herself by menial labour. Medical evidence would indicate that it was necessary for this lady to undergo a serious internal operation in the near future. She had visited her husband merely in order to beg – to beg on her bended knees if necessary – for the wherewithal to feed their children, his children and hers, until such time as she could find strength to go out again and scrub other women's floors to earn the few shillings that she needed to maintain them.

Sumner Concord drew the attention of His Lordship

and the jury to the fact that Mrs Tooth had a separation order but had never received a penny: her forbearance was inspired by mercy and also by fear, because Sidney Tooth, as he was about to prove, had been one of the most murderous bullies and unmitigated scoundrels that ever polluted God's earth. This poor woman, Mrs Tooth, did not care whether she lived or died – her husband by his persistent brutality and ill-treatment had beaten the normal fear of death out of her. Evidence was forthcoming which would prove that this wretched, persecuted woman had for many years gone in terror of her life and had frequently interposed her broken and bruised body between the drunkenly raging Sidney Tooth and the undernourished, trembling bodies of his children. Mother-love was stronger than the terror of bodily harm. Knowing that in a little while her exhausted frame could no longer support the strain imposed upon it – knowing that the time was fast approaching when she must go into hospital – Martha Tooth went to plead with her husband, and he mocked her. He laughed in her face. He struck her. She, driven to desperation, God forgive her, driven to self-destruction, picked up that pair of scissors to stab herself. In doing so she wounded her hand. Then Tooth, who was drunk and who – a brute at the best of times – was murderous when drunk, as evidence would prove, took her by the throat and began to strangle her. She struck out blindly and he let her go. She went weeping, she ran out blindly into the night. Mr Sumner Concord did not deny the validity of the evidence of Mr Wainewright and Mrs Madge. Mrs Tooth believed that she must have killed her husband, and she was horrified at the very thought of it. As for killing him by intention – she could never have thought of that, she loved him too much and she feared him too much. She wanted to kill herself. There was medical evidence to prove that the blood in the hand-basin was her own blood from her own hand which she cut in so blindly snatching the scissors with which Tooth had been killed. That her life was in danger might be indicated by the evidence of eleven witnesses, three of them doctors. . . .

Mr Wainewright, wondering at the complexity of it all, looked away. He looked away from the face of Sumner Concord, scanned the faces of the jurymen (one of them was surreptitiously slipping a white tablet into his mouth) and blinked up at the ceiling. A piece of fluffy stuff, such as comes away from a dandelion that has run to seed, was floating, conspicuous against the panelling. It began to descend. Mr Wainewright's eyes followed it. It came to rest on the judge's wig, where it disappeared. Mr Wainewright was conscious of a certain discontent.

After that nothing of the trial stuck in his mind except Sumner Concord's peroration, and Mr Justice Claverhouse's verdict.

The peroration was something like:

'Here was a beast. He tortured this woman. She trusted him and gave him her life. He accepted it brutally and threw it away. She had been beautiful. He had battered her with his great bony fists into the woman you see before you. That face was offered to Tooth in the first flush of its beauty. He beat it into the wreck and ruin of a woman's face – the wreck, the ruin that you see before you now. She did not complain. He mocked and humiliated her. She was silent. She wept alone. He made her an object of pity, this mad and murderous bully, and she said nothing. He deserted her, leaving her with two young sons whom she loved very dearly: she was sick and weak, and still she never spoke! The prosecution has raised its voice: Martha Tooth suffered in silence. She worked for her children, happy to bring home a little bread in her poor cracked hands.

'You have heard the evidence of those who have known her. She was a woman without stain, a woman undefiled. But when, at last, she went ill – dear God, what was she to do? She wanted nothing for herself. But there were her children. Her husband was prosperous. She asked him only for bread for his children – he laughed in her face. He struck her and ordered her to go. She pleaded – and he beat her. She cried for mercy and he abused her, reproaching her for the loss of her beauty, the beauty he himself had savagely beaten away.

'At last, driven mad by despair, she picks up the first thing that comes to hand, a pair of scissors, and tries – poor desperate woman – to kill herself. Laughing, he takes her by the throat. These hands, strong enough to break a horseshoe, are locked about her frail throat. Imagine them upon your own, and think!

'She struggles, she cannot speak, she can only struggle while he laughs in her face, because these murderous thumbs are buried in her windpipe. She strikes out blindly, and this great furious hulk of bestial manhood collapses before her. Sixteen stone of bone and muscle falls down, while seven stone of wretchedness and sickness stands aghast.

'And looking down she sees the scissors embedded in that bull neck. By some freak of chance – by some act of God – she has struck the subclavian artery and the great beast has fallen. She runs blindly away, weeping bitterly, half demented with anguish, and when the police find her (which was easy, since she had not attempted to conceal herself) she is crying, and the blood in the basin is her own blood. The children lie asleep and she begs the police to take her away, to take her away anywhere out of this world. She asks for nothing but death, and there, there is the pity of it! . . .'

After an absence of twenty-five minutes the jury returned a verdict of Not Guilty.

.   .   .   .   .

Then, although everyone said he had known from the beginning that Martha Tooth would be acquitted, London went wild with delight. The *Sunday Extra* sent Munday Marsh to offer the bewildered woman five hundred pounds for her life-story. Pain of the *Sunday Briton* offered a thousand. She shook her head wearily and dispiritedly. 'Twelve hundred and fifty,' said the *Sunday Briton*. The *Extra* said: 'Fifteen hundred.'

'I can't write stories,' said Martha Tooth. 'Anyway——'

'I can,' said Pain.

'Calm, gentlemen, calm,' said the sardonic voice of John Jacket. They turned, and saw him dangling an oblong of scribbled paper between a thumb and a forefinger. 'I've got it.'

The *Sunday Special* had given Jacket authority to pay as much as two thousand pounds for Martha Tooth's story. Ten minutes before Munday Marsh arrived, Jacket had bought the story for six hundred pounds.

'Oh well,' they said, without malice, and went away. Pain said: 'To-day to thee, to-morrow to me, Jack,' and they shook hands. Ainsworth of *The People* said nothing: he knew that in a year's time the whole business would be forgotten, and then, if he happened to need a human-interest murder-feature, he could re-tell the story from the recorded facts.

So John Jacket wrote fifteen thousand words – four instalments, illustrated with photographs and snap-shots – under the title of *DIARY OF AN ILL-USED WOMAN*. What Jacket did not know he invented: Martha Tooth signed everything – she still could not understand what it was all about. Soon after the first instalment was published she began to receive fan-mail: half a dozen religious leaflets, letters urging her to re-pent, prophecies concerning the Second Coming, and proposals of marriage, together with frantically abusive notes signed *Ill-used Man*. She also received parcels of food and clothes, and anonymous letters enclosing postal orders. An old lady in the West Country, saying that she had wanted to kill her husband every day for forty years, enclosed sixty twopenny stamps.

Martha Tooth was taken in hand by a lady reporter, who carried her off to a beauty parlour, compelled her to have her hair waved, and showed her how to choose a hat. In three weeks she changed; paid attention to her finger-nails and expressed discontent with the Press. The press, she complained, wouldn't leave her alone, and everyone wanted to marry her. Before the fourth instal-ment appeared she had received eleven offers of marriage. Martha Tooth had become whimsical, smiled one-sidedly, and took to lifting her shoulders in a sort of shrug. 'Men,' she said, 'men! These men!'

After the fourth week, however, she got no more letters. She was out of sight and out of mind.

She went to the offices of the *Sunday Special* to see

Jacket. Someone had told her that she ought to have got thousands of pounds for her story, and that there was a film in it. When she told Jacket this, he drew a deep breath and said:

'Mrs Tooth. Your story is written, read, and wrapped around fried fish, and forgotten. You forget it too. Be sensible and forget it. You've lived your story and told your story. Go away and live another story.' He added: 'With a happy ending, eh?'

She went away. Soon, a paragraph on the gossip page of an evening newspaper announced that she had married a man called Booth. Her name had been Tooth – there was the story. Mrs Tooth married Mr Booth. He was a market-gardener, and, strangely enough, a widower. Mr Booth had proposed to her by letter.

John Jacket had forgotten the Tooth case when Mr Wainewright came to see him for the second time, twelve weeks later.

. . . . .

It struck Jacket as odd that Mr Wainewright was wearing a jaunty little green Tyrolean hat and a noticeable tweed suit.

'Is it fair?' asked Wainewright. 'Where do I come in?'

'Come in? How? How d'you mean, where do you come in?'

'Well,' said Mr Wainewright, shuffling his feet, 'I mean to say . . . I hear that Tooth's good lady got thousands and thousands of pounds.'

'A few hundreds, George,' said Jacket.

'It isn't that, Mr Jacket. It's——'

'The credit?' asked Jacket, twitching an ironic lip.

'Who is *she* to be made a heroine out of?' asked Wainewright, looking at his finger-tips.

'What exactly are you trying to get at, George?' asked Jacket.

'Get at? Who, me? Nothing, Mr Jacket.'

'Then what do you want? What do you want me to do?'

Mr Wainewright looked at the ball of his right thumb and shook his head. 'There was nothing about me at all in the papers,' he said. 'I've got a story, too.'

'Be a pal,' said Jacket, 'and go away. I've got work to do, George, old man, work. So be a pal.'

'Right.' Mr Wainewright got up.

'Don't be angry with *me*. Things come and things go,' said Jacket, 'and a story is a nine-days' wonder. Wash this murder out of your head.'

Mr Wainewright said: 'Well, you know best. But I've also got a story——'

A telephone bell rang. 'See you some other time,' said John Jacket, lifting the receiver. 'So long for now, George.'

Wainewright went out without saying good day. Shortly after he had gone, John Jacket, hanging up the telephone, found himself wondering about something. There had been something wrong with Wainewright. What?

Jacket gnawed a fat black pencil.

He had eaten his way to the last letter of the pencil-maker's name before he knew what he was trying to remember. He laughed, and said to himself: *That silly little man has gone and got himself up in a furry green hat and a tweed suit. What on earth for?*

Jacket felt that he was on the verge of a discovery – not

a *Sunday Special* story, but something interesting all the same.

Then his telephone rang. By the time he had stopped listening new things were in his head, and Mr Wainewright, being gone, was forgotten.

.   .   .   .   .

Three weeks later, as Jacket was leaving the office at lunch-time, he heard Mr Wainewright's voice again. The little man came breathlessly out of the cover of a doorway and said: 'Mr Jacket, sir. Please. One moment. Just *one* moment.'

'Well, what is it?' said Jacket, looking down at him with an expression of something like loathing. 'What is it now, Wainewright?'

'It's something important, sir. Something very important. I give you my word, my word of honour, you'll never forgive yourself if you don't listen to me.'

'I'm in a hurry.'

'I've been waiting for you here in the street for an hour and a half,' said Mr Wainewright.

'You should have telephoned.'

'If I had, you wouldn't have spoken to me.'

'True,' said Jacket. Then he blinked, and said: 'What the devil have you been doing to yourself?'

Mr Wainewright was dressed in a tight-fitting, half-belted jacket of white stuff like tweed, an orange-coloured shirt and a black satin tie with a diamond horseshoe pin, blue flannel trousers, a panama hat, and brown-and-white buckskin shoes. He had trimmed his moustache to a fine straight line, above and below which Jacket could see a considerable area of tremulous white lip, beaded with perspiration. And he could smell lavender-water and whisky.

'Doing to myself? Nothing, sir,' said Mr Wainewright.

'I like your hat.'

'It's real panama.'

'Um-um!' Jacket considered him for a second or two, and then said: 'Come on, then. Tell me all about it. Come and have a drink.'

'It's very private,' said Mr Wainewright. 'It's not something I could talk about if there was anybody around. Look, Mr Jacket, it'll be worth your while. Come home with me, just for a few minutes.'

'*Home* with you?'

'To Bishop's Square – ten minutes in a taxi, no more. I've got plenty of drinks at home. Have a drink there. Ten minutes. I'll show you something. . . . I'll tell you something. Please do! Please do, Mr Jacket.'

'All right, then. But I haven't long,' said Jacket.

They got into a taxi. Neither of them spoke until Mr Wainewright said: 'After you,' as he unlocked the street door of Number 77, Bishop's Square. 'Lead the way,' said Jacket. The little man bobbed in a shopwalker's obeisance. They passed through a clean, dim passage hung with framed caricatures out of *Vanity Fair*, and climbed sixteen darkly-carpeted stairs to the first floor. Mr Wainewright opened another door. 'This used to be my auntie's room,' he said, rather breath-lessly.

'Charming,' said Jacket, without enthusiasm.

'It was Tooth's room, too.'

'Oh I see. The room in which Tooth was murdered, eh?'

'Yes, sir. It's my bedroom now.'

'And is this what you brought me here to see?' asked Jacket.

'No, no,' cried Mr Wainewright, splashing a quarter of a pint of whisky into a large tumbler, and pressing the nozzle instead of the lever of a soda-water syphon. 'Please sit down.'

'That's a massive drink you've given me,' said Jacket. He observed that his host's drink was not much smaller.

'No, not at all.'

'Cheers.' Jacket emptied his glass in two gulps. Mr Wainewright tried to do the same, but choked; recovered with a brave effort, and forced the rest of his drink into his mouth and down his throat. Jacket could hear his heavy breathing. 'Now, tell us all about it,' he said.

'There was,' said Mr Wainewright, swaying a little in his chair, 'there was a . . . an astounding miscarriage of justice.'

'In what way, Wainewright?'

'In every way, Mr Jacket, sir. In every way. What I have to say will shock you.'

'Go ahead.'

'Sid Tooth died just about on the spot where you are sitting, sir.'

'Well?'

'The rug, of course, is a new one. They couldn't clean the old one. . . . But your glass is empty.'

'I'll pour drinks. You go on,' said Jacket, rising.

'Listen,' said Mr Wainewright. . . .

.   .   .   .   .

Mr Wainewright said, dreamily:

'What I want to know is this: where's your justice?

Where's your law? If justice is made a mockery of, and law is tricked – what do I pay rates and taxes for? The world's going mad, sir. A woman is accused, sir, of killing her hubby with a pair of scissors. It's proved that she did it, proved beyond doubt, Mr Jacket! And what happens? This woman, a nobody, mind you; this woman does not pay the penalty of her crime, sir. No. She is made a heroine of. She is cheered to the echo. She has her picture in all the papers. She has her life-story published. She marries again, lives happy ever after. Is that fair? Is that right?'

'What's on your mind, Wainewright? It was pretty well established as a clean-cut case of self-defence.'

Mr Wainewright, with extraordinary passion, said: 'She was lying! Tooth was still alive when she left this house! He was hale and hearty as you or me, after the street door closed behind Martha Tooth. Alive and laughing, I tell you. She's a perjurer . . . a perjuress. She's a liar. She got what she got under false pretences: all that money, all that sympathy. "Ill-Used Woman", as you called her! She never killed Tooth. The world must be going mad.'

'What about your evidence?' asked Jacket, skilfully pouring half his drink into his host's glass.

Mr Wainewright snapped: 'Evidence! Don't talk to me about evidence!'

'You drink up your nice drink,' said Jacket, 'and go over it all again.'

'I hated that man,' said Mr Wainewright. 'Who did he think *he* was, that Sid Tooth? He was no good. And all the women were in love with him. He was a bully, a dirty bully. A drunkard, a bad 'un – bad to the backbone. He practically forced his way into this house. A laugh, a joke, a drink, a bang on the back – and before I knew where I was, there was Tooth, in auntie's old room. I'm not used to that sort of thing, Mr Jacket, sir. I'm not used to it. He borrowed money in cash, and ran up bills. He told me he'd done a deal with a new department store, for weighing machines – over a thousand pounds in commission he had to collect. So he said. All lies, sir, all lies, but I swallowed 'em. I swallowed everything Tooth said. Bad, sir, bad! He was bad to the backbone.'

Jacket asked: 'Why didn't you tell him to get out?'

'I meant to,' said Mr Wainewright, 'but he always saw it coming. Then it was a laugh, and a joke, and a drink, and a bang on the back. . . . To-morrow: he'd pay me to-morrow. And to-morrow, he said, to-morrow. And then he had to go to Leeds, or Bristol. It was drinks and women with him, sir, all the time. He used to bring women into this very room, Mr Jacket, sir, into this very room. And I was next door. No woman ever looked twice at me, sir. What's the matter with *me*? Have I got a hump on my back, or something? Eh? Have I?'

Jacket said: 'Far from it, old friend.'

'And I sat in my room, next door, with nothing to do but get my scrap-book up to date.'

'What scrap-book?' asked Jacket, refilling the little man's glass.

Mr Wainewright giggled, pointing to a neatly-arranged pile of red-backed volumes on a shelf by the bed. Jacket opened one, and riffled the pages. Mr Wainewright had meticulously cut out of cinematic and physical-culture magazines the likenesses of young women in swimming suits. He had gummed them in and smoothed them down. Here, between the eight covers of four scrap-books, lay his seraglio. His favourite wife, it appeared, was Ann Sheridan.

'You think I'm pretty terrible,' he said, rising uncertainly and taking the book out of Jacket's hands.

'Go on,' said Jacket.

'No, but I don't want you to think . . .'

'I'm not thinking anything. Go on, pal, go on.'

'I think there's something *artistic* in the human form, sir. So for a hobby, you see, I collect it in my scrap-books.'

'I understand, I understand,' said Jacket. 'You were sitting in your room next door to this, with nothing to do but get your scrap-books up to date, when – go on, go on, George.'

'I asked you here to tell you this,' said Mr Wainewright. 'You don't need to . . . to draw me out. I'm telling you something. A story – worth a fortune. No need to screw your face up. No need to pretend to treat me with respect. I know what you think. You think I'm nothing. You think I'm nobody. Let me tell you.'

'You were sitting in your room——'

'I was cutting out the picture of the young lady called Pumpkins Whitaker, sir – an artistic figure – when Mrs Tooth came to visit *him*.'

He pointed to the floor under Jacket's chair.

'Go on.'

'Yes, Mr Jacket. I listened. What happened was as I said in court. They quarrelled. She cried. He laughed. There was a scuffle. In the end Mrs Tooth ran out. Just like I said, sir.'

'Well?'

Mr Wainewright leaned forward, and Jacket had to support him with an unobtrusive hand.

'Then, sir, I went into Tooth's room, this very room, sir. I knocked first, of course.'

'And there was no answer?'

'There was an answer. Tooth said "Come in." And I came in, Mr Jacket.'

'You mean to say Tooth was alive when you came in here, after his wife had left?'

'Exactly, sir. I was curious to know what had been going on. I made up an excuse for coming to see him just then. I'd borrowed his scissors, you see, the ones she is supposed to have killed him with. I'd been using them – they were very sharp – for cutting things out. They were part of a set – scissors and paper-knife in a shagreen case. I came to give them back – it was an excuse. Actually, I wanted to know what had been going on.'

'Go on, George,' said Jacket, quietly.

Mr Wainewright said: 'He was sitting on the bed, just about where you are now, in his shirt-sleeves, laughing and playing with the paper-knife. He started telling me all about his wife, Mr Jacket, sir – how much she loved him, how much the barmaid at the "Duchess of Douro" loved him, how much every woman he met loved him. His collar was undone.' Mr Wainewright paused and moistened his lips. 'His collar was undone. He had one of those great big thick white necks. I had that pair of scissors in my hand. He threw his head back while he was laughing. I said: "Here's your scissors." He went on laughing, and coughing – he was a cigarette-smoker – at the same time. "Here's your scissors," I said. I think he'd been drinking. He roared with laughter. And then, all of a sudden, something got hold of me. I hit him with my right hand. I couldn't pull my hand away. It was holding on to the scissors, and they were stuck in his neck, where his collar was open. He made a sort of noise like *Gug* – as if you'd pushed an empty glass into a basin of water, sir, and simply went down. I hadn't intended to do it. I hadn't even shut the door of this room when I came in. But as soon as I saw what I'd done I wiped the scissors with my handkerchief, in case of fingerprints, and I slipped out, shutting the door from the outside, and went back to my room. Do you see?

'Martha Tooth never killed anybody. It was me. I killed Sid Tooth, Mr Jacket, in this very room.

'And so you see, sir. There was a miscarriage of justice. Martha Tooth hasn't got any right to be made a heroine out of. She never killed that beast, sir. I killed Tooth. But she,' said Mr Wainewright, with bitterness, '*she* gets acquitted. *She* is made a fuss of. *Her* life-story is all over your paper. *Her* picture and *her* name is all over the place. And the honest truth of it is, that *I* did it!'

John Jacket said: 'Prove it.'

.   .   .   .   .

Mr Wainewright drew a deep breath and said: 'I beg pardon, sir?'

'Prove it,' said Jacket. 'Prove you did it.'

'Do you think I'm crazy?' asked Mr Wainewright.

'Of course you're crazy,' said Jacket.

'I swear before the Almighty,' said Mr Wainewright, with passionate sincerity, 'I swear, so help me God, that I killed Tooth!'

Jacket, who had been watching his face, said: 'I believe you, Wainewright. I believe you *did* kill Tooth.'

'Then there's your story,' Mr Wainewright said. 'Eh?'

'No,' said Jacket. 'No story. It's proved that Martha Tooth killed her husband and was justified in killing him. It's all weighed and paid. It's all over. You can't prove a thing. I believe you when you say you killed Tooth. But if you weren't a lunatic, why should you go out of your way to tell me so after everything has been resolved and poor Martha Tooth has been comfortably provided for?'

Mr Wainewright sat still and white. He was silent.

Jacket rose, stretched himself, and said: 'You see, George old man, nobody in the world is ever going to believe you now.' He reached for his hat.

'Still, I did it,' said Mr Wainewright.

'I begin,' said Jacket, 'to understand the way you work. Tooth was a swine, a strong and active swine. I see how you envied Tooth's beastly strength, and shamelessness. I think I get it. *You* wanted to ill-treat Tooth's wife and betray his girl friends. You were jealous of his power to be wicked. You wanted what he had. You wanted to be Tooth. No? So you killed Tooth. But all the while, George, in your soul, *you were Tooth*! And so you've gone and killed yourself, you poor little man. You tick unheard, George; you move unseen – you are a clock without hands. You are in hell, George!'

John Jacket put on his hat and left the house.

He did no work that afternoon. At five o'clock he telephoned Chief Inspector Dark, at Scotland Yard, and said: '. . . Just in case. That little man Wainewright has just been telling me that *he* killed Tooth in Bishop's Square.'

Chief Inspector Dark replied: 'I know. He's been telling the same story around here. He was in yesterday. The man's mad. Damned nuisances. Happens every time. Dozens of 'em always confess to what they haven't done every time somebody kills somebody. Have to make a routine investigation, as you know. But this Tooth business is nothing but a lot of Sweet Fanny Adams. Pay no attention to it. Wainewright's stone crackers, plain crazy. Forget it.'

'Just thought I'd tell you,' said Jacket.

'Right you are,' said the chief inspector, and rang off.

.   .   .   .   .

So Jacket forgot it. Great things were happening. Everyone knew that England was about to go to war against Germany. The nights were full of menace, for the lights were out in the cities. London after dark was like something tied up in a damp flannel bag. Jacket, who preferred to work a little ahead of time, was preparing certain articles which, he was certain, were going to be topical. He wrote a thousand words about a gas attack, under the title *They Thought This Was Funny*, and had it set up, illustrated with a cartoon from a 1915 issue of *Simplicissimus*. He wrote an impassioned obituary on the first baby that was to be killed in London, for immediate use if and when the war broke out. He compiled and elaborated monstrously scurrilous biographical articles about Hitler, Goebbels, Goering, etcetera.

But one evening, as he sat refreshing himself with a glass of beer and a sandwich in the 'Duchess of Douro', he saw Mr Wainewright again. Mr Wainewright could not see him: a twelve-inch-square artificial mahogany pillar stood between them, and the hot, smoky bar was crowded. Mr Wainewright, dressed in a tight-fitting black suit with red chalk-stripes, was conversing with a thick-set sweaty man in a light tweed sports coat.

The conversation had touched the perils and the

dangers of the coming night. The thick-set man was saying:

'Buy torches! Buy bulbs, buy bulbs and batteries! At any price – any price at all, wherever you can lay your hands on them. Buy torches, bulbs, and batteries. Prices are going up by leaps and bounds. A good torch is going to be worth its weight in gold. Everybody is stumbling about in the dark. There's going to be accidents in the black-out. Mark my words. Accidents. And crime. Look out for crime.'

'Crime?' said Mr Wainewright.

'Crime. Forgive me if I can't offer you a drink,' said the thick-set man.

'Oh please, have one with me.'

'No, no! Well, a small one. You're very kind. . . . Yes, crime. Robberies, murders – the black-out sets the stage for robberies and murders.'

The barmaid whom Tooth had called Baby said, as she put down two drinks: 'Are you still on about murders?'

Mr Wainewright, paying her, said: 'You look out. This gentleman is right. You can't be too careful. What's to stop anybody following you home in the dark and sticking a knife in you?'

The thick-set man said: 'Exactly, sir. Exactly.'

'I don't go home. I've got no home,' said the barmaid. 'I live here. You and your murders!'

'Yes, but you go out sometimes,' said the thick-set man.

'Only on Tuesday,' said the barmaid, with a tired laugh. 'If you want to stick a knife in me, you'd better wait till Tuesday.' She pushed Mr Wainewright's change across the bar and served another customer.

'Tuesday,' said Mr Wainewright.

The thick-set man was pleased with his idea. He said: 'I'm a man who is as it were *professionally* interested in crime.' He looked sideways and laughed.

'Oh, indeed?' said Mr Wainewright.

'As a *writer*,' said the thick-set man, suddenly grave. 'My name is Munday Marsh. You may have come across one or two of my little efforts in the *Roger Bradshaw Detective Library*.' He cleared his throat and waited. Mr Wainewright said:

'Oh yes, yes I have indeed!'

'I hate to have this drink with you because I can't return it. . . . No, no – not again! You're *very* good! As I was saying. Assume there is a sort of Jack the Ripper; a murderer without motive – the most difficult sort of killer to catch. The lights are out in this great city. The streets are dark. Dark, and swarming with all kinds of men from everywhere. Now, say a woman – Blondie there, for instance——'

'She is called Baby,' said Mr Wainewright.

'Baby. Baby is found dead, killed with a common kitchen knife. There are thousands of kitchen knives. I've got half a dozen at home myself. Say I kill Baby with such a knife. All I need is nerve. I walk past her, stab suddenly, and walk on, leaving the knife in the wound. If necessary I turn back as the lady falls and ask "What's the trouble?" Do you get the idea? I simply kill, and walk coolly on. Who could swear to me in this black-out, even if anyone saw me? Eh?'

'What a clever man you must be!' exclaimed Mr Wainewright.

Jacket, who could see his face, saw that the scanty eye-brows arched upwards, and observed a strange light in the colourless eyes.

'Of course,' Mr Wainewright continued, thoughtfully, 'you'd use – in your story, I mean – any sort of knife. Something anyone could get anywhere. A common French cook's knife, say: a strong knife with a point. Um?'

'Any knife,' said the writer who called himself Munday Marsh. 'Anything. You don't wait to get your victim alone. No. All you need is nerve, sir, nerve! A quick, accurate stab, and walk calmly on your way. I'd write that story, only I can see no means of catching my murderer.'

The barmaid heard the last word and said: 'My God, why is everybody so morbid? Murder, murder, murder – war, war, war. What's the matter with you? You got a kink or something?'

'Wait and see,' said Mr Wainewright. 'I'm not so kinky as you think.'

Jacket, still watching, saw Mr Wainewright's pale and amorphous mouth bend and stretch until it made a dry smile. For the first time he saw Mr Wainewright's teeth. He did not like that smile.

The barmaid raised her eyes to the painted ceiling with languid scorn. Jacket observed that she looked downward quickly. Then he heard the *whup-whup-whup* of the swinging door, and noticed that Mr Wainewright was gone.

.   .   .   .   .

A week passed. John Jacket was eating and drinking at the bar of the 'Duchess of Douro' before one o'clock in the afternoon, the day being Wednesday.

'How's life?' he asked the barmaid.

'So-so,' she said.

'Doing anything exciting?'

She hesitated, and said: 'I ran into a friend of yours last night.'

'A friend? Of mine?'

'That little man. What's his name? A little man. You *remember*! That funny little man. Old Murders – I forget what he calls himself. The one that gets himself up like a gangster. Used to go about in a bowler hat. Talks about murders. What *is* his name?'

'You mean Wainewright?'

'That's it, Wainewright.'

'How did you manage to run into him, Baby?'

'It was a funny thing. You know Tuesday's my day off. I generally go to see my sister. She lives near High Road. Tottenham. I left here about eleven in the morning and there was little what's-his-name. Wainewright. I walked along Charing Cross Road to get the tram at the end of Tottenham Court Road – you like to stretch your legs on a nice morning like yesterday, don't you?'

'Well?'

'I walk to Hampstead Road, and there he is again.'

'Wainewright?'

'Yes. Well, I pay no attention, I catch my tram, I go to my sister's and spend the afternoon, and we go to the pictures. We get the tram back and go to the Dominion. And when we get out, there he is again!'

'Wainewright?'

'That's right. There he is. So my sister says: "A nice night like this – let's walk a bit. I'll walk back with you." So we walk back here. Well, when we get to the National Gallery, we wait for the lights to change before we cross the road – there he is again.'

'There Wainewright is again?'

'Uh-huh. So I say to him: "Hallo." And he says "Hallo," and walks off again along Charing Cross Road. It was almost as if he was following us.'

'That's funny,' said John Jacket.

'Coincidence, I dare say. But he's a funny little man. Do you like him, Mr Jacket?'

'No, Baby, I can't say I do.'

'Well,' said the barmaid, reluctantly, 'he seems to be all right. But somehow or other I don't seem to like him very much myself. What's the matter? What're you thinking about, all of a sudden?'

'Nothing, Baby, just nothing.' Jacket finished his drink, and said: 'He was outside here. He was at the tram-stop in Hampstead Road. He was at the Dominion. And then he was here again. Is that right?'

'Yes. Why?'

'Nothing. When's your next day off?'

'Tuesday.'

'Are you going to your sister's again?'

'I generally do,' said Baby, turning away to serve a soldier.

'What time d'you get out?' asked Jacket, when she returned.

'About eleven or so. Why?'

'I just wondered. And you get back before the pub closes, I suppose? Before half-past eleven, I mean. Eh?'

'We've got to be in before twelve o'clock, you know,' said Baby. 'Why do you ask?'

'Curiosity. Your movements fascinate me,' said Jacket.

Then the lunch-hour rush began to come into the 'Duchess of Douro', and Jacket went out.

He went to see Chief Inspector Dark. 'Listen, Dark,' he said, 'you know me.'

'Well?' said the chief inspector.

'You know I'm not crazy.'

Chief Inspector Dark pursed his lips and said: 'Well?'

'You remember that crazy little man Wainewright, the witness in the Tooth case?'

'Well?'

'I think he's getting to be dangerous.'

'How?'

'You remember how he kept confessing to the killing of Tooth?'

'Well?'

'Well, Dark, I believe he really did do it.'

'Well?' said Chief Inspector Dark.

'If I were you I'd keep an eye on Wainewright.'

'Why?'

'Because I believe that Wainewright's gone really mad, dangerously mad at last, Dark.'

'What makes you think so?'

Having explained why he thought so, Jacket concluded: 'Wainewright's feelings are hurt. He is determined to make you believe, at any cost.'

'Look,' said Chief Inspector Dark. 'With one thing and another I'm rushed off my feet. I'm short-handed, and I'm busy. Is this all you've got to say?'

'Keep an eye on Wainewright,' said Jacket. 'He's after the barmaid, Baby, at the "Duchess of Douro".'

'Following her about? So would I, if I wasn't a married man, and had time to spare,' said Dark. 'Keep an eye on Wainewright yourself. I don't think there's anything to it. I'm short-handed, and I'm busy, Jacket. Will you take a hint?'

Jacket said: 'Oh well, I can't blame you for not seeing my point.'

'Much obliged,' said Dark. 'See you some other time.'

Jacket left, grinding his teeth. *I'll keep close to Baby myself,* he said to himself, as he waited for a taxi in Whitehall. *I'll show them. I'll make Dark feel small!*

But on the following Sunday, Mr Chamberlain announced that England was at war with Germany, and ten days passed before John Jacket had time to think of Baby and of Mr Wainewright.

By then, something had happened.

.   .   .   .   .

It happened on the night of 5 September 1939. The Germans had destroyed the 7th Polish Division, and the French Army had engaged the Germans between the Rhine and the Moselle. U-boats had sunk British merchant ships. The blonde called Baby had her day off, and Mr Wainewright followed her. She did not leave until half-past five that day.

He had learned something of the technique of pursuit. Instinct had warned him to put on again his dark suit and his bowler hat. He wore, also, a grey overcoat. The blonde called Baby could be kept in sight without his being seen. Mr Wainewright knew how to play his cards. He saw her coming out of the side entrance of the 'Duchess of Douro', and kept her in sight: she wore a fur that resembled a silver fox, and a diminutive yellow hat. It was not difficult to keep her within your range of vision.

Mr Wainewright followed her to St Martin's-in-the-Fields, and right, into Charing Cross Road. Something had happened to the current of life in the town. There was a new, uneasy swirl of dark-clothed civilians, like tea-leaves in a pot, together with a rush of men in khaki uniforms.

Baby walked on: she had to walk. Once she tried to stop a taxi, but the driver waved a vague hand and drove towards Whitehall. So she walked, until she caught her tram. Baby climbed to the upper deck to smoke a cigarette. Mr Wainewright sat below. When she got out, he got out. She disappeared into a little house beyond Seven Sisters corner. He waited.

As he waited he thought:

'Nobody believes me. I've confessed to a murder. They throw me out. They laugh at me. They take me for a lunatic. To the police, I'm one of those madmen who go about confessing – saying they've committed crimes they haven't committed. I killed Tooth, and I tell them so. But no! I'm crazy, they say. Good. I'll kill her. I'll kill her with a common knife. When the papers report it, I'll mark it with a pencil and go along and confess again. Nobody will believe.'

The light was fading. Keeping his right eye on the ground-floor window of the house into which Baby had disappeared, Mr Wainewright stepped sideways into the road. He put his right hand under his coat and chuckled. Then he heard something coming. He hesitated, leapt backwards – saw that the truck had swerved into the middle of the street to miss him, and tried to jump back to the pavement.

But the driver, having seen his first leap in that treacherous autumnal light, spun back to the left-hand side of the road, and knocked Mr Wainewright down.

The light truck squealed to a standstill as its rear wheels came back to the surface of the road with a soft, sickening jolt. Somewhere a woman screamed, and a man shouted. A policeman came running, and as he ran he switched on the beam of an electric torch which waggled in front of him.

A few minutes later an ambulance came, with a high, flat clangor of bells. Mr Wainewright was carried away.

He was horribly crushed. But he also had a knife-wound. A long, wide, triangular cook's knife – what they call a French knife – was embedded in his stomach.

The surgeon came to the conclusion that Mr Wainewright must have been carrying the knife in his inside breast pocket.

.   .   .   .   .

When, at last, Mr Wainewright opened his eyes he knew that he was dying. He did not know how he knew, but he knew. A cool hand was upon his left arm, and he could discern – in a big, shadowy place – a white coat and a white face.

'I killed Sid Tooth,' he said.

'There, there,' said a voice.

'I tell you I killed Sid Tooth!'

'That's all right, there, there . . .'

Something pricked his left arm, hesitated, went in deep, and threw out a sort of cold dullness.

Pain receded, tingled, and went away.

Mr Wainewright said: 'I swear I did it. Believe me, do please believe me – I did it!'

'There, there, there,' said a whisper.

Looking down at his blank, white, featureless face, the surgeon was reminded of the dial of a ruined clock, a mass-produced clock picked to bits by a spoiled child, and not worth repairing.

Men Without Bones

WE were loading bananas into the *Claire Dodge* at Puerto Pobre, when a feverish little fellow came aboard. Everyone stepped aside to let him pass – even the soldiers who guard the port with nickel-plated Remington rifles, and who go barefoot but wear polished leather leggings. They stood back from him because they believed that he was afflicted-of-God, mad; harmless but dangerous; best left alone.

All the time the naphtha flares were hissing, and from the hold came the reverberation of the roaring voice of the foreman of the gang down below crying: 'Fruta! Fruta! *FRUTA!*' The leader of the dock gang bellowed the same cry, throwing down stem after stem of brilliant green bananas. The occasion would be memorable for this, if for nothing else – the magnificence of the night, the bronze of the negro foreman shining under the flares, the jade green of that fruit, and the mixed odours of the waterfront. Out of one stem of bananas ran a hairy grey spider, which frightened the crew and broke the banana-chain, until a Nicaraguan boy, with a laugh, killed it with his foot. It was harmless, he said.

It was about then that the madman came aboard, un-hindered, and asked me: 'Bound for where?'

He spoke quietly and in a carefully modulated voice; but there was a certain blank, lost look in his eyes that suggested to me that I keep within ducking distance of his restless hands which, now that I think of them, put me in mind of that grey, hairy, bird-eating spider.

'Mobile, Alabama,' I said.

'Take me along?' he asked.

'None of my affair. Sorry. Passenger myself,' I said. 'The skipper's ashore. Better wait for him on the wharf. He's the boss.'

'Would you happen, by any chance, to have a drink about you?'

Giving him some rum, I asked: 'How come they let you aboard?'

'I'm not crazy,' he said. 'Not actually . . . a little fever, nothing more. Malaria, dengue fever, jungle fever, rat-bite fever. Feverish country, this, and others of the same nature. Allow me to introduce myself. My name is Goodbody, Doctor of Science of Osbaldeston University. Does it convey nothing to you? No? Well then; I was assistant to Professor Yeoward. Does *that* convey anything to you?'

I said: 'Yeoward, Professor Yeoward? Oh yes. He was lost, wasn't he, somewhere in the upland jungle beyond the source of the Amer River?'

'Correct!' cried the little man who called himself Goodbody. 'I saw him get lost.'

Fruta! – Fruta! – Fruta! – Fruta! came the voices of the men in the hold. There was rivalry between their leader and the big black stevedore ashore. The flares spluttered. The green bananas came down. And a kind of sickly sigh came out of the jungle, off the rotting river – not a wind, not a breeze – something like the foul breath of high fever.

Trembling with eagerness and, at the same time, shaking with fever chills, so that he had to use two hands to raise his glass to his lips – even so, he spilled most of the rum – Doctor Goodbody said: 'For God's sake, get me out of this country – take me to Mobile – hide me in your cabin!'

'I have no authority,' I said, 'but you are an American citizen; you can identify yourself; the Consul will send you home.'

'No doubt. But that would take time. The Consul thinks I am crazy too. And if I don't get away, I fear that I really will go out of my mind. Can't you help me? I'm afraid.'

'Come on, now,' I said. 'No one shall hurt you while I'm around. What are you afraid of?'

'Men without bones,' he said, and there was something in his voice that stirred the hairs on the back of my neck. 'Little fat men without bones!'

I wrapped him in a blanket, gave him some quinine, and let him sweat and shiver for a while, before I asked, humouring him: 'What men without bones?'

He talked in fits and starts in his fever, his reason staggering just this side of delirium:

'. . . What men without bones? . . . They are nothing to be afraid of, actually. It is they who are afraid of you. You can kill them with your boot, or with a stick. . . . They are something like jelly. No, it is not really fear – it is the nausea, the disgust they inspire. It overwhelms. It paralyses! I have seen a jaguar, I tell you – a full-grown jaguar – stand frozen, while they clung to him, in hundreds, and ate him up alive! Believe me, I saw it. Perhaps it is some oil they secrete, some odour they give out . . . I don't know . . .'

Then, weeping, Doctor Goodbody said: 'Oh, nightmare – nightmare – nightmare! To think of the depths to which a noble creature can be degraded by hunger! Horrible, horrible!'

'Some debased form of life that you found in the jungle above the source of the Amer?' I suggested. 'Some degenerate kind of anthropoid?'

'No, no, no. *Men!* Now surely you remember Professor Yeoward's ethnological expedition?'

'It was lost,' I said.

'All but me,' he said. '. . . We had bad luck. At the Anaña Rapids we lost two canoes, half our supplies and most of our instruments. And also Doctor Terry, and Jack Lambert, and eight of our carriers. . . .

'Then we were in Ahu territory where the Indians use poison darts, but we made friends with them and bribed them to carry our stuff westward through the jungle . . . because, you see, all science starts with a guess, a rumour, an old wives' tale; and the object of Professor Yeoward's expedition was to investigate a series of Indian folk tales that tallied. Legends of a race of gods that came down from the sky in a great flame when the world was very young. . . .

'Line by criss-cross line, and circle by concentric circle, Yeoward localised the place in which these tales had their root – an unexplored place that has no name because the Indians refuse to give it a name, it being what they call a "bad place".'

His chills subsiding and his fever abating, Doctor Goodbody spoke calmly and rationally now. He said, with a short laugh: 'I don't know why, whenever I get a touch of fever, the memory of those boneless men comes back in a nightmare to give me the horrors. . . .

'So, we went to look for the place where the gods came down in flame out of the night. The little tattooed

Indians took us to the edge of the Ahu territory and then put down their packs and asked for their pay, and no consideration would induce them to go further. We were going, they said, to a very bad place. Their chief, who had been a great man in his day, sign-writing with a twig, told us that he had strayed there once, and drew a picture of something with an oval body and four limbs, at which he spat before rubbing it out with his foot in the dirt. Spiders? we asked. Crabs? What?

'So we were forced to leave what we could not carry with the old chief against our return, and go on unaccompanied, Yeoward and I, through thirty miles of the rottenest jungle in the world. We made about a quarter of a mile in a day . . . a pestilential place! When that stinking wind blows out of the jungle, I smell nothing but death, and panic. . . .

'But, at last, we cut our way to the plateau and climbed the slope, and there we saw something marvellous. It was something that had been a gigantic machine. Originally it must have been a pear-shaped thing, at least a thousand feet long and, in its widest part, six hundred feet in diameter. I don't know of what metal it had been made, because there was only a dusty outline of a hull and certain ghostly remains of unbelievably intricate mechanisms to prove that it had ever been. We could not guess from where it had come; but the impact of its landing had made a great valley in the middle of the plateau.

'It was the discovery of the age! It proved that countless ages ago, this planet had been visited by people from the stars! Wild with excitement, Yeoward and I plunged into this fabulous ruin. But whatever we touched fell away to fine powder.

'At last, on the third day, Yeoward found a semi-circular plate of some extraordinarily hard metal, which was covered with the most maddeningly familiar diagrams. We cleaned it, and for twenty-four hours, scarcely pausing to eat and drink, Yeoward studied it. And, then, before the dawn of the fifth day he awoke me, with a great cry, and said: "It's a map, a map of the heavens, and a chart of a course from Mars to Earth!"

'And he showed me how those ancient explorers of space had proceeded from Mars to Earth, via the Moon. . . . To crash on this naked plateau in this green hell of a jungle? I wondered. "Ah, but was it a jungle then?" said Yeoward. "This may have happened five million years ago!"

'I said: "Oh, but surely! it took only a few hundred years to bury Rome. How could this thing have stayed above ground for five thousand years, let alone five million?" Yeoward said: "It didn't. The earth swallows things and regurgitates them. This is a volcanic region. One little upheaval can swallow a city, and one tiny peristalsis in the bowels of the earth can bring its remains to light again a million years later. So it must have been with the machine from Mars . . ."

' "I wonder who was inside it," I said. Yeoward replied: "Very likely some utterly alien creatures that couldn't tolerate the Earth, and died, or else were killed in the crash. No skeleton could survive such a space of time."

'So, we built up the fire, and Yeoward went to sleep. Having slept, I watched. Watched for what? I didn't know. Jaguars, peccaries, snakes? None of these beasts climbed up to the plateau; there was nothing for them up there. Still, unaccountably, I was afraid.

'There was the weight of ages on the place. *Respect old age,* one is told. . . . The greater the age, the deeper the respect, you might say. But it is not respect; it is dread, it is fear of time and death, sir! . . . I must have dozed, because the fire was burning low – I had been most careful to keep it alive and bright – when I caught my first glimpse of the boneless men.

'Starting up, I saw, at the rim of the plateau, a pair of eyes that picked up luminosity from the fading light of the fire. *A jaguar,* I thought, and took up my rifle. But it could not have been a jaguar because, when I looked left and right I saw that the plateau was ringed with pairs of shining eyes . . . as it might be, a collar of opals; and there came to my nostrils an odour of God knows what.

'Fear has its smell as any animal-trainer will tell you. Sickness has its smell – ask any nurse. These smells compel healthy animals to fight or to run away. This was a combination of the two, plus a stink of vegetation gone bad. I fired at the pair of eyes I had first seen. Then, all the eyes disappeared while, from the jungle, there came a chattering and a twittering of monkeys and birds, as the echoes of the shot went flapping away.

'And then, thank God, the dawn came. I should not have liked to see by artificial light the thing I had shot between the eyes.

'It was grey and, in texture, tough and gelatinous. Yet, in form, externally, it was not unlike a human being. It had eyes, and there were either vestiges – or rudiments – of head, and neck, and a kind of limbs.

'Yeoward told me that I must pull myself together; overcome my "childish revulsion", as he called it; and look into the nature of the beast. I may say that he kept a long way away from it when I opened it. It was my job

227

as zoologist of the expedition, and I had to do it. Microscopes and other delicate instruments had been lost with the canoes. I worked with a knife and forceps. And found? Nothing: a kind of digestive system enclosed in very tough jelly, a rudimentary nervous system, and a brain about the size of a walnut. The entire creature, stretched out, measured four feet.

'In a laboratory I could tell you, perhaps, something about it . . . with an assistant or two, to keep me company. As it was, I did what I could with a hunting-knife and forceps, without dyes or microscope, swallowing my nausea – it was a nauseating thing! – memorising what I found. But, as the sun rose higher, the thing liquefied, melted, until by nine o'clock there was nothing but a glutinous grey puddle, with two green eyes swimming in it. . . . And these eyes – I can see them now – burst with a thick *pop*, making a detestable sticky ripple in that puddle of corruption. . . .

'After that, I went away for a while. When I came back, the sun had burned it all away, and there was nothing but something like what you see after a dead jellyfish has evaporated on a hot beach. Slime. Yeoward had a white face when he asked me: "What the devil is it?" I told him that I didn't know, that it was something outside my experience, and that although I pretended to be a man of science with a detached mind, nothing would induce me ever to touch one of the things again.

'Yeoward said: "You're getting hysterical, Goodbody. Adopt the proper attitude. God knows, we are not here for the good of our health. Science, man, science! Not a day passes but some doctor pokes his fingers into fouler things than that!" I said: "Don't you believe it. Professor Yeoward, I have handled and dissected some pretty queer things in my time, but this is something repulsive. I have nerves? I dare say. Maybe we should have brought a psychiatrist . . . I notice, by the way, that you aren't too anxious to come close to me after I've tampered with that thing. I'll shoot one with pleasure, but if you want to investigate it, try it yourself and see!'"

'Yeoward said that he was deeply occupied with his metal plate. There was no doubt, he told me, that this machine that had been had come from Mars. But, evidently, he preferred to keep the fire between himself and me, after I had touched that abomination of hard jelly.

'Yeoward kept himself to himself, rummaging in the ruin. I went about my business, which was to investigate forms of animal life. I do not know what I might have found, if I had had – I don't say the courage, because I didn't lack that – if I had had some company. Alone, my nerve broke.

'It happened one morning. I went into the jungle that surrounded us, trying to swallow the fear that choked me, and drive away the sense of revulsion that not only made me want to turn and run, but made me afraid to turn my back even to get away. You may or may not know that, of all the beasts that live in that jungle, the most impregnable is the sloth. He finds a stout limb, climbs out on it, and hangs from it by his twelve steely claws; a tardigrade that lives on leaves. Your tardigrade is so tenacious that even in death, shot through the heart, it will hang on to its branch. It has an immensely tough hide covered by an impenetrable coat of coarse, matted hair. A panther or a jaguar is helpless against the

229

passive resistance of such a creature. It finds itself a tree, which it does not leave until it has eaten every leaf, and chooses for a sleeping place a branch exactly strong enough to bear its weight.

'In this detestable jungle, on one of my brief expeditions – brief, because I was alone and afraid – I stopped to watch a giant sloth hanging motionless from the largest bough of a half-denuded tree, asleep, impervious, indifferent. Then, out of that stinking green twilight came a horde of those jellyfish things. They *poured up* the tree, and writhed along the branch.

'Even the sloth, which generally knows no fear, was afraid. It tried to run away, hooked itself on to a thinner part of the branch, which broke. It fell, and at once was covered with a shuddering mass of jelly. Those boneless men do not bite: they suck. And, as they suck, their colour changes from grey to pink and then to brown.

'But they are afraid of us. There is race-memory involved here. We repel them, and they repel us. When they became aware of my presence, they – I was going to say, ran away – they slid away, dissolved into the shadows that kept dancing and dancing and dancing under the trees. And the horror came upon me, so that I ran away, and arrived back at our camp, bloody about the face with thorns, and utterly exhausted.

'Yeoward was lancing a place in his ankle. A tourniquet was tied under his knee. Near-by lay a dead snake. He had broken its back with that same metal plate, but it had bitten him first. He said: "What kind of a snake do you call this? I'm afraid it is venomous. I feel a numbness in my cheeks and around my heart, and I cannot feel my hands."

'I said: "Oh, my God! You've been bitten by a jara-jaca!"

' "And we have lost our medical supplies," he said, with regret. "And there is so much work left to do. Oh, dear me, dear me! . . . Whatever happens, my dear fellow, take *this* and get back."

'And he gave me that semi-circle of unknown metal as a sacred trust. Two hours later, he died. That night the circle of glowing eyes grew narrower. I emptied my rifle at it, time and again. At dawn, the boneless men disappeared.

'I heaped rocks on the body of Yeoward. I made a pylon, so that the men without bones could not get at him. Then – oh, so dreadfully lonely and afraid! – I shouldered my pack, and took my rifle and my machete, and ran away, down the trail we had covered. But I lost my way.

'Can by can of food, I shed weight. Then my rifle went, and my ammunition. After that, I threw away even my machete. A long time later, that semi-circular plate became too heavy for me, so I tied it to a tree with liana-vine, and went on.

'So I reached the Ahu territory, where the tattooed men nursed me and were kind to me. The women chewed my food for me, before they fed me, until I was strong again. Of the stores we had left there, I took only as much as I might need, leaving the rest as pay-ment for guides and men to man the canoe down the river. And so I got back out of the jungle. . . .

'Please give me a little more rum.' His hand was steady, now, as he drank, and his eyes were clear.

I said to him: 'Assuming that what you say is true: these "boneless men" – they were, I presume, the

Martians? Yet it sounds unlikely, surely? Do inverte-brates smelt hard metals and——'

'Who said anything about Martians?' cried Doctor Goodbody. 'No, no, no! The Martians came here, adapted themselves to new conditions of life. Poor fellows, they changed, sank low; went through a whole new process – a painful process of evolution. What I'm trying to tell you, you fool, is that Yeoward and I did *not* discover Martians. Idiot, don't you see? *Those boneless things are men. We are Martians!'*

The Brighton Monster

I FOUND one of the most remarkable stories of the century – a story related to the most terrible event in the
history of mankind – in a heap of rubbish in the corridor
outside the office of Mr Harry Ainsworth, editor of the
People, in 1943.

Every house in London, in those dark, exciting days,
was being combed for salvage, particularly scrap metal
and waste paper. Out of Mr Ainsworth's office alone
came more than three hundred pounds of paper that,
on consideration, was condemned to pulp as not worth
keeping.

The pamphlet I found must have been lying at the
bottom of a bottom drawer – it was on top of the salvage
basket. If the lady, or gentleman, who sent it to the
People will communicate with me I will gladly pay her
(or him) two hundred and fifty English pounds.

As literature it is nothing but a piece of pretentious
nonsense written by one of those idle dabblers in
'Natural Philosophy' who rushed into print on the
slightest provocation in the eighteenth century. But the
significance of it is formidable.

It makes me afraid.

.   .   .   .   .

The author of my pamphlet had attempted to tickle
his way into public notice with the feather of his pen by

writing an account of a Monster captured by a boatman
fishing several miles out of Brighthelmstone in the
county of Sussex in the summer of the year 1745.

The name of the author was the Reverend Arthur
Titty. I see him as one of those pushing self-assertive
vicars of the period, a rider to hounds, a purple-faced
consumer of prodigious quantities of old port; a man of
independent fortune, trying to persuade the world and
himself that he was a deep thinker and a penetrating
observer of the mysterious works of God.

I should never have taken the trouble to pocket his
*Account of a Strange Monster Captured Near Bright-
helmstone in the County of Sussex on August 6th in the
Year of Our Lord 1745* if it had not been for the coincidence of the date: I was born on 6 August. So I pushed
the yellowed, damp-freckled pages into the breast pocket
of my battledress, and thought no more about them
until April 1947, when a casual remark sent me running, yelling like a maniac, to the cupboard in which my
old uniforms were hanging.

The pamphlet was still in its pocket.

.   .   .   .   .

I shall not waste your time or strain your patience
with the Reverend Arthur Titty's turgid, high-falutin'
prose or his references to *De rerum* – this, that and the
other. I propose to give you the unadorned facts in the
very queer case of the Brighthelmstone Monster.

Brighthelmstone is now known as Brighton – a large,
popular, prosperous holiday resort delightfully situated
on the coast of Sussex by the Downs. But in the
Reverend Titty's day it was an obscure fishing village.

If a fisherman named Hodge had not had an unlucky

234

night on 5 August 1745, on the glass-smooth sea off Brighthelmstone, this story would never have been told. He had gone out with his brother-in-law, George Rodgers, and they had caught nothing but a few small and valueless fishes. Hodge was desperate. He was notorious in the village as a spendthrift and a drunkard, and it was suspected that he had a certain connection with a barmaid at the Smack Inn – it was alleged that she had a child by him in the spring of the following year. He had scored up fifteen shillings for beer and needed a new net. It is probable, therefore, that Hodge stayed out in his boat until after the dawn of 6 August because he feared to face his wife – who also, incidentally, was with child.

At last, glum, sullen, and thoroughly out of sorts, he prepared to go home.

And then, he said, there was something like a splash – only it was not a splash: it was rather like the bursting of a colossal bubble: and there, in the sea, less than ten yards from his boat, was the Monster, floating.

George Rodgers said: 'By gogs, Jack Hodge, yon's a man!'

'Man? How can 'a be a man? Where could a man come from?'

The creature that had appeared with the sound of a bursting bubble drifted closer, and Hodge, reaching out with a boat-hook, caught it under the chin and pulled it to the side of the boat.

'That be a Merman,' he said, 'and no Christian man. Look at 'un, all covered wi' snakes and firedrakes, and yellow like a slug's belly. By the Lord, George Rodgers, this might be the best night's fishing I ever did if it's alive, please the Lord! For if it is I can sell that for

235

better money than ever I got for my best catch this last twenty years, or any other fisherman either. Lend a hand, Georgie-boy, and let's have a feel of it.'

George Rodgers said: 'That's alive, by hell – look now, and see the way the blood runs down where the gaff went home.'

'Haul it in, then, and don't stand there gaping like a puddock.'

They dragged the Monster into the boat. It was shaped like a man and covered from throat to ankle with brilliantly coloured images of strange monsters. A green, red, yellow and blue thing like a lizard sprawled between breast-bone and navel. Great serpents were coiled about its legs. A smaller snake, red and blue, was picked out on the Monster's right arm: the snake's tail covered the forefinger and its head was hidden in the armpit. On the left-hand side of its chest there was a big heart-shaped design in flaming scarlet. A great bird like an eagle in red and green spread its wings from shoulder-blade to shoulder-blade, and a red fox chased six blue rabbits from the middle of his spine into some unknown hiding place between his legs. There were lobsters, fishes, and insects on his left arm and on his right buttock a devil-fish sprawled, encircling the lower part of his body with its tentacles. The back of his right hand was decorated with a butterfly in yellow, red, indigo and green. Low down, in the centre of the throat, where the bone begins, there was a strange, incomprehensible, evil-looking symbol.

The Monster was naked. In spite of its fantastic appearance it was so unmistakably a male human being that George Rodgers – a weak-minded but respectable man – covered it with a sack. Hodge prised open the

Monster's mouth to look at its teeth, having warned his brother-in-law to stand by with an axe in case of emergency. The man-shaped creature out of the sea had red gums, a red tongue and teeth as white as sugar.

They forced it to swallow a little gin – Hodge always had a flask of gin in the boat – and it came to life with a great shudder, and cried out in a strange voice, opening wild black eyes and looking crazily left and right.

'Tie that up. You tie that's hands while I tie that's feet,' said Hodge.

The Monster offered no resistance.

'Throw 'un back,' said George Rodgers, suddenly overtaken by a nameless dread. 'Throw 'un back, Jack, I say!'

But Hodge said: 'You be mazed, George Rodgers, you born fool. I can sell 'e for twenty-five golden guineas. Throw 'un back? I'll throw 'ee back for a brass farthing, tha' witless fool!'

There was no wind. The two fishermen pulled for the shore. The Monster lay in the bilge, rolling its eyes. The silly, good-natured Rodgers offered it a crust of bread which it snapped up so avidly that it bit his finger to the bone. Then Hodge tried to cram a wriggling live fish into its mouth, but 'the Monster spat it out *pop*, like a cork out of a bottle, saving your Honour's presence.'

Brighthelmstone boiled over with excitement when they landed. Even the Reverend Arthur Titty left his book and his breakfast, clapped on his three-cornered hat, picked up his cane, and went down to the fish-market to see what was happening. They told him that Hodge had caught a monster, a fish that looked like a man, a merman, a hypogriff, a sphinx – heaven knows what. The crowd parted and Titty came face to face with the Monster.

Although the Monster understood neither Hebrew, Greek, Latin, Italian nor French, it was obvious that it was a human being, or something remarkably like one. This was evident in its manner of wrinkling its forehead, narrowing its eyes, and demonstrating that it was capable of understanding – or of wanting to understand, which is the same thing. But it could not speak; it could only cry out incoherently and it was obviously greatly distressed. The Reverend Arthur Titty said: 'Oafs, ignorant louts! This is no sea monster, you fools, no *lusus naturae*, but an unfortunate shipwrecked mariner.'

According to the pamphlet, Hodge said: 'Your Reverence, begging your Reverence's pardon, how can that be, since for the past fortnight there has been no breath of wind and no foreign vessel in these parts? If this be an unfortunate shipwrecked mariner, where is the wreck of his ship, and where was it wrecked? I humbly ask your Reverence how he appeared as you might say out of a bubble without warning on the face of the water, floating. And if your Honour will take the trouble to observe this unhappy creature's skin your Reverence will see that it shows no signs of having been immersed for any considerable period in the ocean.'

I do not imagine for a moment that this is what Hodge really said: he probably muttered the substance of the argument in the form of an angry protest emphasised by a bitten-off oath or two. However, the Reverend Arthur Titty perceived that what the fisherman said was 'not without some show of reason' and said that he proposed to take the Monster to his house for examination.

Hodge protested vigorously. It was his Monster, he

said, because he had caught it in the open sea with his own hands, in his own boat, and parson or no parson, if Titty were the Archbishop himself, an Englishman had his rights. After some altercation, in the course of which the Monster fainted, the Reverend Arthur Titty gave Hodge a silver crown piece for the loan of the Monster for philosophical observation. They poured a few buckets of sea water over the Monster which came back to consciousness with a tremulous sigh. This was regarded as positive proof of its watery origin. Then it was carried to Titty's house on a hurdle.

It rejected salt water as a drink, preferring fresh water or wine, and ate cooked food, expressing, with unmistakable grimaces, a distaste for raw fish and meat. It was put to bed on a heap of clean straw and covered with a blanket which was kept moistened with sea water. Soon the monster of Brighthelmstone revived and appeared desirous of walking. It could even make sounds reminiscent of human speech.

The Reverend Arthur Titty covered its nakedness under a pair of his old breeches and one of his old shirts . . . as if it had not been grotesque-looking enough before.

He weighed it, measured it, and bled it to discover whether it was thick or thin-blooded, cold or hot-blooded. According to Titty's fussy little account the Monster was about five feet one and three-quarter inches tall. It weighed exactly one hundred and nineteen pounds, and walked upright. It possessed unbelievable strength and superhuman agility. On one occasion the Reverend Arthur Titty took it out for a walk on the end of a leather leash. The local blacksmith, one of Hodge's boon companions, who was notorious for his gigantic muscular power and bad temper – he was later to achieve nation-wide fame as Clifford, who broke the arm of the champion wrestler of Yorkshire – accosted the Reverend Arthur Titty outside his smithy and said: 'Ah, so that's Hodge's catch as you stole from him. Let me feel of it to see if it be real,' and he pinched the Monster's shoulder very cruelly with one of his great hands – hands that could snap horseshoes and twist iron bars into spirals. The inevitable crowd of children and gaping villagers witnessed the event. The Monster picked up the two-hundred-pound blacksmith and threw him into a heap of scrap iron three yards away. For an anxious second or two Titty thought that the Monster was going to run amok, for its entire countenance changed; the nostrils quivered, the eyes shone with fierce intelligence, and from its open mouth there came a weird cry. Then the creature relapsed into heavy dejection and let itself be led home quietly, while the astonished blacksmith, bruised and bleeding, limped back to his anvil with the shocked air of a man who has seen the impossible come to pass.

Yet, the Monster was an extremely sick Monster. It ate little, sometimes listlessly chewing the same mouthful for fifteen minutes. It liked to squat on its haunches and stare unblinkingly at the sea. It was assumed that it was homesick for its native element, and so it was soused at intervals with buckets of brine and given a large tub of sea water to sleep in if it so desired. A learned doctor of medicine came all the way from Dover to examine it and pronounced it human; unquestionably an air-breathing mammal. But so were whales and crocodiles breathers of air that lived in the water.

Hodge, alternately threatening and whimpering,

claimed his property. The Reverend Arthur Titty called in his lawyer, who so bewildered the unfortunate fisherman with Latin quotations, legal jargon, dark hints and long words that, cursing and growling, he scrawled a cross in lieu of a signature at the foot of a document in which he agreed to relinquish all claim on the Monster in consideration of the sum of seven guineas, payable on the spot. Seven guineas was a great deal of money for a fisherman in those days. Hodge had never seen so many gold pieces in a heap, and had never owned one. Then a travelling showman visited the Reverend Arthur Titty and offered him twenty-five guineas for the Monster, which Titty refused. The showman spoke of the matter in the Smack, and Hodge, who had been drunk for a week, behaved 'like one demented', as Titty wrote in a contemptuous footnote. He made a thorough nuisance of himself, demanding the balance of the twenty-five guineas which were his by rights, was arrested and fined for riotous conduct. Then he was put in the stocks as an incorrigible drunkard, and the wicked little urchins of Brighthelmstone threw fish-guts at him.

Let out of the stocks with a severe reprimand, smelling horribly of dead fish, Hodge went to the Smack and ordered a quart of strong ale, which came in a heavy can. Rodgers, to whom Hodge had given only twelve shillings, came in for his modest morning draught, and told Hodge that he was nothing better than a damned rogue. He claimed half of the seven golden guineas. Hodge, having drunk his quart, struck Rodgers with the can, and broke his skull; for which he was hanged not long afterwards.

The Brighthelmstone Monster was an unlucky Monster.

The Reverend Arthur Titty also suffered. After the killing of Rodgers and the hanging of Hodge the fishermen began to hate him. Heavy stones were thrown against his shutters at night. Someone set fire to one of his haystacks. This must have given Titty something to think about, for rick-burning was a hanging matter, and one may as well hang for a parson as for a haystack. He made up his mind to go to London and live in politer society. So he was uprooted by the Monster. The fishermen hated the Monster too. They regarded it as a sort of devil. But the Monster did not care. It was languishing, dying of a mysterious sickness. Curious sores had appeared at various points on the Monster's body – they began as little white bumps such as one gets from stinging-nettles, and slowly opened and would not close. The looseness of the skin, now, lent the dragons and fishes a disgustingly lifelike look: as the Monster breathed, they writhed. A veterinary surgeon poured melted pitch on the sores. The Reverend Titty kept it well soaked in sea water and locked it in a room, because it had shown signs of wanting to escape.

At last, nearly three months after its first appearance in Brighthelmstone, the Monster escaped. An old man-servant, Alan English, unlocked the door, in the presence of the Reverend Arthur Titty, to give the Monster its daily mess of vegetables and boiled meat. As the key turned the door was flung open with such violence that English fell forward into the room – his hand was still on the door-knob – and the Monster ran out, crying aloud in a high, screaming voice. The Reverend Arthur Titty caught it by the shoulder, whereupon he was whisked away like a leaf in the wind and lay stunned at the end of the passage. The Monster ran out of the house. Three responsible witnesses – Rebecca North, Herbert George and Abraham Herris (or Harris) – saw it running towards the sea, stark naked, although a north-east wind was blowing. The two men ran after it, and Rebecca North followed as fast as she could. The Monster ran straight into the bitter water and began to swim, its arms and legs vibrating like the wings of an insect. Herbert George saw it plunge into the green heart of a great wave, and then the heavy rain fell like a curtain and the Brighthelmstone Monster was never seen again.

It had never spoken. In the later stages of its disease its teeth had fallen out. With one of these teeth – probably a canine – it had scratched marks on the dark oak panels of the door of the room in which it was confined. These marks the Reverend Arthur Titty faithfully copied and reproduced in his pamphlet.

The Brighthelmstone fishermen said that the sea devil had gone back where it belonged, down to the bottom of the sea to its palace built of the bones of lost Christian sailors. Sure enough, half an hour after the Monster disappeared there was a terrible storm, and many seamen lost their lives. In a month or so Titty left Brighthelmstone for London. The city swallowed him. He published his pamphlet in 1746 – a bad year for natural philosophy, because the ears of England were still full of the Jacobite Rebellion of '45.

Poor Titty! If he could have foreseen the real significance of the appearance of the Monster of Brighthelmstone he would have died happy . . . in a lunatic asylum.

Nobody would have believed him.

· · · · ·

Now in April 1947 I had the good fortune to meet one of my oldest and dearest friends, a colonel in Intelligence who, for obvious reasons, must remain anonymous, although he is supposed to be in retirement now and wears civilian clothes, elegantly cut in the narrow-sleeved style of the late nineteen-twenties, and rather the worse for wear. The Colonel is in many ways a romantic character, something like Rudyard Kipling's Strickland Sahib. He has played many strange parts in his time, that formidable old warrior; and his quick black eyes, disturbingly Asiatic-looking under the slackly-drooping eyelids, have seen more than you and I will ever see.

He never talks about his work. An Intelligence officer who talks ceases automatically to be an Intelligence officer. A good deal of his conversation is of sport, manly sport – polo, pig-sticking, cricket, rugby football, hunting, and, above all, boxing and wrestling. I imagine that the Colonel, who has lived underground in disguise for so many years of his life, finds relief in the big wide-open games in which a man must meet his opponent face to face yet may, without breaking the rules, play quick tricks.

We were drinking coffee and smoking cigarettes after dinner in my flat and he was talking about oriental wrestling. He touched on wrestling technique among the Afghans and in the Deccan, and spoke with admiration of Gama, the Western Indian wrestler, still a rock-crusher at an age when most men are shivering in slippers by the fire, who beat Zbyszko; remarked on a South-Eastern Indian named Patil who could knock a strong man senseless with the knuckle of his left thumb; and went on to Chinese wrestlers, especially Mongolians, who are tremendously heavy and powerful, and use their feet. A good French-Canadian lumberjack (the Colonel said), accustomed to dancing on rolling logs in a rushing river, could do dreadful things with his legs and feet, like the Tiger of Quebec, who in a scissors-hold killed Big Ted Glass of Detroit. In certain kinds of wrestling size and weight were essential, said the Colonel. The Japanese wrestlers of the heavy sort – the ones that weighed three or four hundred pounds and looked like pigs – those big ones that started on all fours and went through a series of ritual movements; they had to be enormously heavy. In fact the heavier they were the better.

'No, Gerald my lad, give me ju-jitsu,' he said. 'There is no one on earth who can defeat a master of ju-jitsu – except someone who takes him by surprise. Of course, a scientific boxer, getting a well-placed punch in first, would put him out for the count. But the real adept develops such wonderful co-ordination of hand and eye that if he happens to be expecting it he can turn to his own advantage even the lightning punch of a wizard like Jimmy Wilde. He could give away eight stone to Joe Louis and make him look silly. Georges Hackenschmidt, for instance, is one of the greatest catch-as-catch-can wrestlers that ever lived, and one of the strongest men of his day. But I question whether he, wrestling Catch, might have stood up against Yukio Tani? Oh, by the way, speaking of Yukio Tani, did you ever hear of a wrestler called Sato?'

'I can't say that I have. Why? Should I have heard of him?'

'Why, he is, or was, a phenomenon. I think he was a better wrestler than Tani. My idea was to take him all round the world and challenge all comers – boxers, wrestlers, even fencers, to stand up against him for ten minutes. He was unbelievable. Furthermore, he *looked* so frightful. I won a hundred and fifty quid on him at Singapore in 1938. He took on four of the biggest and best boxers and wrestlers we could lay our hands on and floored the whole lot in seven minutes by the clock. Just a minute, I've got a picture in my wallet. I keep it because it looks so damn funny. Look.'

The Colonel handed me a dog-eared photograph of an oddly assorted group. There was a hairy mammoth of a man, obviously a wrestler, standing with his arms folded so that his biceps looked like coconuts, beside another man, almost as big, but with the scrambled features of a rough-and-tumble bruiser. There was one blond grinning man who looked like a light heavy-weight, and a beetle-browed middle-weight with a bulldog jaw. The Colonel was standing in the background, smiling in a fatherly way. In the foreground smiling into the camera stood a tiny Japanese. The top of his head was on a level with the big wrestler's breast-bone, but he was more than half as broad as he was tall. He was all chest and arms. The knuckles of his closed hands touched his knees. I took the picture to the light and looked more closely. The photographer's flash-bulb had illuminated every detail. Sato had made himself even more hideous with tattooing. He was covered with things that creep and crawl, real and fabulous. A dragon snarled on his stomach. Snakes were coiled about his legs. Another snake wound itself about his right arm from forefinger to armpit. The other arm was covered with angry-looking lobsters and goggle-eyed fishes, and on the left breast there was the conventionalised shape of a heart.

It was then that I uttered an astonished oath and went running to look for my old uniform, which I found, with the Reverend Arthur Titty's pamphlet still in the inside breast pocket. The Colonel asked me what the devil was the matter with me. I smoothed out the pamphlet and gave it to him without a word.

He looked at it, and said: 'How very extraordinary!' Then he put away his eye-glass and put on a pair of spectacles; peered intently at the smudged and ragged drawing of the Brighthelmstone Monster, compared it with the photograph of Sato and said to me: 'I have come across some pretty queer things in my time, but I'm damned if I know what to make of this.'

'Tell me,' I said, 'was your Sato tattooed behind? And if so, in what way?'

Without hesitation the Colonel said: 'A red-and-green hawk stooping between the shoulder-blades, a red fox chasing six blue-grey rabbits down his spine, and an octopus on the right buttock throwing out tentacles that went round to the belly. Why?'

Then I opened Titty's pamphlet and put my finger on the relevant passage. The Colonel read it and changed colour. But he said nothing. I said: 'This is the damnedest coincidence. There's another thing. This so-called Monster of Brighton scratched something on the door of the room where he was locked up, and the old parson took a pencil rubbing of it. Turn over four or five pages and you'll see a copy of it.'

The Colonel found the page. The spongy old paper was worn into holes, blurred by time and the dampness of lumber-rooms and the moisture of my body. He said: 'It looks like Japanese. But no Japanese would write like that surely . . .'

'Remember,' I said, 'that the Brighton Monster scratched its message with one of its own teeth on the panel of an oak door. Allow for that; allow for the fact that it was weak and sick; take into consideration the grain of the wood; and then see what you make of it.'

The Colonel looked at the inscription for ten long minutes, copying it several times from several different angles. At last he said: 'This says: *I was asleep. I thought that it was all a bad dream from which I should awake and find myself by the side of my wife. Now I know that it is not a dream. I am sick in the head. Pity me, poor Sato, who went to sleep in one place and awoke in another. I cannot live any more. I must die. Hiroshima 1945.*'

'What do you make of that?' I asked.

The Colonel said: 'I don't know. I only know the bare facts about Sato because, as I have already told you, I was trying to find him. (a) He had a wife, and a home somewhere in Hiroshima. (b) He was in the Japanese Navy, and he went on leave in August 1945. (c) Sato disappeared off the face of the earth when they dropped that damned atom bomb. (d) This is unquestionably a picture of Sato – the greatest little wrestler the world has ever known. (e) The description of the tattooing on the back of this Monster tallies exactly with Sato's . . . I don't know quite what to make of it. Sato, you know, was a Christian. He counted the years the Christian way. *Hiroshima 1945.* I wonder!'

'What do you wonder?'

'Why,' said the Colonel, 'there can't be the faintest shadow of a doubt that Sato got the middle part of the blast of that frightful atom bomb when we dropped it on Hiroshima. You may or may not have heard of Dr Sant's crazy theories concerning Time in relation to Speed. Now imagine that you happen to be caught up – without disintegrating – in a species of air-pocket on the fringe of an atomic blast and are flung away a thousand times faster than if you had been fired out of a cannon. Imagine it. According to the direction in which you happen to be thrown you may find yourself in the middle of Tomorrow or on the other side of Yesterday. Don't laugh at me. I may have been frying my brains in the tropics most of my life, and I may be crazy; but I've learned to believe all kinds of strange things. My opinion is that my poor little Sato was *literally blown back* two hundred years in time.'

I said: 'But why blown backwards only in time? How do you account for his being struck by the blast in Hiroshima and ending in Brighton?'

'I'm no mathematician,' said the Colonel, 'but as I understand, the earth is perpetually spinning and Space is therefore shifting all the time. If you, for example, could stand absolutely still, here, now, where you are, while the earth moved – if you stood still only for one hour, you'd find yourself in Budapest. Do you understand what I mean? That atomic blast picked little Sato up and threw him back in Time. When you come to think of that, and remember all the curious Monsters they used to exhibit in Bartholomew's Fair during the eighteenth century – when you think of all the Mermaids, Monsters, and Mermen that they picked out of the sea and showed on fair-grounds until they died . . . it makes you think.'

'It makes you think.'

'Do you observe, by the way,' said the Colonel, pointing to the Reverend Titty's pamphlet, 'that poor little

Sato was sick with running sores, and that his teeth were falling out? Radio-activity poisoning: these are the symptoms. Poor Sato! Can you wonder why he got desperate and simply chucked himself back into the sea to sink or swim? Put yourself in his position. You go to sleep in Hiroshima, in August 1945 and then – *Whoof!* – you find yourself in Brighton, in November 1745. No wonder the poor wretch couldn't speak. That shock would be enough to paralyse anyone's tongue. It scares me, Kersh, my boy – it puts a match to trains of thought of the most disturbing nature. It makes me remember that Past and Future are all one. I shall really worry, in future, when I have a nightmare . . . one of those nightmares in which you find yourself lost, struck dumb, completely bewildered in a place you've never seen before – a place out of this world. God have mercy on us, I wish they'd never thought of that disgusting Secret Weapon!'

.   .   .   .   .

You are free to argue the point, to speculate and to draw your own conclusions. But this is the end (or, God forbid, the beginning) of the story of the Brighton Monster.

Frozen Beauty

Do *I* believe this story?

I don't know. I heard it from a Russian doctor of medicine. He swears that there are certain facets of the case which – wildly unbelievable though it sounds – have given him many midnight hours of thought that led nowhere.

'It is impossible,' he said, 'in the light of scientific knowledge. But that is still a very uncertain light. We know little of life and death and the something we call the Soul. Even of sleep we know nothing.

'I am tired of thinking about this mad story. It happened in the Belt of Eternal Frost.

'The Belt of Eternal Frost is in Siberia.

'It has been cold, desperately cold, since the beginning of things . . . a freak of climate.

'Did you know that a good deal of the world's ivory comes from there? Mammoth ivory – the tusks of prehistoric hairy elephants ten thousand years dead.

'Sometimes, men digging there unearth bodies of mammoths in a perfect state of preservation, fresh enough to eat after a hundred centuries in the everlasting refrigerator of the frost.

'Only recently, just before Hitler's invasion, Soviet scientists found, under the snow, a stable complete with horses – standing frozen stiff – horses of a forgotten tribe that perished there in the days of the mammoths.

'There were people there before the dawn of history;

but the snow swallowed them. This much science knows. But as for what I am going to tell you – only God knows.'

(I have no space to describe how the good doctor, in 1919, got lost in the Belt of Eternal Frost. Out of favour with the Bolsheviks, he made a crazy journey across Siberia towards Canada. In a kind of sheltered valley in that hideous hell of ice, he found a hut.)

'I knocked. A man came; shaggy and wild as a bear, but a blond Russian. He let me in. The hut was full of smoke, and hung with traps and the pelts of fur animals.

'On the stove – one sleeps on the brick stove in the Siberian winter – lay a woman, very still. I have never seen a face quite like hers. It was bronze-tinted, and comely, broad and strong. I could not define the racial type of that face. On the cheeks were things that looked like blue tattoo-marks, and there were rings in her ears.

' "Is she asleep?" I asked, and my host replied: "Yes, for ever." "I am a doctor," I said; and he answered: "You are too late."

'The man betrayed no emotion. Maybe he was mad, with the loneliness of the place? Soon he told me the woman's story. Absolutely simply, he dropped his brief sentences. Here is what he said:

.   .   .   .   .

I have lived here all my life. I think I am fifty. I do not like people around me.

About fifteen . . . no, sixteen years ago I made a long journey. I was hunting wolves, to sell their skins. I went very far, seven days' journey. Then there was a storm. I was lucky. I found a big rock, and hid behind it from the wind. I waited all night. Dawn came. I got ready to go.

Then I see something.

The wind and storm have torn up the ground in one place, and I think I see wood. I kick it. I hit it with my axe. It is wood. It breaks. There is a hole.

I make a torch with some old paper that I have, and drop it down. There is no poisonous air. The torch burns. I take my lamp, and, with a little prayer, I drop down.

There is a very long hut. It is very cold and dry. I see in the light of my lamp that there are horses. They are all standing there, frozen; one with hay or something, perhaps moss, between his teeth. On the floor is a rat, frozen stiff in the act of running. Some great cold must have hit that place all of a sudden – some strange thing, like the cold that suddenly kills elephants that are under the snow for ever.

I go on. I am a brave man. But this place makes me afraid.

Next to the stable is a room. There are five men in the room. They have been eating some meat with their hands. But the cold that came stopped them; and they sit – one with his hand nearly in his mouth; another with a knife made of bronze. It must have been a quick, sudden cold, like the angel of death passing. On the floor are two dogs, also frozen.

In the next room there is nothing but a heap of furs on the floor, and sitting upon the heap of furs is a little girl, maybe ten years old. She was crying, ever so long ago. There are two round little pieces of ice on her cheeks, and in her hand a doll made of bone and a piece of old fur. With this she was playing when the Death Cold struck.

I wanted more light. There was a burnt stone which

was a place for a fire.

I look. I think that in the place where the horses are there will be fodder. True; there is a kind of brown dried moss. The air is dry in that place! But cold!

I take some of this moss to the stone, and put it there and set light to it. It burns up bright, but with a strong smell. It burns hot. The light comes right through the big hut, for there are no real walls between the rooms.

I look about me. There is nothing worth taking away. Only there is an axe made of bronze. I take that. Also a knife, made of bronze too; not well made, but I put it in my belt.

Back to the room with the furs in it, where the fire is blazing bright. I feel the furs. They are not good enough to take away. There is one fur I have never seen, a sort of grey bear-skin, very coarse. The men at the table, I think, must have been once, long ago, strong men and good hunters. They are big – bigger than you or me – with shoulders like Tartar wrestlers. But they cannot move any more.

I stand there and make ready to go. There is something in this place I do not like. It is too strange for me. I know that if there are elephants under the frost, still fresh, then why not people? But elephants are only animals. People, well, people are people.

But as I am turning, ready to go, I see something that makes my heart flutter like a bird in a snare. I am looking, I do not know why, at the little girl.

There is something that makes me sorry to see her all alone there in that room, with no woman to see to her.

All the light and the heat of the fire is on her, and I think I see her open her eyes! But is it the fire that flickers? Her eyes open wider. I am afraid, and run.

Then I pause. *If she is alive?* I think. *But no,* I say, *it is the heat that makes her thaw.*

All the same, I go back and look again. I am, perhaps, seeing dreams. But her face moves a little. I take her in my arms, though I am very afraid, and I climb with her out of that place. Not too soon. As I leave, I see the ground bend and fall in. The heat has loosened the ice that held it all together – that hut.

With the little girl under my coat, I go away.

No, I was not dreaming. It is true.

I do not know how. She moves. She is alive. She cries. I give her food; she eats.

That is her, over there, master. She was like my daughter. I taught her to talk, to sew, to cook – everything.

For thousands and thousands of years, you say, she has lain frozen under that snow – and that this is not possible. Perhaps it was a special sort of cold that came. Who knows? One thing I know. I found her down there and took her away. For fifteen years she has been with me – no, sixteen years.

Master, I love her. There is nothing else in the world that I love.

.   .   .   .   .

'That's all,' the doctor said.

'No doubt the man was mad. I went away an hour later. Yet I swear – her face was like no face I have ever seen, and I have travelled. Some creatures can live, in a state of suspended animation, frozen for years. No, no, no, it's quite impossible! Yet, somehow, in my heart I believe it!'

Carnival on the Downs

WE are a queer people: I do not know what to make of us. Whatever anyone says for us is right; whatever anyone says against us is right. A conservative people, we would turn out our pockets for a rebel; and prim as we are, we love an eccentric.

We are an eccentric people. For example: we make a cult of cold baths – and of our lack of plumbing – and a boast of such characters as Dirty Dick of Bishopsgate, and Mr Lagg who is landlord of The White Swan at Wettendene.

Dirty Dick of Bishopsgate had a public house, and was a dandy, once upon a time. But it seems that on the eve of his marriage to a girl with whom he was in love he was jilted, with the wedding breakfast on the table. Thereafter, everything had, by his order, to be left exactly as it was on that fatal morning. The great cake crumbled, the linen mouldered, the silver turned black. The bar became filthy. Spiders spun their webs, which grew heavy and grey with insects and dirt. Dick never changed his wedding suit, nor his linen, either. His house became a byword for dirt and neglect . . . whereupon, he did good business there, and died rich.

Mr Lagg, who had a public house in Wettendene, which is in Sussex, seeing The Green Man, redecorated and furnished with chromium chairs, capturing the carriage trade, was at first discouraged. His house, The White Swan, attracted the local men who drank nothing but beer – on the profit of which, at that time, a publican could scarcely live.

Lagg grew depressed; neglected the house. Spiders spun their webs in the cellar, above and around the empty, mouldering barrels, hogsheads, kilderkins, nipperkins, casks, and pins. He set up a bar in this odorous place – and so made his fortune. As the dirtiest place in Sussex, it became a meeting place for people who bathed every day. An American from New Orleans started the practice of pinning visiting cards to the beams. Soon, everybody who had a card pinned it up, so that Lagg's cellar was covered with them.

When he went to town, Lagg always came back with artificial spiders and beetles on springy wires, to hang from the low ceiling; also, old leather jacks, stuffed crocodiles and spiky rays from the Caribbean gulfs, and even a dried human head from the Amazon. Meanwhile, the cards accumulated, and so did the bills advertising local attractions – cattle shows, flower shows, theatricals, and what not.

And the despisers of what they called the 'great Un-washed' congregated there – the flickers-away of specks of dust – the ladies and gentlemen who could see a thumb print on a plate. Why? Homesickness for the gutter, perhaps – it is an occupational disease of people who like strong perfumes.

I visited The White Swan, in passing, on holiday. The people in Wettendene called it – not without affection – The Mucky Duck. There was the usual vociferous gathering of long-toothed women in tight-cut tweeds, and ruddy men with two slits to their jackets howling confidences, while old Lagg, looking like a half-peeled beetroot, brooded under the cobwebs.

He took notice of me when I offered him something to drink, and said: 'Stopping in Wettendene, sir?'

'Overnight,' I said. 'Anything doing?'

He did not care. 'There's the flower show,' he said, flapping about with a loose hand. 'There's the Christian Boys' Sports. All pinned up. Have a dekko. See for yourself.'

So I looked about me.

That gentleman from New Orleans, who had pinned up the first card on the lowest beam, had started a kind of chain reaction. On the beams, the ceiling, and the very barrels, card jostled card, and advertisement advertisement. I saw the card of the Duke of Chelsea overlapped by the large, red-printed trade card of one George Grape, Rat-Catcher; a potato-crisp salesman's card half overlaid by that of the Hon. Iris Greene. The belly of a stuffed trout was covered with cards as an autumn valley with leaves.

But the great hogshead, it seemed, was set aside for the bills advertising local attractions. Many of these were out of date – for example, an advertisement of a Baby Show in 1932, another of a Cricket Match in 1934, and yet another for 'Sports' in 1923. As Mr Lagg had informed me, there were the printed announcements of the Christian Boys' affair and the Flower Show.

Under the Flower Show, which was scheduled for 14 August, was pinned a wretched little bill advertising, for the same date, a 'Grand Carnival' in Wagnall's Barn on Long Meadow, Wettendene. Everything was covered with dust.

It is a wonderful place for dust. It is necessary, in The

Mucky Duck cellar, to take your drink fast or clasp your hand over the top of the glass before it accumulates a grey scum or even a dead spider: the nobility and gentry like it that way. The gnarled old four-ale drinkers go to The Green Man: they have no taste for quaintness.

I knew nobody in Wettendene, and am shy of making new acquaintances. The 'Grand Carnival' was to begin at seven o'clock; entrance fee sixpence, children half price. It could not be much of a show, I reflected, at that price and in that place: a showman must be hard up, indeed, to hire a barn for his show in such a place. But I like carnivals and am interested in the people that follow them; so I set off at five o'clock.

Long Meadow is not hard to find: you go to the end of Wettendene High Street, turn sharp right at Scott's Corner where the village ends, and take the winding lane, Wettendene Way. This will lead you, through a green tunnel, to Long Meadow, where the big Wagnall's Barn is.

Long Meadow was rich grazing land in better times, but now it is good for nothing but a pitiful handful of sheep that nibble the coarse grass. There has been no use for the barn these last two generations. It was built to last hundreds of years; but the land died first. This had something to do with water – either a lack or an excess of it. Long Meadow is good for nothing much, at present, but the Barn stands firm and four-square to the capricious rains and insidious fogs of Wettendene Marsh. (If it were not for the engineers who dammed the river, the whole area would, by now, be under water.) However, the place is dry, in dry weather.

Still, Long Meadow has the peculiarly dreary atmosphere of a swamp and Wagnall's Barn is incongruously sturdy in that wasteland. It is a long time since any produce was stocked in Wagnall's Barn. Mr Etheridge, who owns it, rents it for dances, amateur theatrical shows, and what not.

That playbill aroused my curiosity. It was boldly printed in red, as follows:

!!! JOLLY JUMBO'S CARNIVAL!!!
!! THE ONE AND ONLY !!
COME AND SEE
!! GORGON, The Man Who Eats Bricks & Swallows Glass !!
!! THE HUMAN SKELETON !!
!! THE INDIA RUBBER BEAUTY –
She Can Put Her Legs Around Her Neck & Walk On Her Hands !!
!! A LIVE MERMAID !!
!! ALPHA, BETA, AND DOT. The World-Famous Tumblers
With The Educated Dog! !
! JOLLY JUMBO !
!! JOLLY JUMBO !!

I left early, because I like to look behind the scenes, and have a chat with a wandering freak or two. I remembered a good friend of mine who had been a Human Skeleton – six foot six and weighed a hundred pounds – ate five meals a day, and was as strong as a bull. He told good stories in that coffee-bar that is set up where the Ringling Brothers and Barnum and Bailey Combined Circuses rest in Florida for the winter. I 'tasted sawdust', as the saying goes, and had a yearning to sit on the ground and hear strange stories. Not that I expected much of Wettendene. All the same the strangest people turn up at the unlikeliest places. . . .

Then the rain came down, as it does in an English summer. The sky sagged, rumbled a borborygmic threat of thunderstorms, which seemed to tear open clouds like bags of water.

Knowing our English summer, I had come prepared with a mackintosh, which I put on as I ran for the shelter of the barn.

I was surprised to find it empty. The thunder was loud, now, and there were zigzags of lightning in the east; what time the pelting rain sounded on the meadow like a maracca. I took off my raincoat and lit a cigarette – and then, in the light of the match flame, I caught a glimpse of two red-and-green eyes watching me, in a far corner, about a foot away from the floor.

It was not yet night, but I felt in that moment such a pang of horror as comes only in the dark; but I am so constituted that, when frightened, I run forward. There was something unholy about Wagnall's Barn, but I should have been ashamed not to face it, whatever it might be. So I advanced, with my walking-stick; but then there came a most melancholy whimper, and I knew that the eyes belonged to a dog.

I made a caressing noise and said: 'Good dog, good doggie! Come on, doggo!' – feeling grateful for his company. By the light of another match, I saw a grey poodle, neatly clipped in the French style. When he saw me, he stood up on his hindlegs and danced.

In the light of that same match I saw, also, a man squatting on his haunches with his head in his hands. He was dressed only in trousers and a tattered shirt.

Beside him lay a girl. He had made a bed for her of his clothes and, the rain falling softer, I could hear her breathing, harsh and laborious. The clouds lifted. A little light came into the barn. The dog danced, barking, and the crouching man awoke, raising a haggard face.

'Thank God you've come,' he said. 'She can't breathe. She's got an awful pain in the chest, and a cough. She can't catch her breath, and she's burning. Help her, Doctor – Jolly Jumbo has left us high and dry.'

'What?' I said. 'Went on and left you here, all alone?'

'Quite right, Doctor.'

I said: 'I'm not a doctor.'

'Jumbo promised to send a doctor from the village,' the man said, with a laugh more unhappy than tears. 'Jolly Jumbo promised! I might have known. I did know. Jolly Jumbo never kept his word. Jumbo lives for hisself. But he didn't ought to leave us here in the rain, and Dolores in a bad fever. No, nobody's got the right. No!'

I said: 'You might have run down to Wettendene yourself, and got the doctor.'

' "Might" is a long word, mister. I've broke my ankle and my left wrist. Look at the mud on me, and see if I haven't tried. . . . Third time, working my way on my elbows – and I am an agile man – I fainted with the pain, and half drowned in the mud. . . . But Jumbo swore his Bible oath to send a physician for Dolores. Oh, dear me!'

At this the woman between short, agonised coughs, gasped: '*Alma de mi corazan* – heart of my soul – not leave? So cold, so hot, so cold. Please, not go?'

'I'll see myself damned first,' the man said, 'and so will Dot. Eh, Dot?'

At this the poodle barked and stood on its hindlegs, dancing.

The man said, drearily: 'She's a woman, do you see, sir. But one of the faithful kind. She come out of Mexico. That *alma de mi corazan* – she means it. Actually, it means "soul of my heart". There's nothing much more you can say to somebody you love, if you mean it. . . . So you're not a doctor? More's the pity! I'd hoped you was. But oh, sir, for the sake of Christian charity, perhaps you'll give us a hand.

'She and me, we're not one of that rabble of lay-abouts, and gyppos, and what not. Believe me, sir, we're artists of our kind. I know that a gentleman like you doesn't regard us, because we live rough. But it would be an act of kindness for you to get a doctor up from Wettendene, because my wife is burning and coughing, and I'm helpless.

'I'll tell you something, guv'nor – poor little Dot, who understands more than the so-called Christians in these parts, she knew, *she* knew! She ran away. I called her: "Dot – Dot – Dot!" – but she run on. I'll swear she went for a doctor, or something.

'And in the meantime Jolly Jumbo has gone and left us high and dry. Low and wet is the better word, sir, and we haven't eaten this last two days.'

The girl, gripping his wrist, sighed: 'Please, not to go, not to leave?'

'Set your heart at ease, sweetheart,' the man said. 'Me and Dot, we are with you. And here's a gentleman who'll get us a physician. Because, to deal plainly with you, my one-and-only, I've got a bad leg now and a bad

arm, and I can't make it through the mud to Wettendene. The dog tried and she come back with a bloody
mouth where somebody kicked her . . .'

I said: 'Come on, my friends, don't lose heart. I'll
run down to Wettendene and get an ambulance, or at
least a doctor. Meanwhile,' I said, taking off my jacket,
'peel off some of those damp clothes. Put this on her.
At least it's dry. Then I'll run down and get you some
help.'

He said: 'All alone? It's a dretful thing, to be all
alone. Dot'll go with you, if you will, God love you!
But it's no use, I'm afraid.'

He said this in a whisper, but the girl heard him, and
said, quite clearly: 'No use. Let him not go. Kind voice.
Talk' – this between rattling gasps.

He said: 'All right, my sweet, he'll go in a minute.'

The girl said: 'Only a minute. Cold. Lonely——'

'What, Dolores, lonely with me and Dot?'

'Lonely, lonely, lonely.'

So the man forced himself to talk. God grant that no
circumstances may compel any of you who read this to
talk in such a voice. He was trying to speak evenly; but
from time to time, when some word touched his heart,
his voice broke like a boy's, and he tried to cover
the break with a laugh that went inward, a sobbing
laugh.

Holding the girl's hand and talking for her comfort,
interrupted from time to time by the whimpering of the
poodle Dot, he went on:

.   .   .   .   .

They call me Alpha, you see, because my girl's name
is Beta. That is her real name – short for Beatrice

Dolores. But my real name is Alfred, and I come from Hampshire.

They call us 'tumblers', sir, but Dolores is an artist. I can do the forward rolls and the triple back-somersaults; but Dolores is the genius. Dolores, and that dog, Dot, do you see?

It's a hard life, sir, and it's a rough life. I used to be a Joey – a kind of a clown – until I met Dolores in Southampton, where she'd been abandoned by a dago that ran a puppet show, with side-shows, as went broke and left Dolores high and dry. All our lives, from Durham to Land's End, Carlisle to Brighton, north, south, east, west, I've been left high and dry when the rain came down and the money run out. Not an easy life, sir. A hard life, as a matter of fact. You earn your bit of bread, in this game.

Ever since Dolores and me joined Jolly Jumbo's Carnival, there was a run of bad luck. At Immersham, there was a cloudburst; Jumbo had took Grote's Meadow – we was two foot under water. The weather cleared at Athelboro' and they all came to see Pollux, the Strong Man, because, do you see, the blacksmith at Athelboro' could lift an anvil over his head, and there was a fi'-pun prize for anybody who could out-lift Pollux (his name was really Michaels).

Well, as luck would have it, at Athelboro' Pollux sprained his wrist. The blacksmith out-lifted him, and Jolly Jumbo told him to come back next morning for his fiver. We pulled out about midnight: Jumbo will never go to Athelboro' again. Then, in Pettydene, something happened to Gorgon, the man that eats bricks and swallows glass. His act was to bite lumps out of a brick, chew them up, wash them down with a glass of water, and crunch up and swallow the glass. We took the Drill Hall at Pettydene, and had a good house. And what happens, but Gorgon breaks a tooth!

I tell you, sir, we had no luck. After that, at Firestone, something went wrong with the Mermaid. She was my property, you know – an animal they call a manatee – I bought her for a round sum from a man who caught her in South America. A kind of seal, but with breasts like a woman, and almost a human voice. She got a cough, and passed away.

There never was such a round. Worst of all, just here, Dolores caught a cold.

I dare say you've heard of my act, Alpha, Beta and Dot? . . . Oh, a stranger here; are you, sir? I wish you could have seen it. Dolores is the genius – her and Dot. I'm only the under-stander. I would come rolling and somersaulting in, and stand. Then Dolores'd come dancing in and take what looked like a standing jump – I gave her a hand-up – on to my shoulders, so we stood balanced. Then, in comes poor little Dot, and jumps; first on to my shoulder, then on to Dolores' shoulder from mine, and so on to Dolores' head where Dot stands on her hind legs and dances. . . .

The rain comes down, sir. Dolores has got a cold in the chest. I beg her: 'Don't go on, Dolores – don't do it!' But nothing will satisfy her, bless her heart: the show must go on. And when we come on, she was burning like a fire. Couldn't do the jump. I twist sidewise to take the weight, but her weight is kind of a deadweight, poor girl! My ankle snaps, and we tumbles.

Tried to make it part of the act – making funny business, carrying the girl in my arms, hopping on one foot, with good old Dot dancing after us.

That was the end of us in Wettendene. Jolly Jumbo says to us: 'Never was such luck. The brick-eater's bust a tooth. The mermaid's good and dead. The strong-man has strained hisself . . . and I'm not sure but that blacksmith won't be on my trail, with a few pals, for that fi'-pun note. I've got to leave you to it, Alph, old feller. I'm off to Portsmouth.'

I said: 'And what about my girl? I've only got one hand and one foot, and she's got a fever.'

He said: 'Wait a bit, Alph, just wait a bit. My word of honour, and my Bible oath, I'll send a sawbones up from Wettendene.'

'And what about our pay?' I ask.

Jolly Jumbo says: 'I swear on my mother's grave, Alph, I haven't got it. But I'll have it in Portsmouth, on my Bible oath. You know me. Sacred word of honour! I'll be at The Hope and Anchor for a matter of weeks, and you'll be paid in full. And I'll send you a doctor, by my father's life I will. Honour bright! In the mean-time, Alph, I'll look after Dot for you.'

And so he picked up the dog – I hadn't the strength to prevent him – and went out, and I heard the whips cracking and the vans squelching in the mud.

But little Dot got away and come back. . . .

I've been talking too much, sir. I thought you was the doctor. Get one for the girl, if you've a heart in you – and a bit of meat for the dog. I've got a few shillings on me.

.　　　.　　　.　　　.　　　.

I said: 'Keep still. I'll be right back.' And I ran in the rain, closely followed by the dog Dot, down through that dripping green tunnel into Wettendene, and rang long and loud at a black door to which was affixed the brass plate, well worn, of one Dr MacVitie, *M.R.C.S., L.R.C.P.*

The old doctor came out, brushing crumbs from his waistcoat. There was an air of decrepitude about him. He led me into his surgery. I saw a dusty old copy of *Gray's Anatomy*, two fishing rods, four volumes of the Badminton Library – all unused these past twenty years. There were also some glass-stoppered bottles that seemed to contain nothing but sediment; a spirit lamp without spirit; some cracked test-tubes; and an ancient case-book into the cover of which was stuck a rusty scalpel.

He was one of the cantankerous old Scotch school of doctors that seem incapable of graciousness, and grudging even of a civil word. He growled: 'I'm in luck this evening. It's six months since I sat down to my bit of dinner without the bell going before I had the first spoonful of soup half-way to my mouth. Well, you've let me finish my evening meal. Thank ye.'

He was ponderously ironic, this side offensiveness. 'Well, out with it. What ails ye? Nothing, I'll wager. Nothing ever ails 'em hereabout that a dose of castor oil or an aspirin tablet will not cure – excepting always rheumatism. Speak up, man!'

I said: 'There's nothing wrong with me at all. I've come to fetch you to treat two other people up at Wagnall's Barn. There's a man with a broken ankle and a girl with a congestion of the lungs. So get your bag and come along.'

He snapped at me like a turtle, and said: 'And since when, may I ask, were you a diagnostician? And who are you to be giving a name to symptoms? In any case, young fellow, I'm not practising. I'm retired. My son runs the practice, and he's out on a child-bed case. . . . Damn that dog – he's barking again!'

The poodle, Dot, was indeed barking hysterically and scratching at the front door.

I said: 'Doctor, these poor people are in desperate straits.'

'Aye, poor people always are. And who's to pay the bill?'

'I'll pay,' I said, taking out my wallet.

'Put it up, man, put it up! Put your hand in your pocket for all the riffraff that lie about in barns and ye'll end in the workhouse.'

He got up laboriously, sighing: 'Alex is over Iddlesworth way with the car. God give us strength to bear it. I swore my oath and so I'm bound to come, Lord preserve us!'

'If—' I said, 'if you happen to have a bit of meat in the house for the dog, I'd be glad to pay for it——'

' – And what do you take this surgery for? A butcher's shop?' Then he paused. 'What sort of a dog, as a matter of curiosity would ye say it was?'

'A little grey French poodle.'

'Oh, aye? Very odd. Ah well, there's a bit of meat on the chop bones, so I'll put 'em in my pocket for the dog, if you like . . . Wagnall's Barn, did ye say? A man and a girl, is that it? They'll be some kind of vagrant romanies, or gyppos, no doubt?'

I said: 'I believe they are some kind of travelling performers. They are desperately in need of help. Please hurry, Doctor.'

His face was sour and his voice harsh, but his eyes were bewildered, as he said: 'Aye, no doubt. I dare say, very likely. A congestion of the lungs, ye said? And a fractured ankle, is that it? Very well.' He was throwing drugs and bandages into his disreputable-looking black bag. I helped him into his immense black mackintosh.

He said: 'As for hurrying, young man, I'm seventy-seven years old, my arteries are hard, and I could not hurry myself for the crack of doom. Here, carry the bag. Hand me my hat and my stick, and we'll walk up to Wagnall's Barn on this fool's errand of yours. Because a fool's errand it is, I fancy. Come on.'

The little dog, Dot, looking like a bit of the mud made animate, only half distinguishable in the half dark, barked with joy, running a little way backwards and a long way forwards, leading us back to the Barn through that darkened green tunnel.

The doctor had a flash-lamp. We made our way to the barn, he grumbling and panting and cursing the weather. We went in. He swung the beam of his lamp from corner to corner, until it came to rest on my jacket. It lay as I had wrapped it over poor Dolores, but it was empty.

I shouted: 'Alpha, Beta! Here's the doctor!'

The echo answered: '*Octor!*'

I could only pick up my jacket and say: 'They must have gone away.'

Dr MacVitie said, drily: 'Very likely, if they were here at all.'

'Here's my jacket, damp on the inside and dry on the outside,' I said. 'And I have the evidence of my own eyes——'

'No doubt. Very likely. In a lifetime of practice I have learned, sir, to discredit the evidence of my eyes, and my other four senses, besides. Let's away. Come!'

'But where have they gone?'

'Ah, I wonder!'

'And the dog, where's the dog?' I cried.

He said, in his dour way: 'For that, I recommend you consult Mr Lindsay, the vet.'

So we walked down again, without exchanging a word until we reached Dr MacVitie's door. Then he said: 'Where did you spend your evening?'

I said: 'I came straight to the Barn from The White Swan.'

'Well, then,' he said, 'I recommend ye go back, and take a whisky-and-water, warm; and get ye to bed in a dry night-shirt. And this time take a little more water with it. Good-night to ye——' and slammed the door in my face.

I walked the half mile to The White Swan, which was still open. The landlord, Mr Lagg, looked me up and down, taking notice of my soaking wet clothes and muddy boots. 'Been out?' he asked.

In Sussex they have a way of asking unnecessary, seemingly innocent questions of this nature which lead to an exchange of witticisms – for which, that night, I was not in the mood.

I said: 'I went up to Wagnall's Barn for Jolly Jumbo's Carnival. But he pulled out, it seems, and left a man, a woman, and a dog——'

'You hear that, George?' said Mr Lagg to a very old farmer whose knobbed ash walking-stick seemed to have grown out of the knobbed root of his earthy, arthritic hand, and who was smoking a pipe mended in three places with insulating tape.

'I heerd,' said old George, with a chuckle. 'Dat gen'lemen'll been a liddle bit late for dat carnival, like.'

At this they both laughed. But then Mr Lagg said,

soothingly, as to a cash customer: 'Didn't you look at the notice on the bill, sir? Jolly Jumbo was here all right, and flitted in a hurry too. And he did leave a man and a girl (not lawfully married, I heerd) and one o' them liddle shaved French dogs.

'I say, you'm a liddle late for Jolly Jumbo's Carnival, sir. 'Cause if you look again at Jolly Jumbo's bill, you'll see – I think the programme for the Cricket Match covers up the corner – you'll see the date on it is August the fourteenth, 1904. I was a boy at the time; wasn't I, George?'

'Thirteen-year-old,' old George said, 'making you sixty-three to my seventy-two. Dat were a sad business, but as ye sow, so shall ye reap, they says. Live a vagabond, die a vagabond. Live in sin, die in sin——'

'All right, George,' said Mr Lagg, 'you're not in chapel now . . . I don't know how you got at it, sir, but Jolly Jumbo (as he called hisself) lef' two people and a dog behind. Hauled out his vans, eleven o'clock at night, and left word with Dr MacVitie (the old one, that was) to go up to Wagnall's Barn.

'But he was in the middle o' dinner, and wouldn't go. Then he was called out to the Squire's place, and didn't get home till twelve o'clock next night. And there was a liddle dog that kep' barking and barking, and trying to pull him up the path by the trousis-leg. But Dr Mac-Vitie——'

'Dat were a mean man, dat one, sure enough!'

'You be quiet, George. Dr MacVitie kicked the liddle dog into the ditch, and unhooked the bell, and tied up the knocker, and went to bed. Couple o' days later, Wagnall, going over his land, has a look at that barn, and he sees a young girl stone dead, a young fellow dying, and a poor liddle dog crying fit to break your heart. Oh, he got old Dr MacVitie up to the barn then all right, but t'was too late. The fellow, he died in the Cottage Hospital.

'They tried to catch the dog, but nobody could. It stood off and on, like, until that pair was buried by the parish. Then it run off into the woods, and nobody saw it again——'

'Oh, but didn't they, though?' said old George.

Mr Lagg said: 'It's an old wives' tale, sir. They *do* say that this here liddle grey French dog comes back every year on August the fourteenth to scrat and bark at the doctor's door, and lead him to Wagnall's Barn. And be he in the middle of his supper or be he full, be he weary or rested, wet or dry, sick or well, go he must. . . . *He* died in 1924, so you see it's nothing but an old wives' tale——'

'Dey did used to git light-headed, like, here on the marshes,' said old George, 'but dey do say old Dr Mac-Vitie mustn't rest. He mus' pay dat call to dat empty barn, every year, because of his hard heart. Tomorrow, by daylight, look and see if doctor's door be'nt all scratted up, like.'

'George, you're an old woman in your old age,' said Mr Lagg. 'We take no stock of such things in these parts, sir. Would you like to come up to the lounge and look at the television until closing time?'

Teeth and Nails

'MADAME, I have the honour of wishing you a very good night,' said Ratapoil, kissing his wife's fingers. She curtsied graciously. Tessier started then, for a three-branched candlestick seemed to detach itself, of its own accord, from the shadows in a far corner of the dining-room. It was only a slave lighting Madame Ratapoil upstairs, but he was dark and silent as smoke out of a magical Arabian bottle.

The lady having been bowed out, Ratapoil threw off his gold-buttoned blue coat, and loosened his waistcoat, and the waist-band of his trousers, too. Tessier said dryly: 'Aie, Ratapoil, old wolf! You stand on ceremony nowadays!'

Ratapoil said, half apologetically: 'Tessier, old comrade, in a savage country it is a gentleman's duty to preserve the Decencies.'

'You have done well for yourself,' said Tessier, draining his glass. 'You have come a long way, Ratapoil, since you and I dined off dried dates and crawling green water under the Pyramids . . . not that it is much cooler here in New Orleans——' A great black hand came down over his shoulder, and filled his glass from a crystal decanter. '– Eh, Ratapoil! Is that a man, or a ghost? Send him to bed, for God's sake! I hate people coming up behind me like that.'

Ratapoil dismissed the slave with a jerk of the head.

'Not a bad boy, that one,' he said. 'He is worth five dollars a pound, and weighs a hundred and ninety-five; but I won him at piquet, as against three hogshead of rum.'

'What, so now he deals in rum and slaves! Molière gave us the *Bourgeois Gentilhomme*; Ratapoil gives us the *Gentilhomme Bourgeois*! Ratapoil turns tradesman. Aie, but times have changed indeed!'

Ratapoil said: 'So they have, old fellow. And one must move with them; although, of course, if anyone but you called me a tradesman he should feel a few inches of my sword in his tripes within ten minutes. . . .' He sighed. 'But nobody would dare. Here, as heretofore, I am still Ratapoil, the Jack of Swords. Nobody dares to challenge me in New Orleans, any more than they did in Paris in the old days; unless they happen to be very drunk. Then, I pink them in the arm to teach them better manners; or, if they are very young, simply disarm them. Oho, I assure you, Tessier, the Creoles treat me with the respect to which I am accustomed. But among themselves they fight like the very devil, either with the *colchemarde* or else the sword-cane. . . . Not your line, eh, old comrade?'

Tessier shook his head, and said: 'No, I used to have a tolerably light hand with a rapier, fifteen or twenty years ago. Your *colchemarde*, however, you can keep – it is nothing but a triangular pig-sticker. I am an artillery-man, when all is said and done. Well . . . I take it that you have not made your fortune exclusively as Master of Arms in New Orleans? . . . For example, this fine house, "three hogshead of rum" for a slave in livery, etcetera——'

' – Oh, one thing leads to another,' said Ratapoil. 'In

this country one finds oneself becoming a tradesman in spite of oneself. If you want to twist the play titles of Molière, you can call me *Le Bourgeois Malgré Lui*. . . . Clever, eh? I opened my little Académie in the Vieux Carré, in the spring of 1813. It was not done, I may say, without a little bloodshed. The Master of Fence at that time was a Swiss named Harter. One word led to another, we measured swords, he was buried the following day (nothing keeps long in this humidity), and I took over. I challenged a Spanish Fencing Master and, on his decease, accommodated his pupils also. By way of advertisement, I then challenged the entire Army of His Majesty, the King of Spain, to come on, one at a time, with sabre, rapier or *colchemarde*, for the honour of France. Only half a dozen Spaniards took up the challenge; if that child's play had gone on, His Catholic Majesty would have had to abdicate for lack of soldiers. Meanwhile, I played a little at cards and dice. Nobody dared to cheat me. I won. The stakes were money, or money's worth – rum, molasses, cane-sugar, coffee, or what not. What do you do with a storehouse-full of such truck?'

'Sell it,' said Tessier.

'Exactly; thereby becoming a kind of merchant. For example, I bought this house with tobacco. I may also mention that at this time we were living at the Saint Timothy Hotel, at a cost of thirty dollars a month. You may remember that my dear wife Louise was brought up by a most respectable aunt, who used to let elegant furnished apartments to unmarried gentlemen in one of the best quarters of Paris——'

' – I remember your attic room,' said Tessier.

'To cut a long story short,' said Ratapoil. 'Louise said:

"They are robbing us, my dear. I could provide accommodation twice as good for twenty dollars a month. The steamboats are on the river now; elegant ladies and gentlemen are coming into New Orleans in place of the *Kaintoucks*, the flat-boat men. Let us build a fine hotel, stylishly furnished." "To provide good food and lodging, twice as good as at the Saint Timothy, for twenty dollars a month?" I asked. She said: "No; for forty dollars a month. . . . And, since you must gamble, why not do it under your own roof? We could set apart a nicely-appointed room for cards and so forth, strictly for the nobility, and with you to keep order. . . ." In brief, old comrade: I am merchant, hotelier, and anything you like. I am rotten rich. And I take this opportunity of telling you that, with the exception of my wife and my toothbrush, everything I have is yours to command.'

'I do not want a wife,' said Tessier, 'and I have no need for a toothbrush.' He bared his toothless gums.

'You used to have excellent teeth,' said Ratapoil.

'I have none left that show – I was kicked in the face by a horse.'

'You shall have the best teeth that money can buy,' said Ratapoil, 'the teeth of a healthy young negress, fresh-pulled; and Dr Brossard will fit them into your jaws, so that you'll never know the difference. Meanwhile, drink, Tessier, drink. Brandy needs no chewing.'

Tessier drank, muttering: 'The devil take all horses, and, in particular, dapple-grey mares that show the whites of their eyes. . . . Believe me, Ratapoil, men, women and horses are never to be trusted when they show the whites of their eyes below the iris. . . . Also, beware of Roman noses, they also are signs of danger in men, women, and horses. . . . Damn that roman-nosed dapple-grey mare from throat-latch to croup; and damn her rolling eyes!'

'I detest horses,' said Ratapoil. 'But then I am an infantryman, born and bred. I'd rather trust myself to my own two legs than to the four legs of that most hysterical and cowardly of beasts, the horse. I can at least rely on these feet of mine not to bolt with me if a rabbit starts up under my nose in the moonlight; or not to kick my teeth out when I stoop to cut their toe-nails . . . Still, horses have their place in the world, also.'

'You are even beginning to *think* like a bourgeois,' said Tessier. 'All the same, you are right. Every grain of sand has its assigned position in the Scheme of Things——'

'– I should say so! Do you remember when I fought LeGrand with pistols in Egypt? A grain of sand flew into my eye just as the handkerchief dropped, so that I missed him clean; otherwise I should certainly have shot him. As it turned out, I was in the wrong; and LeGrand and I became good friends, until he was killed at Eylau. How old is a grain of sand, and how many grains of sand are there in a desert? And how long had that grain in particular been lying there, awaiting instructions to fly up and prevent an injustice? It goes to show . . . But what were you doing on horseback at your time of life, Tessier?'

'Taking my place in the Scheme of Things,' said Tessier, sombrely, 'dust that I am.'

His pale, toothless mouth pulsed like a frog's throat as he sucked his cigar alight at a candle. Then he went on:

.   .   .   .   .

. . . You, Ratapoil, were always a Legitimist at heart. I, *au fond*, was always a good Republican. But both of us loved France, first and foremost; therefore we gave of our best to Napoleon for the greater glory of France. Our health, our youth, our blood, our marrow – what we had, we gave! And after we had grown old in his service Buonaparte brushed us off, like dust from his cuffs; you for breach of discipline, me as a political suspect. Then we said, in effect: *Beware of the Dust, O Emperor! The Wrath of God waits in the Dust!* (only you said 'God', and I said 'History'.) And we joined little anti-Napoleonist clubs.

You were in the Malet Plot; I was a member of the Brutus Club. Still, we were old comrades and helped each other. You escaped from France by the skin of your teeth, in 1812, and came here to America. I stayed, more fool me!

I still clung to some mad hope of a Republican *coup*. If that hope had been realised – which it could not have been, because the time was not ripe for it – I should now be a General. As events occurred, Louis XVIII came back to France when Napoleon went to Elba.

You, wisely, stayed in New Orleans. But, where was I to go? Whichever way the cat jumped, I was the mouse. At that time the Bonapartists hated me; the Legitimists hated me; the Republicans, driven underground, split into a hundred tiny sects, every one of which execrated me as a heretic, a Republican of the old-fashioned Classical School.

I got out of Paris and wandered, living from hand to mouth. For a while I was a waiter in Antwerp, and then I worked for a bookseller in England, compiling a French Grammar and Phrase-Book for Young Ladies. Then I

went to Belgium, as courier and what-you-will to an
Anglo-Indian gentleman. But, not long after Napoleon
returned from Elba and the Infantry hailed him, again,
as Emperor, my nabob paid me off and made for Flushing and the sea in a light carriage, leaving me with a
trunkful of soiled linen, and one of his horses – a dapple-
grey mare named Cocotte.

She had cast a shoe on that appalling stretch of road
between Marchienne and Fontaine l'Evêque, by the
River Sambre: a most desolate and dreadful place, a
brooding brown plain under a sky such as must have
hung over Sodom before the fire fell from Heaven. Only,
in this case, the heavens were full of water, but none the
less black for that. It was a wet spring, that spring of
1815, and nowhere wetter or more sombre than at
Marchienne, where the Sambre runs from above Landres
to join the Meuse at Namur.

We had put up at a questionable kind of inn. Originally, it had been named 'L'Aiglon', the Imperial Eagle.
As soon as Napoleon was deposed, the landlord had
painted out his sign, leaving it blank. Later, he had
daubed on a Fleur-de-Lys. When we arrived, he was trying to smear back the Eagle: the news of the Emperor's
return from Elba had already broken.

'If we scraped off a few strata of paint,' I said to him,
'no doubt we should come to the *Liberté, Egalité,
Fraternité.*'

He said: 'I am only a poor inn-keeper, I am a neutral –
I move with the times.'

This inn-keeper's name was Morkens, and he was a
boor. He had some arrangement with the local blacksmith: if a traveller lost a tyre, a horseshoe, or the merest
lynch-pin, the blacksmith would detain him, so that he

was compelled to stay with Morkens. Morkens charged the traveller treble, and the blacksmith charged him quintuple; each paid the other commission.

We paused at this inn (call it what you will), intending to stop for two hours. Two days later, the mare was still unshod. 'Is it my fault?' whines this execrable Morkens. 'If milord is in a hurry, I can sell him a horse——'

'Do so,' says my master; and Morkens sells him an abominable screw for the price of a thoroughbred, swearing that he is taking the bread out of his children's mouths.

'I'll pay!' cries my nabob, dashing down golden guineas. Then, to me: 'Here's your money, my good man. Can't take you with me. Travelling light – can't spare weight. Here's another ten guineas for you.'

'Your trunk, milord? The mare?' I asked.

'Oh, damn the trunk and confound the damned mare! Keep 'em! I'm away!' cries he.

And off he went, bumping over the most dismal and treacherous road in the world, leaving me standing under an equivocal sign that creaked outside the world's worst inn, rubbing elbows with the meanest rogue in muddy Flanders: Morkens.

The chaise was not out of sight when this Morkens turned to me, and said: 'The linen he left behind in that trunk is of the finest cambric——'

' – How do you know?' I asked.

'Oh,' said Morkens, 'I gathered as much from the quality of the stuff your master had on his back. Why do you ask? Would *I* look in his trunks?'

'Of course not,' I answered.

You understand; my instinct warned me to continue

to play the perfect courier-cum-*valet de chambre* with this Morkens. I spoke primly, but at the same time gave him a sidelong glance, smiling with the right-hand corner of my mouth, while I winked with the left eye, falling impassive, again, upon the instant.

'Now, look here,' said he, 'then we'll go halves.'

'Halves? Of what?' I asked.

'Oh, linen and what-not,' said Morkens. 'The linen, the horse . . .'

'But milord gave the horse and the linen to me, my friend,' I said. 'You heard him.'

He shouted: 'Hey, Marie!' and his wife came out. She was good-looking in the Flemish style – a skin like cream, and hair like copper. The cream soon goes cheesy, and the copper tarnishes; still, while their looks last, Flemish women, as you know, are very pretty, if you like something to get hold of (if you understand what I mean). Marie Morkens must have been a good twenty years younger than her hogshead of a husband, and she had the sleek look and something of the colouring of a fine, healthy, tortoise-shell cat. I remember that she had golden eyelashes; never trust a woman with fair eyelashes.

'My darling,' said Morkens, 'did we hear milord giving his horse and his linen to this gentleman?'

She answered: 'Of course not, my dear. . . . Hey, Cornelys, come here!' Her voice was husky, yet penetrating, not unlike a cowbell in a mist.

Cornelys, the blacksmith, whose smithy was only twenty yards away, came running, hammer in hand, and stood open-mouthed, a veritable Vulcan with his leather apron and his blackened face. He stood, grinning like an idiot, rolling his inflamed eyes at the inn-keeper's

wife, with whom he was obviously head over heels in
love.

'Cornelys,' said she, 'you did not hear the English
milord giving his horse and his linen to this gentleman
here, did you?'

'No.'

'You heard him giving them to my husband, didn't
you?'

'Did I? Oh yes, I remember now. That's right; to
your husband, certainly,' said this idiot.

Morkens said: 'So there you are!'

You know, my friend, that I am nicknamed 'The Fox'.
I am supposed to be incredibly clever. In point of fact, I
am not; I pass as clever only because, in an emergency, I
keep a cool head, hold my tongue, keep my temper, and
wait to see which way the cat jumps. I hold by the old
apophthegm *To the ignorant much is told,* moreover. I
give away as little as possible, and prefer to profess, above
all, an abysmal ignorance of foreign languages when in
out-of-the-way places. In Flanders, for example, I pretended not to understand Flemish, although I understand it perfectly; thus I overheard many interesting
things, as will soon be evident.

Now the woman turned to her husband and in the
barbarous dialect of the locality – it always reminds me
of a dog with a bone in his throat – said: 'Joris, give him
the horse. One side or the other will be advancing or
retreating, any day now, and horses will be com-
mandeered anyway.'

'Give him the horse? Are you out of your mind, wife?'

She purred in her throat: 'Give him the horse, I say,
husband; and sell him a saddle.'

'You are right, my heart.'

'I am not your heart, you fat lump; I am your brain, you fool. Let me handle this,' said she. Then to me, in French: 'Nevertheless, monsieur, it is not in my character to see a traveller stranded in this God-forsaken mud. My husband is willing to lend you milord's horse. A light rider like yourself can easily overtake milord's coach, which will be going heavily, the roads being as they are. You can join milord at Flushing, and all's well that ends well. No?'

I said, with simulated reluctance: 'Very well. I see that I am outnumbered here. Shoe me the mare, and let me go.'

The blacksmith said: 'Oh, as for that – ten minutes! The shoe is made.'

So I led the dapple-grey mare out of the stable, and to the forge. Madame Morkens accompanied me. She stood, hugging herself as if in secret delight at some incommunicable titillating thought, as such women will, while Cornelys went to work with rasp and hammer. That lovesick clown's mind was not on his work. Every other second he paused to make sheep's eyes at Madame Morkens. Once, indeed, while he was driving home the first nail, the mare Cocotte almost kicked him into his own fire.

'Easy, there!' I said. 'Do you want to lame the beast?'

'She's vicious,' he said.

'You are clumsy,' said I, 'you are not nailing a plank to a joist!'

He cursed me obscenely in Flemish, and when I said: 'I beg pardon?' he said in French: 'I was simply saying "You are quite right, monsieur."'

So, at last, Cocotte was shod and I led her back to the inn. Madame Morkens lingered for a few seconds. I heard the smack of a boorish kiss, and when she joined me she was wiping soot from her face with her apron. And then the rain came down again – but what rain! Every drop hit the mud with a smack and a splash like a musket-ball.

The landlord had prepared some pleasant concoction of mulled spiced wine. He said: 'Well, so now you have your horse, all right and tight. . . . No doubt monsieur is an expert bareback rider, like the ladies in the circus?' I asked him what he meant, as if I did not know. He continued: 'Monsieur proposes, no doubt, to ride to Flushing without a saddle?'

'Oh – oh!' said I. 'I never thought of that. Oh dear!'

'As luck will have it,' he said, 'I have a fine English hunting saddle, almost brand-new. I can let you have it dirt-cheap, if you like.'

'I'd like to have a look at it,' I said.

You see, it was my intention to have him saddle and harness Cocotte, and then, pretending to try the saddle for comfort, to get my feet in the stirrups, give the mare the edge of my heel, and so away.

But he said: 'Oh, the saddle's in the stable, and the rain is coming down in bucketfuls. Let it give over. Why hurry?'

The saddle was in the stable, then; that was something worth knowing.

She said: 'In any case it will soon be dark, monsieur, and the roads are terrible. Best take your dinner at your ease and stay the night, and make a good start at daybreak,' and gave her husband a quick, sidelong look that chilled my blood.

She had seen milord give me my pay, thirty guineas, and ten guineas over and above that, for a *pourboire*;

besides, I had twenty guineas more in my purse, some of it my own money and some of it petty cash for travelling expenses with which milord had entrusted me and of which I had neglected to remind him. And I have seen a throat cut for five francs in wayside inns in Flanders!

Morkens muttered in Flemish: 'It's dangerous. . . .'

'Fool!' she said. 'In a few days, after the battle, the whole countryside will be littered with stabbed carcasses. Who will count one more or less?'

I said: 'I beg pardon?'

She said: 'I was saying "More haste, less speed," and telling my husband to go and kill a capon for dinner.'

'Oh well,' I said, 'no doubt you are right. The weather is, as you say, impossible. I will go to my room and pack my little valise in readiness for the morning.'

They had given me a horrid little closet of a room overlooking the yard, and smelling abominably of the stable; but I was glad of it now. If the window was too small to let the daylight in, it was not too small to let me out, and if I hung by my hands from the sill, I should have only a six-foot drop to the yard. So far, so good.

Also, I had another idea. You know that I am still troubled periodically with my old Egyptian dysentery. When it begins to trouble me, I take ten drops of tincture of laudanum, which is nothing more nor less than opium. In case of emergency, I always carry a vial of it wherever I go. I took this vial out of my valise now, and slipped it into my pocket – a good two ounces of the stuff.

Then I went downstairs and waited. Madame Morkens was roasting the chicken and her husband was setting the table. I guessed that their plan was to make me comfortably drowsy with good food and wine – he had brought up a couple of sealed bottles of his best from the cellar – and then, quite simply, knock me on the head. The woman alone would have been more than a match for a shrimp like me, to say nothing of her ox of a husband. I carried a little pair of pocket pistols, it is true, but I always keep my small-arms for use if all else fails.

So. While we were picking the bones of the capon, I, pretending to be a little lively with wine, said: 'Upon my word, madame, you are a cook fit for a king, and beautiful as a queen! And you, Monsieur Morkens, are a jolly good fellow! I'll tell you what – I'll stand you a bowl of rum punch in the English style, and mix it myself according to Lord Whiterock's own secret recipe. . . . You, old fellow, will be so good as to fetch me a bottle of rum, a bottle of brandy, and a bottle of port wine. You, madame, will get me lemons and sugar, nutmeg and ginger, cinnamon and cloves . . . and I see a fine old ale-bowl over there which will be the very thing to mix it in!'

It worked. He went to fetch the spirits and the wine; she took her keys to the spice cupboard; and I, uncorking my bottle, emptied it rapidly into the bowl. It went without a hitch. In fifteen minutes the punch was mixed. Laudanum has a bitter, cloying taste, but the rum, the brandy, the port, the sugar and the spices that I mixed in that punch would have disguised it if it had been so much asafoetida. I insisted on filling immense bumpers. You understand – I had been taking laudanum therapeutically for twenty years or so, so that what I swallowed in my punch was merely a homeopathic dose. But the effect of the drug on the Morkenses soon became apparent. Their minds wandered; the pupils of their eyes contracted. They drank again and again, not knowing or caring how much they drank, never noticing that I had taken no more than one glass. All the same, they were tough, those two!

It was eleven o'clock before Madame Morkens became unconscious. Her husband saw her fall across the table. He pointed at her, chuckling stupidly, and then rolled sideways out of his chair and fell to the floor with a crash. '*Hodi mihi, cras tibi,*' I said, 'today to me, tomorrow to thee, my friends. . . . And now I think I will punish you a little. A vindictive man would burn your inn over your heads. But I . . .'

. . . In short, I went through their pockets, etcetera, for their keys. As I had guessed, it was the woman who had in her keeping the most important of the keys – one in particular, a little one, suspended on a piece of string which she wore about her neck. The key of the cash box, evidently. And where would they hide their cash box, these two? Unquestionably, under their bed. It was so. After twenty years in the Grande Armée one acquires experience in looting, eh?

I found the loose plank, and had that cash box open in five minutes. It contained banknotes and gold to the value of about seventy thousand *livres*, which I stuffed into my pockets.

Then I took my little valise, and put on my cloak and my hat, and went out. The landlord and his wife were stertorously snoring, almost as if their skulls had been smashed. I had nothing to fear from them. The great dog in the yard barked furiously, but luckily for me he was chained. I got into the stable with the aid of Morkens's key, and lit the lantern, by good luck, in no time at all. I always keep my tinderbox dry, as you know. The saddle was hanging on a nail. It was a mouldering old English hunting saddle, but I made shift to buckle it on the mare Cocotte.

I had my left foot in the stirrup, and was ready to mount, when I heard another horseman approaching.

Now, the *manner* of his approach made me pause. A bona-fide traveller, coming to an inn at night, makes a noise, shouts 'Landlord! Landlord!' – is, in fact, in a devil of a hurry to get in out of the rain; especially on such a night as this was. Furthermore, I heard him speak to the dog in Flemish, and the dog was silent. A friend of the family, evidently. He tried the front door, and found it locked. Then, leading his horse, which was very weary, he came round to the back.

Believe me when I tell you that I slid out of the stirrup and into the hay as I heard that fellow approach. His horse, alone, came into the stable before him; he had been there before – he knew his way. I could not see him; he was of the colour of the darkness, an iron-shod shadow, only I heard him walking and breathing.

Also, I heard the rider knocking upon the back door of the inn, and calling in a kind of subdued shout: 'Morkens, Morkens!' There was no answer. He came stumbling and splashing back, cursing at the end of his teeth, and I heard him call the name of Cornelys. The rain washed most of his voice away; all the same, I heard him between the drops . . . 'Cornelys! . . . Cornelys! . . .'

Here, you may say, was the time to get out. So it was. But you know that there are times when curiosity is somewhat stronger than the desire to live. I had guessed that this night-bird, since he was in the confidence of Morkens, who was a cut-throat, must be some sort of highway robber – especially since he came quietly by night, on an exhausted horse. I wanted to know more, quite simply; therefore I waited, particularly after I heard him call for Cornelys the blacksmith, who was another thorough-going rascal.

Cornelys came soon, with a lantern. By the sound of him I knew that he was booted and spurred: a nice way for a simple blacksmith to be, at that time of night, on a lonely road! Furthermore, his voice had changed somewhat since last I had heard it; now he spoke hard and tight. Following the newcomer into the stable, Cornelys said: 'What's this? What's the matter with Morkens and Marie?'

He spoke in Flemish, and in Flemish the other man replied: 'Dead drunk in the kitchen.'

'Impossible,' said Cornelys. 'Can't be. Not now!'

'No? Go and see.'

He went, but soon returned, grunting incredulously: 'This night of all nights!' The other man groaned. 'What's the matter with you, Klaes? Are you hurt?' asked Cornelys.

'No; tired, dead tired, Cornelys. Dropping where I stand,' said the man who had been addressed as Klaes. Indeed, he sounded tired.

'Makes no difference,' said Cornelys the blacksmith. 'In any case, it was I who was to carry the word. I am ready. . . . Well?'

'Well,' said the man called Klaes, speaking very deliberately, like a man who is drunk or used up. 'Get it right the first time, Cornelys, because I swear I'm in no condition to repeat it . . . oh, dear God, how tired I am! . . . Listen carefully, now; the password is the English word, Ditch. Have you got that?'

'*Ditch,*' said Cornelys.

'You will pass that word to Collaert's vedettes,' said Klaes.

'Where?' asked Cornelys.

'Between here and Braine le Comte,' Klaes said.

'I will pass the word *Ditch* to Collaert's vedettes between here and Braine de Comte,' Cornelys said. 'And then?'

'Then you will be conducted at once to General Collaert of the cavalry, by his aide-de-camp, Brigadier de Beukelaer, who will have a fresh horse waiting. You will tell your message to Collaert in person. This is what you will say: *That you come from Jan Klaes* (that, of course, is myself). *That Klaes has been compelled to take devious roads because he has been shadowed. That Jan Klaes has been forty-eight hours in the saddle, and therefore sends you to deliver to Collaert a message which should have gone in advance to Wellington at Brussels.* . . . Is this fixed in your mind?'

Cornelys repeated it, word-perfect. He was not the fool that he pretended to be. . . . Or was he? I don't know. I have known congenital idiots, and nagging women, who had that same curious knack of repeating, with just such exactitude, precisely what vibrated the nerves of their ears. Empty domes throw back the most perfect echoes. . . . This Cornelys repeated the very inflection of the man Klaes, who, in something between a groan and a yawn, expressed approval, and then went on.

'Excellent. You will say this to Collaert, then: *Our man de Wissembourg, whom Collaert knows, has taken the place of Lacoste, as Napoleon's guide. Napoleon is completely ignorant of the terrain around St Lambert. It is reasonably certain that the Emperor will deploy his cavalry before the plateau of Mont St Jean. This force*

*of cavalry will consist mainly of Milhaud's cuirassiers –
twenty-six squadrons, supported by Lefebre Desnouette's
division. Altogether, between three and four thousand of
the cream of Napoleon's heavy cavalry. . . .* Have you got
that?'

'I have. Continue.'

'Good. Listen again: *'If Wellington makes a show of
English infantry on the plateau of Mont St Jean, behind
a light covering fire of canister from the masked batteries
on the Nivelles road, the odds are that Napoleon will
make one of his master-strokes – his heavy cavalry, en
masse, will charge the English infantry line, with a view
to smashing it and cutting the Allies in two, before the
German reinforcements arrive; Blücher and Bülow
being already delayed. . . .* Is that clear?'

'Perfectly clear – not that I understand. Go on. It is
written in my head as on a slate.'

'You are neither expected nor required to understand, only to remember. Listen again: *Before the
French cavalry can reach the English infantry, therefore,
they must cross a certain little road that runs across the
plain from Ohain to Mont St Jean——*'

'Cross it, how?' said Cornelys. 'I know the Ohain road.
Road? It is a ditch, twelve feet deep, banked up steep
on either side. Mountaineers cross such a road, not
cavalry. I know the Ohain road.'

'All the better. Tell Collaert so, and answer clearly
any questions he may ask. Meanwhile, remember again:
*If Wellington, having arranged his foot-guards above the
Ohain road, draws the main charge of Napoleon's heavy
cavalry, he will break the head off Napoleon's sledge-
hammer, and break off the jaws of his tongs, too. It is
Jan Klaes who says so, having received word from de*

Wissembourg, alias Lacoste, Napoleon's own guide. . . .
For God's sake, is all I have said impressed upon your
memory, Cornelys?'

'Every word,' said the blacksmith, 'firm as print, clear
as ink – aie – aie! What's this?——' He had put out his
hand, instinctively stroking and stroking as blacksmiths
will, feeling the back of the mare Cocotte. ' – Why, may
I die, if Morkens hasn't saddled the Englishman's mare!'

'What Englishman? What mare?' Klaes asked.

'A bony dapple-grey, sixteen hands. I shod her myself
today. Fed like a fighting-cock. Broken to shafts and
saddle, and good for anything; a horse for a lady or a
gentleman.'

'What Englishman?'

'Oh, a millionaire, a nabob. He left the horse as a tip
for his valet; simple as that! Not to go into details: I
guess that Morkens had her saddled and ready, knowing
that my little gelding is a little too light for my weight.
This dapple-grey will carry two hundred pounds over
fifty miles of mud. A good idea!' said Cornelys.

'The Englishman is gone. And the valet?' Klaes asked.

Cornelys said: 'I think the valet won't be needing the
dapple-grey tonight.' I almost felt the darkness contract
and expand as he winked unseen.

'Good,' said Klaes. 'To horse and away, hell for
leather! Be off!'

But now Cornelys became insolent and, quoting some
clownish proverb, 'Patience, fleas, the night is long!' he
then said: 'Those two sots have left the best part of half
a bowl of punch, eh?'

'Hurry,' said Klaes.

But Cornelys insisted: 'A stirrup-cup first, and then
we're off!' – and splashed back to the house.

293

Crouching in the hay with my hands on my pistols, I was almost sorry then for the man Klaes, squatting on his truss of straw; for I perceived the weary misery of him when (believing himself to be alone in the dark) he moaned '. . . Oh Lord, Lord, Lord! . . . Is it for me to choose Your instruments? . . . I can no more, I have done my best. . . .' Wow, but that man was tired!

Then the oaf Cornelys came back chuckling, saying: 'May the Lord forgive all the sins of the man who mixed that punch! It goes down well on a night like this. I finished it to keep out the damp. . . .'

So Cornelys had drunk the rest of my punch, then! Good.

'Away with you!' cried Klaes. The blacksmith swung himself into Cocotte's saddle, said *au revoir*, and was off.

I kept still in the hay, working over in my mind the tremendous significance of the message which Klaes had conveyed to Cornelys, and which Cornelys was to carry to Wellington. The weight of this message crushed the breath out of me, because the fate of an Empire depended upon it! I knew that this messenger Cornelys must, at all costs, be intercepted and his message diverted. But, I ask you – how? Violence is not in my line – I live or die by my wits. He was a powerful and resolute man, mounted on a strong, fresh horse. I was a shrimp of a man with nothing to put between my thighs but an exhausted scrub. True, I had a pair of pistols in my pockets; so, without doubt, had Cornelys.

But the odds, as I counted them, were evened by the laudanum in the punch Cornelys had drunk. He had told Klaes that he had drunk half a bowl of the mixture; so he had (the shallower half of the bowl, which was, therefore, only a third of the total volume); still, that

should be sufficient, in a literal sense, to tip the balance –
Cornelys's equilibrium – in my favour.

In a flash, you realise, I had seen my duty. I did not
like Napoleon; indeed, in my time I had plotted against
him. But in this moment I saw him not as the renegade
Republican, not as the ingrate, not as the ambitious little
deserter of Egypt and of Russia; I saw him as the old
eagle hatched again. I saw in him something symbolic of
the Spirit of the Man that goeth Upwards. In this extraordinarily indomitable little rogue returned from Elba
to confront the gathered might of the Allies I saw – forgive the comparison – something of myself. I recaptured
a little of the old enthusiasm. Yes, old comrade, I saw
again the red dawn of Egypt. I knew then that I must,
by hook or by crook, warn Napoleon of the menace at
his elbow.

Ah, if only I had had with me then you, or any one of
half a dozen other stout fellows I could name! Then I
should have let Cornelys carry his message to Collaert,
while you carried to Napoleon the intelligence of that
message well in advance. Thus forewarned, having
allowed the English infantry to form, Napoleon would
have fallen upon their left flank and carried the plateau
of Mont St Jean!

But I was alone, and only one course was open to me:
I must intercept Cornelys, before he reached Collaert,
and cut him down. This, as a first move, was the wisest
for me, situated as I was. I had something like a dog's
chance of overtaking Cornelys, and then, mounted on the
mare Cocotte, making my way to the French lines. And
this I resolved to do.

Hence, when the tired man Klaes dragged himself
back to the inn, I mounted that weary horse of his, and,

using my pen-knife as a spur, made after the blacksmith. That horse had heart. He drew a long breath, and hit the road.

And do you know what, old comrade-in-arms? Then it was as if I had shed the weight of a quarter of a century. I felt as I had felt on a certain dawn in the spring of 1795, when, seeing sunlight through the powder-smoke, I first realised that I was a grown man, and therefore too old to be afraid. . . . Then my heart, which had been flapping and fluttering somewhere below my belt, found its wings and soared, singing to high heaven; Fear of Death was a shadow in the valley far below and far behind me; and I laughed and cried, delighting in my new-found freedom from that fear. . . .

So I felt, then, when I nudged and goaded Klaes's weary horse back into the mud and the darkness. Ah, but that was an enchanted moment – how good it was to feel that rain, and to see so far away that struggling, watery moonlight!

The horse seemed to catch my exhilaration. He was winded, so that I might have been sitting astride Cornelys's own heaving, wheezing bellows; but still he galloped. All the same, exaltation apart, my reason had not deserted me. The blacksmith was mounted on Cocotte, who was strong and fresh, and had the start of my poor nag. But I had not forgotten that, within the hour, Cornelys should be most insecure in that little hunting saddle, if he were seated at all. By the time I overtook him, he must in any case be too befuddled to aim a pistol; and then I should have him.

I planned to put a ball in his thick head, take his mount, and ride belly-to-earth north-east to the first French outpost where I would pass the word: *The so-*

called Lacoste, the Emperor's guide, is an enemy agent –
beware the sunken road between Ohain and Braine le
Leud, between the French front and the plateau of Mont
St Jean!

. . . So, I rode, only God knows how, for that road
was rutted inches deep under a layer of red clay whipped
by the rain and mashed by a million wheels and hoofs
into a most dangerous mire. And then, that rain! The
Deluge was come again. I believe that summer of 1815
was the wettest summer in the history of the world. It
was as if Fate, in a sporting mood, seeing two tremendous adversaries coming to hand-grips had said: 'You shall
wrestle in the Indian style, my children – in a pit of
slippery mud, just to make the game a little more difficult. . . .'

A storm broke, and at every clap of thunder the whole
black sky splintered like a window struck by a bullet –
starred and cracked in ten thousand directions letting in
flashes of dazzling light, so that I was stunned and bewildered. Dr Mesmer (he, also, dressed all in black) used
to daze his subjects with little mirrors revolving before
their eyes in order to put them to sleep. So the elements
under the black cloak of the night seemed resolved to
mesmerise me.

But my brave horse carried me on until, at a bend in
the road, he stumbled and shuddered; went down on his
knees, and rolled over on his side. I sprang clear just in
time . . . tugged at the reins, shouting encouraging words;
then let go his head. He was dead. He had burst his
heart.

I stood by my dead horse, sick with hopelessness. But
then the lightning flashed again, and I saw, not a hundred paces in front of me, the big grey mare Cocotte,

walking very slowly, riderless, in the rain. I made my way to her, and you may rest assured that I had my hands on my pistols under my cloak. When I reached her, I saw in the light of another flash why she was walking slowly: the blacksmith Cornelys had tumbled out of the saddle, his left foot had caught in the stirrup, and she was dragging his enormous bulk in the clinging mud.

Hope flamed high again. I was sure then that Fate was on my side. Cornelys was not dead, only drugged and stunned. In a little while he would recover and continue on his errand as best he could. But first he would have to find another horse; he would be seriously delayed. Before he could be well on the road again to carry his message to Collaert at Braine le Comte I should be half-way to Genappe, where Napoleon was!

I disengaged his boot from the stirrup. His ankle was broken. So much the better! I sprang into the little hunting saddle on the back of the grey mare, turned her head, cried: *Hue! – Hue! – Hue, Cocotte!* and galloped back down the road over which I had travelled . . . away, away, past that accursed inn, through Fontaine l'Evêque, and so in the direction of our French outposts . . . past Drapceau, through St Estelle-sur-Ruth; and, as I rode, I dreamed fine dreams and even – could I have mixed that punch too strong even for my own head? – made up little songs which I sang inside myself to Cocotte's hoof-beats . . .

> *Rataplan, rataplan,*
> *Napoléon*
> *Eveille, éveille,*
> *Tessier*

Au tron, au tron,
Napoléon . . .

And then, not far from Trois Ruisseaux – you know my luck – the rhythm halted and changed. The mare Cocotte had gone lame, and was limping on her off hind-leg.

I assumed that she had picked up a flint, or, perhaps, a bit of a broken spike, from those deplorable roads. So, saying: 'Patience, Cocotte, my darling; we will put you right in no time at all, and you shall yet help Tessier to save France' – I dismounted, took out my pocket-knife, and, lifting up the mare's lame hoof, explored it with my finger-tips, since there was no light to see by. I could feel nothing amiss. Then I remembered how Cocotte had started and kicked while Cornelys the blacksmith, driving home a nail, was making eyes at the inn-keeper's wife, and my heart sank. He had lamed her through his inattention, the accursed idiot! I realised then that I would have done better to let Cornelys go unpursued to find myself stuck in the mud with a lame mare, while I took my chance in the direction of the French lines. . . . But I ask you, how was I to have foreseen this?

Full of bitterness, I let go Cocotte's hoof.

She shook her leg, and kicked me in the face.

I do not know, my friend, how long I lay unconscious in the ditch. I know that when I came to myself I was lying on my back, blinking at a dirty sky from which the rain was no longer falling, and that for the moment I thought that I was again in Spain, when the English stormed the battery and an infantryman knocked me down with the butt of his musket. I was in the most atrocious pain, and my throat was full of blood. It was this very blood, this very pain, that brought me back to consciousness; for the blood made me cough, and the cough shook my head, and my lower jaw was badly broken. Several of my teeth were embedded in my tongue, which was half bitten through.

I have, in my time, been wounded in almost every conceivable way. I have survived grape-shot in my ribs, a musket-ball in the stomach, a pistol-ball in the shoulder and, most miraculous of all, a *biscaien* ball in the hip (I say nothing of the bayonet-thrust, or a sabre-cut, here and there) and I have had most of the fluxes, dysenteries and agues that our frail flesh is heir to; together with a rheumatic fever which, I believed, was the *ultima Thule* of punishment. But the gathered might of all my enemies, my friend, never inflicted upon me one-half of the anguish I suffered under the hoof of that white-eyed devil of a dapple-grey mare! The pain of the broken bones in my face was terrible. The agony of my bitten tongue was worse. But worst of all was the pain of a shattered nerve on the left-hand side of my face. It was as if some fiend had delicately pushed a wire into my left nostril, up through some fine passage at the back of the eyeball, and out at the ear – and then applied a powerful current of electricity. My face twitched and jerked like Galvani's frog. . . .

However, never mind that. I took off my cravat and tied up my jaws, and then staggered away in search of my horse. Puzzle: find her! She had bolted, God knows where, sore foot and all. Blind with misery and the night, I walked, I cannot tell you how far or for how long, until at last I saw the lights of a wayside inn.

With my muddy, bloody, smashed face, and my sodden black cloak, I must have looked like the Angel of Death himself, for the inn-keeper fell back a pace when he saw me. I tried to speak, but I could not, so I pushed past him, seated myself, put down a gold napoleon and, taking out tablet and pencil, wrote the word: *Cognac.*

He shook his head: he could not read. Then, as best I could, I drew the outline of a bottle and a glass. I am no draughtsman, but he understood, and brought me *eau-de-vie* and a glass. Heavens above, but the raw spirit stung like a swarm of bees! Yet it stung me alert. I beckoned the man to my side, and drew the outline of something like a horse, saddled; and put down on the table a handful of Morkens's gold.

He said: 'Monsieur wants a horse? Monsieur is in luck, then. I have one only, a beautiful grey mare. She belonged to a Belgian colonel of cavalry. I could not part with her for less than a hundred *louis d'or* – but, seeing it's you, I'll throw in the saddle, a beautiful light saddle, the property of Milord Wellington himself. He brought it over from England when he hunted the fox in a blue coat to pass the time away, at the time of the Spanish blockades. The mare has been eating her head off in my stable for the past six months – God strike me dead if I lie! Well?'

I counted the rascal out his hundred gold pieces, and followed him to the stable.

'I had her shoed only this morning,' said he, holding high his lantern.

And what did I see? You have guessed. Cocotte, hook-nosed and supercilious as a camel, rolling her eyes at me in the dim yellow light.

There was nothing to be gained by argument: there was no time to lose, and I was growing weaker and weaker. Cursing the inn-keeper in my heart, I mounted, thinking: *Filthy Cocotte! If I get off your back between this and Genappe, it will be to fall dead into the road. And, curse you, if you cannot take me there on four legs, by God you must carry me on three!*

So, I rode again, still mounted on Cocotte. The rain was falling again, and now every drop of cold water on my sore head was like a blow with a hammer. Somewhere between my eyes, something was revolving like one of those children's rattles composed of a springy strip of wood and a cogged wheel. . . .

Brother, when you were a boy at school you learned the nature of the ancient Roman catapult? It was a system of stiff, springy beams mounted on a ponderous base. With ropes and winches the ancient artillerymen dragged down the topmost end of the upright beam until it was bent almost to breaking point. To this beam was fastened a cup. In this cup they played a great net bag filled with loose stones to the weight of about sixty pounds. The catapulter pulled a trigger. The agonised, bent beam snapped upright, struck the crossbeam with a horrible jolt, thus sending the bag of stones whirling away in a giddy parabola. . . . You remember? Believe me, I remembered! My spine was the strained upright, my shoulders were the crossbeam; my skull was the cup, my brains were the rattling stones; and every step Cocotte took pulled a trigger. . . . I was too wretched even to cry out, because when I cried my tongue vibrated, and I could not bear that.

Yet, agonised as I was, I continued to think, asking myself: *Dumb, wounded beast that I am, how shall I pass the sentries? How shall I deliver my message to the Emperor?*

I answered myself: *How, but in writing? . . . I must*

write a series of messages on little pieces of paper; keep
these messages in separate pockets of my waistcoat, and
present them in their proper order.

I stopped again at a wretched farmhouse. Staying in
the saddle – I should not have had the strength to re-
mount – by the light of a lantern I wrote my notes, and
put them into their respective pockets. After that, I
bullied Cocotte back to the road, and so we struggled,
splashing, on our way.

What was the name of that Greek who was doomed
to push a great boulder up a steep hill for ever and for
ever? I think his name was Sisyphus. I drink, comrade-
in-arms, to Sisyphus; I think I know something of what
he went through. It seemed to me – pain of bitten
tongue and broken jaw apart – that I was condemned to
ride eternally, through blinding rain and endless night,
upon a lame mare, on a mission of honour, slipping back
two paces for every pace that I covered. Soon I felt
Cocotte weakening under me. Ah well, poor beast, she
too had her troubles!

I remembered that my great cloak, sodden with the
rain, must weigh heavy, so I unclasped it at the throat
and let it fall behind me. . . . Everything was spinning,
and spitting sparks. There were fireworks in my head, I
tell you! Still, I remembered that it is the odd, super-
fluous pound of weight that tries you at the last mile
. . . and I was carrying in my pockets something like
thirty thousand *livres* in gold, and forty thousand in
good paper. My friend, it was not entirely delirium that
inspired me to put my hands in my pockets and scatter
to the mud and the rain more gold than I had ever
touched in my life. The tail-pockets of my coat were
heavy with the stuff, after I had emptied the side and

breast-pockets; these same coat-tails were slapping heavily against Cocotte's belly. My mind was set now on my objective. I unbuttoned my coat, and let that fall, too, and felt lighter for the loss of it. Gold and bank-notes were in that coat, and my pistols too. . . . I tore off my watch and chain, which also I tossed into the ditch. I would have kicked off my boots, only I dared not take my feet from the stirrups.

Now, then, I was riding in my shirt, trousers, and waistcoat; there was no more to jettison. All the time, notwithstanding, Cocotte went slower and slower.

At last – it was dawn, I think – to my infinite relief, I heard a hoarse voice cry: '*Qui va là?*'

I could not speak, of course, so I pulled out my first written message. It said:

I have intelligence of the utmost importance to the Emperor. Conduct me to him immediately.

Tessier,
Colonel, Artillery.

A mounted trooper took the paper, and handed it to another man. Seen through the curtain of the road, through my tired eyes, he looked like one of those terra-cotta soldiers on terra-cotta horses that we used to play with when we were children; he was so plastered with mud. But he spoke very civilly in the French of Paris, saying: 'What is your message, Colonel Tessier?'

I felt myself fainting, fading away. I had done all that I could do. I tapped my right-hand waistcoat pocket. It seems, then, that I slid out of the saddle; because I know that I had a sensation of falling, as it were, down the side of a mountain, and uppermost in my mind was a dread of what I should feel when my cracked face hit the road.

The terra-cotta man caught me. I heard him cry: 'Hold up there, sir!'

I became senseless, as much from horror as from pain and exhaustion.

He had cried out in English.

When I came to life again, I was lying on the floor in the kitchen of a farmhouse. My clothes had been stripped off, and I was wrapped in a dry cloak. They had put me by the fire, which was blazing bright. I saw, still dimly, a tight-faced officer in a blue uniform, sitting at a table between two pair of candles. Standing beside him and behind him were four other officers in blue. I recognised that tight face: it belonged to Collaert of the Allied cavalry.

Also, I saw my muddy waistcoat and trousers on a chair. Collaert was holding between a fastidious thumb and forefinger a little piece of paper which I knew. It was my second note. It said:

Sire! Your guide Lacoste is a spy. His name is de Wissembourg. He is in the pay of the Allies. He intends to misdirect you between Genappe and the plateau of Mont St Jean. Wellington will place his infantry there, behind a sunken road, which leads from Ohain to Braine le Leud. For God's sake, make reconnaissance of this terrain, against which Wellington hopes you will send cavalry. . . .

> *Tessier,*
> *Colonel (late), Artillery.*

It was anguish of spirit that made me cry out at this,

not pain of the body. Someone put something like a
rolled-up greatcoat under my head, and the voice of the
terra-cotta man murmured in English: 'No shame in
missing your way on a night like last night, in weather
like this. Cheer up, monsieur; better luck next time!'
He was Captain Conconnel of Lord Wellington's staff,
but I did not learn that until later.

I made certain unmistakable motions with my fingers.
The Englishman said: 'He wants to write something.'

They gave me pencil and paper, and I wrote: *Please
give me a pistol and allow me to kill myself.*

But they did not. Couriers were dispatched to Wellington with the intelligence which I had believed I had
delivered to Napoleon. A doctor came to set my jaw, and
later, locked in a bedroom, guarded by a grizzled old
English trooper, I lay and listened to the rain on the
shutters; and soon I heard the guns of Waterloo, and oh,
but I wept bitterly! I had not the strength to lift my
hand to wipe my eyes. The trooper came and wiped
them for me: he had no handkerchief, so he offered me
his cuff, saying: 'Easy does it, mounseer – steady on,
froggie. You'll be a man before your mother yet. . . .'
But he, also, was listening to the guns. . . .

I need not tell you what happened. Blücher was
delayed, indeed. The English cavalry was cut to pieces,
and we had the balance of artillery in our favour. It remained only to break that infernal English infantry, and
the battle was in our hands. Napoleon knew this, and
therefore he ordered that terrible charge of cuirassiers
at the plateau of Mont St Jean. The guide Lacoste – in
other words the spy de Wissembourg – was at his elbow
at the very moment when he gave that order. Lacoste, as
he is called, omitted to mention the 'hollow road' of

Ohain. There is no stopping a full charge of armoured cavalry, as you know. Before they could begin to pull up, two thousand cuirassiers were in the ditch of Ohain; the remainder were flying in disorder under volley upon volley of musket-fire; demoralisation had set in; the English had re-formed and were attacking; and that was the end of us. Napoleon fled.

So, brother, France fell: I blame myself for that.

.   .   .   .   .

Tessier sighed, and lit a fresh cigar. Ratapoil said: 'Come now, old moustache – how can you talk like that? There are more causes than one to any conclusion. You might, for example, also say that Cornelys the black-smith won the battle of Waterloo because, making eyes at the inn-keeper's wife, he lamed your mare. No one is to blame . . . though, had I been you——'

'Don't say it,' said Tessier. 'You asked me to tell you how I lost my teeth, and I have told you. And now, with your kind permission, I will go to bed.'

In a Room Without Walls

'IF it could only be like this for ever!' said the quiet
girl called Linda, looking over Jimmy's shoulder at the
dim grey face of the clock. 'Oh, Jimmy, this is heaven!
How happy I am! What can I have done, to deserve
such happiness?'

She felt Jimmy smiling. 'Are you happy too?' she
asked Jimmy. He nodded, observing the reflection of the
clock face in the long mirror on the wardrobe door. He
had been grimacing.

Last year, he thought chafing and trying not to fidget,
*I made a hundred and four thousand five hundred
pounds. All that money in three hundred and sixty-five
days. It works out at . . . what? . . . Twelve-pound-
ten an hour. I have given this girl twenty-five pounds'
worth of my time, at that rate. Four shillings and twopence a minute – nearly a penny a second. I've thrown
away twenty-five pounds, being gracious to Linda for
two hours. And she talks of this going on for ever – for
ever, at a penny a second! There isn't that much money
in the world!*

Linda, with a luminous glory behind her somewhat
faded face, closed her eyes and, resting her chin upon his
shoulder and caressing his cheek with her forehead, said:
'How sweet, Jimmy! How sweet! How can I ever tell
you how grateful I am to you for making me so happy?
Ah, my dear darling – now, just now, do you know what?

I'm so full of love and happiness that another tiny bit would be too much . . . I'd die. But this is Heaven: I'll never want any Heaven but this – to be here, with you, exactly like this, loving you as I do and knowing that you love me. You do love me?'

Jimmy was inclined to say: 'Oh, nonsense! Love? Ha! You? Bah! What, *me?* Love *you?* Who are you? A laundress. I am Jimmy – you know who I am – Jimmy the Star. I could have world-famous actresses, take my choice of the beauties of five continents. The world is mine, and all the women in it. Titled women, even. Because a whim takes hold of me, and I beckon to a poor pale creature in a clutching crowd of infatuated fans – because I, like a god, confer upon you the glory of my intimacy for a moment you talk of love? Love? My love? For you? At four-and-twopence a second, do you realise what a lingering look is worth?'

But he said: 'Of course I love you,' and he looked at the reversed reflection of the clock that told the time.

'All my life,' said Linda, 'all my life I've dreamt of such a moment. Don't laugh – I felt somehow that it *might* happen to me. I never dared to say to anybody that I had a dream of love. They would have laughed; I'm so plain and ordinary, Oh, dear God, but I love you, Jimmy! You're too good for me!'

In spite of his seething distaste, Jimmy muttered: 'Nothing of the sort. Charming girl!'

'Ah, my own dear love! My dream-come-true! Do you know what? I believe you if you say so. I believe! I believe! I believe in you. This morning I was washing sheets, and you were only a picture, a splendid vision. And now I'm here, with you, in your arms, hearing you telling me you love me. There *is* a God! Where is yesterday? Where is the grey when the sunlight bleaches it away? *Why* do you love me?'

'Sweet,' said Jimmy, with his eye on the time. The movement of the big hand was worth thirty-four shillings an inch.

He was in an ecstasy of boredom and visitation. *Oh, to be rid of this ridiculously happy woman!* he thought. *Why did I do it? Why? Why?*

'Tell me why you love me,' she said. 'No, never mind. Just say it again.'

What was Jimmy to say? If he could have said: 'I only said so to please you. It tickled my vanity to beckon you out of the mob around the stage door. You helped me to condescend, you made me feel greater' – then he would have been talking like an honest man. If he had had the courage to say: 'You were such a whole-hearted worshipper that I wanted to be a god,' then he would not have been where he was at that moment. If he could have told the truth he would have been an honest man – not a man in anguish, caressing a woman with his hand while he gritted his teeth and watched the clock.

But he said: 'Of course I love you!'

There was a silence: it seemed to cling to his ears for a lifetime. Then it came away with a sort of thick sucking noise, and he heard the sharp tick of the round white clock. His face looked drawn in the darkening mirror. He had a desperate yearning to speak a little truth.

'And you promise to stay with me always?' Linda asked.

He had meant to say 'No,' but heard himself muttering: 'Mm.'

'Jimmy! Hold me!'

Although he had intended to get up and go away,

Jimmy found himself embracing Linda and looking into her eyes.

'Always?' she whispered.

He answered: 'Always.' Candour stuck in his throat.

'Oh, Jimmy, if this could go on for ever!'

Unutterably weary, he muttered: 'Uh-uh; sure!' He was sick, sick to the heart, of pent-up truth.

'Did you say "sure"? Do you mean it?'

'Yes.'

'If you say you mean it, I know you mean it,' said Linda. 'Dearest, there *is* a God. There *is* a Heaven!'

'Oh yes, yes. Sure, sure,' said Jimmy, with a half-laugh. 'This *is* Heaven, isn't it?'

He shifted, meaning to pull himself away from her. Something happened; he moved in the wrong direction. Linda was in his arms.

'It is! It is!' she whispered.

He sneered. 'And hell? Where's hell?'

Something comparable to a bladder, a grey strained veinous membrane, seemed to burst in a splash of pure, cold light. Out of the indefinable centre of this light a grave, clear voice said: 'Think!'

Jimmy looked at the clock. Its hands still marked seven minutes to four of a drizzling February afternoon.

He remembered that there had been a judgement, a hundred thousand years ago. Linda, on his shoulder, had achieved paradise; and he was damned. And for all eternity the clock had stopped.

The Oxoxoco Bottle

THE fact that the intensely red colour of the glaze on the Oxoxoco Bottle is due to the presence in the clay of certain uranium salts is of no importance. A similar coloration may be found in Bohemian and Venetian glass, for example. No, the archæologists at the British Museum are baffled by the shape of the thing. They cannot agree about the nature or the purpose.

Dr Raisin, for example, says that it was not designed as a bottle at all, but rather as a musical instrument: a curious combination of the ocarina and the syrinx, because it has three delicately curved slender necks, and immediately below the middle neck, which is the longest, there is something like a finger-hole. But in the opinion of Sir Cecil Sampson, who is a leading authority on ancient musical instruments, the Oxoxoco Bottle was never constructed to throw back sounds. Professor Miller, however, inclines to the belief that the Oxoxoco Bottle is a kind of tobacco pipe: the two shorter necks curve upwards while the longer neck curves downwards to fit mouth and nostrils. Professor Miller indicates that smouldering herbs were dropped in at the 'finger-hole' and that the user of the bottle must have inhaled the smoke through all his respiratory passages.

I have reason to believe that Professor Miller has guessed closest to the truth although, if the document in my possession is genuine, it was not tobacco that they burned in the squid-shaped body of the bottle.

It was intact, except for a few chips, when I bought it from a mestizo pedlar in Cuernavaca in 1948. 'Genuine,' he said; and this seemed to be the only English word he knew: 'genuine, genuine.' He pointed towards the mountains and conveyed to me by writhings and convulsions, pointing to earth and sky, that he had picked the bottle up after an earthquake. At last I gave him five pesos for it, and forgot about it until I found it several years later while I was idling over a mass of dusty souvenirs: sombreros, huaraches, a stuffed baby alligator, and other trifles, such as tourists pick up in their wanderings, pay heavily for, and then give away to friends who consign them to some unfrequented part of the house.

The straw hats and other plaited objects had deteriorated. The stitches in the ventral part of the little alligator had given way, and the same had happened to the little Caribbean sting-ray. But the vessel later to be known as the Oxoxoco Bottle seemed to glow. I picked it up carelessly, saying to a friend who was spending that evening with me: 'Now what this is, I don't know——' when it slipped from between my dusty fingers and broke against the base of a brass lamp.

My friend said: 'Some sort of primitive cigar-holder, I imagine. See? There's still a cigar inside it. . . . Or is it a stick of cinnamon?'

'What would they be doing with cinnamon in Mexico?' I asked, picking up this pale brown cylinder. It had a slightly oily texture and retained a certain aromatic odour. 'What would you make of a thing like that?'

He took it from me gingerly, and rustled it at his ear between thumb and forefinger much in the manner of a would-be connoisseur 'listening to' the condition of a cigar. An outer leaf curled back. The interior was pale yellow. He cried: 'Bless my heart, man, it's paper – thin paper – and written on, too, unless my eyes deceive me.'

So we took the pieces of the bottle and that panatella-shaped scroll to the British Museum. Professor Mayhew, of Ceramics, took charge of the broken bottle. Dr Wills, of Ancient Manuscripts, went to work on the scroll with all the frenzied patience characteristic of such men, who will hunch their backs and go blind working twenty years on a fragment of Dead Sea scroll.

Oddly enough, he had this paper cigar unrolled and separated into leaves within six weeks, when he communicated with me, saying: 'This is not an ancient manuscript. It is scarcely fifty years old. It was written in pencil, upon faint-ruled paper torn out of some reporter's notebook not later than 1914. This is not my pigeon. So I gave it to Brownlow, of Modern Manuscripts. Excuse me.' And he disappeared through a book-lined door in the library.

Dr Brownlow had the papers on his table, covered with a heavy sheet of plate-glass. He said to me, in a dry voice: 'If this is a hoax, Mr Kersh, I could recommend more profitable ways of expending the Museum's time and your own. If this is not a hoax, then it is one of the literary discoveries of the century. The Americans would be especially interested in it. They could afford to buy it, being millionaires. We could not. But it is curious, most curious.'

'What is it?' I asked.

He took his time, in the maddening manner of such men, and said: 'Considering the advanced age of the putative author of this narrative, there are certain discrepancies in the handwriting. The purported author of this must have been a very old man in about 1914, at

314

which I place the date of its writing. Furthermore, he suffered with asthma and rheumatism. Yet I don't know. If you will allow me to make certain inquiries, and keep this holograph a few days more . . . ?'

I demanded: 'What man? What rheumatism? What do you mean?'

He said: 'Beg pardon, I thought you knew. This –' and he tapped the plate-glass ' – pretends to be the last written work of the American author, Ambrose Bierce. I have taken the liberty of having it photographed for your benefit. If we may keep this until next Monday or so for further investigation . . . ?'

'Do that,' I said, and took from him a packet of photographs, considerably enlarged from the narrow notebook sheets.

'He was a great writer!' I said. 'One of America's greatest.'

The Modern Manuscripts man shrugged. 'Well, well. He was in London from 1872 to 1876. A newspaperman, a newspaperman. They used to call him "Bitter" Bierce. When he went back to America he worked – if my memory does not deceive me – mainly in San Francisco, wrote for such publications as *The Examiner, The American, Cosmopolitan*, and such-like. Famous for his bitter tongue and his ghostly stories. He had merit. Academic circles in the United States will give you anything you like for this – if it is genuine. If . . . Now I beg you to excuse me.' Before we parted, he added, with a little smile: 'I hope it is genuine, for your sake and ours – because that would certainly clear up what is getting to be a warm dispute among our fellows in the Broken Crockery Department . . .'

.   .   .   .   .

Mount Popocatepetl looms over little Oxoxoco which, at first glance, is a charming and picturesque village, in the Mexican sense of the term. In this respect it closely resembles its human counterparts. Oxoxoco is picturesque and interesting, indeed; at a suitable distance, and beyond the range of one's nostrils. Having become acquainted with it, the disillusioned traveller looks to the snowy peak of the volcano for a glimpse of cool beauty in this lazy, bandit-haunted, burnt-up land. But if he is a man of sensibility, he almost hopes that the vapours on the peak may give place to some stupendous eructation of burning gas, and a consequent eruption of molten lava which, hissing down into the valley, may cauterise this ulcer of a place from the surface of the tormented earth, covering all traces of it with a neat poultice of pumice stone and a barber's dusting of the finest white ashes.

They used to call me a good hater. This used to be so. I despised my contemporaries, I detested my wife – a feeling she reciprocated – and had an impatient contempt for my sons; and for their grandfather, my father. London appalled me, New York disgusted me, and California nauseated me. I almost believe that I came to Mexico for something fresh to hate. Oxco, Taxco, Cuernavaca – they were all equally distasteful to me, and I knew that I should feel similarly about the (from a distance enchanting) village of Oxoxoco. But I was sick and tired, hunted and alone, and I needed repose, because every bone in my body, at every movement, raised its sepulchral protest. But there was to be no rest for me in Oxoxoco.

Once the traveller sets foot in this village, he is affronted by filth and lethargy. The men squat, chin on knee, smoking or sleeping. There is a curious lifelessness about the place as it clings, a conglomeration of hovels, to the upland slope. There is only one half-solid building in Oxoxoco, which is the church. My views on religion are tolerably well known, but I made my way to this edifice to be away from the heat, the flies, and the vultures which are the street cleaners of Oxoxoco. (In this respect it is not unlike certain other cities I have visited, only in Oxoxoco the vultures have wings and no politics.) The church was comparatively cool. Resting, I looked at the painted murals. They simply christen the old bloody Aztec gods and goddesses – give them the names of saints – and go on worshipping in the old savage style.

A priest came out to greet me. He radiated benevolence when he saw that I was wearing a complete suit of clothes, a watch-chain, and boots, however down at heel. In reply to his polite inquiry as to what he could do for me, I said: 'Why, padre, you can direct me out of this charming village of yours, if you will.' Knowing that nothing is to be got without ready cash, I gave him half a dollar, saying: 'For the poor of your parish – if there are any poor in so delightful a place. If not, burn a few candles for those who have recently died of want. Meanwhile, if you will be so good as to direct me to some place where I can find something to eat and drink, I shall be infinitely obliged.'

'Diego's widow is clean and obliging,' said he, looking at my coin. Then: 'You are an American?'

'I have that honour.'

'Then you will, indeed, be well advised to move away from here as soon as you have refreshed yourself, because there is a rumour that Zapata is coming – or it may be Villa – what do I know?'

'Presumably, the secrets of the Infinite, padre, judging by your cassock. Certainly,' I said, 'the secrets of Oxoxoco. Now, may I eat and drink and go on my way?'

'I will take you to Diego's widow,' said he, with a sigh. 'Up there,' said he, pointing to the mountain slope, 'you will certainly be safe from Villa, Zapata, and any other men in these parts. No one will go where I am pointing, *señor* – not the bravest of the brave. They are a superstitious people, my people.'

'Not being superstitious yourself, padre, no doubt you have travelled that path yourself?'

Crossing himself, he said: 'Heaven forbid!' and hastily added: 'But you cannot go on foot, *señor*?'

'I'd rather not, padre. But how else should I go?'

His eyes grew bright as he replied: 'As luck will have it, Diego's widow has a *burro* to sell, and *he* knows the way anywhere. Come with me and I will take you to Diego's widow. She is a virtuous woman, and lives two paces from here.'

The sun seemed to flare like oil, and at every step we were beset by clouds of flies which appeared not to bother the good priest who seemed inordinately concerned with my welfare. His 'two paces' were more like a thousand, and all the way he catechized me, only partly inspired (I believe) by personal curiosity.

'*Señor*, why do you want to go up *there*? True, you will be safe from bad men. But there are other dangers, of which Man is the least.'

'If you mean snakes, or what not——' I began.

' – Oh no,' said he, 'up *there* is too high for the reptiles and the cats. I see, in any case, that you carry a pistol and a gun. Oh, you will see enough snakes and cats when you pass through the Oxoxoco jungle on your way. That, too, is dangerous; it is unfit for human habitation.'

'Padre,' said I, 'I have lived in London.'

Without getting the gist or the point of this, he persisted: 'It is my duty to warn you, *señor* – it is very bad jungle.'

'Padre, I come from San Francisco.'

'But *señor*! It is not so much the wild beasts as the insects that creep into the eyes, *señor*, into the ears. They suck blood, they breed fever, they drive men mad——'

'– Padre, padre, I have been connected with contributors to the popular press!'

'Beyond the second bend in the river there are still surviving, unbaptized, certain Indians. They murder strangers slowly, over a slow fire, inch by inch——'

'– Enough, padre; I have been married and have had a family.'

His pace lagged as we approached the house of Diego's widow, and he asked me: 'Do you understand the nature of a *burro*, a donkey?'

'Padre, I attended the Kentucky Military Institute.'

'I do not grasp your meaning, but they are perverse animals, bless them. Tell them to advance, and they halt. Urge them forward, they go sideways.'

'Padre, I was drummer-boy with the Ninth Indiana Infantry.'

'Ah well, you will have your way. Here is Diego's widow's house. She is a good woman.' And so he led me into a most malodorous darkness, redolent of pigs with an undertone of goat.

The widow of Diego, as the padre had said, was unquestionably a good woman, and a virtuous one. With her looks, how could she have been other than virtuous? She had only three teeth, and was prematurely aged, like all the women hereabout. As for her cleanliness, no doubt she was as clean as it is possible to be in Oxoxoco. A little pig ran between us as we entered. The padre dismissed it with a blessing, and a hard kick, and said: 'Here is a gentleman, my daughter, who requires refreshment and wants a *burro*. He is, of course, willing to pay.'

'There is no need of that,' said the widow of Diego, holding out a cupped hand. When I put a few small pieces of money into her palm she made them disappear like a prestidigitator, all the while protesting: 'I could not possibly accept,' etcetera, and led me to a pallet of rawhide strips where I sat, nursing my aching head.

Soon she brought me a dish of enchiladas and a little bottle of some spirits these people distil, at a certain season, from the cactus. I ate – although I knew that the hot, red pepper could not agree with my asthma; and drank a little, although I was aware that this stuff might be the worst thing in the world for my rheumatism. The flies were so numerous and the air so dense and hot that I felt as one might feel who has been baked in an immense currant bun, without the spice. She gave me a gourd of goat's milk and, as I drank it, asked me: 'The *señor* wants a *burro*? I have a *burro*.'

'So the reverend father told me,' said I, 'and I hear no good of him.'

'I have never seen such a *burro*,' said she. 'He is big and beautiful – you will see for yourself – almost as big as a mule, and all white. You can have him for next to nothing. Five silver dollars.'

'Come now,' said I, 'what's wrong with this animal that has all the virtues in the world and goes for next to nothing? I have lived a very long time in all parts of the world, *señora*, and one thing I have learned – never trust a bargain. Speak up, what's the matter with the beast? Is he vicious?'

'No, *señor*, he is not vicious, but the good people in Oxoxoco are afraid of him, and nobody will buy him. They called him a ghost *burro*, because his hair is white and his eyes and nose are red.'

'In other words, an albino donkey,' I remarked.

At the unfamiliar word, she crossed herself and continued: '. . . And what need have I for a *burro, señor?* A few goats, a pig or two, a little corn – what more do I want? Come, *caballero*, you may have him for four dollars, with a halter and a blanket thrown in.'

'Well, let me see this famous *burro*, widow. I have ridden many a ghost in my time, and have been ridden by them in my turn.'

So she led me to a shady place near-by where stood a large white donkey, or *burro* as they call them, haltered, still, and seemingly contemplative. 'Where did you get him?' I asked.

The question seemed to embarrass her, but she replied: 'He strayed from up *there* –' pointing to the mountain ' – and since no one has claimed him in three years I have the right to call him mine.'

'Well,' said I, 'I am going up there. No doubt someone will recognise him and claim him, and I'll be short one donkey. But give me the blanket and the halter, and I will give you three dollars for the lot.'

Diego's widow agreed readily. I could see what was passing in her mind: the *burro* was economically valueless, and if Villa broke through, which seemed likely, his commissariat would take the donkey away to carry ammunition or, perhaps, to eat. She could not hide a donkey, but she could hide three dollars. Hence, she produced an old Indian blanket and a rawhide halter. Also, she filled my canteen with water and offered me a stirrup-cup of mescal, and pressed into my pockets some cakes wrapped in leaves. '*Vaya con Dios*, stranger,' she said, 'go with God. When you pass the bend in the river and find yourself in the jungle, look to your rifle. But where the path forks, where the trees get thin, *turn left, not right*.' Then she threw over my head a little silver chain, attached to which was a small silver crucifix. I felt somewhat like the man in young Bram Stoker's *Dracula* (which might have been an excellent novel if he could have kept up to the quality of the first three or four chapters), but I thanked her, and offered her another dollar which she refused. Perhaps, after all, she really was a good woman, as the priest had said?

The inhabitants of Oxoxoco came out of their divers lethargies to cross themselves as I passed, mounted on the white *burro*. But soon I was in the jungle, following a barely perceptible path up the mountain.

I detest the indiscriminately growing, perpetually breeding, constantly rotting, useless and diseased life of the jungle. It reminds me too much of life in the poorer quarters of such great cities as London and New York. Jungles – whether vegetable or of brick-and-mortar – are to hide in, not to live in. Where there is too much life there is too much death and decay. The Oxoxoco jungle was full of useless forms of life. The trees grew to an immense height, racing neck for neck to the sunlight; meeting overhead and grappling with one another branch to branch, locked in a stranglehold, careless of the murderous vines that were twining themselves about their trunks and sucking their life-sap while they struggled. There was no light, but there was no shade; only a kind of evil steam. In places I thought I would have to cut my way with my machete, but the donkey seemed to know his way through what, to me, seemed hopelessly impenetrable places. He paused, sometimes, to drink out of some little pool or puddle that had dripped from the foliage above. But he went on very bravely. I never spent three dollars on a better bargain, and wished now that I had not haggled with Diego's widow who, I was by now convinced, was not merely a virtuous woman but a generous one. Or a fool. And I had reason to bless her forethought in filling my canteen with water and my pocket with cakes, because three laborious days passed before the air became sweeter and the vegetation more sparse.

But long before we got out of the jungle I heard myself talking to myself, saying: 'So, you old fool, you have got what you deserve. Live alone, die alone . . .' There being no unlicked journalists to puncture with my tongue, I turned it against myself; and I believe that at last I met my match in piercing acrimony, because I was tongue-tied against my own onslaughts.

Then, having drunk the last drop of my water (which immediately sprang out again through the pores of my skin) I gave myself up for lost and started to become delirious. I thought that I was back in the log cabin in which I was born in Meigs County, Ohio, with my poor crazy father and my eight brothers and sisters . . . and I had made up my mind to run away . . .

Then, miraculously, there were no more trees, and the air was clean and cold. The white *burro* broke into a gallop, then a trot, then a walk, and so came to a halt. I raised my drooping head and saw, standing in our path, a tall, lean man dressed all in white, holding up a hand in an imperious gesture. He said, in a sonorous voice: 'So, you bad *burro*, you have come home? Well, I will forgive your going astray since you have brought us a guest.' Then, to me, in pure Castilian: 'Allow me to help you to dismount, *señor*. I fear you are exhausted, and your face is badly scratched by the thorns.'

I managed to croak, in English: 'For God's sake, water!'

Mine was the semi-imbecile astonishment of the help-lessly played-out man when I heard him reply in perfect English: 'Of course, sir. I am extremely thoughtless.' I suppose he made some gesture, because two men lifted me, very gently, and put me in a shady place, while the gentleman in white held to my lips a vessel – not a gourd, but a metal vessel – of pure ice-cold water, admonishing me to drink it slowly.

It revived me wonderfully, and I said: 'Sir, you have saved my life, and I am grateful to you – not for that, but for the most delicious drink I have ever tasted.' Then my eyes fell upon the cup from which I had drunk. The outside was frosted, like a julep-cup, but the inside was not. Then I noticed the colour and the weight of it. It was solid gold.

A servant refilled it from a golden ewer and I drained it again. The gentleman in the white suit said: 'Yes, it is very good water. It comes unadulterated from the snows, which are unpolluted. But your voice is familiar to me.'

I was travelling incognito, but in courtesy I had to give my host some name to call me by, so I said: 'My name is Mark Harte——' borrowing from two of my con-temporaries the Christian name of one and the surname of the other. Then I fainted, but before I quite lost con-sciousness I heard the gentleman in the white suit utter some words in a strange language and felt myself, as it were, floating away. I know that somebody put to my lips a cup of some bitter-tasting effervescent liquid. Then, curiously happy, I fell into oblivion as lightly as a snowflake falls upon black velvet.

.   .   .   .   .

It was one of those sleeps that might last an hour or ten thousand years. When I awoke I was lying on a bed of the most exquisite softness, in a cool and spacious chamber simply but luxuriously furnished in a style with which I was unacquainted. My only covering was a white wrapper, or dressing-gown of some soft fabric like cashmere. There was a kind of dressing-table near the window upon which stood a row of crystal bottles with gold stoppers containing what I presumed to be perfumes and lotions. Above the dressing-table hung a large bevelled mirror in a golden frame, wonderfully wrought in designs which seemed at once strange and familiar. My face, in the mirror, was miserably familiar. But my month-old beard was gone. Only my moustache remained; and my hair had been trimmed and dressed exactly as it was before I left San Francisco and came to Mexico to die. There were bookshelves, also, well filled with a variety of volumes. With a shock of surprise – almost of dismay – I recognised some works of my own. Upon a low table near the bed stood a golden ewer and cup, and a little golden bell. This last named I picked up and rang. The door opened and two servants came in carrying between them a table covered with a damask cloth and laid with a variety of dishes, every dish of gold with a gold cover. One of them placed a chair. Another unfolded a snowy napkin which he laid across my knees as I sat. Then he proceeded to lift the covers, while the other brought in a wine-cooler of some rich dark wood curiously inlaid in gold with designs similar to those in the frame of the mirror. Everything but the wine-glasses was of massive gold; and these were of crystal, that beautiful Mexican rock crystal. I picked up a champagne glass and observed that it had been carved out of one piece, as had the hock glass, claret glass, port-wine glass, and liqueur glass, etcetera. Many months of patient, untiring, and wonderfully skilful craftsmanship must have gone into the making of every piece. Gold never meant much to me, except when I needed it; and such a profusion of it tended even more to debase that metal in *my* currency. But those wine-glasses, carved and ground out of the living crystal – they fascinated me.

While I was admiring them, I touched a goblet with a tentative fingernail and was enjoying its melodious vibrations when the *sommelier*, the wine waiter, went out on tiptoe and returned, wheeling a three-tiered wagon, upon every shelf of which was ranged a number of rare wines of the choicest vintages. It seems that I had touched a sherry glass; in any case he filled the glass I had touched from an old squat bottle. 'Hold hard, my friend,' I said, in Spanish. But he only bowed low and made a graceful gesture towards the glass. I believe that that sherry was in the hogshead before Napoleon came to hand-grips with the Duke of Wellington at Badajoz. Sherry is the worst thing in the world for rheumatism, and I meant to take no more than one sip. But that one sip filled me so full of sunlight that I felt myself responding to it as if to Spanish music, and my appetite came roaring back. I ate as I had never eaten before. With each course came an appropriate wine. At last I was served with coffee and brandy. The table was removed. In its place they brought in a low round table, inlaid like the wine-cooler, and upon a great gold tray, crystal glasses, a decanter, and all that goes with a Sèvres coffee-pot.

Now my host came in, and I had an opportunity to observe him more closely. 'I trust that you have refreshed yourself, Mr Harte,' said he.

I replied: 'My dear sir, it is you who have refreshed me. Never have I, in my wildest dreams, imagined such heliogabalian hospitality. I do not know how to thank you.'

He replied: 'You thank me by your presence. You reward me, Mr Mark Harte. Let us take coffee and cognac together. I hope you slept well. I thought that it might please you, when you awoke, to find yourself looking a little more like the gentleman whose conversation I – inadvertently but with vast pleasure – happened to overhear in the Imperial Café in London, in the spring of 1873; and later at the Ambassador, not many years ago. But do taste this brandy. It was distilled, I think, about the time when Napoleon was a cadet –

> *Napoleon with his stockings half down*
> *Is in love with Giannaconnetta . . .*

– You heard the jingle? Yes, Mr Harte, the wine merchants speak of "Napoleon Brandy", but I possess the last few dozen authentic bottles in the world.'

'You have been so kind to me,' said I, 'that I feel bound to tell you: my name is not Mark Harte.'

'Oh, but I knew that two days ago – yes, you slept forty-eight hours – and I was quite aware that you were neither Mark Twain, nor Bret Harte, nor any imaginable combination of the two. You are Mr Ambrose Bierce and, to be frank with you, I would rather have you under my roof than the other two put together.'

Always of an irritable turn, though somewhat mellowed by deep rest, good food and fine wine, I repeated what I must have said elsewhere a thousand times before: that Bret Harte was a cheap slangy upstart who had wheedled his way; and that Sam Clemens (Mark Twain) was better, but not much, or he would never have written such a puerile work as *Huckleberry Finn*.

I drew a deep breath, whereupon one of my asthmatic attacks took hold of me. An asthmatic should know better than to draw a deep breath too suddenly, even when he is about to launch a diatribe against his rivals. A certain mockery pervades such occasions. You need at least two good lungsful of air to blow up the epigram, which is, of course, the most brilliant thing that ever came to the tip of your tongue. Then your respiratory tracts close as surely as if a Turk had a bow-string about your throat, and the air you have inhaled refuses to come out. Suddenly, you develop the chest of a blacksmith and the complexion of a general. It is at once the most ridiculous and the most wretched of maladies torturing as it does sufferer and bystander alike. My host rang the little golden bell and in a moment an old woman came in.

He said to her three or four words in that unknown tongue which I had heard before, and she darted away to return with a most curious bottle with three necks, a small gallipot, and a vessel of boiling water. The contents of the gallipot she poured into a hole in the body of the bottle and added what I presume to be boiling water. Then, inserting two of the necks of the bottle into my nostrils and the middle neck between my lips, she applied her own to the hole in the body of the bottle and steadily blew. I was first aware of something disagreeably pungent. Then the pungency became pleasurable. She withdrew the bottle and I found myself breathing, with a most charming sense of peace.

But my witticisms had been completely driven out of my mind.

'It is only asthma,' my host said, in his powerful but gentle voice. 'We can cure you of that, Mr Bierce.'

'Thank you, sir, thank you,' I said. I was about to add that, with such a formula, he might make his fortune in the north; but I remembered that profusion of pure gold and said, instead: 'It was that, that drove me here – that, and rheumatism. I thought that the hot, high, dry air . . .'

My host said, in his gentle voice: 'Indeed, yes, Mr Ambrose Bierce. You are right, as usual – and, as usual, somewhat wrong. Remember your story entitled *The Damned Thing* in which you indicate that there are sounds inaudible to the human ear and colours invisible to the human eye. If my memory does not deceive me, you concluded with the words: "God help me, the Damned Thing is of such a colour!" Correct me if I am wrong. Listen, Mr Bierce – up here we can hear the high and the low, the squeak of the bat and the rumblings under the earth; and we know, believe me, we *know*.' His eyes were like coals, but his face was bland as he said: 'What do you know, Mr Ambrose Bierce? . . . Let us change the subject. Tell me of your experiences in the Oxoxoco jungle. Were you troubled?'

'Excepting hunger and thirst,' I said, 'not a bit. Once or twice I thought I saw some red-brown faces peering at me, but then they disappeared almost as if they were afraid of me.'

My host laughed, and said: 'Do forgive me, Mr Bierce. Those savages were not afraid of you, they were afraid of Tonto.'

'I thought it might be my guns that frightened them,

sir. But who is Tonto?'

'Tonto is a Spanish word meaning: silly, irresponsible, stupid. It is the name of the *burro* upon which you rode here – and for bringing you I will forgive all that perverse donkey's sins. Allow me to assure you, however, that if you had been riding any ordinary ass, both you and it, by now, would have been butchered, eaten, and forgotten. Thank Tonto. When those jungle beasts see one of my white *burros* – and they know them, the dogs – they hide their heads.' Then he mused, 'Tonto was always a curiously rebellious animal. That is why we call him Tonto. Cross-grained. A donkey is not called a donkey without reason, sir.' He laughed. 'It would be no use beating him even if I were so disposed. One must earn the affection of a donkey or a mule; otherwise they will stand and be beaten to death rather than take an order. Not that I have ever beaten beast or man. We are humane here, sir, and loathe violence. Mr Bierce, sir, let it be quite plain that you do here as you will.'

'I like that donkey, or *burro*,' said I. 'Somehow I find him sympathetic.'

'Then he is yours,' said my host.

After some interchange of courtesies, I said: 'Here is something I do not understand, sir: you live here in the wilds, near a jungle inhabited by savages. Yet you live in a magnificent stone house, attended by servants who would be worth their weight in gold even in Mexico City. I speak of gold – you eat off gold platters, drink out of gold cups or glasses of pure rock crystal. You are an accomplished man; you speak several languages with remarkable purity. This, I do not understand.'

'Mr Bierce, I am the head of a very ancient family, indeed – possibly the most ancient family extant upon the

330

face of the earth. No, wait! I see, springing to your lips, an inquiry unworthy of you, which would not do justice to me. Did I come over with the Conquistadores? Were my predecessors with Cortez? The answer is, no. Then you will ask whether my forebears, the ancient Aztecs, came up here to escape from the Spaniards and their horses. Sir, you may believe me when I tell you that the Aztecs were mere upstarts by *my* family reckoning. The very house in which I have the honour of sheltering you is almost as old as the pyramids in Yucatan. Do not speak to me, sir, of the Aztecs – without entering into the detail, they were a foolish people though numerous. *My* people were kings, sir, before the Aztecs crept out of the jungle. The little they knew of architecture, carving, and so forth, they derived from *us*. You have seen the Yucatan pyramids? Have you ever seen anything so crude? The Aztec carvings? Put your fingers in the corners of your mouth, pull, and roll your eyes. They are out of drawing, too, if you observe the limbs. . . .

'Now this house is made of volcanic rock – fused by the fires that die not – cut in cubes, mathematically precise, each side of the cube as long as my stride, which is about thirty-two inches. No baking, no plastering. It is not a house (humble though it may seem to you), it is an ancient jewel. The pyramids of Egypt themselves would, on analysis, look foolish beside this little house. . . . Now you will ask me about gold, etcetera. Sir, Mr Bierce, we have almost inexhaustible funds of gold, and take it for granted. In effect, we of the Old People scarcely regard it except as a medium of exchange . . . and for certain other purposes. Personally, for utility, I prefer silver. Silver, I find, is lighter and more agreeable. And while I drink out of crystal – my men grind it to its proper proportions with wet sand, as the Chinese shape jade – I prefer a mixture of silver, gold and copper for my dishes. This is firmer than tedious gold. I would like to make an admixture with tin, which might be a very good thing. But I bore you.'

'I assure you, not in the least, sir,' I said. 'I was only about to remark that you seem to have travelled greatly. You say that you have seen me in London, in San Francisco, and so forth——'

' – Why not, Mr Bierce? Necessarily so, sir. You may have observed that we live, here, in something of a civilised way. You took (and I hope you enjoyed it) champagne, for example, with your meal. Where does it come from? Necessarily, France. How do I get it? Very simple; I exchange gold, of which I have an immense supply. There you have it.'

'But, my dear sir, you are a man of the world. It seems to me,' said I, 'that you speak every language fluently – even including languages I have never heard spoken.'

'Oh, I move, here and there as necessity dictates. But this is my home. Not only do I speak languages, Mr Bierce – I speak accents and dialects.' Then he made a chewing motion with his jaws, let the right-hand side of his mouth droop loosely, and spoke in the accents of a Calaveres prospector and pretended to spit as he said: 'Mr Ambrose Bierce, sir! Me and my folks sure would admire to have you for supper!'

I replied, in the same intonation: 'Yes *sir*, you *bet*!'

We shook hands in the California style. His handshake was exploratory – he seemed to be feeling my hand joint by joint. Said he: 'But we were speaking of rheumatism. We can first alleviate, then cure that. Nothing simpler, if you overcome your modesty.'

'My modesty apart,' said I, 'what is your process?'

My host said: 'There are two processes. The preliminary process is a form of massage. You have been massaged, no doubt, by shampooers in Turkish baths and Hummumms in various cities. But only by ten fingers. Now *my* masseuses have seventy fingers. That is to say, there are seven of them. Each takes a joint, a muscle, or a place where certain nerves cross. The seven women – I am sorry, but only women can do it – work at the same time, in perfect co-ordination. They were trained from childhood, bred to the business. They will prepare you for the second treatment, which is sonic.'

'Sonic? That, sir, should pertain to *sound*.'

'Just so, Mr Bierce. My masseuses will prepare you for the sound treatment that will take away the crystals that come between certain joints and fibres, and make you uncomfortable. With all your perspicacity you do not understand? Here, I'll demonstrate.'

This extraordinary man now picked up a crystal water glass, and threw it down. It bounced – while I winced – and rocked itself still, undamaged. He picked it up and set it on the low table, saying: 'To all intents and purposes, Mr Bierce, apart from a sudden shock this crystal is indestructible. But observe me closely.' While I watched, he rang the glass with a fingernail. It gave out a gloriously melodious note, somewhere in the scale of *D* major. He listened intently; then, filling his lungs, which were the enormous lungs of the man who lives in the rarefied air of the uplands, he sang into the glass precisely the same note as it had sounded. Only that one note, and he sang it with tremendous volume and power. The glass quivered, appeared to dance – then suddenly burst asunder, fell to pieces.

He said: 'One must take into consideration the natural cohesion of particles. The particles, or atoms, of all matter, living or dead, are obedient to certain natural laws of cohesion. They respond to their own vibrations, Mr Bierce. By means of sound, and sound alone, I could – for example – have made that glass very light or very heavy. And when you are relaxed, almost inert, I will find the right vibration and, by the proper application of sound, I will break the tiny nodules and disperse the antagonistic acids that cause you so much pain . . . with your permission, let it be understood – not without your permission.'

'If you can rid me, sir, of these aches and pains as you have rid me of this asthmatic attack, you have my permission to do anything.'

He rang the little golden bell. A manservant came in, immediately, to whom he gave an order in that tantalisingly familiar yet utterly foreign tongue of the household. Then he said to me, in his impeccable English: 'I must ask you, if you will be so kind, to remove your robe. I may say, by the bye, that the clothes in which you came have been cleaned and mended, so that they are as good as new; your boots likewise. They are in the cupboard by the door, together with your gun, your revolver, and your machete. Understand me: it is my desire that you be perfectly content. You have only to express a wish and it will be granted. . . . You may think this odd, Mr Bierce?'

'Delightfully so,' I said.

'Yes, by common standards it is. But I am of the Old People, and we live by the spirit of the great. I have sent out messages, north, south, east and west, to my scattered family. They will assemble here in a month, and

334

then——'

But then eight women came into the room. An anthropologist would have been hard put to it to define their race. Presumably their heads had been bound at birth, because their skulls were curiously conical. Their faces were of the neutral colour of weak coffee, and quite expressionless. While I lay on the bed, seven of them took positions around me. The eighth carried a golden bowl of some kind of aromatic oil, which she offered to the others who steeped their hands in it.

Then began the massage as my host had explained it – inch by inch, line by line, nerve by nerve and muscle by muscle – seventy skilled fingers working in perfect co-ordination. There used to be a masseur with a red beard in the Turkish bath at Covent Garden whom I regarded as a master of his profession. He could take away indigestion, muscular pains, or a headache simply by the application of his supple and intelligent hands. His name was Jim. Any one of these seven women was worth ten Jims. I had been tolerably comfortable before they went to work. But they brought to me a sense of tranquillity of which I should never have thought myself capable.

I fell asleep while they were still working. How long they worked I do not know, but the sun was setting when I awoke, and I was hungry and thirsty again. I rang my little bell and the two men who had previously attended me, came in again, this time with a larger table which they set for two. Now, my host dined with me, anticipating my every want. 'With this meal,' he explained, 'you may eat only white meats – merely poultry of various sorts, unborn veal, fish, omelettes, etcetera. Hence, only white wine. Because, after an hour for digestion and a good cigar, you must come with me and we will complete the treatment. There will be no more rheumatism, no more arthritis, no more gout. Believe me, Mr Bierce, we live by the spirit here and once purged of pain and hate, relieved of the necessity to earn a living, yours is the greatest spirit of the age and I want you to become one of us. We will make you perfect.'

It was in my heart to say that I did not want to be perfect; that perfection was for saints and gods, and I had no ambition in that direction; for they used to call me 'Bitter' Bierce, not without reason. Certain souls thrive on bitter fruit; only fools love sugar, only madmen hope for perfection. But I was too comfortable to argue the point, and my host had been somewhat more than kind to me. I may have been born a farmer's boy, but I have some of the instincts of a gentleman.

'A cigar, if you will, but no brandy until later. Then, anything you like. Later, nothing will hurt you, Mr Bierce. I have had a steer killed, and the *filet* hung; likewise a five-year-old sheep, well fed, well penned, well killed – we shall eat the saddle . . .'

So, eventually, having dressed me in a suit similar to his own, he led me through a labyrinth of corridors, down and down from door to door, into the bowels of the mountain, and there we came into a great cave. One might put St Paul's Cathedral in London, entire, into the dome of St Peter's in Rome; but St Peter's itself might have been lost in the vastness of that cave. It was occupied by something, the sight of which impelled me to ask: 'Is this an organ, sir?'

'An organ, of a kind,' said my host, 'but of such a kind that I venture to say that its like will never be seen again. I suppose you know that the Indians in Yucatan, etcetera, have what they call "water-pipes". These are a series of pottery jars of varying sizes, to the tops of which are attached a certain kind of whistle. By means of a primitive sort of spigot they regulate a flow of water into the largest jar, first of all. The water, rising, compresses the air which, being forced out through the whistle, makes a certain sound – what time the water, having reached a certain level, pours into the next jar . . . and so on, until the air is full of mysterious music. It must be,' he mused, 'a race memory. Crude, yes; primitive, unquestionably. But derived from the Old People, who used sound in its proper application before Atlantis sank into the sea. Now these things which seem to you to be the pipes of some colossal organ are water-pipes. They are grey only with the encrustations of age, but they are mostly of pure gold. The largest one, which is about the size of five hogsheads, is of massive gold. The next is of silver. The following five are of gold and bronze. There are ninety-three in all. You yourself, Mr Bierce, have written of colours the human eye cannot see, and sounds the human ear cannot hear. You cannot hear the great pipe because it is too deep; and you cannot hear the ninety-third pipe, which is thinner than a pencil, because its note is higher than the squeak of a bat. . . . Now you must take off your clothes and lie down on this pallet. Shut your eyes, open your mouth, and wait while I control the flow.'

I asked: 'What happens now?'

'There are sounds which it is not vouchsafed to man to hear, Mr Bierce. You won't hear them – you will scarcely feel them. Breathe deeply, and let us have done with discussion. Listen and tell me what you hear.'

'I hear,' I said, 'a pouring of water. A tinkling of water conjoined to something strangely compounded of melody and thunder.'

'Aha! The great pipe fills. Now wait——'

My host held to my lips that bitter, effervescent drink which I so clearly remembered, and then as it were through a veil I sensed an agreeable numbness while, from basso to alto, the pipes made their music. I felt them rather than heard them. The first sensation was in the back of my head, in my *cerebellum*; then it was in my wrists and my elbows, my hips and knees and ankles. Soon this fabulous vibration, controlled as it was by my host, as it seemed took hold of the front of my throat. If I had the will of ten men I could not have resisted this spell. It is not that I swooned – I very gently became unconscious. It is common knowledge that I am a man of a certain strength of will: I held on to my senses as long as I could; was aware of strange vibrations in all my joints; and finally floated out of the world in a black sleep. The last thing I remember in this gigantic cave was the intolerably thin whistle of the smallest pipe, queerly compounded with the dull thunder of the great pipe. It was as if I were melting.

' – We only want your spirit,' said my host.

I could not speak, but I remember saying within myself: 'I hope you may get it.'

Soon the music died. All I could hear was a sound of water running away. Somebody wrapped me in a soft blanket and I was carried away again, back through those labyrinthine passages, to my bedroom where I fell into a profound slumber. I did not awaken until about noon next day. One of my silent attendants led me to a bath of warm water delicately perfumed with something like sandalwood. Again, they shaved me while I slept. He had laid out a fresh white suit, a fine silk shirt, and a black cravat. Studs, cuff-buttons, and scarf-pin were of matched pearls. He was setting the table again, so that I had my choice of a dozen dishes. My host came in when I was dressed. 'Now, Mr Bierce,' said he, 'confess that our treatment is efficacious.'

'I never felt so well in all my life,' I said.

'I dare say not. And you will feel better yet. We will not need to repeat yesterday's treatment. Only, after you have taken luncheon and rested a little, I might advise the use of the bottle again. Two or three repetitions, and there will be an end to your asthma. Your rheumatism, sir, you may regard as cured for ever; but if you will allow me I shall have the Seven Sisters repeat the massage every night before you retire, to make you plump and supple. Repose, repose – refresh, refresh! Pray be seated with a good appetite. Will you take a glass of sherry with me? . . . Aha – here, I see, is this saddle of mutton. You must try it. It is of Welsh breed. Do you prefer capers or red-currant jelly? You must eat, Mr Bierce, and relax and be happy. Soon my family (what is left of it) will be here, and then we shall have a real feast, and you shall be one of us. . . . Allow me to serve you . . .'

After we had drunk each other's health he left me. The mutton was excellent. I also ate something which, if it was not real Stilton cheese matured with port wine, was remarkably like it. I opened the cupboard by the door and there, indeed, were my old clothes rejuvenated. Only they had thrown away my old straw sombrero and replaced it with a magnificent Panama lined with green silk. There was my gun cleaned and oiled, and my revolver too; both fully loaded. My machete stood in its scabbard, but they had burnished the leather with a bone, as soldiers in England burnish their bayonet scabbards, so that it shone like glass. For my convenience, my host had placed next to it a walking-stick of some rare jungle vine with a handle of pure gold in the form of a lizard with emeralds for eyes. So I put on my hat and picked up the stick and prepared to go for a walk.

An attendant conducted me into the open. The air was keen and refreshing. Far below lay the dense and foetid jungle; but up here everything was sweet and fresh. I saw that the house, although it was only one storey high, covered an immense area. Some distance away there stood a smaller, somewhat humbler, house which, as I guessed, was for the servants. Beyond there were erected other buildings, all of that ancient, diamond-hard volcanic stone. From one of these buildings came the braying of an ass. I strolled over. There were horses and mules, all white; and, segregated, a number of white *burros*, all beautifully clean and well fed. I called: 'Hello there, Tonto!——' and sure enough, my old friend that I had bought for three dollars, blanket and halter and all, came running towards me to be stroked. I spoke to him with affection. 'Well, Tonto, old friend,' said I, 'I believe I owe you a debt of gratitude, little *burro*, because you certainly did me a good turn when you brought me here. Yes, Tonto, you and I must have something in common. A restlessness, eh? Eh, Tonto? A misanthropy? Which, I wonder, is the donkeyest donkey of us two? You must be an ass, you know, to run away from a cosy crib like this to go to Oxoxoco – however virtuous Diego's widow may be. *Hasta luego*, my friend; *hasta la vista*, Tonto.' Then I went slowly back to the house, twirling my stick.

But I was aware of a vague disquiet, which I could not define. My host was waiting for me. He too was wearing a Panama hat, but the handle of his walking-stick was of a translucent glowing red. He saw my curious glance and said: 'It is cut out of a solid ruby. In Paris, say, a ruby like this would be worth a fortune. Here, its value is merely symbolical. Here, let us exchange walking-sticks. Carry it in good health. I beg.' He took away my gold-headed stick and pressed into my hand the ruby-headed one. I have seen rubies one-twentieth of the size that were valued at ten thousand dollars. Then, with many compliments he, followed by two attendants, con-ducted me to my room, saying: 'You must rest. Yester-day's treatment shakes the very fabric of one's being. You have lived in England; have you acquired the English habit of taking afternoon tea? In any case, it shall be sent up, with buttered toast and cinnamon buns. I want to see you plump and hearty, Mr Bierce, solid and vital, bursting with life. You must not over-exert yourself.'

'I was not, sir. I was only making my courtesies to the *burro* that brought me here.'

'Ah, little Tonto? He is an unpredictable *burro*, that one; temperamental, spasmodically seized with an itch to travel. Please rest, and if there is anything at all that you desire, you have only to ring the bell. But before you lie down' – he beckoned and an attendant brought a cup of that bitter, effervescent stuff – 'drink this. It re-laxes the nerves, it is good for the blood, and improves the appetite. In a manner of speaking, it loosens and clarifies the spirit.'

I drank it, and lay down. But even as the soporific effect of that draught took hold, disquietude came back. I was on the verge of sleep when I sat up and snapped my fingers, having hit upon the cause of it. Simply, I was too contented – a condition to which I was unaccus-tomed, and which aroused in me the direst suspicions.

Maddeningly incomplete yet indescribably sinister thoughts passed through my mind. In spite of the comforts with which I was surrounded and the charming courtesy and respect with which I was treated, I felt that something, somewhere, was wrong – wrong in a mad, unearthly way.

However, I slept very peacefully and awoke only when the seven masseuses and their cup-bearer came in. Again, when I was massaged and dressed, the attendants brought the table and my host came in, smiling. 'I will wager,' said he, 'that you feel as you look – thirty years younger. I am delighted to see you looking so well, and I hope that you will do justice to the *filet*. My little herd is of interesting stock, part Hereford, part Scottish. I keep it only for my table, of course.'

'I have the appetite of an ostrich,' said I, 'and his digestion too. I am sure that I am getting fat.'

'By the time the rest of my family are gathered here you will be in perfect condition, Mr Bierce. Then we will have a true banquet –' he stopped himself abruptly and added ' – of the spirit, of the spirit.' He looked at me with curious intensity and begged me to try an avocado pear with a particularly rich and savoury stuffing.

In spite of my nameless misgivings I ate like a fifteen-year-old boy. My host dined with me; but tonight he seemed to be beset with a kind of neurasthenic lassitude. He said: 'I am in low spirits, this evening. Yes, I am in need of spiritual refreshment . . . Ah well, it will not be long now.' And he poured me a glass of that superlative cognac, saying: 'I will take a glass with you, and then I must sleep. You must rest, too. In a little while they will bring you your draught, and so good-night and pleasant dreams to you.'

But I did not drink my draught that night. I say, I was weary of idleness and contentment, and wanted to think. I drowsed a little, however, and should eventually have slept – but then a frightful thought occurred to me, which jerked me like a hooked fish, cold and wet with panic, into bright consciousness. I remembered what my host had said when he had imitated the accents of the California squatter: *Me and my folks sure would admire to have you for supper* . . . and the peculiar expression of veiled mockery that flashed across his face when he said it. Then, I remembered all his talk about the banquet, the impending 'feast of the spirit', and I recalled again certain cannibalistic practices of some ancient races who believed that partaking of a portion of the flesh of a dead friend or enemy, they absorb some of his spiritual and intellectual attributes. And now I began to understand the deadly terror in which the people up here were regarded. Also I perceived for the first time the nature of the pleasant-smelling oil with which I had been so carefully shampooed; I detected in its odour thyme, sage, basil, marjoram, hyssop and mint – herbs, in fact, which belong not to the art of healing, but to the art of cookery. This was enough. . . .

So, to clear my thoughts and to pass the time, I wrote the above in my notebook. I propose, in case I am caught and searched, to roll these thin pages into a tight little scroll and put it where no one will ever think of looking for it: into one of the necks of the inhaler-bottle which stands on my dressing-table. Then I will put on my own clothes, take up my old arms, go to the stable and call the *burro* Tonto. He found his way to Oxoxoco once; he may do so again. One thing is certain: no savage will touch me while I am mounted on his back. And once in the jungle, given a three hours' start, I shall have nothing but thirst to fear. I am reluctant to leave the stick with the ruby head but, although I was born an Ohio farmer's boy, nevertheless I trust I have the instincts of a gentleman. In any case, with my other equipment, I shall find it inconvenient to carry. The moon is setting. Gun, revolver, machete, canteen; and then, to horse.

(Signed) Ambrose Bierce.

May (?) 1914.

And that is the manuscript that was found in the Oxoxoco Bottle. The authorities have been reluctant to publicise it for fear of a hoax. The farce of the Piltdown skull still rankles in many academic minds. But, in my opinion, it is genuine. The holograph is undoubtedly in Ambrose Bierce's writing. The fact that it is no longer the writing of an old man may be attributed to the circumstance that he was relieved of his rheumatism up there, when the man in the white suit was making him 'perfect' for the ghoulish 'spiritual supper'.

But exactly how one of the greatest American writers of his time died we still do not know. It may be – I hope not – that they pursued him and led him and Tonto back. It may be that he died in the jungle. It may be that he reached Oxoxoco and there – as is generally believed – was shot by Pancho Villa. One thing is certain: and that is, that the gentleman in the white suit, his house, his riches, and his tribe were wiped out when Popocatepetl erupted some years later, and now are covered by an unknown depth of hard volcanic rock, so that no solution is to be looked for there.

Still I am convinced that this is the only authentic account of the last days of 'Bitter' Ambrose Bierce.